The desert shei
primal – dare

Warm desert wind
subtle scents, u
all available in the arms of an all-powerful,
irresistible sheikh…

Three marvellous novels by three bestselling
and beloved writers: Lynne Graham, Jane Porter
and Sarah Morgan

BRIDES

LYNNE GRAHAM

JANE PORTER

SARAH MORGAN

Harlequin Mills & Boon Limited, Eton House,
18-24 Paradise Road, Richmond, Surrey TW9 1SR

ISBN: 978 0 263 87717 5

25-0110

Harlequin Mills & Boon policy is to use papers that are natural, renewable and recyclable products and made from wood grown in sustainable forests. The logging and manufacturing processes conform to the legal environmental regulations of the country of origin.

Printed and bound in Spain
by Litografia Rosés S.A., Barcelona

The Sheikh's Innocent Bride

LYNNE GRAHAM

Lynne Graham was born in Northern Ireland, and has been a keen Mills & Boon® reader since her teens. She is very happily married, with an understanding husband who has learned to cook since she started to write! Her five children keep her on her toes. She has a very large dog, which knocks everything over, a very small terrier, which barks a lot, and two cats. When time allows, Lynne is a keen gardener.

Look out for Lynne Graham's latest exciting novel, *Ruthless Magnate, Convenient Wife*, available in January 2010 from Mills & Boon® Modern™.

CHAPTER ONE

HIS SERENE HIGHNESS, Prince Shahir bin Harith al-Assad, reached his vast estate in the Scottish Highlands shortly before eight in the morning.

As usual, every possible arrangement had been put in place to smooth his arrival with the seamless luxury that had been his right since birth. A limousine with blacked-out windows had collected him from the private airfield where his Lear jet had landed. At no stage had anyone sought to breach his reserve with unwelcome dialogue, for he valued his privacy beyond all other things and his staff worked hard at keeping the rest of the world at bay. Offered a seat in the limo, his estate manager, Fraser Douglas, had answered several questions and then embraced a self-effacing silence.

The only road to Strathcraig Castle stretched for more than fifteen miles, through tawny moorlands surrounded by spectacular purple-blue mountains. The lonely silence of the majestic landscape and the wide blue sky that filled the horizon reminded Shahir of the desert that he loved with an even greater passion. After the frenetic bustle and buzz of the business world, the wild, natural emptiness refreshed his eyes.

As the limo began its descent into the remote forested glen of Strathcraig the passage of a flock of sheep forced the powerful vehicle to a halt. A white-haired woman with a bicycle was also waiting by the side of the road. Only when she turned her head did Shahir appreciate that the woman had barely left her teenage years behind: her hair was not white, it was a very pale platinum-blonde, drawn back from her delicate features in smooth wings. Slender and graceful, she had wide, intelligent eyes and a sensitive, full pink mouth. Even her drab clothing could not conceal the fact that she was as proud and pure in her beauty as an angel he had once seen in an illuminated manuscript. There was, however, nothing reverent about the instant charge of lust that she ignited in Shahir. He was startled by the unfamiliar intensity of his desire, for it had been a long time since a woman had excited his interest to that extent

'Who is that?' he asked the estate manager seated opposite him.

'Kirsten Ross, Your Highness,' the square-faced older man advanced, and when the silence lay gathering dust, in a way that implied he had answered too briefly, he hastened to offer more facts. 'I believe she's employed as a domestic at the castle.'

Shahir would not have dreamt of bedding an employee, and the news that she worked for him in so menial a capacity struck an even less welcome note, for he was a fastidious man. 'I haven't seen her before.'

'Kirsten Ross isn't the sort to draw attention to herself.'

Hard cynicism firmed Shahir's well-sculpted mouth. He was a connoisseur of beautiful women, and had yet to meet one unaware of her power. 'She must be accustomed to the attention her looks excite.'

'I shouldn't think she's ever been encouraged to pay much heed to a mirror,' Fraser Douglas responded with a wry grimace. 'Her father is a religious fanatic with a reputation for being very strict on the home front.'

Realising in some surprise that he was still staring at

the exquisite blonde, Shahir averted his attention with punctilious care from her. The car drove on.

The older man's censorious reference to the girl's father had surprised him, for where did religious devotion end and fanaticism begin? After all, to an outsider village life in Strathcraig appeared to revolve round the church and its activities. The local community followed a very different code of values from the more liberal ways of high society circles. Indeed, the tenants on the estate had a conservative outlook that struck visitors as distinctly grim and outdated, and was probably the result of the glen's isolation from the wider world.

Yet Shahir was more at home at Strathcraig than he was within a more *laissez-faire* culture. Dhemen, the Middle Eastern kingdom of his birth, was equally strait-laced. Right was right and wrong was wrong and community welfare always took precedence over the freedom of the individual. Within that clear framework few dared to stray, and those who did were punished by the opprobrium they attracted.

In much the same way Shahir accepted the limitations that fate had chosen to place on his own prospects of happiness. Any woman he took to his bed could only be a poor substitute for the one he really desired, he acknowledged wryly. He loved a woman who could never be his, and casual sexual affairs were his only outlet. But he was thirty-two years old, and that was not how he had planned to live his life.

Concerned relatives kept on lining up the names of promising bridal prospects, and the more broad-minded set up casual meetings with suitable females on his behalf. Perhaps, he reflected grimly, it was time for him to bite the bullet and choose one of those candidates. His darkly handsome features firmed. An Arabian woman would devote her energies 24/7 to the pursuit of being his wife. In return she would expect children, wealth, and the prestige of great position. Love wouldn't come into the equation and why should it? Marriage in his world had much more to do with the practicalities of status, family connections and, primarily, the provision of an heir. His father had been extremely sympathetic towards his son's desire to remain single for as long as possible but, as the next in line to the throne, Shahir was well aware that he could not stave off the inevitable for much longer.

It was fortunate that there was not an atom of romance in his soul, Shahir conceded with bleak satisfaction. His hot-blooded temperament and powerful sex-drive had always been kept in line by his strong principles and his discriminating tastes. He was a man who faced the truth, no matter how unpalatable it was. He was not a man who made foolish mistakes. Born into the very heart of a royal family, he knew what his duty entailed and he was proud of his heritage. His keen intelligence told him that accepting the need to acquire a wife would be a much more sensible option than eying up a gorgeous but totally unsuitable Western woman—particularly one who worked for him in so lowly a capacity…

'You're living in Cloud-cuckoo-land,' Jeanie Murray told Kirsten with blunt conviction as she sat on the worn wooden counter, smoking a cigarette in flagrant disregard of her rules of employment. 'Your father will never let you live away from home to go to college.'

Kirsten continued to wash a bone-thin Sevres china saucer with gentle and careful hands, her classic profile intent. 'I think that now that he's married to Mabel he might be prepared to consider it.'

'Aye, all that kneeling and praying didn't stop your dad from courting a new bride before your poor mum was cold in her grave. Folk say he likes his home comforts on tap.' Impervious to her companion's discomfiture, the plump, freckled redhead rolled her eyes and vented a laugh. 'But why should he agree to you moving out? You're bringing home a tidy pay packet. Don't tell me that that isn't welcome to Angus Ross—we all know how tight his hold is on his wallet!'

Kirsten tried not to wince at the news that her father's stinginess was a living legend locally. Jeanie's frankly uttered opinions and tactless remarks often caused friction with other members of staff. Kirsten, however, could forgive her much, for she valued the other woman's warm-hearted friendliness. 'Jeanie…'

'Don't go all goody-goody on me just because you think you should. You know it's true. I've heard a story or two about what your home life's like, and that's no picnic by all accounts—'

'But I don't discuss my family with anyone,' Kirsten slotted in swiftly.

Jeanie rolled her eyes with unblemished good humour. 'I bet you're still doing all the cooking and cleaning at home. Old sourpuss Mabel won't want you to move out either. Face up to it, Kirsten. You're twenty-two years old and the only way you're ever going to get a life of your own is by running away as fast as your legs can carry you from the pair of them!'

'We'll see.' Kirsten bent her head and said nothing more.

It would take a hefty sum of money to enable her to set up home elsewhere. Running away would be the coward's way out, and doing so without sufficient funds would be foolish, for it would land her straight into the poverty trap. She wanted to be able to rent somewhere decent and plan her future. She just had to be patient, she reminded herself sternly. She was only six weeks into her very first job, and with her father taking a large slice of her wages to cover her keep it would be a few months before her savings could cover any sort of a move.

She could wait until then; her job, humble as it was, still felt like a lifeline to her. She loved working in the medieval splendour of the historic castle. The magnificent surroundings were an endless source of fascination to her. Even riding her bike into work every morning gave her a freedom that had long been denied her. The chance to mix freely with other people was even more welcome. But she was equally conscious that she wanted more out of life than a post as a cleaner, and that she needed qualifications and training to aspire to anything more.

Yet the prospect of having to blatantly defy her father's rigid rules of conduct was challenging and frightening, for she had been taught from childhood to offer him unquestioning obedience. He was a cold, intimidating man, with a violent temper that she had once struggled to protect her late mother from. Her lovely face shadowed, for she was still grieving for that loss.

Isobel Ross had become ill when her daughter was thirteen years old, and her long, slow decline had been matched by her ever greater need for care. That responsibility had fallen on Kirsten's shoulders. Her father had not been prepared to assist with what he saw as 'women's work', and her older brother, Daniel, had been kept too busy doing farm work to be in any position to help. Once the brightest child in her class, Kirsten had begun to miss a great deal of school and her grades had slowly worsened.

Fed up with the restrictions imposed by their father's

increasingly obsessive absorption in religion, her brother had finally quarrelled with him and moved out. As soon as it was legally possible, Angus Ross had removed his daughter from school so that she could nurse her mother and take charge of his household.

For the following five years Kirsten had only left the farm to attend church and do the weekly shop. Her father disapproved of social occasions and had discouraged all visitors. Exactly a year after her mother's death her father had married Mabel. The other woman was sour and sharp-tongued. But Kirsten was grateful that Mabel's eagerness to see more money coming into the household had prompted her stepmother to persuade her husband to allow Kirsten to seek employment outside the home.

'We'll have to see if we can get you a proper thrill this week, while our gorgeous desert sheikh is in residence,' Jeanie remarked brightly.

A surprisingly mischievous smile curved Kirsten's lips. 'I've had my treat for the week: I saw the Prince's limousine, and very impressive it was too.'

'Never mind the limo. We'll hide you somewhere to get a glimpse of the man himself! I've only seen him a couple of times, and at a distance, but I'm telling you he'd make a sinner out of any saint.' Jeanie groaned, with a lascivious look in her eyes, as she disposed of her cigarette and put the ashtray back in its hiding place. 'He's a right sex god.'

'I'll be keeping well out of his way. I wouldn't want to lose my job.' Kirsten had been warned when she was hired that all domestic tasks at the castle were to be carried out with as much silence and invisibility as was humanly possible. It had been made equally clear to her that if her phenomenally rich and royal employer was to appear in the same corridor she was to hastily vacate it, so she didn't think there would be much chance of her bumping into him!

'If I had your face and body I'd be tripping over myself to accidentally fall in His Serene Highness's way!' Jeanie gave her a broad wink.' If he fancied you he could take you away from all this and set you up in a house somewhere. You'd be *made*, because he's minted! Think of the clothes you could have, and the jewels, and a real macho man in your bed into the bargain. You're really beautiful, Kirsten. If anyone could pull Prince Shahir, you could!'

Kirsten studied her in bewilderment, her colour rising. 'I'm not like that—'

'Well, you'd be much better off if you were,' the redhead told her roundly. 'At least I know how to have a bit of fun and I can enjoy a good laugh. If you don't watch out your father will turn you into a dried-up old spinster!'

Having finished washing the Sevres dinner service, Kirsten dried it piece by piece with great care. Even so, her thoughts were miles away. She felt so out of step with Jeanie. Kirsten had been brought up in a house where the only spoken reference to sex had related to what her father referred to as 'the sin of fornication'. The content of the newspapers and magazines she had glimpsed since starting work at the castle had initially shocked her, for the only written matter in her home consisted of the Bible and religious tracts, and it was many years since her father had got rid of the television. Yet she was guiltily aware that she was sorely tempted by the fashionable clothes and the exotic places that she had seen in those publications.

If only her father were a more reasonable man. If only he would allow her to go out and about and enjoy mixed company, like other women her age. After all, he must have dated her late mother to have married her—and surely that could not have been morally wrong?

Her father was growing terrifyingly unreasonable in his attitudes and his demands. After a dispute with the church elders, the older man would no longer attend church, and Kirsten and Mabel had been forced to stay home as well. Kirsten loved music. One of her few pleasures had been her radio, and he had broken that in a fit of rage when Mabel complained that her stepdaughter spent so much time listening to it that she was late making breakfast. Mabel had been shaken by her husband's reaction, though, Kirsten recalled heavily. It was small comfort for her to suspect that her stepmother was not wholly content with her hasty second marriage.

'Would you like it?' At lunchtime another member of staff extended the magazine she had been reading to Kirsten. 'It's OK…I'm finished with it.'

Her face suffused with self-conscious pink, Kirsten accepted the item with a muttered word of thanks. As she left the basement staffroom, she heard the woman say, 'It's a pity about her, isn't it? Angus Ross should be hung for treating her the way he does! She's scared of her own shadow!'

No, I'm *not*, Kirsten thought, frantically pedalling away her hurt pride and resentment as she headed home on her bike. She was not scared of her own shadow—but neither was she mad enough to go head to head with her father before she had the means to leave his home.

The beauty of the early summer day soon calmed her temper and raised her spirits. After all it was a Friday, and her favourite day of the week. On Fridays she finished work early, and the house would be empty whilst Mabel and her father did the weekly grocery shopping.

Afterwards they would visit Mabel's elderly mother, and remain with her for their evening meal. Kirsten decided to take her dog for a walk and read the magazine.

Half an hour later she walked through her father's fields, which led right up to the edge of the forest. She was dismayed to see that fresh tyre tracks had torn up the soft ground, leaving messy furrows of mud that would fill with water when the rain came. Her father had been outraged a few weeks earlier, when a pair of yobs on motorbikes had torn up a newly sown field. News of a second visit and further damage to the land would put Angus Ross into the kind of temper that made Kirsten suck in her breath in dismay.

Deciding that it would be wiser to let her father discover the damage for himself, she crossed the stile that marked the boundary of the farm and followed a little-used path up through the forest to the top of the hill. She kicked off her shoes, undid a couple of buttons at the neck of her blouse, and loosened her hair to relax in the sunshine. Her dog, Squeak, a small, short-legged animal of mixed ancestry, sank down in the middle of the grassy path, for the steep climb had exhausted him. His perky little ears did not prick up at the distant growl of an engine across the valley for as his age had advanced his hearing had steadily become more impaired.

Kirsten began to devour her magazine, and before very long was absorbed to the exclusion of all else in the delightful world of celebrities, fabulous fashion and wicked gossip.

One minute she was dreaming in the sunlight, the next she was jerking up from her reclining position with a stricken exclamation as a giant black motorbike burst with a roar over the hill and headed straight for Squeak. Kirsten made a violent lunge at the old dog to grab him out of the way. Mere feet from her, the bike skidded at fantastic and terrifying speed off the track, and the rider went flying up into the air. Horror stopped her breathing. But, in what seemed like virtually the same moment, he hit the ground and rolled with the spectacular, almost acrobatic ease of a jockey taking a fall.

Kirsten looked on wide-eyed as the rider, who was clearly uninjured, vaulted back upright again. Her shock was engulfed by a flood of unfamiliar anger.

'You're trespassing!' she heard herself yell at the impossibly tall black-leather-clad figure approaching her as she scrambled up.

Shahir was furious with her for sitting in the middle of a track, like a target waiting for a direct hit from on high. She was very fortunate not to have been killed. He could not credit that she was shouting at him—nobody ever shouted at him—but, perhaps fortunately for her, the alluring picture that she made clouded that issue. Her shimmering silvery blonde hair was loose round her narrow shoulders and fell almost to her waist in a stunning display of luxuriance. He encountered eyes that were not the Celtic blue he had expected, but the verdant green of emerald and moss. His attention was by then irretrievably locked to her, and he noticed that she was surprisingly tall for a woman. As tall as his Berber ancestors himself, he stood six feet five in his socks, but barefoot she was still tall enough to reach his chin.

'In fact, not only are you trespassing—'

'I am not a trespasser,' he countered, his dark, deep voice muffled by the black helmet which concealed his face from her.

'This is private ground, so you *are* trespassing.' As far as Kirsten was concerned his failure to offer an immediate apology merely added insult to injury, and her soft mouth compressed. 'Don't you realise how fast you were going?'

'I know exactly what my speed was,' Shahir confirmed.

He might behave like a yob, but he didn't speak quite as she had assumed he would. His accent was unmistakably English and upper class, his crystal-clear vowel sounds crisply pronounced in spite of the helmet. She told herself off for being so biased in her expectations. A tourist toff could be just as much of a hooligan as a yob out for a day biking through the hills. Her chin took on a stubborn tilt.

'Well, you frightened the life out of me and my dog!' she asserted, lowering her arms to let Squeak down , his solid little body having become too heavy for comfort.

Far from behaving like a traumatised animal, Squeak padded over to Shahir's booted feet, nuzzled them, wagged his tail in a lazily friendly fashion and then ambled off to curl up and sleep in the sunshine.

'At least he's not shouting at me as well.' Shahir said dryly.

'I wasn't shouting.' Her lilting accent took on a clipped edge of emphasis. His refusal to admit fault was testing even Kirsten's tolerant nature. 'You could have killed me…you could have killed yourself!'

Shahir flipped up his visor. Kirsten stilled. Her first thought was that he had the eyes of a hawk from the castle falconry: steady, unblinking, unnervingly keen. But his gaze was also a spectacular bronze-gold in colour, enhanced by lashes lush as sable and dark as ebony. Her heart jumped behind her breastbone and suddenly she was conscious of its measured beat. Indeed, it was as if her every sense had gone on to super-alert and time had slowed its passage.

'Don't exaggerate,' Shahir drawled.

'You were travelling at a crazy speed...' she framed breathlessly.

Shahir watched the sun transform her hair to a veil of shining silver that he longed to touch. He was so taken aback by the inappropriate desire that for the first time in his life he forgot what he was about to say. 'Was I?'

He pulled off his helmet and smoothed back his ruffled black hair with long brown fingers. Kirsten's mouth ran dry. He was so exceptionally handsome that she simply stared. He also had the most unforgettable face. His fantastic bone structure was composed of high, slashing cheekbones and sleek planes and hollows, divided by a strong, masculine nose and defined by level dark brows. His bronzed complexion and very black hair suggested an ancestry at variance with his beautifully enunciated English. Every aspect of him offered a source of immediate fascination to her. She felt dizzy, as if she had been spinning round and round like a child and had suddenly stopped to find her balance gone. A tiny twist of something she had never felt before pulled low in her pelvis.

'Were you what?' she mumbled, belatedly striving to recall the conversation.

The hint of a smile tilted the beautiful curve of his mouth. She was as enchanted by the movement of his sculpted lips as though a magic wand had been waved over her.

'I always travel at a crazy speed on the motorbike. But I'm a very safe rider.'

Kirsten made a frantic attempt to rescue her wits. 'But you couldn't even see where you were going,' she reminded him.

Shahir was not accustomed to a consistent reminder of his apparent oversight, and he fought back. 'Should I expect to find a woman and a dog parked in the centre of the track?'

'Perhaps not…but you *are* on private land—'

'I know—and I knew there were no livestock up here. This is *my* land.'

Kirsten giggled. 'No, it's not. I live just down the hill, and you can't fool me.'

'Can't I?' Shahir watched amusement light up her exquisite face and realised that she assumed he was teasing her. She genuinely had no idea of his identity.

But the sound of that unfamiliar light-hearted giggle emerging from her own lips had startled Kirsten. Her eyes veiled, and dropped from his in dismay. She was finally recalling the furrows ploughed on her father's ground at the foot of the hill, and she was dismayed that she had contrived to forget what she had seen.

'This isn't your first visit here, though, is it?' she said tautly. 'You and your motorcycle have already made a mess of the field below the forest!'

Incredulous at the sudden accusation, Shahir surveyed her with narrowed eyes that had the subtle gleam of rapier blades. 'Now you are talking nonsense. I respect the field boundaries. I am not a teenage vandal.'

Kirsten coloured, but persisted. 'Well, it seems to me that it's too much of a coincidence to be anyone else but you who was responsible. Someone has been in that field within the last few days, and there's been a lot of damage done.'

'It was not I. You should not make such an allegation without evidence to support it,' Shahir condemned, with a gravity that was very much at odds with the apparent casualness of his motorbike leathers. 'I find it offensive.'

His measured intonation made her pale. His dark gaze was uncompromisingly direct, and he spoke with a clear authority that unnerved her. Involuntarily, for she had lowered her scrutiny, she stole a glance at him. Her eyes glittered like jade in the pale oval of her face. 'I find it offensive that you haven't even said sorry for giving me the fright of my life.'

The silence lay like a charge of dynamite already lit.

An almost imperceptible touch of colour highlighted his superb cheekbones; Shahir had always cherished the belief that he was innately courteous. 'Naturally I offer you my apologies for scaring you.'

'Well, if it wasn't you who cut up my father's field,' Kirsten said doubtfully, 'I'm sorry I suggested it was.'

Shahir bent down with fluid grace and swept up the magazine lying abandoned on the ground and extended it to her. 'You were reading?'

'Yes…thanks.' Suddenly aware of his keen regard, Kirsten blushed to the roots of her hair and dragged her attention from him, wondering in a panic of embarrassment if he was staring at her only because she had been staring at him.

A sweet, savage hunger gripped Shahir as he studied her downbent head and luscious pink mouth. He let his attention roam to the pouting fullness of her small full breasts. His body hardened with an ardent masculine urgency that shook him.

Kirsten was conscious of the tense atmosphere, and of the inexplicable sense of excitement trying to pull at her senses. She did not understand its source, for it filled her with too much confusion. While one part of her wanted to run away, the rest of her wanted to prolong the meeting. She fumbled frantically for something to say. 'Is your motorbike going to be all right?'

'I believe so.' He had mastered his hunger with fierce self-discipline, and Shahir's drawl was as cool and discouraging as a shower of rain. He was annoyed by his own brief loss of control. Admittedly, she was very beautiful, but he was used to gorgeous women. Perhaps, he reasoned, there was something especially appealing about such natural loveliness and unmistakable modesty when he was usually accustomed to meeting with boldness.

'Have you far to go?' Kirsten muttered, scarcely crediting her own daring. But at that moment all she was aware of was that he was about to walk away and she didn't want him to.

'Only to the castle.' Shahir strode over to the fallen machine and hauled it up out of the flattened grass with strong hands. He could have told her who he was, but he saw no point in embarrassing her when it was unlikely that they would ever meet again. Someone else would soon tell her of the mistake she had made.

He was staying at Strathcraig Castle as a guest? Why hadn't that occurred to her before? It was, after all, the most obvious explanation for the presence of a well-spoken stranger in the glen. Dismay replaced the daze that she had been wrapped in and her skin chilled. She had offended him, hadn't she? Would he complain about her? Say she had been rude to him? Accusing him of vandalism had certainly not been the way to demonstrate a hospitable welcome to a visitor. What on earth had come over her? She shouldn't have said a single critical word to him. After all, if she was sacked she would never find another job locally, and her father would be outraged.

Shahir replaced his helmet and fired the engine of the powerful motorbike, looking back at her only for an instant before he took off back down the track again. With him travelled the image of glorious green eyes pinned to him with anxious intensity. He wondered what sort of a life she had, with the fanatical father his estate manager had mentioned. She looked scared and unhappy.

A split second later, without any warning whatsoever of the trick his cool and rational brain was about to play on him, Shahir was startled to find himself wondering how Kirsten Ross might adapt to being a mistress. *His* mistress. The instant the idea occurred to him he was exasperated by the vagaries of his own mind; that type of arrangement was certainly not his style. He was a generous lover, who offered commitment for the duration of an affair. But the affairs began and ended without touching his heart or even his temper. Sex was a pleasure to be savoured, but his libido did not control him and he sought nothing more lasting from the women who entertained him in bed.

In short, a mistress would be a radical new departure for him. She would have a semi-permanent role in his life, and would be dependent on him in a way that he had never allowed a woman to be. It was an insane idea for a male who enjoyed his freedom to the extent that he did, Shahir acknowledged with a brooding frown. What was more Kirsten Ross was an employee, and as such strictly out of bounds; Shahir was a man of honour. What the hell was the matter with him? One minute he was thinking of taking a wife, the next a mistress—and all in the space of twenty-four hours!

Having dug a hole in the soft ground below the trees and buried the magazine, Kirsten ran most of the way home, with Squeak gasping at her heels. Unlocking the back door, she sped through it, only to be brought up short by the dismaying sight of the thickset man lodged in stillness at the back of the sparsely furnished kitchen.

'I wasn't expecting you to be home this early…is

something wrong?' Kirsten asked, dry-mouthed with fright at the tension in the air.

'Mabel's mother took ill and she's staying the night with her. Where have you been?' Her father's harsh-featured face was ruddy with angry colour and his sharp eyes bright with suspicion.

'I went for a walk…I'm sorry—'

'If I'd been here you'd not have been idling away your time,' he growled. 'What have you been up to?'

Kirsten was rigid. 'Nothing.'

'You had better not be, girl,' he warned her, closing a powerful hand round her thin forearm with bruising force. 'Now, go and make my dinner. Then we'll study the Lord's Book and we will pray for you to be cleansed of the sin of idleness.'

When Angus Ross had stomped out of the kitchen Kirsten rubbed her aching arm with a shaking hand. She was trembling. Her father had never raised a hand to her in anger. She told herself that she had no reason to be so afraid of the older man. It was true that his temper was violent. And in a rage he ranted and raved and stormed up and down in a very frightening manner, but he had never yet become physically abusive with her—or indeed anyone else. So why did she get the feeling that that was in the process of changing?

CHAPTER TWO

FOUR days later, Shahir sprang out of bed at three in the morning and stalked into the luxurious *en suite* bathroom to take another cold shower. A more primitive male might have believed he had been bewitched by an enchantress no human male could resist, but Shahir told himself no such comforting tales.

As the cooling water streamed down over the heated length of his bronzed, muscular body, he groaned out loud in furious frustration. Never before had a woman disturbed Shahir's sleep. But something about Kirsten Ross had fired his imagination to new erotic heights of creativity. The very idea of her as his mistress had become a sexual fantasy he could not shake. Even while he slept his disobedient brain rehashed their brief meeting into an intimate encounter of a wildly uninhibited if unlikely variety that appealed most to the male sex. His inability to control his own subconscious mind infuriated him.

Resting his arrogant dark head back against the cool stone surround, he thought about Faria instead. It was rare for him to indulge himself with reflections about what could not be, for he knew how pointless it was to lament the inevitable. Faria, with her laughing dark eyes and compassionate heart, could never become his wife. Although Faria and he were not related by blood, Faria's mother had briefly acted as Shahir's foster mother when he was very young. And Shahir's religion forbade the marriage of a man to his foster-sister.

He had not known what love was before the day he had glanced across a courtyard at an interminable wedding and seen a very pretty brunette entertaining the children with magic tricks. Faria had grown up while he'd worked abroad, and she had trained as a teacher. He hadn't even recognised her. On the last occasion he had seen her she had still been a little girl.

While Faria had been brought up in the knowledge that Shahir was her foster-brother, *he* had barely heard the matter mentioned. Shahir was royalty, and all too many people claimed to have a connection with him. And, having enjoyed a brief period of intimacy with the royal family in the aftermath of tragedy, Faria's parents, who had never been socially ambitious, had soon returned to their quiet lives. Meeting her as an adult, Shahir had immediately recognised that Faria was exactly the kind of young woman he wanted to marry. In that very acknowledgement the damage had been done—even before he could appreciate that he had mistakenly set his heart on a woman who rightly regarded him as an honorary brother.

Was his nature innately perverse? Shahir asked himself now, his lean strong face shadowed by a dark frown. Although he would not mention his lust for Kirsten Ross in the same sentence as his unspoken admiration for Faria, he could not avoid registering that once again he was guilty of desiring a woman who was forbidden to him. Even that vague similarity disturbed him. In another sense it also challenged him, for Kirsten Ross was by no means out of reach.

Perhaps, Shahir reflected in exasperation, he had become too careful—too fastidious in his refusal to let his libido rule him. Almost certainly he was suffering from the effects of too much sexual denial, and the most effective cure for the foolish fantasies assailing him in the middle of the night would be a welcoming and hopefully very wanton woman.

And he knew exactly who was most likely to qualify in that department. Lady Pamela Anstruther, his nearest neighbour at Strathcraig, invariably acted as his hostess when he entertained at the castle. The arrangement suited them both. Pamela was clever and amusing, a strikingly attractive widow with champagne tastes, struggling to get by on a small income. Shahir respected her honesty and her survival skills. Pamela had never hidden the fact that she wanted him, and that sentiment would not complicate the issue.

At morning break, later that same day, Jeanie frowned at Kirsten. 'You look like you're sickening for something,' she scolded. 'You have dark shadows under your eyes. Aren't you sleeping properly?'

'I'm fine…' Uneasy with telling even that minor lie, Kirsten dropped her head. Several disturbed nights of sleep had left their mark on her face, and she was ashamed of her inability to get the motorcyclist out of her head. Time and time again their encounter would replay in her memory, and when she went to sleep her dreams took over. The disturbing and horribly embarrassing content of them she would not have shared with a living soul.

'Is something wrong at home?'

'No.' Kirsten chewed tautly at the soft underside of her lower lip before finally surrendering to the pressure of her curiosity and saying, as artlessly as she could contrive, 'There was a guy riding a motorcycle up our way last Friday afternoon. I think he was staying at the castle…'

'There's always a bunch of new faces staying in the service wing.' The other woman's attention was concentrated on the large scone she was liberally spreading with butter. 'I bet it was that old tubby guy with the pigtail. You know…the one here to write a history book about the castle. Someone told me that either him or the photographer arrived on a motorbike, dressed like a Hell's Angel.'

'He doesn't sound much like the man I saw.' Kirsten focused on Jeanie's scone, which was being cut into tiny slices so that the pleasure of eating it could be extended. 'He was young, and he looked like he might have originally come from another country—'

'Oh…*him*!' Jeanie's eyes lit up like a row of winning symbols in a fruit machine. 'That'll be the Polish builder working on the stable block. Tall, dark, tanned, superfanciable?'

Kirsten nodded four times in eager succession, like a marionette.

'I saw him on a motorbike in the village on Saturday night.' Jeanie gave her an earthy grin. 'You've got a pair of eyes in your head at last, have you?'

Kirsten had flushed to the roots of her hair, but could not restrain the all-important question brimming on her lips. 'Do you know if he's married?'

'Kirsten Ross—you shameless hussy, you!' Jeanie guffawed with noisy appreciation. 'No, he's not married. That was checked out by an interested party on his first day. No wonder you're away with the fairies this morning. I spoke to you twice and you didn't notice. Did you get talking to him? I hear he speaks great English. Did you fall madly in love at first sight?'

Kirsten was squirming with embarrassment. 'Jeanie! I

was out for a walk and we only spoke for a minute. I was just being curious.'

'Course you were…' Jeanie was merrily grinning at the prospect of what she saw as entertainment. 'Right, with your face getting off with that builder will be no problem—but somehow I think that getting past your dad is likely to be the biggest challenge.'

'So it's just as well that I'm not thinking of trying to get off with anyone!' Kirsten whispered in feverish interruption. 'Look, please don't go talking about this, Jeanie. If my dad hears any gossip about me he'll go mad! He does not have a sense of humour about things like that.'

'Kirsten…' Jeanie leant across the table, her plump face arranged in lines of sympathy. 'I don't think *anyone* would repeat gossip about you to your father. Since he had that row with the minister and the church elders and left the congregation folk have been very wary of rousing his temper.'

Kirsten jerked her head in mortified acknowledgement of the point.

When the housekeeper signalled her from the doorway, she was glad of the excuse to leave the table and go and speak to the older woman. Offered the chance to work extra hours to cover for a sick colleague, Kirsten accepted gratefully and phoned her stepmother to say that she would be late home.

It was a welcome distraction to be sent to a section of the castle that was new to her. The extensive service wing had been converted to provide state-of-the-art office facilities and a conference center, as well as accommodation for the constant procession of tradesmen and businessmen who visited the remote estate in a working capacity.

Unfurling a floor polisher in a corridor, Kirsten hummed a nameless snatch of music below her breath. *He* was from Poland; a builder from Poland. Had she imagined that upper class accent? But then from whom had he learned the language? Perhaps that had influenced the way he spoke? Suddenly she wanted to know everything there was to know about Poland. Her own ignorance embarrassed her.

At the same time she didn't really know whether she was on her head or her heels. Why on earth was she thinking about a man she would never see again? He worked outside; she worked inside. The castle was huge, the staff extensive. In all likelihood they wouldn't bump into each other again unless he sought her out—and why would he do that? She had shouted at him. Of course if she was the shameless hussy Jeanie had teased her for being she would seek him out for herself. Only thankfully she wasn't. But the thought of never laying eyes on him again made her tummy feel hollow, and filled her with the weirdest sense of panic.

Without warning the floor polisher was switched off, and she straightened from her task in surprise.

'Look, miss. We're having a very important meeting in here, and that machine's damn noisy…couldn't you go and clean elsewhere?' a young man in a suit demanded angrily.

'Yes, of course,' Kirsten muttered, cut to the bone.

Another man appeared behind him, and murmured with glacial cool, 'Don't let me hear you address another member of staff in that tone or in that language again.'

'No, of course not, Your Highness,' the first man framed in dismay, his complexion turning a dull dark red at that cold rebuke.

Kirsten had stopped breathing when the second male

emerged into view, for he was taller, broader and altogether more impressive in stature. Her entire being was wrapped in the sheer challenge of recognition: it was the man on the motorbike. But she could not believe that it could be the same person for he looked so very different, in a formal dark business suit the colour of charcoal: sophisticated, dignified, the ultimate in authority.

Belatedly she registered the significance of the title the younger man had awarded him and incredulity sentenced her to shaken stillness. The guy she had met on the hill above the farm was the Prince? Prince Shahir—the enormously rich owner of Strathcraig and its ninety-odd-thousand acres? Surely that was impossible? *This is my land,* he had said, but she had assumed he was joking. How could she have possibly guessed that a young man, casually clad in biker leathers, might be so much more than he seemed?

Refusing to allow herself to look back at him, she began to reel in the cable of the floor polisher. Her hands were all fingers and thumbs, and clumsy with nerves. She seized a hold on the weighty machine, in preparation for carting it off to a less contentious area, but her perspiring palms failed in their grip and it toppled back on to the ground again, with a noisy clatter that made her wince in despair. She was supposed to be silent and invisible around him, she recalled in steadily mounting frustration. Was she supposed to abandon the polisher and just run?

'Let me help you with that…'

'No!' Kirsten yelped in horror, when she raised her head to find him standing over her, and she backed away in panic, hauling up the polisher before the lean brown hand he had extended could get anywhere near it. 'Sorry…'

Moving as fast as she could with the unwieldy machine, Kirsten hurried away and sped through the first set of fire doors. For a split second Shahir hesitated, a frown of annoyance and surprise at her behaviour pleating his brows, and then he strode after her.

'Kirsten…' he breathed, before she could reach the next set of fire doors.

Unnerved by the unfamiliar sound of her name on his lips, Kirsten whirled round. She was breathing heavily, her lovely face pink with the effort of carting the cleaner with her. 'You're not supposed to speak to me!'

'Don't be ridiculous,' Shahir retorted crisply.

'I'm not being ridiculous! What do you want from me? An apology? Right, you've got it. I'm sorry I told you off for riding that bike like a maniac. I'm sorry if I interrupted your important meeting…OK, Your—er—Highness?' And, with that almost pleading completion, Kirsten continued to back away, until she hit the doors with her behind, then twisted round and quickly made her way through them.

Shahir followed her at speed, and long before she could draw near the next set of doors he spoke and arrested her in her tracks. 'No—don't move one further step,' he murmured, with a quietness that was misleading; every syllable of that warning somehow contrived to bite into her like a whiplash. 'When I'm speaking to you, you will stand still.'

Kirsten groaned. 'But that's against the rules!'

Shahir vented an unappreciative laugh. 'What rules?'

'The household rules. People like me are supposed to vanish when you appear—'

'Not when I'm trying to speak to you,' Shahir asserted in dry interruption.

'But you're going to get me into trouble… Nobody

knows we've even met, and I don't want to be seen talking to you.'

'That's not a problem.' Shahir opened the nearest door and thrust it wide. 'We'll talk in here.'

Kirsten sucked in a steadying breath and walked into an empty meeting room furnished with a polished table and chairs. 'Why do you want to speak to me?'

Shahir thought he had never heard a more insane question. Any man between fifteen and fifty would have wanted to speak to her. Her head was bent, her face half turned away from him, her spectacular hair tied back. But nothing could hide the silken shine of that pale hair, the stunning perfection of her profile or the flawless clarity of her complexion. Nor could a dreary overall conceal the fluid, willowy grace of her highly feminine figure.

But on another level her sheer lack of vanity and her naivety shook him. He had never had to pursue a woman before. Even without his encouragement women gave Shahir a great deal of attention. Many were so enthusiastic that he had to freeze them out with a façade of cold formality. Others were more subtle, but equally obvious in their eagerness to demonstrate their availability to him. If he showed even the smallest interest to the average young woman she would fall over herself to respond to him and roll out the welcome mat.

'Why did you tell no one that we had met?'

Kirsten focused on his superb leather shoes. 'I wasn't supposed to be on the hill.'

'Why not?'

Kirsten continued to study his feet with fixed attention. She did not know what to say. She did not want to admit that her father policed her every move, and the alternative of lying was anathema to her.

Her seeming defiance challenged Shahir. 'I asked a question.'

A sudden rush of frustrated tears burned the back of Kirsten's eyes, and she threw her head up, green eyes blazing at his persistence. 'I wasn't supposed to be there because my father doesn't like me going out without his permission. I was also reading a magazine, and he won't allow anything like that in the house!'

'I apologise. I should not have pried,' Shahir acknowledged in a tone of regret that he should have embarrassed her. 'But I was curious.'

The thickness in her tight throat would not allow her to swallow. The slight rough edge to his rich, dark drawl feathered down her spine as if he had touched her. Obeying a prompting she wasn't even aware of, she glanced up and was entrapped by brilliant dark golden eyes. 'I was curious about you too…'

Shahir tensed, the honest admission challenging his self-discipline. But he knew that it was his fault—for he had crossed the line and brought down a barrier by getting too personal. He was her employer, he reminded himself fiercely. She had accompanied him into a room where they were alone because he was her employer and she trusted him. What sort of a man would take advantage of such a situation? It did not matter that the attraction between them was mutual. It did not matter that the awareness made the blood pound through his veins like a war drum beaten with intent. That was a cruel trick of fate and not to be acted on.

'When we met, you mentioned damage to your father's field,' Shahir said with flat determination. 'I have had the matter investigated.'

Kirsten simply nodded. That he should have approached her for such a reason made complete sense to her, although she was surprised that he had bothered. She could not take her eyes from his. Never had she been so tense. Her back hurt with the strain of her rigid stance. Her breath was coming in little fast, shallow bursts, her lips were slightly parted, and there was a knot low in her tummy that was tight enough to make her feel uncomfortable. And yet it was a kind of discomfort that was in the strangest way enjoyable.

'It has been established that someone working here at Strathcraig has been biking over that land. He has now been made aware of his mistake and it won't happen again. My estate manager will call on your father to tell him that the damage will be made good at our expense.' His deep rich voice had been husky in intonation as Shahir surveyed her with shimmering intensity, for the more she looked at him the more aroused he became, and it took every atom of his will-power to remain businesslike and distant.

'Oh…' Kirsten framed abstractedly.

His bright gaze narrowed, for it was a challenge to believe that she had not been paying attention to what he had said. 'What did I just say?' he heard himself ask in the sizzling silence.

'Something about the field…' Her answer was uneven in tone and she was leaning almost infinitesimally closer. The soft peaks of her breasts had stirred into straining tightness beneath her clothing and she was hugely conscious of that tingling sensation.

'You really aren't listening.' An instinctive charge of masculine satisfaction lanced through Shahir. He liked the fact that she couldn't concentrate around him. He loved it that she was barely breathing. In fact all of a sudden he felt like a marauding pirate on the loose, for his desire for her was primal in its force. He wanted to lift her into his arms, spread her over the table and ravish her glorious body with the kind of exquisite pleasure that would enslave her for ever.

His slow-burning smile hooked Kirsten like a fish. A split second later she found herself wondering what it would feel like if he pressed that beautifully moulded mouth of his down on hers.

It was only then that she realised what was the matter with her, and she was shocked by her own ignorance. With difficulty she dredged her gaze from the burning hold of his and lowered her head. She was appalled that she had been standing there yearning for his touch like the brazen hussy Jeanie had teased her for being. How could she not have guessed immediately that she was attracted to him?

'I'd better get back to work,' she mumbled, half under her breath, but her legs refused to move her in the direction of the door.

'That's not what you were thinking,' Shahir murmured thickly.

His insight shattered her. 'No, it wasn't…'

'So what were you thinking about?' Shahir persisted, his voice husky and low, so intent on her that he could see his own reflection in her dilated pupils.

Kirsten trembled, both frightened and wildly exhilarated by the charge in the atmosphere. Her body felt unbearably taut and sensitive. She could not take her eyes from him for a second.

'Tell me…' Shahir pressed thickly. 'I trust you not to lie to me.'

The revelation of the desire that held her on the edge of painful anticipation had brought down her barriers. She was still in shock. 'I was wondering what it would feel like if you kissed me…'

Shahir muttered something in fierce Arabic and then closed his lean strong hands over hers to ease her slowly closer. He was on automatic pilot, his blood rushing through his veins like a runaway juggernaut, and although at the back of his mind caution was shouting to be heard his sheer hunger slammed the door on that warning voice. 'Let me *show* you...'

His beautifully shaped mouth came down on hers. His kiss was hard and hungry and demanding, but somehow not quite hard enough to satisfy the terrible yearning that was flaming up from the very depths of Kirsten's being. A low moan sounded in her throat and she closed her arms round him, stretching up on tiptoe to intensify their contact. Her hand slid up from his shoulder to sink its fingers into the ebony luxuriance of his hair, and spread there to hold him to her.

She was in the centre of a storm, and it was whipping faster and faster around her. Excitement had dug feverish claws of need into her quivering length for the first time, and unleashed a wildness she had not known she possessed. Nothing mattered but the potent feel of his lean, powerful body against her softer curves, the crushing strength of his arms and the glorious taste of him.

When he parted her velvety soft lips with his tongue and delved deep into the moist tenderness within the sensual shock of that tender assault roared through her. She shivered violently, a muffled little cry escaping her. She was so caught up in what she was experiencing that the sound of a voice on the inter-office call system made her flinch and gasp in surprise.

That intervention in Arabic had the same effect on Shahir as a bucket of cold water, and he had faster reactions. He lifted his tousled dark head, spared one glance for the dazed expression on her exquisite face, and immediately released her from his hold. Caught unprepared, she stumbled and almost fell. Instantly he reached out to steady her again with careful hands.

Breathing shallowly, she backed away into the cold support of the wall behind her while she made a great effort to get her brain back into gear. The confusion created by the sound of the foreign language being spoken on the call system did not help.

'What is he saying? What is it?' she muttered feverishly.

'My PA is informing me that someone has arrived to see me,' Shahir breathed, not quite evenly.

The silence hung around them, suspended, heavy with uneasy undertones. Kirsten could not meet his eyes. Indeed, she could not bring herself to look at him at all. With a sudden moan of unconcealed distress, she sped past him to yank the door open, and she fled as though an avenging angel was in pursuit of her.

Shahir drank in a deep, shuddering breath. Every natural instinct urged him to go after her and apologise for what had transpired, but his staff were already looking for him and Kirsten was obviously upset. It would be foolish to risk a scene that would attract adverse attention to her and increase her embarrassment. What the hell had got into him? He was furious at his loss of control, and could not work out how it had happened. It was as though his libido had hit an override button that had switched off all moral restraint.

Waiting in the elegant reception hall, Lady Pamela Anstruther tapped an impatient foot. Through the glass insert in the fire doors she watched a breathtakingly beautiful blonde girl emerge pell-mell from an office along the corridor. The doors flipped back noisily one by one until the youthful blonde finally rushed past her in tears.

A minute later Shahir came out of the exact same doorway, a forbidding reserve stamped on his devastatingly handsome features.

The attractive brunette's calculating gaze hardened and veiled as she angrily considered what she had just seen and came up with the most likely explanation.

Kirsten stared at herself in the cloakroom mirror. Her green eyes were raw with guilt and shock. Her lips were red and slightly swollen, and tingling. Her body felt hot and tight and wickedly different. Shame engulfed her in a terrible drowning flood. Prince Shahir had been talking gravely about the damage to her father's field. She remembered the way she had been looking at him while he spoke and she wanted to die on the spot. He had asked her what she was thinking about because he had noticed that she wasn't listening properly. Only a very bold woman would then have told him that she was wondering what it would be like if he kissed her! How much more obvious an invitation could a woman give a man? It had been the provocative equivalent of telling him outright that she fancied him. Inwardly she cringed. She was to blame for what had transpired because she had tempted him into touching her.

Finding an empty office, she got on with the job of emptying the bins and dusting and vacuuming. But, as hard as she tried, her response to that kiss kept on coming back to seize hold of her thoughts. In her whole life it had never occurred to her that a man could make her feel like that, and she was shattered by the passion that had lurked undiscovered inside her until that moment of revelation. She was even more devastated by the excitement and pleasure she had felt in his arms. He was a stranger, she didn't even know him, and yet she had found him irresistible—had been so lost in the delight of it that he could have done anything he wanted to her! She felt even worse that it had been him and not her to call a halt to their intimacy.

It was a relief to finish for the day. The staff locker room was very quiet because her usual shift had finished hours earlier. Buttoning her jacket, Kirsten crossed the coach yard to her bicycle. A man who had climbed out of an opulent sports car a few yards away was staring at her in a way that made her feel uncomfortable, and she dropped her head and quickened her step.

'Hold on a minute…' the man urged as she reached for her bike. 'Let me have a proper look at you.'

A bewildered frown denting her smooth brow, Kirsten focused on the tall, thin man in jeans approaching her. 'Sorry…were you speaking to me?'

'You are stunning…' He walked slowly round her, staring at her from every angle with frowningly intent eyes. 'If you're photogenic as well, I can make you the discovery of the decade!'

'I don't know what you're talking about.' Detaching her bike from the stand, Kirsten began to wheel it swiftly away.

'Look, I'm Bruno Judd.' The man hurried after her. 'You may well have heard of me—I *am* an internationally acclaimed fashion photographer. I don't act as a modelling scout in the normal way, but you're very eye-catching and I'd like to take some photographs of you.'

'No, thank you.' Eager to get rid of him, for she thought he was a weirdo, Kirsten climbed on to her bike in haste.

'Did you hear what I said?'

'Please leave me alone!' she muttered fiercely, and pedalled away, leaving him standing staring after her with an air of disbelieving annoyance.

CHAPTER THREE

'I WANT you to find out where Kirsten Ross is working today and I want to speak to her in private. Arrange it, but do so with the utmost discretion,' Shahir instructed his most senior PA, who concealed his surprise at the order with difficulty and bowed out of the room.

Alone again, and restive, Shahir studied the pink roses in the vase by the window. He let a fingertip stroke gently down over the satiny smooth petal of a single perfect bud and thought of the ripe flavour of Kirsten's lips, and the subtle scent and softness of her skin, and swore under his breath almost simultaneously. Her passion had surprised but enthralled him, but he would not allow his thoughts to linger on that fact.

Pamela Anstruther knocked and entered with a suggested guest list for the house party to be held at Strathcraig the following month. Her china-blue eyes met his and she gave him a playful smile, tossing her head so that her glossy brown hair bounced on her shoulders. Her heart-shaped face was very pretty. She was small and curvaceous, and the low-necked summer dress she wore displayed the plump fullness of her breasts and was tight enough to make it obvious that she was wearing the bare minimum of underwear.

He smiled, but the smile was perfunctory and not encouraging—he didn't want her. Indeed, the racy brunette's pert and provocative style was so blatant in comparison to Kirsten's more natural charms that Shahir was repelled.

At that moment Kirsten was seated with a group of other employees on the rough area of grass that lay behind the coach yard. It was hot, and a couple of the young men had removed their shirts. Kirsten hugged her knees and studied her feet—for, having been raised to cover as much of her own skin as possible, she was ill at ease when other people stripped.

'Do you like to go for walks?' the dark-haired man beside her asked quietly.

Her face flamed as the Polish builder addressed her again. He had come over to sit beside her, and everybody had stared, and now he had started to make conversation. She could feel Jeanie's expectant glare like a blow torch on her profile. 'I don't go out very much,' she muttered in a stifled voice, feeling guilty for wishing he would go away and leave her alone.

'Why didn't you make more effort with him?' Jeanie demanded when the lunch break was over. 'I dropped a hint or two on your behalf with one of the guys working with him.'

'Oh, Jeanie...*no*!' Kirsten gasped in mortification.

'Well, I thought you fancied him.' Annoyance was making the other woman sound sharp. 'And why wouldn't you? I wouldn't say no.'

'He's not the guy I met on the hill,' Kirsten cut in abruptly.

'He's *not*?' The redhead frowned, the sharp edge fading from her voice. 'Maybe the lad you met wasn't staying at the castle and was just passing through.'

'Maybe so.' Kirsten hoped that would be the end of Jeanie's attempt to establish the identity of the mysterious biker.

'You'll have to stop being so shy and awkward around men. I mean, don't take this the wrong way, Kirsten—'

her companion sighed '—but you're hopeless. When you won't look at a guy, and then you give him the silent treatment, he thinks you're not interested and that's that. He won't come back for a second helping.'

Kirsten went back to cleaning windows in the long gallery. Every so often she spared the baby grand piano at the foot of the vast room a reflective glance. Would she still be able to play? It had been years since she had had the opportunity. In any case, she wouldn't dare touch any valuable antique at the castle without permission.

Her mother had been a music teacher before her marriage, and had ensured that her daughter had grown up an accomplished pianist. Occasionally Kirsten had stood in for the regular organist at church, but when people had complimented her on her skill her father's face had begun to darken with disapproval. Inevitably Angus Ross had decided that the playing of music was frivolous, and an exercise in vanity, and soon after that the piano had been sold. Her invalid mother had been heartbroken. That was the day that Kirsten had determined that somehow, some way, she would own a piano again and play it every day—for hours at a time if she so chose.

A door opened off the gallery. A dark, stocky man in a business suit waved a hand at her to attract her attention and addressed her in accented English. 'I have dropped a tray…may I please have your assistance?'

Kirsten almost laughed at the drama of that announcement, but she hurried into the room he had indicated, well aware that some of the carpets were extremely valuable. Mercifully only a few pieces of china had fallen on to the wooden floor. Nothing appeared broken, and just a small pool of liquid needed mopping up.

Wielding a cloth from her trolley of cleaning utensils, she proceeded to get on with the task. The man had already departed, and she rested back on her heels for a moment to appreciate her surroundings. She was in a gracious sitting room, with a beautiful plasterwork ceiling, picked out in pretty shades of lemon and green. Fresh flowers and comfortable sofas as well as an open fire offered a warm welcome. However, the presence of a cheerfully burning fire in the month of June made her smile. She could only be in a room that *he* retained for personal use.

Kirsten had begun to listen with interest to the occasional facts that other more informed staff let drop about Strathcraig's wealthy owner. Apparently, even in summer, Prince Shahir liked fires to be lit in the main reception rooms. He did not like the cold.

A door in the corner of the room opened just as Kirsten was getting ready to wheel her trolley out again. Shahir appeared in the doorway. When she saw who it was, she lost every scrap of colour in her cheeks as her eyes travelled from the top of his handsome dark head and down the magnificent length of him to his polished loafers. He looked so gorgeous her mouth ran dry.

'I hope you will forgive me for setting up this meeting,' Shahir murmured levelly, his dark golden eyes absorbing her tension and her pallor.

Her brow pleated. 'You set it up? I don't understand. I was called in here because some china had been dropped…'

His strong jawline clenched. 'I suspect that was merely an excuse to allow me this opportunity to talk to you again in private. I had to see you, to offer you my sincere apologies for my behaviour when we last met. What I did on that occasion was inappropriate and wrong.'

Kirsten was stunned by that forthright declaration. 'But I—'

'You must not attach blame to yourself in any way,' Shahir asserted.

Kirsten knew that such an admission of fault could not come easily to him. In fact she could see the strain of the occasion marked in the tautness of his superb bone structure and the brooding darkness of his gaze. He was a very proud man. Yet he had still gone to the trouble of arranging this meeting so that he could express his regret. She was hugely impressed by the reality that he had not allowed his pride to hold him back. Neither his great wealth and status nor her far more modest position in life had deflected him from his purpose. Even though it would have been much easier for him to forget the incident, he had listened to his conscience and acted on it without hesitation.

'But I was at fault too.' Kirsten lifted her chin, her eyes green as emeralds above the delicate pink that overlaid her cheekbones as she made the admission.

'No. You're very young. Innocence is not a fault,' he murmured in gentle disagreement.

As Kirsten gazed up at Shahir he remembered how she had looked on the hill, with her wonderful silvery pale hair cascading over her shoulders. It was a dangerous recollection, for it awakened the hunger he had rigorously repressed. He gritted his teeth, incredulous at the effect she had on him. He was not a randy teenage boy, living in a world of erotic fantasy. He was a man in full control of his own needs.

'I—'

'I know you would not wish your presence here with me to be noticed and remarked on,' Shahir cut in smoothly. 'It would be unwise for us to linger here chatting.'

Feeling unmercifully snubbed and put back into her place, Kirsten dropped her head and grabbed the trolley.

'I don't like to see you engaged in such heavy work,' Shahir breathed in a driven undertone. 'You do not look strong.'

A startled laugh fell from Kirsten's lips and she glanced back at him, green eyes dancing with helpless amusement. 'I'm as healthy as a carthorse—but I suppose I shouldn't tell you that because it's not very feminine to say so!'

Shahir studied her exquisite face for several taut moments before veiling his gaze. He removed a business card from his jacket and crossed the room to extend it to her. 'If you should ever be in a situation where you need help of any kind, I can be reached at this number.'

Mastering her surprise, she accepted the gilded card from his lean brown fingers. He wasn't flirting with her. His tone and expression were serious and above reproach. The sudden awareness that she was longing for him to flirt with her, touch her and kiss her, shook her rigid. Ashamed of a craving that now felt more wrong than ever after what he had just said, she crammed the card into the pocket of her overall. Hot tears were prickling at the back of her eyes because she suddenly felt unbearably sad.

'Thanks...' she managed tightly, and went back to cleaning windows without another word or look.

Early the following week she was cycling home when the rear tyre of her bike went flat. She had no pump with her, and groaned out loud when it started to rain heavily. Even though she wheeled the bike at as fast a pace as she could contrive she was still soaked through to the skin within minutes.

When a big car drew up beside her and the window went down, she peered at it in bewilderment.

'I'll give you a lift.' It was Shahir, his lean strong face firm with determination.

It bothered her that she could not think of him as Prince Shahir, and discomfiture made her reluctant to get into his limousine. His chauffeur, however, had already received his instructions from his employer, and the bike was removed from her hold and wedged without further ado into the vehicle's large boot.

'Honestly—you shouldn't have stopped. I could've walked home fine… I'm so wet I'll make a mess of your car…' Kirsten was gabbling nervously as she climbed into the rear of the sumptuous car. But she fell suddenly silent and flushed to the roots of her dripping hair when she realised that Shahir was not travelling alone.

'Pamela Anstruther,' the dainty brunette seated beside him said chattily. 'And you're…?'

'Kirsten Ross, ' Kirsten filled in shyly, well aware of who the other woman was.

After all, Pamela's ancestors, the Drummonds, had built Strathcraig and lived there for a couple of hundred years. Unfortunately for Pamela, however, her father's debts had forced the sale of the estate while she was still a child, and the family had moved down to London.

'You're very wet. Take this…' Shahir passed Kirsten a pristine white handkerchief in a graceful gesture. Wet, her hair was the colour of gunmetal, and accentuated the dramatic symmetry of her oval face.

Kirsten pushed a sodden strand of hair off her cool brow and dabbed awkwardly at her rain-washed face. Only then did she dare to steal a glance at him, doing so with as much guilt as though it was a forbidden act.

Her eyes, as luminous as jewels, collided unwarily

with his narrowed dark golden gaze, and her heartbeat increased as if someone had punched a switch. 'Thank you…'

'It was nothing,' Shahir murmured politely, lush black lashes semi-veiling his spectacular eyes.

Her soft pink lips curved into a helpless smile of appreciation.

Pamela Anstruther coughed, and Kirsten instantly dragged her attention from Shahir. Realising that she had been caught in the act of staring, Kirsten turned cherry-red and dropped her head.

'Prince Shahir mentioned that you're on the cleaning staff at the castle,' Lady Pamela remarked brightly. 'You look like a very capable young woman. Do you think you could manage work that was a little more testing?'

'I hope so…but this is my first job.' Kirsten was already looking anxiously out of the window to see where they were, not wanting the limo to take her right to the door of her home. Her father would almost certainly make a fuss about her having accepted a lift.

'Oh, I've just had the most wonderful idea!' Lady Pamela carolled. 'Why doesn't Kirsten help me to organise the party at the castle?'

Kirsten's attention settled back on the brunette in astonishment. 'Me…?'

'Why not? You could run errands for me, and handwrite the invitations. It would be run-of-the-mill stuff—nothing you couldn't handle.'

'I'd love to help.' Kirsten was thrilled by the prospect of doing something other than cleaning.

Lady Pamela rewarded her with a smile. 'I really *love* acting as the Prince's social hostess, but there is a lot of work involved and you could be really useful to me.'

'I'm not sure the housekeeper would be willing to spare me, though.'

Kirsten wanted to look at Shahir, who had said nothing throughout this exchange. But why should he be interested? He might be her employer, but she was at the bottom of a large staff pyramid and she was not so naive as to believe that he had any firsthand knowledge of the castle's domestic arrangements. He paid others to take care of such practicalities, and no doubt Pamela Anstruther was quite free to pluck a junior member from the lower ranks if it suited her to do so.

The limousine came to a halt. Kirsten glanced out of the window and froze, her face draining of colour: her father was glowering on the doorstep, his ruddy face rigid with dour disapproval.

'Oh, dear, who's the nasty old codger?' Lady Pamela asked with an appreciative giggle. 'Ye olde farm labourer?'

Kirsten had already risen to leave the car. The quip mortified her, but she was not surprised that her father's scowling stance had roused such amused comment.

Shahir's attention rested on Angus Ross's aggressively clenched fists. His measuring gaze was cool and his jawline squared. He vacated the limo only a step in Kirsten's wake. As she hovered in obvious apprehension while her bike was being unloaded, Shahir introduced himself to her father. Prompted by Shahir's careful courtesy, Pamela awarded the older man a gracious wave of acknowledgement from the limo. Kirsten was intensely relieved to see her parent's anger banished by the attention he had received from his landlord.

'So the Prince has got that harlot working for him,' Angus Ross commented with an unpleasant laugh when he went back indoors. 'The nerve of yon woman, waving at me like she's the queen! She's hoping to wed the Prince and get the castle back into her family, but she's wasting her time. He must know she's a greedy trollop!'

'Aye, I'd think so. They say he's no fool,' Mabel, a thin-faced woman in her early fifties, agreed with sour enjoyment. 'Before that husband of hers died Lady Pamela had one man after another staying up at that lodge with her! Naturally Sir Robert left her next to nothing on his death.'

'It was God's judgement on her,' the older man pronounced with satisfaction.

Kirsten fondled Squeak's greying ears and wished that her father and her stepmother would be a little more charitable about other people. There were few secrets in so small a community, and she knew the brunette's history too. A good ten years had passed since Pamela had married Sir Robert Anstruther, a wealthy businessman more than twice her age. Pamela had returned to the glen that had once belonged to her family but spiteful tongues had been quick to suggest that she was an unscrupulous gold-digger.

For years Sir Robert had owned an old hunting lodge in the glen, which he had used as a holiday home. Keen to take up full-time residence there, Pamela had renovated and extended the lodge. And while her husband had continued to spend most of his time in London, she had often entertained friends at their highland home. When the older man had died, the gossip had become even more malicious after it became clear that Sir Robert had left the lion's share of his worldly goods to the children of his first marriage.

Kirsten, however, believed that Pamela Anstruther deserved the benefit of the doubt. The other woman had seemed perfectly pleasant to her, and, after all, nobody that Kirsten had heard spreading scandal had ever seen any definitive proof that the lively brunette had been an unfaithful wife *or* was a gold-digger.

'I'm really not interested in being photographed,' Kirsten proclaimed impatiently, four days later, when she was waylaid in the quadrangle that lay behind the service wing.

Jeanie, her hands planted on her ample hips, released a belly laugh at the look of incomprehension on Bruno Judd's thin mobile face. 'Mr Judd, if you knew Kirsten's dad you'd know better than to ask her to model for you in a miniskirt! I'm her friend, and even I haven't seen her knees or her elbows—so what chance do you think you have?'

'You don't understand what an opportunity I would be giving her. There is nothing offensive about my request either. I hate to see potential talent going to waste,' the older man argued in growing frustration. 'Kirsten might have what it takes to become a famous model—'

'Might!' Jeanie emphasised with rich cynicism as the two women walked on, and then she dropped her voice to a whisper, 'Do you think he could be for real?'

Kirsten shrugged. 'Who cares? When I leave Strathcraig it'll be to go to college, so that I can get a better-paying job. I'm not going to waste my time chasing some stupid pipe dream. I bet only one in a thousand girls who want to be a model actually gets to be one.'

'You're too sensible,' the redhead scolded. 'How's it going with Lady Posh?'

'Don't call her that…she's been very nice to me,' Kirsten protested uncomfortably.

'Odd, that, don't you think…when everyone else says she's a total bitch?'

'I think they're being very unkind.'

Ignoring Jeanie's unimpressed snort of disagreement, Kirsten mounted the stairs to the suite Pamela Anstruther used when she was staying at the castle. Kirsten had spent two of the past four days working for Pamela, and she was enjoying the chance to get a break of a few hours here and there from her usual duties. She had answered the phone, run messages and organised the mess on Pamela's desk. She had also unpacked and ironed the other woman's clothes and tidied her room. Pamela treated her more like a casual friend than an employee and Kirsten couldn't help wanting to please her.

A dark frown of disapproval stamped on his lean, powerful face, Shahir watched Bruno Judd finally abandon his attempt to recapture Kirsten's attention as she crossed the quadrangle. There could be no mystery as to the source of the photographer's interest, and Shahir was concerned by what he had seen. The older man was not known for his scruples.

As Shahir turned away from the window, wondering whether or not he should intervene, Pamela Anstruther telephoned to request an immediate meeting with him.

A few minutes later Shahir rose from behind his desk to award the highly strung brunette his reluctant attention. 'What *is* the problem that you prefer not to discuss on the phone?'

Pamela winced. 'It's rather delicate. I'm afraid a piece of jewellery has gone missing from my bedroom.'

Shahir looked grave. 'The police must be called.'

'I don't want to upset the staff by involving the police. Really, the brooch isn't worth very much!'

'Monetary value has no bearing on the matter. I will not tolerate theft.'

'But it is still possible that I have mislaid the stupid thing. Let's not inform the police yet. I'll ask Kirsten to search my suite for it.'

'As you wish.' For an instant Shahir wondered why she had chosen to approach him before an adequate search had been conducted. 'Is the guest list complete yet?'

'Almost. Why don't you join us for coffee today?' Pamela suggested brightly. 'We could make it a working break.'

On the brink of refusal, Shahir hesitated. 'In thirty minutes, then.'

Kirsten was troubled when Pamela told her about the brooch, because she knew that when anything of value went missing everyone who had entered the castle would come under suspicion. 'Of course I don't mind looking for it.'

'Do this room now,' the brunette instructed. 'Then, when the Prince arrives, you can go next door and search my bedroom. Thank you so much. Let's hope you can find it for me.'

Kirsten was down on her hands and knees on the carpet when she heard the deep dark sibilance of Shahir's drawl carrying through from the adjoining reception room. Her throat thickened. She sucked in a jerky breath. No matter how hard she tried not to, she thought about him a lot. Not thinking about him sometimes seemed an impossible challenge, for the instant she relaxed her mental vigilance her thoughts would immediately race back to him again.

Her fingers curled round something small and she looked down in bemusement to see the small brooch that had been lying on the carpet.

'I found it… Oh, sorry!' Kirsten came to a paralysed

halt in the doorway when Shahir sprang upright at her entrance. 'I'm sorry. I didn't mean to interrupt you.'

'My goodness—don't mind that. You found my brooch?' Pamela hurried over to examine it. 'I don't believe it! I went over every inch of that room before you arrived this morning. Where was it?'

'On the floor by the dressing table.'

'But that's *impossible*!' The brunette was frowning in apparent astonishment. 'Of course I'm very grateful not to have to call the police, but I don't understand how I could have missed seeing it there.'

'It happens. Congratulations, Kirsten.' Shahir's calm intercession stole both women's attention.

Kirsten's bewilderment at the other woman's attitude evaporated from her mind when she let herself look at Shahir properly for the first time. Meeting his brilliant dark golden gaze, she felt her tummy muscles clench, and she could barely breathe for excitement. She studied him, feverishly absorbing every tiny facet of his appearance: the way the sun coming through the window behind him found light in his cropped black hair, the amazing bronze clarity of his eyes, the hint of a smile that stole the gravity and reserve from his darkly handsome features. He was so very tall that she wouldn't be able to look down on him even if she were to acquire and get to finally *wear* high heels, she thought abstractedly

'Yes, I'm very grateful.' Pamela Anstruther treated Kirsten to a bright smile of approval. 'Could I have a word with you outside, please? Please excuse us, Your Highness.'

Mystified by the request, Kirsten followed her out into the corridor.

'I just had to get you out of there.' The smaller woman dealt Kirsten a scornful appraisal that bore no resemblance to her usual sweetly sympathetic approach. 'You haven't got a clue, have you? You were seriously embarrassing Prince Shahir and making a fool of yourself. Don't you know better than to gape at the man like a stupid schoolgirl?'

Aghast at the unexpected attack, Kirsten stared at the other woman, and then swiftly lowered her shaken gaze. Her stomach rolled with the nausea of extreme mortification. She was appalled that she had let herself down to such an extent that her behaviour had attracted attention. How could she have been so foolish?

But almost as quickly a spirit of defiance stirred within Kirsten. While she would humbly accept full responsibility for a mistake, she felt that there was some excuse for her lack of composure in Prince Shahir's radius. It was very hard not to be madly aware of the one and only man who had ever kissed her. And, also in her defence, hadn't he stared at her too? For just as long? Was anyone about to slap *his* wrist and rake him down for the same offence?

'Of course I noticed that you had a giant crush on the Prince that day he gave you a lift home. That's hardly surprising. He's a staggeringly handsome man. But I'm quite sure that you don't want people to start laughing at you.'

Kirsten lifted her chin. 'I don't think I made myself ridiculous.'

The cold china-blue eyes narrowed at that quiet comeback. 'I suppose you think I've been brutal, but someone had to warn you for your own good. Look, why don't you finish early today and go home?'

Kirsten did nothing of the sort. One or two of her co-workers had been less than impressed by her newly flexible employment conditions, and she deemed it wisest to head down to the staff locker room in the basement, don her overall and finish up her usual shift.

While she worked she began to revise her initial favourable impression of Pamela Anstruther. Perhaps she had been a touch naive about the imperious brunette, she acknowledged ruefully. Whatever—it was obvious that she had really angered Pamela. She could only suppose that there was truth in the rumour that Pamela was interested in Shahir, for she felt there had been no need for Pamela to humiliate her to that extent.

When she was pulling on her jacket to go home she was told that the housekeeper was looking for her.

'You're wanted back in the service wing,' the older woman informed her ruefully. 'I did say it was your finishing time, but you're to wait in Reception there.'

Kirsten was dismayed by the news. Was she in trouble about something? Had she so annoyed Lady Pamela that the brunette wished to dispense with her assistance? She had barely sat down in the waiting area when one of Shahir's office staff appeared and indicated that she was to follow him. She was mystified right up until the moment she was shown into a large, imposing office and saw Shahir poised by the window.

Her fine facial bones tensed beneath her smooth porcelain skin. She felt torn apart: she wanted to see him and she didn't want to see him. Her heart hammered behind her breastbone and her green eyes feasted on him while her brain battled against any acknowledgement of the sheer charisma of his dark good looks. But every time she saw him she was afraid it would be the last time, and that honed her interest in him to a desperate edge.

For the merest instant Shahir pictured her slender loveliness spread across his bed, her beautiful hair loose in silver streamers he could bury his fingers in, that luscious soft pink mouth ripe and ready for his. Even as he angrily suppressed that unwelcome flight of erotic fancy his body punished him with a raw masculine response. He was the descendant of a long line of fierce warrior ancestors, and self-denial figured nowhere in his genes, he acknowledged grimly. His hunger for her might be in his blood, like a primitive fever, but he was proud of the fact that only regard for her wellbeing had persuaded him that this meeting was necessary.

Shahir rested steady dark bronze eyes on Kirsten. 'You must be wondering why I wished to see you?'

'Yes.' But the familiar frisson of sweet tightness was already curling in Kirsten's tummy and she was deliciously tense. He had sought her out again, and that pleased her so much she felt that she was floating ten feet off the ground. If she smiled she knew she might not be able to stop. For the first time ever a sense of her power as a woman was flaring through her, and it shook her to recognise that questionable feeling for what it was.

'I saw Bruno Judd trying to speak to you.' His husky dark drawl was incisive in tone. 'I understand that it is not the first time he has approached you, and I was concerned.'

His explanation took Kirsten entirely by surprise. She came down from her fluffy mental cloud of irresistibility with a resounding crash and her face flamed. She could not credit that she had been so vain as to assume that he had had a more personal motive for wishing to see her.

In an effort to conceal her discomfiture, she burst straight into speech. 'He wants to take some photographs of me. He thinks I might have what it takes to become a fashion model.'

'Very well. It will be my pleasure to ensure that you aren't troubled by Mr Judd again,' Shahir informed her.

Kirsten was already feeling silly and hurt, and mortified to the depths of her soul, and his high-handed statement of intent sent her flying from miserable awkwardness to angry defensiveness. What right had he to assume that she would not be interested in Bruno Judd's proposition? She might be forced to accept her father's tyranny at home, but she saw no reason why anyone else should be allowed to take decisions on her behalf, or assume the right to tell her how she ought to behave.

'But Mr Judd isn't troubling me,' Kirsten countered in flat rebuttal. 'And if he was I could quite easily send him about his business if I wanted to.'

'But of course you must want to.' Shahir's conviction of his own greater wisdom came as naturally to him as breathing. 'You're not streetwise enough to survive in the modelling world. The fashion industry is tough and corrupt, and it favours very young teenagers. Judd won't stand by you if your face fails to make his fortune. He is a talented photographer, but he has few scruples.'

Kirsten flung up her head, green eyes sparkling like polished gemstones. 'I can look after myself!'

Shahir studied her with dark eyes cool as ice. 'Please don't raise your voice to me. I do not tolerate impertinence.'

Kirsten lowered her lashes. She was as chagrined as a child who had been told off and sent to stand in the corner, and embarrassment struggled with resentment inside her. Her usually even temper sparked. She felt angry with the world in general. And the knowledge that she could not speak freely and could not even risk raising her voice had the same effect on her as a gag. The silence fairly sizzled with undertones.

'My only wish is to protect you from exploitation,' Shahir murmured with icy gravity.

That cold intonation of his wounded her even more. 'Maybe I'm more streetwise than I look.' Hurt and bitterness rose like a tide inside her, and she stole a burning emerald glance at him. 'Maybe I *want* to take my chance at becoming a model!'

Her mouth ran dry as she met the smouldering gold of his appraisal. Anticipation coursed through her in a wicked helpless surge: she felt as though her heart was in her throat, choking her with its accelerated beat. A dam-burst of tension was pooled up inside her, like oil waiting for a flame to ignite it.

'Naturally that must be your decision.' And with that unemotional assurance Shahir opened the door for her departure.

As a victory it rang hollow for Kirsten. She bent her head, her hands clenching in on themselves with unbearable tension, her emotions erratic. She dimly understood that in teaching her to want him he had destroyed her peace of mind. By making her crave what she could not have he had made her vulnerable to pain and dissatisfied with what she had. Even being polite to him was a challenge for her. Indeed, something very like hatred powered the deep sense of rejection she was experiencing. Never in her life had she felt so bereft. But she walked away with her head held high.

On the way out of the building she checked her pigeonhole and found a magazine. Brand-new, and still sealed in its wrapper, it was the same publication that Shahir had found her reading on the hill. She did not know how, but she was immediately convinced that he was responsible for the anonymous gift.

Just as quickly she found that she was able to see their recent encounter in another light. He had been worried about her. She might not have appreciated the way he chose to express his opinion, but the very existence of his concern touched her. Her anger evaporated. Suddenly the world no longer seemed such a cold and hostile place. His indifference would have wounded her intolerably. But the mysterious arrival of the magazine allied to his attempt to protect her felt comforting. In that lighter mood, she headed home.

She knew something was wrong the instant she entered the kitchen. Her father was seated alone at the table, his weathered face set like granite. 'You're late. What have you been doing?'

'I was held up at work.' Uneasily conscious of the older man's accusing stare, Kirsten struggled to behave normally. 'That's all.'

'Don't lie to me!' Angus Ross slammed a clenched fist down on the worn table and made her jump. 'That man Judd was here!'

Wholly unprepared for that announcement, Kirsten stared at her father in bewilderment. 'Mr Judd came...*here*?'

'Thanks to you, he brought his dirty suggestions into my home.' Kirsten flinched back a hasty step as the older man reared upright and came towards her. 'What have you to say about that?'

'I had nothing to do with him coming here,' she protested in a nervous rush, appalled by the news that the photographer had been foolish enough to approach her father in the hope of winning his support. 'I have no idea why he would have done such a thing—'

'He thought he could fool me into letting you go down to London with him!' the older man snarled. 'He showed me pictures of shameless half-naked women. He defiled a God-fearing household with his filth.'

'I'm sorry he upset you, but he's just a pushy man with silly ideas. He doesn't know anything about me.'

'You're lying, girl. He knew where you lived. You told him you'd need my permission to leave home. You put him up to it, didn't you?'

'No, I didn't. He must have asked someone where I lived. I told him I wasn't interested in being photographed. I'm sure he didn't mean to insult you—'

'It's you who's insulted me! You must've encouraged him!' His rage was unabated by her efforts to calm him down.

'But I didn't!'

'You're lying to me and I won't stand for it!'

With that roared declaration, Angus Ross raised a fist the size of a sledgehammer and thumped her.

CHAPTER FOUR

THE next morning Kirsten would have avoided going into work if she could have done. Her cheekbone was bruised and swollen, and she knew that someone was sure to ask what had happened. She also knew that unless she was prepared to report her father to the police she would have to lie.

Had she not turned her head, so that the main force of the blow was deflected, her nose might easily have been broken. She was equally conscious that, having hit her once, her father might just as easily hit her again. Her tummy flipped when she recalled the older man's intractable fury. He hadn't cared that he had hurt her, and he hadn't been ashamed either.

Hearing Kirsten cry out, Mabel had rushed downstairs, and had seemed very much shocked by what she found there. Yet within an hour of that distressing episode Mabel had been laying the blame for Bruno Judd's visit and her husband's violence at Kirsten's door.

Her eyes were hot and scratchy from the silent tears that had seeped under her eyelids the night before. Her father had never been a soft man, but he had not been a brutal one either. In fact he had once been reasonably well-respected in the community and she was deeply ashamed that he had struck her.

Evidently Jeanie had been right to be cynical about the prospects of Kirsten managing to leave home with her father's approval. But the need for her to move out was now a matter of greater urgency, and it was obvious that she would have to plan a secret departure. Unfortunately her cash reserves were still pitifully low. She decided that she would put her name down to work extra hours whenever possible.

'My word…what happened to your face?' Pamela Anstruther asked in a hushed tone of enquiry within minutes of Kirsten's arrival.

'I tripped and hit myself on the edge of a table…I was lucky not to break anything,' Kirsten stated with an uneasy shrug.

The brunette gave her a sympathetic look that was reassuringly empty of suspicion. 'Poor old you. Look, I only need you for an hour this morning. You can tidy my bedroom and then go back to your usual duties when we're done.'

Kirsten repressed a stab of disappointment and resentment. So this was to be yet another day when she did not get to help with the party arrangements. She had always liked to think of herself as ready and willing to turn her hand to most tasks. But the brunette had taught her that there were tasks…and tasks. Pamela always left her room like a rubbish tip, and Kirsten really disliked being used as her personal maid.

His handsome mouth compressed into a hard line, Shahir studied the letter he had received that morning from a cousin. And then, with a sudden bitter laugh, he crunched the item up and tossed it in the bin.

It seemed a fitting footnote to his non-relationship with Faria that he should have learned quite accidentally that the only woman he had ever cared about had just become the wife of another man. He had not even been aware that she was betrothed!

But, owing to the recent death of a relative, Faria's

wedding had been a small, quiet affair, staged at speed to facilitate the bridal couple's departure for London, where the bridegroom had taken up a surgical post.

It had been inevitable that Faria would marry, Shahir acknowledged bleakly, and she was no more out of his reach now than she had ever been. He refused to allow himself to feel unsettled by the news of his foster-sister's marriage. He was strong, not weak, he reminded himself with grim resolve.

An hour later Pamela Anstruther arrived, to collect the corrected guest list from him.

'I think that Kirsten Ross has been up to no good,' she remarked with a suggestive roll of her eyes.

Shahir elevated a cool ebony brow that would have silenced a less bold woman.

Predictably, Pamela continued to talk with animation. 'You see, I did hear a rumour that Kirsten was sneaking out to meet the Polish builder working here. The life she leads, I certainly don't blame her for trying to hide something like that. Unfortunately for her, though, it seems that her nasty old father has got wind of her promiscuous behaviour—'

'I have a strong dislike of rumour and gossip,' Shahir sliced in dryly.

Pamela gave him a sweet smile of apology. 'I gathered that you felt sorry for the girl—that's the only reason I mentioned it. You see, Kirsten isn't looking quite as pretty today as she usually does.'

Shahir levelled unreadable dark eyes on the brunette. 'Get to the point, Pamela.'

'Well, the poor girl looks like somebody punched her in the face, and I suspect her gruesome old dad is responsible.' Pamela watched Shahir and was disappointed by the fact that his lean strong face remained impassive.

'Did she say so?'

'Of course not…she trotted out the old ''I tripped'' chestnut. But I reckon that her daddy found out that she was doing what healthy farm girls do with a man when they get off the leash!' Pamela vented an earthy laugh that had the subtlety of a brick hitting glass. 'You disapprove of that kind of speculation, but it *is* the most likely explanation—and who could fault her for it? From what I understand she's not allowed any freedom at all, and that's not natural for a girl of her age.'

When the brunette had gone, Shahir released his breath in a measured hiss. He would have a member of his senior staff raise the matter of Kirsten's welfare with the housekeeper. He would ensure that all possible advice and assistance was offered to her. What need was there for him to involve himself in any more direct way?

But was it true that Kirsten was involved with a man? That she had already acquired a name for being promiscuous? Distaste assailed Shahir. What did he really know about Kirsten Ross? Regard for her good name had prevented him from discussing her or her background with anyone. He had assumed that she was an innocent, and vulnerable. But now he was remembering her passion in his arms and wondering whether it had, in fact, been the response of a more experienced lover.

Could he have been mistaken? He could hardly tell the difference on the basis of one stolen kiss, he conceded abstractedly. And why the hell was he even thinking about such a thing? Virgin or wanton, she was still forbidden to him.

On the other hand, he was one hundred per cent weary of the nonsense attached to his expressing an honest and entirely proper concern for the wellbeing of an employee. Why should he have to act unseen, through intermediaries? Why should he have to tiptoe around the sensibilities of his staff? If Kirsten had been assaulted, why should he not check that shocking fact out for himself? In the palace where he had grown up he would not have hesitated to do so.

After all, his entire upbringing had been geared to the need for him to feel personally responsible, protective and compassionate towards more vulnerable human beings. He had picked up that lesson at a very young age. He had been taught that no person and no problem should ever be considered beneath his notice or too small to warrant his individual attention. An honourable man did what was right, regardless of appearances!

Without further ado, he accessed the housekeeping rota on the computer, to establish where in the castle Kirsten was likely to be. He did not allow it to occur to him that until very recently he had not even known such rotas existed, or where they could be found.

Kirsten was brushing the polished floorboards of the long gallery. For once she had little appreciation for the magnificence of her surroundings. The prospect of going home that afternoon was already filling her with a sense of dread that overshadowed her every thought. What sort of a mood would her father be in?

'Kirsten…'

At the sound of her name she jumped, and the brush fell from her nerveless fingers and hit the floor with a noisy clatter. Her pale head flying up, she focused in surprise on Shahir, who had come to a halt about twenty feet away.

In one glance he saw the fear she could not hide and the purple discolouration that marred one side of her face.

His outrage at what he saw slashed right through his cool reserve.

'What has happened to you?' he breathed, his long stride bringing him to her side within seconds. 'Did your father do this to you?'

His candour thoroughly disconcerted her. All morning she had been horribly aware of the sidelong looks and whispered comments behind her back, but only Pamela Anstruther had dared to question her. 'No—I don't know where you got th-that idea,' she stammered, nervously evading his frowning scrutiny. 'I stumbled and fell against a table.'

Shahir lifted a lean brown hand and let a gentle forefinger brush the edge of the bruise that stood out in livid contrast to the porcelain perfection of her skin. It enraged him that she had been brutalised. Her home life was clearly appalling, and her predicament could not be ignored. Yet if she was allowed to enter staff accommodation at the castle would her father leave his daughter there in peace? Shahir doubted that it would be so simple. Such a man would not easily surrender control over his own flesh and blood.

'I know that is nonsense,' he asserted with quiet conviction. 'You cannot look me in the eye and lie.'

At his touch, which felt like a delicious caress, Kirsten had stiffened in astonishment. Until that moment she had not known that a man could be so gentle. Her emotions felt like dynamite on a hair trigger. Keeping the lid on them demanded every ounce of her self-discipline. His attention, his very interest in her, was already having an intoxicating effect on her. He was so close that she could smell the faint and already surprisingly familiar scent of his skin. Soap? Some expensive shaving lotion? For an instant it was all she could concentrate on: the aromatic mystery of that clean, rich tangy preparation that somehow made her tingle inside her clothes and want to move closer still.

'I'm not lying,' she mumbled in belated response, feeling bereft because he had withdrawn his hand again.

'You have been hurt, and that is not acceptable under any circumstances. No one has the right to inflict injury on you, not even a parent. I must know the truth,' Shahir persisted steadily. 'Without your trust, I cannot help you.'

'You couldn't help me anyway!' The involuntary protest erupted from Kirsten, and stinging tears flooded her eyes and overflowed, her unhappiness unconcealed.

'In that you are wrong.' Years of rigorous royal training prevented Shahir from attempting to comfort her by closing his arms round her, but he had never been more tempted to break the rules. He recognised that it had been very unwise to tackle her on such an emotive matter in a public area of the castle. 'But this is definitely not the place for us to talk about it.'

'We can't talk anywhere!' Kirsten gasped.

In disagreement, Shahir curved a purposeful hand to her spine and guided her along to the door that lay at the foot of the gallery. Beyond that solid mahogany barrier lay his private quarters, maintained solely by his personal retinue, where nothing short of fire or flood would lead to an interruption. His bodyguards, who had been deeply unhappy when their royal charge moved out of their sight and hearing, greeted his reappearance with pronounced relief.

Shahir swept Kirsten past them into the vast sitting room. 'I need you to calm down and tell me what happened to you yesterday.'

'I *can't* tell you…' A stifled sob thickened Kirsten's declaration.

Shahir reached for her hand to draw her to him when she would have turned away in an effort to conceal her distress. 'Loyalty to one's family is always a most admirable trait, but in this case your personal safety is more important. What happened yesterday could happen again, and you could be more seriously hurt.'

'But it's my own fault...I brought it on myself!' Kirsten protested guiltily.

'How could it be your fault?'

'If I'd let you scare off Bruno Judd this wouldn't have happened! But I was mad with you because you interfered, and I thought it was none of your business,' Kirsten admitted shakily, her green eyes glimmering with tears of regret.

'Hush....' Murmuring soothing words in Arabic, Shahir sank down on the arm of a sofa and reached for her other hand in a reassuring gesture. 'Don't be upset. How is the photographer involved in this?'

'That stupid man found out where I lived and called round to introduce himself to my father,' Kirsten volunteered. 'He must've thought that he could persuade Dad that there was no harm in his wanting to take photos of me.'

'Judd visited your home?' Shahir frowned, his lean, powerful face intent on her.

'And showed Dad pictures of "shameless h-half-naked women"!' Kirsten quoted, with a hysterical edge to her shaking voice. 'Can you imagine anything more guaranteed to cause offence? My father was waiting for me to come home. He was in a real rage—'

'No more...stop remembering.' Shahir rested a forefinger in gentle reproach against her quivering lower lip while wondering how it was that the livid bruise should only seem to accentuate her fragile beauty. 'He will not have the opportunity to hurt you again. I will not allow it.'

'But there's nothing you can do,' she whispered unevenly, her breath feathering in her dry throat.

'On my word of honour, I will protect you,' Shahir swore with fierce resolve, but he knew even as he said it that the easiest way to protect her would be to take her away from Strathcraig.

But how would she survive removed from everything and everyone that she knew?

Why should he not look after her? an insidious inner voice queried. Why should he not take her to his bed? What did she have here? What would he be taking her from? Poverty and misery. At the very least he would make her happy. In fact he was convinced he had the power to make her deliriously happy.

Suddenly madly aware of the silence surrounding them, and of his proximity, Kirsten muttered guiltily, 'I shouldn't be here with you.'

Brilliant dark golden eyes flared over her tear-streaked face and held her uncertain gaze with arrogant force of will. 'But you want to be with me…'

It was a fatal statement, for the barrier she had attempted to raise crashed down again. She did want to be with him—and if even he knew that, why should she pretend otherwise? She was in the mood to rebel, and was already asking herself why she shouldn't for once do as she wanted.

The heat of his appraisal sent hot little flames of anticipation twisting and curling through her slender length. The tension was excruciating. She felt as if her own heartbeat was thundering in her ears at a faster and faster pace, making her dizzy and breathless. In an almost infinitesimal movement she shifted closer to him.

Shahir picked up on that feminine encouragement with a hot-blooded masculine appreciation powered by the raw physical charge of his arousal. His mounting conviction that she was not quite the innocent he had believed readily put to flight any lingering thread of restraint. Spiky black lashes semi-cloaked his narrowed gleaming gaze as he focused on the luscious pink fullness of her lips. 'I want you.'

'Do you?' Her breath was feathering in her throat. She was taut with anticipation. He sprang fluidly upright and reached for her with a strength and assurance that exhilarated her. Splaying his hand to the soft curve of her hip, he urged her up against his big powerful frame. Crushed to the hard, muscular heat of his strong body, she trembled. He bent his handsome dark head and captured her parted lips with devastating hunger.

The searching flicker of his tongue against the roof of her mouth made her shiver and gasp. She angled her head back so that he could plunder the tender interior. His lips were warm and skilled, and unbelievably sensual. One kiss left her craving the next with helpless impatience.

'You are as eager for me as I am for you,' Shahir growled, taking her swollen pink mouth again, with a demanding urgency that she found irresistible. Lifting her, he brought her down on the hard cradle of his thighs. Deft fingers released the zip on her overall and pushed the garment from her shoulders to free her from it.

'Oh…' Her dazed green eyes flew wide open as he let an exploring hand travel over the pouting thrust of her small breasts beneath the dark blouse she wore. The straining tips of her tender flesh tightened and swelled within the cups of her bra.

'Oh…' Shahir mimicked her with a sensual mockery

that felt as unreal as everything else that had so far happened between them.

But, unreal or otherwise, she was already in thrall to the insistent demand of her own body. He pressed his knowing mouth to the tiny pulse-spot below her ear and nuzzled the sensitive skin there. Startled by the resulting leap of sensation, she clenched her fingers convulsively into his sleeves.

'I've never been into discomfort.' With that husky declaration, Shahir gathered her up into his arms and stood up as if she weighed no more than a china doll. 'And as a rule I prefer to make love in bed—although I am not saying that I could not be tempted by a more adventurous venue.'

Bed? Never had a single word seemed more graphic in its connotations!

Kirsten tensed in dismay, for she had not thought beyond the defiant act of enjoying kissing and getting close to him. But Shahir chose that exact same moment to bend his well-shaped dark head and let his tongue dip between her parted lips in a provocative and incredibly enervating sneak invasion. Kirsten melted like ice cream on a hot griddle, and did not surface from the grip of that all-encompassing loss of rational awareness until she found herself standing positioned between his splayed thighs while he sat on the edge of a bed. He had already undone the clasp at the nape of her neck to release her hair from confinement.

'I desired you the first time I saw you,' Shahir confessed, skimming lean brown fingers slowly through the shimmering fall of her pale silvery blonde hair. 'Every time I saw you from that moment I desired you even more...'

She was so tense that her knees wobbled beneath her. 'Truthfully?'

'Though you do not seem aware of the fact, you are extraordinarily beautiful.'

The clear green eyes clinging to his lean dark features clouded with sorrow. Her hand fluttered up to touch the ugly bruise. 'Not today, I'm not…'

Shahir enclosed her thin hand in a firm grip. His dark golden eyes were as bright as the heart of a fire. 'Today you seem even more beautiful to me.'

A laugh that wasn't a laugh at all was wrenched from Kirsten. Her eyes glimmered and her throat worked. Suddenly she was tipping herself forward and claiming his perfectly moulded mouth for herself, with passionate urgency. He unbuttoned her blouse, and the fastener on her trousers, tugging her down on to his lap to extract her with smooth expertise from her clothing while his kisses held her imprisoned.

'You wear so many clothes,' he censured thickly, one hand knotted in her silky hair to tip her head back so that his marauding mouth could trace an enterprising trail across the sensitive skin of her throat.

As her bra fell away, and cooler air brushed her nipples, Kirsten went rigid with shock and closed her hands over her exposed breasts.

Shahir stilled and tipped back his handsome dark head. He swept her up and settled her back against the pillows, straightening again by the bed to look searchingly down at her. 'I assumed that you were no stranger to sex. If I am mistaken, tell me, and you can leave without reproach,' he murmured tautly. 'I don't seduce virgins.'

Her lashes lowered over evasive green eyes. She hugged her knees to her chest, silvery fair hair falling round her like a screening veil. Her thoughts were in turmoil.

Growing up in Angus Ross's home had made her familiar with constant disappointment. Virtually everything that might give her pleasure had been denied her. Now she wanted Shahir more than she had wanted anything in her whole life. His candour gave her a choice. If she told him the truth, he would send her away from him, and she could not face that conclusion.

'I'm not a virgin.' she muttered in a rush, telling the lie before she could think through what she was doing and lose her nerve.

Shahir was very much in the mood to be convinced. Though in every way that mattered she was different from every other woman he had ever known. 'You seem very shy…'

Kirsten focused fixedly on her bare toes. 'Do you have a problem with that?'

He surveyed her delicate profile with smouldering golden eyes full of appreciation. 'No.'

'Then could you please close the curtains?'

Taken aback, Shahir raised a questioning brow. 'Do you only make love in the dark?'

Kirsten nodded vehemently.

Torn between a desire to laugh and an uneasy stab of tenderness that discomfited him, Shahir hit the buttons that closed the blinds and the curtains.

In the sudden darkness, Kirsten slid nervously off the bed. Her toes tangled with the garments scattered on the floor and she fell over her own feet.

Winded, she lay there until Shahir picked her up, saying, not quite steadily, 'You may make love in the dark, but I don't think you have night vision.'

'Obviously not…' The lamps on either side of the bed

lit up and she blinked rapidly at the sudden restoration of light.

His attention zeroed straight down to the prominent rosy nipples that crowned the pert thrust of her breasts. 'Why would you seek to hide such perfection?'

He closed his hands over hers before she could cover herself again, and backed her down on to the bed with masculine purpose. He cupped and stroked the small tempting mounds, and let his thumbs rub over the straining crests. She gasped as liquid heat snaked down to her pelvis and pooled there to form a knot of intense physical longing. He lowered his dark head and let his hungry mouth play over the distended pink buds.

She moved trembling fingers into the dense luxuriance of his cropped black hair. 'Shahir…'

'I like the way you say my name…' With a groan of reluctance he vaulted upright and proceeded to strip off his suit jacket and his tie.

Passion-glazed eyes widening, Kirsten watched him pull open his shirt to reveal a bronzed and muscular slice of chest. Off came the shirt, to reveal the hard contours of hair-roughened pectorals and the corrugated flatness of his stomach. He was all male, from the satin-smooth strength of his broad shoulders to his narrow waist and long, powerful thighs.

As he shed his well-cut trousers and stood revealed in black boxers she could feel her face starting to burn with hot colour. She wanted to look and she didn't want to look. The jersey boxers left little to the imagination, and her imagination was already running riot. He peeled them off, and for a split second she stared in apprehension, then quickly shut her eyes tight in mortification. There was too much of him, she thought in a panic. There was no way he was going to fit her, or she was going to fit him.

'I'm not shy,' Shahir confided, quite unnecessarily.

'I know,' she mumbled, not looking within six feet of him and scrambling below the sheet.

'But I find your shyness appealing,' he murmured in a surprised tone of discovery. 'It's very sexy.'

'Oh…'

'Oh…' Shahir mocked again, thrusting back the sheet.

Dark eyes slumberous, he leant over her and ran a slow, possessive hand over the silken swell of her breast down over her quivering tummy to the taut line of a lissom thigh. He let his tongue lash a tantalising pink peak and the breath hissed in her throat as she flung her head back, her back arching.

The knot of desire low in her belly twisted tighter. He parted her legs with gentle resolve, explored the silver curls that screened her feminine mound, and traced the slick smooth folds at the heart of her, where she was tender and swollen. She couldn't stay still. Her hips jerked and shifted on the bed. The hunger was back with a vengeance, fiercer and stronger than she could stand.

'Oh…*yes*,' Shahir breathed with raw satisfaction against her reddened mouth, and he eased a finger into the hot wet welcome that awaited him.

'Please…'

'It's too soon,' he husked.

He toyed with her melting body until whimpers of need were torn from her lips and she was writhing beneath the onslaught of an almost agonising tide of pleasure. Only then did he rise over her and plunge his hard male shaft into the sweet, tight depths of her receptive body. She was aching for him, eager—and completely unprepared for the sudden sharp tearing pain that made her cry out.

Abruptly, Shahir stilled. A lean hand turned her face up to his. Burnished golden eyes clashed with hers, his astonishment unhidden. 'You lied to me? You *are* a virgin?' he bit out incredulously.

Hot-faced, Kirsten shut her eyes tight shut and said nothing.

Shahir gazed down at her in disbelief. Never until that moment had he been aware of just how young she was, and never once had it crossed his mind that she might not tell him the truth. 'Kirsten…'

'Don't stop…' she mumbled, arching up to him in a shamelessly inviting movement that made her face flush with embarrassment. But she couldn't help it; she really couldn't. Somewhere down deep inside her there was an unrelenting throb of desire that was driving her crazy, and she knew that only he could satisfy it.

Torn between anger and a desire that was burning at fever-pitch, Shahir hesitated, his powerful muscles straining with the force of the self-discipline he was exerting over his powerful libido. But, on the edge of withdrawal from the sweet allure of her body, he rebelled against all restraint and slammed back into her with a harsh groan of satisfaction.

She cried out in excitement, sensation rippling through her in heady waves as pain became pleasure. He pushed up her knees, to deepen his penetration, and sank into her over and over again. She abandoned herself to a passion that was pagan in its wildness. He took her to the dazzling heights of sensual ecstasy and a climax of shattering intensity.

Lethargic and happy, stunned by her own capacity for physical enjoyment, Kirsten could barely think straight in the aftermath of her first experience of lovemaking. He held her close, kissed her brow.

She got to revel in that glorious intimacy for perhaps sixty seconds before he pulled back from her again.

At a moment when Kirsten was still floating on mental clouds of bliss, Shahir looked down at her, his stunning dark golden eyes cool and intent. 'Don't ever lie to me again.'

Wholly unprepared for the dynamic verbal condemnation and warning combined in that one pungent sentence, Kirsten gaped at him.

CHAPTER FIVE

'YOU don't have to make such a fuss about it!' Voicing a spirited defence, Kirsten pulled herself up against the tumbled pillows and hugged the sheet to her bare curves, which suddenly felt sinfully naked and exposed.

'Do I not?' Shahir demanded wrathfully, not backtracking a single inch—indeed, seizing the chance to argue the point with the stubborn resolve that was the backbone of his character.

'No, you don't.' Her discomfiture was pronounced. 'I told a little white lie—'

'There is no such thing!' Shahir tossed back the sheet and vaulted out of bed. 'I said I would not touch you if you were a virgin, and you chose to lie rather than tell me the truth. That was an act of deceit, and unfair to me.'

Taken aback by his cutting candour, and by the aggressive masculinity of his naked bronzed body, Kirsten flushed a deep guilty pink and averted her eyes from his powerful physique. 'It was my choice.'

'But it would not have been *my* choice to destroy your innocence. That was a betrayal of the principles that I respect,' Shahir imparted grimly, striding into the dressing room to gather up clean clothes and then continuing on into the adjoining bathroom.

Kirsten heard the sound of a shower running. She still had a convulsive grip on the sheet. A surge of stinging moisture was washing the back of her eyes and she swallowed the painful lump in her throat. She had acted wrongly, and the punishment for her misbehaviour was coming even faster than she had feared it would. She had surrendered her virginity to a man who didn't want it and who did not feel even remotely appreciative of the fact that she had given it to him because she felt he was special.

In what way was he special now? She crushed back that daunting reflection of her own ignorance when it came to men and tried to concentrate.

But it was a challenge. Here she was, desperate for some reassurance from him, even a little warmth and affection, and he was acting as if she had murdered someone. He had also called her a liar and, while strictly speaking that might be true, she really wasn't in the habit of telling lies. Unfortunately she had been upset, and she was very attracted to him, and somehow those two things had combined to wash away her usual level-headed and honest approach to life.

Shahir reappeared, looking formidably elegant and intimidating in yet another dark and beautifully tailored suit.

Kirsten spared him a skimming glance before fixing her attention on the foot of the bed. 'I'm sorry I lied, but I really wasn't thinking about what I was doing,' she admitted in a small, tight voice. 'Now that I am thinking, I wish I hadn't lied to you.'

His brooding gaze lightened several shades at that acknowledgement, but he was determined to drive home his point that he would not tolerate dishonesty. If, as he planned, she became a semi-permanent feature in his life, it was a lesson she needed to learn. 'Lies damage trust,' he pointed out levelly. 'How long do you think it will be before I am prepared to trust your word again?'

Kirsten wasn't listening to him. Having opened up the box of her own regrets, she was now steadily drowning in them. She not only wished that she hadn't lied to him, but was beginning to wish that she had not slept with him. 'I really just wish this hadn't happened—'

'We are not children, Kirsten. We chose to allow it to happen.'

'There's no need to rub it in! It's the worst mistake I ever made in my stupid life…'

'We were both unwise.' Shahir was struggling to silence his conscience while at the same time telling himself that there was no point in agonising over what could not be altered. He had wanted her. Now he had her—in more ways than one. He would be a liar if he overplayed the show of regret. 'But an apparent mistake may yet be turned into a more positive development.'

'I don't see how…' Wrenching the sheet from its moorings, Kirsten wrapped it clumsily round her and clambered off the bed, her lovely face tight with unhappiness.

She longed to have the ability to close her eyes and magically escape from the scene of their intimacy. Why on earth had she not had the sense to flee while he was in the shower? She felt much too ashamed to look him in the face as she stooped to pick up her discarded clothing, piece by mortifying piece. How could she so easily have disregarded every moral rule that had been drummed into her from childhood? She hardly knew him, and yet she had gone to bed with him. She was shattered by that reality, for in her right mind such an act seemed unthinkable to her.

She could see the sheer, terrifying power of her own emotions had combined with sexual attraction to destroy her self-respect. He had looked at her and he had touched her and all her common sense and self control had vanished. How could she continue to deny that she had feelings for him? Was she infatuated with him? Was she in love? He had haunted her thoughts and her dreams from their very first encounter on the hill. But she did not see that as an excuse for what she had allowed to happen between them.

'Stop this…' Catching her slender hand in his, Shahir gently detached her blouse from the fierce hold she had on it.

'But I have to get back to work—'

'No, you do not.' Shahir pressed her down into an upholstered chair. 'I want you to listen to me.'

'I really do need to get dressed—'

'Look at me,' he urged huskily. 'We are lovers now.'

Kirsten froze, the reminder deeply unwelcome. A flush of pained colour washed her cheekbones. She felt utterly wretched. She linked her trembling hands tightly together and made herself look up at him. 'Why do you have to throw that at me? Don't you think I feel bad enough as it is?'

Shahir dropped down in an athletic crouch so that his brilliant dark-as-midnight gaze was on a level with her. 'You should not feel unhappy about what has happened between us—'

'Well, I do,' she cut in unevenly.

'This could be the beginning of a new life for you.'

Her smooth forehead indented. 'How?'

'Obviously after this you can no longer work here. But I won't let you go home to your father again either. From now on I will make myself responsible for you.'

'What are you trying to say?'

'That you can simply get dressed and walk out into the limo with me and never return here.'

Her lashes fluttered up on bewildered green eyes. 'You're asking me to leave Strathcraig with you?'

Shahir wondered why it was that he was finding it difficult to come to the point. 'I'm asking you to continue being my lover.'

Kirsten sucked in a startled breath and attempted to master her astonishment. 'But—'

'Hear me out before you speak. I have an apartment in London. You can live there until you have had the time to choose a new home, of your own. I'll buy you that home and take care of all your needs.'

Shock was rippling through Kirsten as she understood what he was offering her—shock, and the beginnings of anger. 'You really don't have any respect for me, do you? Is that because I work as a cleaner? Or because I went to bed with you before we even got as far as a first date?'

Disconcerted by the unexpectedly volatile response, Shahir murmured flatly, 'Respect doesn't come into this—'

'I noticed! Well, I may have behaved in a very stupid manner today, but I do know the difference between right and wrong! And I may not be a virgin any more either,' Kirsten conceded with fierce discomfiture, 'but there is no way I'm about to turn into some cheap floozy you keep for sex!'

Shahir sprang upright. 'That is a distortion of the facts.'

'For someone who doesn't like lies you can be very imaginative with the truth,' Kirsten muttered bitterly.

'That could be because I very much want you to become a part of my life.'

'No, you don't!' Her eyes were hot with unshed tears but she was quivering with furious pain. 'You think I'm not good enough for anything but sharing a bed with. That's fine. Don't you dare think I care about that. But feeling as you do about me, you should have stayed well away from me!'

With that emphatic accusation, and almost blinded by tears, Kirsten snatched up her clothes, fled through to the bathroom and slammed shut the door. She would have liked a shower but was afraid of getting her hair wet. Even so, she was desperate to make good her escape and get back to work. Having made do with a hurried wash at the vanity unit, she dragged her clothes on over skin that was still damp.

Who would ever have thought that he would invite her to be his mistress? She must have been all right in bed, she reflected painfully. He would not want a repeat performance otherwise. He wouldn't want to offer her a house either. How could he have dared to talk of her becoming part of his life when it was so obvious that all he was interested in sharing with her was sex? When he would essentially be keeping her in return for the use of her body?

That offer was so horribly humiliating. Yet what else had she expected from him? She had not looked before she had leapt. How could she have any kind of normal relationship with a prince? The enormous gulf between them could never be bridged. That was why she should not have slept with him. Playing by the rules and keeping her distance would have protected her. Now her body had an intimate ache that she knew she would never forget.

She suppressed the sob clogging up her throat. She wanted so badly to relive that wonderful moment of togetherness when he had held her close before it all began to go wrong. But that was impossible.

Her home life had been destroyed by her father's violence. Now continuing to work at the castle would feel equally unsustainable. She did not want to see Shahir again. She did not want to work for him in any capacity either. What had once seemed like honest employment would now feel demeaning, she conceded unhappily. Somehow—and soon—she had to find a way to leave the farm and find another job.

Dragging in a shuddering breath of oxygen, she rested her damp brow against the wooden door and then opened it again.

Shahir was pacing the sitting room, his lean, darkly handsome features taut and grave. A heartbeat after Kirsten's flight from his presence, his intelligence had kicked back in and cold logic had prevailed. His perfectly orchestrated and rational existence had gone off the rails and crashed at spectacular speed. He was a disciplined man, and he was not accustomed to finding himself in the wrong, but he had too much integrity to deny the obvious. In retrospect he was sincerely appalled by his own unscrupulous behaviour.

Had he been more disturbed by the news of Faria's nuptials than he was prepared to admit? He saw that it had suited his purpose to give credit to Pamela Anstruther's sleazy suggestion that Kirsten was promiscuous. And he felt it unpardonable that that slur had made Kirsten seem more accessible and his own desire for her more acceptable. Only now that sanity and clear judgement had been restored did Shahir recognise that *nothing* could excuse his having become intimate with an employee.

Yet even that was not a fair appraisal of his misconduct, Shahir acknowledged bleakly. He had taken unprincipled advantage of a virgin—a naive and vulnerable young woman who should have been able to rely on him for support during a troubled period in her life. Instead he had betrayed her trust, and acted in a way that had increased her distress. He could not evade responsibility for the damage that he had caused. And suggesting that she become his mistress had been an even more distasteful act on his part. He was ashamed, and he knew what honour demanded of him in restitution.

Kirsten lodged in the doorway like a nervous fawn, ready to run for the undergrowth at the first sign of threat. 'I'm sorry…I need my overall.'

As she hastened across the room, her eyes screened by her lashes, and stooped to pick up the garment, Shahir addressed her. 'Kirsten, I have to talk to you.'

Kirsten refused to look at him. She was holding herself together, but only just managing, and she would have died rather than break down in front of him. 'You don't need to say anything at all. I bet you'll be relieved to hear that I don't expect to be working here for much longer. In fact I won't even be living at Strathcraig any more.'

'I am not relieved to hear those facts. Where are you planning to go?' Shahir demanded with a frown.

'I have plans.'

'Plans are not enough. Don't allow what happened between us to persuade you into making an impulsive decision. You are suffering a lot of strain right now, and I am aware that I have made the situation worse.'

Pride brought up Kirsten's chin, and she tossed her head. 'Actually…I was coping fine until you suggested that I could enjoy a dazzling future as a whore!'

His superb cheekbones were prominent below his bronzed skin, and faint colour accentuated the proud slant of them. 'I will not attempt to defend myself. I should not have made such a suggestion.'

Flustered by the unexpected admission of fault on his part, Kirsten found it easier to concentrate on putting her overall back on, and then she rushed into the tense silence to break it. 'That's all right…forget it. By the way, I never did say thank you for that magazine you got me.'

'What magazine?'

One glimpse of Shahir's mystified expression was sufficient to tell Kirsten that she had made yet another embarrassing mistake. He had not been responsible for leaving that magazine in her pigeonhole—and why on earth had she assumed that he had? Wishful thinking? Her cheeks burned.

'Never mind… Look, we've got nothing more to say to each other,' she muttered hurriedly.

'In that you are mistaken. I owe you an explanation for my behaviour.'

'I don't think so.'

'Please…'

The sound of that unfamiliar word on his lips allied to the terrible strain in the atmosphere made her eyes sting with tears. She could feel his remorse, and it was as sharp as her own. Oddly enough, his regret at what had happened between them hurt her more than his suggestion that she become his mistress.

She stole a brief glance at him from below her lashes. He was breathtakingly handsome. She remembered his mesmerising smile, the golden sheen of his skin against the white bedlinen, the warmth and the feel of him below her fingertips. Guilty pleasure almost consumed her, and a tiny twist of wicked heat sparked.

She tore her attention away from him in deep shame. Why could she not control her mind and her body?

'I will order coffee.' Shahir was determined to bring a more civilised note to the proceedings.

'No…please, let's just get this over with.'

Shahir studied her pale perfect profile in frustration.

Suddenly it was as though she was locked away from him in a place he couldn't follow. Even when she had been forced to look in his direction he had felt as though she could not quite see him.

'I hate to see you so unhappy. Matters may well have gone awry today because we were both too preoccupied with other events in our lives to be thinking clearly.'

Her attention caught, she glanced at him. 'Other events?'

'Your father had struck you, and I…' His beautifully modelled masculine mouth clenched as he steeled himself to make a personal admission that did not come easily to a male of his reserve. 'I too had some reasons to be disturbed. This morning I learned, quite by accident, that a woman who was important to me had become another man's wife.'

Kirsten could feel the blood draining from below her skin. She dropped her head and stared a hole in the magnificent rug beneath his polished leather shoes. His confession had hit her like a body-blow. It had come out of nowhere and he might as well have plunged a knife into her heart. *A woman important to him?* Obviously he was referring to a woman whom he loved. Yet it seemed almost unimaginable to Kirsten that Prince Shahir could have fallen in love and met with rejection.

Yet he had just told her so. He loved someone else. That thought steadily blocked out every other: Shahir's heart belonged to someone else.

The new awareness blazed a burning, wounding trail of pain across Kirsten's very soul. He loved another woman and, unable to have her, had taken Kirsten to bed instead. She had been a stop-gap, a distraction, a consolation prize. She felt sick with hurt and humiliation.

'What's her name?' she asked shakily.

Shahir had not been prepared either for the lengthy silence that followed his admission or for what he deemed to be the irrelevant question. His ebony brows pleated and his answer was reluctant. 'Faria…'

'You didn't need to tell me about her.' Kirsten could not help wishing that he had remained silent, for in telling her the truth he had lacerated her pride and filled her with a hollow sense of anguish.

'There was a need. I'm not in the habit of behaving as I did today. I took advantage of you and I wish to redress that wrong.' His lean, strong face was set in hard lines of resolve. 'In this situation there is only one way in which I can do that.'

'I don't understand. What's done is done.'

'Marry me,' he murmured levelly. 'Marry me and become my wife.'

Kirsten parted her lips to vent a shaken laugh, but no sound came out. Involuntarily focusing on him, she met dark golden eyes as steady as they were serious. 'But that's the craziest thing I ever heard…'

'It is not. This is not a liberal community, and you are not from a home where sex outside marriage is deemed acceptable. Naturally you are upset by what has happened between us, and you have a right to be. In taking advantage of your trust when you were in an emotional frame of mind I acted with dishonour.'

'But to propose marriage to me…' Words failed her.

She was stunned by the turnaround in his attitude. It was, however, beginning to sink in that his conduct towards her must have been very much out of character. Yet that acknowledgement only made her more painfully aware of his love for Faria. He must have been thinking of Faria when he took her in his arms, and that hurt.

'Why not? Sooner rather than later I must marry someone.'

'But surely not just anyone?' she framed shakily.

'You're very beautiful.'

All over again Kirsten felt the ignominy of being valued for her physical charms alone. Indeed, it seemed to her that the looks that had attracted him to her had extracted a high price from them both. He believed that he had wronged her, but she refused to accept that he was at fault and she totally blameless. Had she admitted her inexperience he would not have slept with her. She was responsible for her own behaviour. She had wanted him. Even knowing that what she was doing was wrong, she had encouraged him to make love to her. Now she had to accept the consequences. He was only asking her to marry him because he felt guilty, and she hoped she had enough pride and decency not to take any man on such discreditable terms.

'Let's just forget about all this.' Her strained green eyes locked to his stubborn jawline and rose no higher. 'You don't owe me anything. I'm not holding you to blame. There's certainly no need for you to be offering me marriage.'

'There is every need,' Shahir countered.

'I appreciate the offer. I really do. I don't want to be rude either… But I'd have to be really desperate to marry anyone without love.' Especially a man madly in love with another woman, Kirsten affixed inwardly.

'This is your decision?'

'Yes. May I go now?' she prompted uncomfortably.

'As you wish.'

Shahir watched her hasty retreat from his presence with grim dark golden eyes and a rare sense of incomprehension. He had expected her to accept his proposal.

Indeed, the prospect of refusal had not crossed his mind. He had already been planning the best terms in which to present such an unequal marriage to his father. He should be relieved that would not now be necessary, and that honour had been satisfied without any degree of personal sacrifice. Disturbingly, however, all he could think about was the fact that there was now no way that Kirsten Ross could ever adorn his bed again.

Kirsten had managed barely three steps down the gallery before Jeanie appeared at the far end and gave her a frantic wave.

'I've been looking everywhere for you. Have you been off some place crying?' the redhead asked with rough sympathy. 'Well, guess what? There's a big panic on in the basement. Something valuable has gone walkabout and the staff lockers are being searched. Everyone has to agree to their locker being checked...but can you imagine how it would look if you refused?'

'Like you were guilty.' Relieved that Jeanie had noticed nothing amiss, Kirsten made a determined effort to behave normally. 'What's gone walkabout?'

'Haven't a clue. The housekeeper and her sidekicks aren't telling.'

So much had happened so fast to Kirsten that she felt disconnected from the world around her. In the midst of the noisy chatter of the staff room she sat in a daze, lost in her own increasingly fantastic thoughts.

Suppose she had been insane enough to say yes to his proposal, she was thinking. Would Shahir really have married her? He would scarcely have asked had he not been prepared to do so. Would she have become a princess? Was there the remotest possibility that she might have made him happy? That he might have fallen out of love with Faria and fallen in love with her instead? How low would it be to marry a man who was only asking out of guilt? Very low, or only a little bit low?

When the senior housekeeper, Mrs Cook, appeared, with her thin face set in severe lines, Jeanie nudged Kirsten to attract her attention. 'Now someone's for it…'

'Kirsten…could I have a word?' Mrs Cook enquired.

Silence spread around Kirsten like a pool of poison. Getting up with a bewildered frown, she followed Mrs Cook into her office, where the older woman's two assistants were waiting.

'This was found in your locker.' A sparkling diamond pendant on a gold chain was placed on the desk in front of Kirsten.

'That's not possible…' Kirsten studied the pendant in disbelief. It was familiar to her, for on at least two occasions she had seen it lying in a careless heap on Pamela Anstruther's dressing table.

'We have a witness who says she saw you hiding it in your locker during your lunch break,' Mrs Cook divulged.

Stunned by that announcement, Kirsten immediately endeavoured to argue her innocence.

What followed was the worst experience of her life. She insisted that she had not entered the locker room since the start of her shift. She declared that it was impossible for there to be a witness to an act that had not happened. She had neither stolen the pendant from Pamela's bedroom, nor attempted to conceal it.

The witness, Morag Stevens, one of the two assistant housekeepers, then stepped forward to tell her story without once looking in Kirsten's direction.

When Kirsten realised that nobody was paying the slightest heed to her protests and defensive explanations she became very scared and upset. But within the hour it was all over. She was informed that she was very lucky that Lady Pamela did not wish to have her prosecuted for theft, and she was dismissed on the grounds of gross misconduct. The contents of her locker were packed into a bag and she was escorted out of the castle.

Jeanie was waiting at the courtyard gate for her. White-faced, Kirsten got off her bicycle to speak to the other woman and tell her about her dismissal. 'I didn't do it, Jeanie. I swear I didn't!'

'I'd be amazed if you did. After all, you'd be the first to be suspected, and you'd have to be a right idiot to think you could get away with it!'

'But why did Morag say she saw me put the pendant in my locker at lunchtime? Why would she lie? Why would she do that to me?'

'Maybe she stole it and then got nervous and hid it in your locker? She has access to the pass keys,' Jeanie reminded her. 'But somehow I'd be more suspicious of Lady Posh.'

'Lady Pamela?' Kirsten interrupted in astonishment. 'Why would she have anything to do with the loss of her own jewellery?'

Jeanie grimaced. 'I first smelt a rat when Lady Posh came over all nice and asked you to work for her. She's never been a nice person. But if she did stitch you up, I can't imagine why or how she did it—and I bet you won't ever be able to prove it. She's a clever one.'

Kirsten bowed her head, thinking of all that Jeanie did not know, and all she did not feel able to tell her. Yes, she acknowledged, she had annoyed Pamela Anstruther by staring at Shahir. But that had just been a little thing, hadn't it? It would be fantastical to suspect that Pamela would deliberately set her up to be falsely accused of theft, sacked and discredited. Yet it did not make any more sense to Kirsten that Morag Stevens would have stolen the pendant, only to conceal it in someone else's locker.

Kirsten's head spun when she attempted to come up with a viable explanation for what she had initially assumed had to be a ghastly misunderstanding or a case of mistaken identity.

'What are you going to do?' Jeanie prompted.

A light switched on in the dark turmoil of Kirsten's thoughts: she would make use of that business card and phone Shahir. She seized on the solution like a drowning swimmer. He would not let her be blamed for something she had not done. He would never believe that she was a thief. If he insisted, the matter would have to be more fully investigated and then surely the truth would emerge.

'Your dad will go bonkers if he finds out you've been done for theft,' Jeanie said worriedly.

'It's Friday. I have the weekend to tell him,' Kirsten mumbled, but her stomach was churning at the very idea.

'Kirsten, you can't tell him. You can't take the risk. No offence intended, but your dad can act like a bit of a nutter. Why don't you come home with me?'

The minibus that ferried castle employees back to the village every day was now within sight.

'I couldn't possibly—'

Jeanie gripped her arm for emphasis. 'You can always phone me. You're welcome any time of the day or night. My dad won't mind you staying with us.'

Kirsten got home as quickly as she could. Breathless, she hurried up to her bedroom, removed the small gilded card from below the mattress and hurried back downstairs to dial Shahir's mobile phone.

When Shahir answered the call, she hurtled straight

into speech. Maybe he had already been told about the pendant, but she was praying that he had not and that her version of events would be the first he heard.

'I have to see you…it's urgent.'

There was a brief moment of silence before he suggested that they meet in an hour's time at the viewpoint which lay about half a mile from her home.

She took strength from the fact that his rich dark drawl sounded the same as usual.

His lean, strong face austere, Shahir set down his phone.

CHAPTER SIX

FROM the viewpoint there was a spectacular panorama of the glen of Strathcraig and the mountains. Surrounded by dense forest, the turreted castle looked like a fairytale palace in a sunlit glade. On the valley floor the water of the loch gleamed as still and as blue as a tear-shaped sapphire.

The silence rushed in Kirsten's ears, and then she heard the faint recognisable purr of a car engine climbing the hill. A couple of minutes later the limousine pulled in to the parking area.

Kirsten started to speak before she even got inside the vehicle. 'I know you must be wondering why I contacted you—'

'No. I am aware of what occurred this afternoon.' Shahir rested impassive dark eyes on her, his absolute calm and composure intimidating her. For a moment it seemed as if the intimacy they had shared earlier that day might never have happened.

That cool, level tone made Kirsten lose colour. 'I *didn't* take that pendant.'

Shahir shifted a lean brown hand in a silencing gesture. 'Although I could not condone theft in any circumstances, I do understand why you did it.'

Kirsten stiffened. 'But I didn't do it!

'Kirsten…I myself witnessed what was probably your first attempt to steal from Lady Pamela.'

Totally taken aback by that astounding claim, Kirsten

whispered, 'My *first* attempt? What are you talking about?'

His bronzed profile took on a grim cast. 'I am referring to the brooch that mysteriously reappeared after Pamela had already conducted a search for it. You luckily found it. Possibly you took fright when she so quickly noticed that the brooch had gone missing and you decided to replace it.'

Her brow had furrowed, an expression of consternation blossoming in her candid gaze. 'Are you saying that you thought I was only pretending to have found the brooch?'

'At the time I did not think that. But I do not place great credence in coincidence.' Shahir regarded her with uncompromising cool.

'Neither do I, but—'

'I must be frank. When I learned that the pendant had been discovered in your locker, I recalled the matter of the brooch. Taking those two incidents into consideration, I would find it impossible to accept that you have been falsely accused of theft.'

That unequivocal declaration slammed into Kirsten like a punch in the stomach: she felt sick and she could hardly catch her breath. She did not know why, or even how, but from somewhere she had managed to acquire immense faith in Shahir's ability to divine the truth. Now that faith seemed impossibly naive. She was in shock as well, because his explanation had added another whole layer of complexity to the theme of her presumed guilt. 'You honestly believe that I'm a thief?'

'There is considerable sympathy for your situation. Had there not been, you would have been prosecuted,' Shahir delivered in a flat undertone 'You are living in distressing circumstances, and naturally you must want to leave your home. Carrying out that objective requires money. Only today you yourself informed me that you did not plan to be at Strathcraig for much longer.'

'Yes, but I didn't mean I was planning to steal jewellery to fund my getaway!' Her head was aching. She wanted to scream with frustration and sob with anger and fear and hurt. She felt horribly isolated and misjudged. She had done nothing wrong, yet a plausible case had still been made against her. People thought she had resorted to pilfering because she was desperate to escape her unhappy home life. No doubt her bruised face had made it even easier for some to believe that she was guilty as charged.

'I intend to give you the financial help that you require to leave your home.'

Her head flew up, green eyes suddenly bright as chipped emeralds as furious mortification took hold of her. 'No, thank you. I won't accept money from you!'

'I want to help. It is only right that I should. I may not be able to condone theft, but I can comprehend your desperation.'

Rage was pumping through Kirsten in an adrenalin rush. She did not trust herself to speak. She tried to open the car door, but it remained infuriatingly closed.

'The door is locked as a security measure. What I have said may be unwelcome to you, but I am not your enemy,' Shahir murmured dryly.

Kirsten flung her head back. 'Oh, yes, you are! I trusted you, I had faith in you, and I don't know why! I had this stupid idea that somehow you would *know* that I didn't take that pendant! Instead you're accusing me of having tried to steal the brooch as well. Let me out of this car!'

'Calm down. You are being foolish.'

'No, I'm not!' Kirsten raged back at him, a flush of

pink mantling her delicate features. 'I'm not a thief, and I don't want your wretched charity. Maybe you'd like me to disappear into thin air because you slept with me, but I'll leave Strathcraig under my own steam and in my own good time—and I don't need anything…least of all help…from you!'

Hard dark golden eyes slammed into hers with the efficacy of a missile hitting a direct target. 'Control yourself. That is *enough*.'

He had not raised his voice. He did not need to do so. His intonation carried enough measured force to quell a riot. Quivering with angry distress, Kirsten sucked in oxygen and expelled it again in a shaken surge. She did not want to control her temper. She was afraid that if her anger dimmed her strength would sink with it, for even in the midst of hating him with all her heart she was conscious of the terrible shock and pain of his misjudgement.

'Whether you accept it or not, I care about what happens to you,' Shahir asserted. 'I would not otherwise have asked you to marry me.'

'Your conscience cares, but you don't *really* care!' Kirsten condemned in fierce argument.

'I would like to know that you are safe and unharmed, and there is no guarantee of that in your current environment.' He settled an envelope down on the seat beside her. 'Use it or burn it. The choice is yours.'

'It's great to have more money than sense, isn't it?'

Shahir ignored that childish crack. 'Are you prepared to press a charge of assault against your father?'

'No.' Kirsten shook her head vehemently.

'Then you cannot be protected from him. Have you no relatives who might intervene on your behalf to reason with him, or who might offer you a home?'

Mute, she shook her head again. Her parents had both been only children. 'I have a brother, Daniel. He quarrelled with my father five years ago and left. I don't know where he is. He hasn't phoned or written home since then.'

'Were you close to your brother?'

'When we were kids, but goodness knows where he is now.'

'It might well be possible to have him traced and found, but that would take time. It would seem that your only immediate option is to leave Strathcraig. I am offering you my support to do that.'

'What support? Your cash? You've let me down.' With pained satisfaction, Kirsten watched his angular masculine jawline clench at that condemnation.

'Regardless of what you believe, I am concerned for your welfare. If you leave the glen, you must let me know where you are.'

'Why would I do that when you don't believe a word I've said?' Kirsten flared back at him. 'I am telling you the truth. I am not a thief and I certainly don't require your advice or your money. I'll manage fine on my own, thank you very much! Now, let me out of this car!'

She was rigid with the amount of emotion that she was holding in. She could not bring herself to touch the envelope. She did need money, but not his. To accept even a blade of grass from him would have hurt like hell.

Scrambling out of the car, she trudged back down the hill. She did not look back. She would not permit her thoughts to rest on Shahir, or on the encounter that had just taken place. That would be a severe waste of mental energy. Had she been foolish enough to believe that her handsome prince would come to her rescue, like some guy in a fairy story? Well, now she knew different. Her world had become a very scary place, and the wound he had inflicted with his mistrust was the most raw of all.

All too well aware that she dared not stay within her own home, she made herself think of practical things. She would pack a small bag, because that was all she could carry on her bike. And she would have to take up Jeanie's offer of hospitality—for the night at least. Would Squeak be welcome as well? She knew that she dared not leave the elderly dog behind, lest he become the focus of Angus Ross's thwarted rage.

Kirsten carted the laden tray past tables packed with lunchtime diners and deposited it in the kitchen.

'You shouldn't be doing that.' Donald's kindly face below his thinning red hair was full of concern as he served up another basket of chips. 'You deal with the bills. Stay away from the heavy work.'

Kirsten just nodded, and waited until he was out of view before massaging the ache in her lower back. The diner was always understaffed, and with the other waitresses struggling to cope, Kirsten refused to sit idle behind the till. She was well aware that she was lucky to still have a job.

It was more than seven months since she had walked out of her home, leaving only a brief note of explanation behind. Donald was Jeanie's brother, and he and his wife, Elspeth, had been very good to Kirsten.

The weekend after Kirsten had left the farm, Donald and Elspeth had visited Strathcraig with a trailer to pick up her personal effects. The couple had given Kirsten a lift down to London. To begin with she had rented their spare room, and she had been grateful to walk straight into a job as a waitress at the café that Donald managed.

She had had to work long hours to save up sufficient to put down a rental deposit for a bedsit.

At first she had felt lost in the city. The sheer volume of the crowds and the traffic and the noise had stunned her. She often pined for the wild grandeur of the mountains and the peace and silence of the glen. But from the outset she had refused to look back with regret, and to satisfy her longing for green places she had explored the London parks with Squeak. While she'd focused on the new and bright future she was determined to carve, she had busily searched out information on further education courses.

It had not been difficult to decide that she should set her sights on training as a music teacher. As a first step in that process she had signed up for a couple of evening classes. Although she already held the required qualifications as a musician, she needed to gain exam passes in other subjects before she could hope to apply for a place on a degree course. She had been happy to face the prospect of several years of studying and living on a very low income. In fact she had felt privileged to have the opportunity, and proud that she had the courage to try and get more out of life than her father had been prepared to allow her to have.

In almost every way her future had looked full of promise, and she had worried that it was all too good to be true. Unfortunately her misgivings had proved correct, for she had soon discovered something that had wrecked all her carefully laid plans and made everything infinitely more complicated.

Another waitress began filling ketchup bottles behind the counter. When Kirsten tried to help, Patsy urged her to sit back down on a stool by the till.

'A good gust of wind and you'd fall over,' the older

woman scolded, closing a motherly hand round Kirsten's thin forearm for emphasis. 'You're too skinny to be healthy. When did you last see the doctor?'

'I've always been thin.' Kirsten sidestepped the question, because she had overslept and missed her last appointment. 'Stop worrying about me.'

'I can't help it. You don't look strong enough to lift a teaspoon, and that baby will be here in another few weeks,' Patsy sighed ruefully.

'I'm fine.'

Kirsten turned away to deal with a customer. The swell of her tummy bumped against the counter. The new awkwardness of her body embarrassed her, and she had yet to adjust to her changed shape. Sometimes she would catch a glimpse of her reflection in a shop window or a mirror and she just wouldn't recognise herself.

Indeed, she had already been four months pregnant by the time she'd discovered that the queasiness she was suffering from was the result of something more than a persistent tummy bug.

Truth to tell, she had been desperately unhappy when she'd first arrived in London, and she had fought her misery every step of the way. Night and day she had waged a battle of denial against the male whose image haunted her every waking hour. She had tried to fill all her time with work or study. The strain of that crazy timetable had destroyed her appetite. It had been ages before she even noticed that her periods had stopped. Believing that stress and weight loss were the cause, she had not been unduly concerned. It had only been when the nausea refused to go away that she'd recognised the need to consult a doctor.

Even at that point it had not occurred to her that she might be carrying a baby. In retrospect her blindness seemed utterly and inexcusably stupid to her. After all, she might have been a virgin, but she was certainly old enough and wise enough to be aware that sexual relations could lead to conception. Unfortunately all such rational considerations had been hampered by the simple fact that just thinking about Shahir reduced her to a useless heap of emotional rubble and self-loathing. In an effort to protect herself from destructive thoughts she had suppressed her every recollection of him—and of the forbidden passion they had shared that day.

Only when the doctor's diagnosis had forced Kirsten to look back to their short-lived intimacy had she realised that she could not recall Shahir having taken the precautions that would have protected her from pregnancy.

The prospect of becoming an unmarried mother had made her feel sick with shame—and very scared. And then she had been so angry with Shahir she had boiled with rage. How could he have been so careless with her? While he might seem to be the ultimate in cool control on the surface, she was aware of a wild, reckless streak underneath. She had seen that side of him on the motorbike—and in bed. An electric frisson of awareness ran through her whenever she recalled the scorching golden glitter of his eyes.

Why should Shahir worry if her life was to be wrecked by the burden of single parenthood? Once the baby was born, how was she to work or attend evening class? With a child to care for it would be a much bigger challenge for her to make ends meet and finish her education.

She had thought about phoning Shahir to inform him that he was destined to become the father of her child. But Shahir had called her a thief and, since she had denied the charge, he had to think that she was a liar into the bargain. His uninhibited regret at having slept with her, not to mention his being hopelessly in love with another woman, had not been in his favour either. What pride she had left had revolted at the idea of announcing her pregnancy to a man who would equate her news with catastrophe.

'How's that little dog of yours doing?' Patsy enquired chattily, breaking into Kirsten's troubled thoughts.

'He's still sleeping a lot. I don't take him walking out as much as I did. The vet says he's just old…' Strain edged Kirsten's voice, for she adored Squeak and she was terrified of losing him: he was her last link with her late mother.

When she'd finished her shift, she walked out on to the street. It was cold, and the street lamps cast a yellow glow over the wet pavement. A few yards ahead of her a car door opened and a man climbed out. Light glinted over his cropped black hair, shadow falling over his lean bronzed profile. Then he straightened to his full imposing height and her breath tripped in her throat. Shock froze her in her tracks, wide green eyes welded to his arrestingly handsome face.

'I seem to have frightened you…that wasn't my intention,' Shahir drawled, as smoothly as if they met and talked on a regular basis.

'How did you find out where I was?' Kirsten exclaimed, busily engaged in buttoning her coat in an instinctive attempt to conceal her protruding stomach.

'Ways and means. Are you feeling all right?' Shahir stared down at her, a frown pleating his ebony brows. 'You're very pale.'

'Am I? This light makes everyone look weird,' she gabbled, striving to act normally. 'What are you doing here?'

'I came to see you.'

She folded her arms, discovered her tummy got in the way of what had once been her waist and hastily dropped her arms again. 'Why?' she asked baldly.

'I did ask you to stay in touch. I was concerned when I didn't hear from you. Let me give you a lift.'

'No, really—there's no need.'

'There is every need. You're shivering with cold.'

She blinked, and realised that he was correct: she *was* shivering, and her light coat offered little defence against the winter chill. She was cold and she was tired and her back was hurting. And, what was more, she thought wretchedly, it was entirely his fault that she was cold, tired and pregnant. Why on earth was she trying to conceal her tummy from the man who had got her into this condition?

In a sudden movement that took him by surprise she stepped past him and clambered into the limousine. The warmth and comfort of the opulent vehicle felt like a cocoon to her weary bones.

'We could dine at my hotel,' Shahir murmured.

'I'd have to go home first…' As Kirsten heard herself virtually agreeing to his invitation, she was disconcerted to appreciate that her tongue seemed to be running ahead of her brain.

Without comment, Shahir asked for her address and passed it to his chauffeur. She watched him from below her lashes the whole time, devouring every aspect of his appearance with a voracious craving for detail. Even the way he sat was graceful, with his proud dark head at an angle, his broad shoulders relaxed back, long lean limbs arranged with careless masculinity. She loved the way he dressed too, with a style that was both elegant and fashionable. His designer suit was perfectly tailored to his powerful physique. He always looked as if he had stepped straight out of a glossy magazine.

He really was incredibly good-looking...sin personified in male flesh, she conceded ruefully. It was little wonder she had fallen stupidly in love and even more stupidly into bed with him.

'I'll only be ten minutes.' Kirsten hurried into the terraced house where she lived.

She lived in a grimy street lined with rundown housing. Shahir had to resist the urge to accompany her. At his nod the bodyguard in the front seat got out and alerted the security team in the car behind. He breathed in slow and deep, his brilliant dark eyes bleak, for he was very much shocked by the change in her appearance. Nothing could steal the haunting loveliness from her flawless face, but her skin was as white as milk and as transparent as glass, while her eyes were hollow and darkly shadowed. She had also become painfully thin. She looked ill.

Kirsten fed Squeak. She knew that she was going to tell Shahir about the baby. Not because it felt like the right thing to do, or because it was silly to feel humiliated by a pregnancy that he had inflicted on her. No, primarily she was going to tell Shahir that she was pregnant because she knew it would ruin his day. There it was—a mean, petty, vengeful and absolutely shameful motive. But that was how she felt at that moment.

All of a sudden she was wondering how many other women he had been with over the past seven months. Had he wined and dined them too? Of course she had just been a lowly cleaner, and while he might have been prepared to take that lowly cleaner to bed he had not been democratic enough to offer to take her out for a meal. Or give her a flower...or, for that matter, even a little magazine! She could not even regard herself as having been a cheap date, because there had not been a date to begin with. That acknowledgement did nothing to raise her sagging self-esteem.

She was convinced that while she had been struggling to survive Shahir had been partying. Household gossip had always implied that he led an astonishingly quiet and boring life at Strathcraig. Didn't drink, didn't smoke, did nothing but work, work and work, what free time he did have absorbed by the charitable foundation he had set up.

Kirsten, however, was unimpressed by that account of clean and decent living. Shahir might not have brought women he slept with to the castle, but he owned other properties round the world, and he had asked her to be his mistress, hadn't he? He had also got her into bed faster than the speed of light, which signified no small amount of experience, she reasoned bitterly. Any man who kept a mistress was a womaniser. He might be a discreet womanizer, but he was a womaniser nonetheless.

Now she had stoked her hatred to new and heady heights, she saw that it was time that he knew exactly what she thought of him!

Squeak had arthritic joints, and had to be lifted into the limousine. Once on board, he curled up in the cosiest corner of the carpeted floor and went straight back to sleep. Kirsten sank heavily into the leather seat opposite Shahir and closed her eyes while she planned the speech she would make to him. Exhaustion weighed her down like a heavy blanket...

The unfamiliar sound of Squeak growling wakened Kirsten from her heavy slumber. Blinking drowsily, she gazed down at Squeak who, having stationed himself protectively in front of her, was baring his teeth at Shahir, leaning forward.

'I was trying to wake you. He is a good watchdog,' Shahir advanced dryly. 'We've arrived at the hotel.'

'Sorry—I must have dozed off.' Running an uneasy hand through her rumpled hair, Kirsten took hold of Squeak's lead. 'Where are we?'

'In the hotel's underground car park. Did you think I was abducting you?'

Kirsten forced a laugh. 'Don't be daft.'

As she walked into the lift, Squeak, agitated by his unfamiliar surroundings, crossed in front of her and she stumbled over his lead. Shahir closed firm hands to her shoulders to steady her before she could tumble forward. 'Careful…'

Without appreciating how close he was to her, Kirsten spun nervously round to face him again. Unfortunately her tummy got in the way of her smoothly completing the movement and rubbed against his hip. She glanced down and was transfixed by the way the fabric of her coat had pulled taut over her projecting midsection to define her fecund shape with cruel accuracy.

Bemused by her tense silence, Shahir followed the path of her gaze. Everything that had confused him fell into place: her ill-health, her unusually clumsy gait, the slowness with which she now moved.

At their feet Squeak growled at the tall dark man's proximity, but he was ignored. Shahir lifted hands that were not quite steady and undid the two buttons on her coat and carefully spread the edges apart. 'You're going to have a baby,' he breathed, his entire focus pinned to the sizeable swell of her belly. 'And soon. Whose baby?'

Kirsten dug her hands into her pockets and used them to whip shut the coat and conceal her stomach again. Her face was as red as fire. 'Whose do you think?' she hissed like a stinging wasp, accusation etched in every syllable.

'Then the baby will be due within the next few weeks…'

'I'm glad you can count,' she commented thinly.

A servant already had the door of his penthouse suite open in readiness.

Shahir felt light-headed. If his calculations were correct, in less than two months he would be a father. He was in shock. So he was not to feature as a statistic in the much-discussed global fall in male fertility. The baby she was carrying was his. Of course it was. Did that explain why she looked so ill? He knew less than nothing about pregnant women. But what he did know sent a cold shiver through him, for his own mother had died bringing him into the world.

Kirsten came to a self-conscious halt in the centre of the luxurious sitting room. 'I want you to know that I hate you for getting me into this situation,' she told him with feverish force. 'I really, really hate you for it!'

Shahir released his breath in a soundless hiss. She was understandably upset, he reasoned. She must have had a rough time in recent months, and she was clearly unwell. But now that he was here to take care of her everything was about to change. The world would literally become her oyster.

He was tempted to scoop her into his arms and race for the airport at speed, but he knew he couldn't take her back to his own country to enjoy the very best of tender care until she was his wife.

'Did you hear me?' Kirsten demanded, a tad shrilly.

'Yes. I acknowledge that we have not enjoyed a conventional relationship—'

'We didn't have a relationship…you slept with me!'

'Dragging up the past in an emotional way at this point is not constructive. You are expecting my child, and that is the key issue at stake here. It is vitally important that we marry as soon as it can be arranged,' Shahir declared without hesitation, lean, powerful features taut. 'Why? Because our baby will be heir to the throne of Dhemen—but *only* if his birth is legitimate.'

Unprepared for either of those two announcements, Kirsten stared back at him in a daze of angry confusion. 'You still haven't said anything about what I said.'

'Right now I would be grateful if you would acknowledge that we currently have a much more pressing duty towards the child you carry.'

'You're still prepared to marry me?' Without warning her mind had circled back to centre on Shahir's earlier proposition, and there her mind stuck—as though her thoughts were lodged in cement. Once again she was getting the chance to marry Shahir. Pride and a strong sense of fairness had made her refuse his first proposal seven months earlier. She had not needed a wedding ring to compensate her for the loss of her virginity. Even loving him, she hadn't wanted him on those humiliating terms.

'Of course I am. '

'Wouldn't it have been simpler just to take precautions and make sure that this didn't happen in the first place?'

'It would have been. But I didn't.' His strong jawline squared. 'I assure you that I have never before been so careless.'

Although the subject embarrassed her, Kirsten was still amazed that a male of his sophistication and experience should have been so careless as to totally disregard the threat of consequences. 'Didn't it occur to you that you might make me pregnant?'

The faintest hint of colour scored his superb cheekbones. 'By the time I appreciated what I had done, it was too late. Afterwards I confess that I underestimated the level of risk. And although I asked you to stay in contact with me, I didn't seriously consider the likelihood of you having conceived.'

'So how do you feel about it now you do know? Cursed? Bitter? Furious?' Kirsten queried, desperate to get a real live human reaction out of him. She was convinced that he had to be feeling such emotions, even if he was determined not to show them.

'I feel that this is our fate and we must accept it with grace,' Shahir countered with rock-solid assurance.

Her teeth gritted at that suave reply. 'You mentioned something about the baby being the heir to...to a throne? What was that about?'

'I am the Crown Prince of my country. My father, Hafiz, is King of Dhemen.' He awarded her a questioning appraisal. 'Surely that cannot be news to you?'

Kirsten was stunned. She had assumed that the royal family he belonged to was a large one, and that he was only one of a whole bunch of princes. She had not been aware that he was the son of a king—or the next in the royal line of succession. In her brief time working at the castle she had not heard anyone mention those facts.

'Let us eat now…'

A door had been quietly opened into an adjoining room and a beautifully laid table awaited them. She sat down, accepted a glass of water, and sipped at it.

'So, Kirsten. Will you set aside your hostility and agree to become my wife?' Shahir prompted gravely.

'I can't believe that you're prepared to marry a thief,' Kirsten heard herself whisper with malicious intent, and she was shocked at herself.

Challenging dark golden eyes flared and met hers in a head-on collision. 'Life is full of surprises.'

Her face flamed, for she had dimly expected him to

backtrack on that issue. 'I didn't steal that pendant…I'm not a thief.'

Shahir said nothing. He watched her shred her roll and leave it untouched.

Kirsten knew that his silence was as good as a statement of his disbelief, and she had to swallow back a hot-headed further comment. Why was it that whenever she tried to score a point with him she ended up sounding wretchedly childish and provocative? She wanted to argue her innocence, but sensed that it would be a waste of what little energy she had left. Right now, his entire focus was on the child she carried.

He wanted to marry her so that the baby would be born within wedlock. She had to be fair to him. The level of his commitment towards their unborn child was impressive, and the speed with which he had accepted responsibility equally so, she acknowledged unhappily. Of course he didn't care about her personally, but what else could she expect? He wasn't even concerned by the reality that she had sworn undying hatred for him. Evidently he was able to rise above such petty personal feelings and concentrate solely on the baby's needs. Shouldn't she be capable of acting with equal unselfishness?

Unfortunately her private emotions did not feel petty. She had fallen madly in love with Shahir bin Harith al-Assad, and he had hurt her terribly. And she only had to look across the table and notice the spectacular bronze of his eyes to be afraid that she was on the brink of being really badly hurt all over again. But she felt horribly guilty for thinking about herself when his example made it clear that she ought only to be considering what was best for the baby.

'So…will you marry me?' Shahir asked again.

'Yes.' Shadowed green eyes screened, Kirsten shrugged her thin shoulders, as if to suggest that she really couldn't care either way. But she doubted that he was taken in by her play of indifference. In the community in which she had been raised the moral rules were narrow and unforgiving, and to have a baby outside the bonds of matrimony could not feel like anything other than a source of shame to her. It was hugely important to her that her child should not suffer the stigma of illegitimacy, and that he or she should have both a father and a father's name.

'I promise that I will not give you cause to regret the decision. I'll make immediate arrangements for our wedding.' The merest hint of a smile tugging at the edges of his sculpted mouth, Shahir stretched a lean brown hand gracefully across the table to engulf hers.

Pale face tensing, Kirsten snaked her fingers hastily back from that threatened contact. 'Let's not be fake,' she said defensively, pushing the soup plate aside after only one spoonful had passed her lips. 'It's not as though it'll be a proper marriage. It'll only be a pretend one, so that we can put on a respectable front.'

Once again Shahir exercised restraint and said nothing. It might have surprised her, but he was renowned as the diplomat of the royal family. Negotiation was an art at his clever fingertips, and one in which he had great skill. Yet around her he was conscious of being as tactless as an elephant running amok in hobnail boots.

He had yet to work out why all judgement and discretion should desert him with such disastrous effect in her radius, so he embraced silence instead.

CHAPTER SEVEN

'I LOOK like a blob with matchstick arms and legs attached.' Strained green eyes full of disappointment, Kirsten turned away from the reflection taunting her in the mirror. She stiffened as a tiny pain curled in her pelvis, but it faded so fast that she thought it nothing to worry about.

Jeanie planted her hands on her ample hips and dealt the younger woman a reproachful appraisal. 'That's a lovely dress, and you look bonny in it!'

'But I'm huge…' Feeling forlorn, and as unlike a bride as it was possible to feel, Kirsten bent down awkwardly to close her suitcase.

She knew she was being unreasonable. She was heavily pregnant, and not even the most cleverly designed outfit could be expected to conceal that reality. Her suit was cream and trimmed with a coffee fringe that was young and stylish, but it was still maternity wear. Just for the space of that morning she would have given virtually anything to look more like a bride than an expectant mother.

A week had passed since she had accepted Shahir's proposal. In the space of that time she had surrendered her job and her bedsit in exchange for a gold credit card, which she had barely used, two bodyguards and a hotel suite. Squeak had taken to a life of luxury with extraordinary ease. Indeed, the little dog trotted about his newly spacious surroundings with a decided hint of cheerful pomposity, but Kirsten still felt as if she was playing a starring role in someone else's drama.

Shahir had applied for a special licence to enable their wedding to take place quickly, and then he had immediately flown home to Dhemen in order to gain his father's consent to the marriage. He had also insisted that she invite Jeanie down for the wedding. He had phoned her every single day too, she reminded herself dully. He was courteous and considerate and…impersonal. He'd asked her how she felt, but not how she thought, and when she had tried to ask him how his father had reacted to his son and heir's desire to marry a very pregnant foreigner, he had smoothly changed the subject. She didn't blame him for doing so, for on reflection she decided that her question had been an incredibly stupid one. After all, there was no earthly way that King Hafiz of Dhemen could possibly be persuaded to look on her as an acceptable bride for his royal son and heir.

'I have something to tell you that will cheer you up,' Jeanie told her with a grin. 'Would you like to guess what the hottest gossip at the castle was when I left yesterday?'

Kirsten shook her head.

'Everyone reckons that Pamela Anstruther framed you as a thief because she realised that Prince Shahir had fallen madly in love with you!'

Kirsten screened her eyes to conceal her pain. On her wedding day of all days she was all too conscious of the fact that her bridegroom did not love her. At the same time, however, she was extremely relieved to hear that the castle staff had started to question and doubt her guilt.

'Is that really what people think?'

'What else could they think? Lady Posh spent two years throwing herself at the Prince, and it didn't matter how short she wore her skirts—she never got to pull him!

She must've been mad with rage and jealousy when she saw the love story of the century happening right under her nose. I mean, you are absolutely besotted with him, aren't you?'

'Yes,' Kirsten mumbled tightly

'Well, it does my heart good to know that all Lady Posh's spite and scheming came to nothing in the end,' Jeanie declared with strong satisfaction.

'How did Morag Stevens react to the news that Shahir and I were getting married?' Kirsten was keen to find out how the assistant housekeeper, whose damning evidence as a witness had convicted her, had behaved.

'When she heard that you were about to become Strathcraig's new mistress she burst into floods of tears and scuttled away,' the redhead shared, with a meaningful roll of her eyes. 'She's scared stiff—that's what she is!'

The phone buzzed. 'The car's waiting for you.' Jeanie grinned. 'Just think—in a couple of hours you'll be a princess.'

Kirsten looked startled. 'Nobody has said anything about that. I honestly don't think it works quite that way—'

'You mean you pulled a prince and you only get to be an ordinary missus?' Wearing an expression of comical disillusionment, Jeanie shook her head as they left the suite. 'What about the baby? Won't it get a title either?'

Kirsten stepped into the lift. 'I really don't know.'

'His family are probably raging that he isn't marrying a royal princess!' Jeanie clamped a guilt-stricken hand to her lips. 'Scratch that—forget I opened my big mouth.'

Kirsten stiffened. 'Why? I bet it's true. Remember how shocked you were when I admitted who the father of my baby was!'

'Yeah…but when I stopped to think about it,' Jeanie answered chirpily, 'Prince Shahir getting off with the most gorgeous good-living virgin under the castle roof is really not that surprising. I mean, there's not a lot else to do at Strathcraig. Now, don't forget that I'm leaving straight after the service at the church with Douglas and Elspeth—'

'Jeanie…that's silly,' Kirsten protested, and not for the first time. 'We're going to a hotel for a meal. Please join us.'

The plump redhead groaned out loud and laughed. 'You won't change my mind about this. No way am I sitting down to eat with a prince…I'd be so nervous I couldn't eat!'

Donald had offered to give Kirsten away at the ceremony, but Kirsten had thanked him and gently refused. It was to be a very quiet wedding, with witnesses only, and she saw no reason to slavishly follow tradition. In fact, she thought that plain and simple suited the nature of the occasion best. It did hurt that she had not a single relative to attend. She would have loved to have had her brother Daniel with her, but she had no idea where he was. After mustering her courage she had phoned her father to tell him that she was getting married, but Angus Ross had put the phone down the minute he had heard his daughter's voice.

She had told herself that such things scarcely mattered. After all, it was to be a marriage of convenience, forged primarily for their baby's benefit. The ring she would receive would not be given with love, or even with respect, she conceded painfully. Shahir still believed that she was a thief, so how could he possibly respect her?

Even so, she had felt that his misconception should not prevent her from recognising their child's right to the legitimate birth that would enable him to be fully accepted by his father's family. But his lack of faith in her still stung like acid. On the other hand the gossip that Jeanie had mentioned made the situation look a good deal brighter. Surely if other people suspected Lady Pamela, and Morag Stevens had lied, Shahir would eventually accept her innocence?

'Go get him, girl!' Jeanie whispered cheekily in Kirsten's ear as she began to move down the aisle of the church.

Her cheeks warming, Kirsten made a covert appraisal of the tall, dark and extravagantly handsome male at the altar. There was a younger man standing by Shahir's side, but she spared the stranger the merest glance because it had been a week since she had last seen Shahir and to her it felt like half a lifetime.

There was no point denying it any longer, she thought ruefully. All that talk about loathing him had just been a brick to hurl for want of any other—a face-saving, juvenile lie. The truth was that she was crazy about him. The sound of his voice on the phone gave her butterflies. When he smiled it was as if wings were attached to her heart.

Spectacular eyes that were the colour of bronze in the dim interior met hers, but he did not smile and she lowered her gaze again.

The service was short. As she made her responses she found that she was very nervous, and she wondered if that was why her skin felt so oddly clammy.

Shahir slid a ring on to her wedding finger and tears flooded her eyes. He was her husband now. She blinked, terrified he would notice her tears and wonder what was the matter with her. Lowering her lashes, however, she hovered lest he wanted to seize the opportunity to kiss her.

'You're as a white as a ghost,' Shahir remarked in a taut undertone, making it evident that kissing could not have been further from his mind.

A single tiny compliment, even a hint of a compliment, would have been sufficient to make the day a happy one for Kirsten. But to be told she resembled the living dead when she had made so much effort to look the very best she could was the equivalent of having a vampire's stake driven through her heart.

'I suppose that is why you look as if you're attending a funeral rather than your own wedding?' his bride whispered back flatly.

'It is a solemn occasion.' His hand closed over hers, his thumb resting against a slender wrist which felt as fragile as the bones of a tiny bird in his careful hold.

Shahir was seriously worried about her health. When he asked her how she was she always said she was fine, but she looked really ill to him. She *had* admitted that nausea spoiled her appetite, and perhaps that was all that was the matter. If he expressed his concern he might worry her, and upset her, and he was reluctant to take that risk. In a few hours they were leaving for Dhemen. There, the need for her to meet her new gynaecologist would ensure that she could enjoy an immediate check-up.

Kirsten was reflecting that he hadn't even thought to give her a bouquet to carry. Suddenly her empty hands seemed to emphasise all that their wedding so conspicuously lacked. Love was the obvious missing component—and she had better get used to that, hadn't she? There was no point hankering after what she could not have.

In the church porch, a lively male voice complained, 'How much longer do I have to wait to meet my sister-in-law?'

Kirsten had been so preoccupied with her own feelings that she had forgotten Shahir's companion at the altar.

'Kirsten…' Shahir fell still. 'This is my younger brother, Raza.'

'Had I met you first, Shahir would be the one acting as best man!' Laughing brown eyes twinkled down at her, and then narrowed with an astonishment he couldn't hide when he registered the unmistakable swell of her stomach. 'But obviously I would have had to meet you quite a long time ago to be in with a chance,' he completed, in a teasing recovery.

Shahir said something in his own language, his demeanour and tone as cold and crushing as ice. Kirsten went red, and then white, and hastily turned away to conceal her discomfiture. He had not even told his brother that she was pregnant. Obviously he was ashamed of her, and of her condition, and she felt cut to the bone. Her back was hurting. As she resisted the urge to massage the spot she felt a dragging pain stir low in her tummy, and a slight gasp escaped her.

'What is it?' Shahir asked instantly.

'Pain,' she framed breathlessly. 'It's really bad!'

His magnificent bone structure set hard below the bronzed skin. He addressed his brother in urgent Arabic and then bent down to lift Kirsten slowly and gently up into his arms. 'You should be lying down.'

'Shahir, I'm scared…the baby!' she sobbed fearfully, and then she bit back any further words—for he scarcely needed to be told that she was afraid that she was having a miscarriage.

It was not a fear Kirsten had had to deal with before.

But it swiftly became a terror that engulfed her in a tidal wave of bitter regret. She had taken the stability of her pregnancy and the health of her unborn child for granted while she complained about the nagging nausea that continually spoiled her appetite. That acknowledgement filled her with guilt and dread. She had hardly dared to appreciate the miracle of conception, or look forward to the birth of her future son or daughter. Her rigid upbringing had inhibited such free thinking. She had been desperately ashamed of being an unmarried mother-to-be, and she had punished herself by refusing to find anything positive in her situation.

Was this, then, to be the price she paid for her blindness? she asked herself in a panic. Was she about to lose her baby?

Her fingers splayed against the taut curve of her stomach. Right from the beginning she had loved the tiny life growing inside her with protective intensity. But she had not allowed herself to visualise a little boy with Shahir's silky black hair and raw energy, or a little girl with a feminine version of his imperious brows and the dazzling gift of his charisma. That would have been a step too far for her—an exercise in self-indulgence that she could not allow herself to enjoy.

Choking back a sob, she squeezed her eyes tight shut and prayed.

Shahir made her lie down full-length in the limousine, and positioned himself by her head. He wound her fingers comfortingly within his. 'We will be at the hospital within five minutes, and the best of care will be yours.'

'I bet you weren't expecting this today,' Kirsten muttered jaggedly.

'Try to keep calm…' Shahir smoothed the hair back from her temples in a soothing gesture. 'When I am with you, you should not be afraid. I will not allow any harm to come to you, and no trouble is so hard to bear when it is shared.'

Kirsten tried to comfort herself with the hope that her pregnancy was far enough advanced for the baby to have a good chance of survival if she went into premature labour. But what if there was something wrong and she was losing their child?

The medical facility she entered was unlike any hospital she had ever visited. The last word in high-tech gleaming luxury, it was a private clinic attached to the charitable foundation that Shahir ran. She was whisked into an examination room at speed. A consultant arrived, and told her that she would have to be admitted and that the following few hours would be crucial.

Helped into bed by a nurse, Kirsten was relieved that the cramping little pains which she had been suffering seemed to be in the process of subsiding.

'You should go and get something to eat,' Kirsten told Shahir, when he entered her private room ten minutes later.

He studied her in polite astonishment. 'Are you joking?'

'There's no reason why you should go hungry.'

'Right now I'm staying here with you.'

'You don't have to,' she told him, but she didn't mean it; just at that moment she did not want to let him out of her sight.

'No matter what, I'll be here.'

That declaration impressed her, and the worst of her tension seeped away. She made herself a little more comfortable in the bed, and a yawn crept up on her out of nowhere. 'I'm so tired…' she whispered apologetically.

'Then try to sleep,' Shahir suggested. 'I'll wake you up if anything happens.'

A drowsy giggle escaped her as she tried to imagine what could happen that she might contrive to sleep through.

She had not actually believed that she would sleep, but she did manage to doze for a while. When her eyes opened fuzzily again the first thing she noticed was her own hand, where it rested on the pillow, and her wedding ring glinting shiny and new on her finger. Shahir was lodged by the window, his back turned to her. Raw tension was etched into the set line of his broad shoulders and the spread of his long powerful legs.

'I bet this isn't how you planned to spend your wedding day…'

Shahir swung round, glittering golden eyes zeroing in on her with an amount of concern that surprised her and made her regret her tart comment. 'If you are well at the end of it, I will have no complaints. You don't look so pale. Any more pains?'

She shook her head slowly. She was finding it a challenge to remove her attention from him. He was incredibly attractive.

A relieved smile curving his handsome mouth, he approached the bed and gazed down at her. 'You are strong, and so is our child.'

'Will I have to stay in here tonight?'

His dark, deepset eyes narrowed, black eyelashes glinting. 'Yes. Would you like something to eat now?'

'No, thanks.'

'I am worried about the amount of weight you have lost, and so is the doctor,' he reminded her gently.

'Feeling sick all the time makes for a very effective diet. Have you eaten yet?'

'I have been so troubled about you that I haven't even felt hungry,' Shahir confided.

Her green eyes clung to his lean strong face and she sighed. 'All right. I get the message. I will try to eat.'

She managed a small meal, and even savoured half of a chocolate mousse before drifting off to sleep again.

Somewhere in the middle of the night she wakened. A shaded lamp shed light into the corner of the room. Shahir was sprawled in a chair by the bed, and she studied him with admiring eyes. A dark shadow of blue-black stubble roughened his jawline and emphasised the beautiful curve of his expressive masculine mouth.

'Why are you still here?' she whispered, amazed that he had not left her to the care of the medical staff.

Angling his proud head back, Shahir rested dark-as-midnight eyes on her, his surprise at the question unconcealed. 'Where else would I be? You're my bride, and this is our wedding night.'

Kirsten was stunned by that response. She had expected him to say something about his duty of care towards her and the child she carried, or to mention the risk of her going into premature labour. 'I'd forgotten that…'

'I hadn't.' He stretched out a hand and enclosed her fingers in his. 'Go back to sleep.'

Even badly in need of a shave he looked quite astoundingly good-looking. 'Yes, boss.'

He laughed softly, sexily. 'I like the sound of that.'

'I should've known you'd take it the wrong way,' she groaned. 'Will you see that Squeak is looked after?'

'Our staff will take care of him.'

'But he'll be lost without me,' Kirsten pointed out anxiously.

'I will personally check that Squeak is OK. How long has he been with you?'

'My mother gave him to me as a puppy, when I was nine years old. He's thirteen now,' she shared.

'A venerable age. Now, stop worrying.'

Over the following five days it slowly sank in on Kirsten that she had no choice other than to be ultra-careful for what remained of her pregnancy.

'When will we be flying out to Dhemen?' she asked Shahir.

'It would be most unwise for us to attempt the journey now. I am resigned to remaining in London until after the birth,' he countered, with a wry shrug of acceptance. 'It is imperative that you rest. Every day that our child stays in your womb makes him or her stronger, though you will find such inactivity frustrating.'

But Kirsten knew that she would only have to live with those limitations for a matter of weeks, and she was willing to do anything that would help her baby to be born safely and in good health. 'Whatever it takes… Will I have to remain here in the clinic?'

His dark golden eyes were grave. 'No. If you promise to be sensible, you can stay in our London apartment. Nurses will be engaged to care for you.'

'I'll be sensible,' she swore.

Thirty-six hours later, Kirsten left the clinic and was installed in the penthouse apartment, where she enjoyed a rapturous reunion with Squeak and met the first of the three nurses engaged to watch over her in shifts.

The apartment was very large indeed, and furnished for slick city living with not an antique or a traditional rug in sight. Kirsten was soon ensconced in an opulent divan in a vast bedroom which enjoyed a spectacular view of the Thames.

Mid-morning, several large lingerie boxes were delivered. The boxes contained a selection of pure silk and lace nightwear in her favourite pastel shades, and a hand-signed gift card from Shahir. Encouraged by the nurse looking after her, she immediately donned a pale green nightdress with a matching jacket, and submitted to having her hair brushed for his promised visit at lunchtime.

'Do you think you will be comfortable here?' Shahir strode in, coolly immaculate in a light grey business suit. 'My family use this as a base when they visit London. Raza stayed here while he was at university, but he has his own apartment now. Perhaps it is time for me to acquire a more private dwelling?'

As Shahir moved deeper into the room the nurse slipped out, with a coy smile that only embarrassed Kirsten.

'That nurse is acting like we're honeymooners, desperate to be alone with each other,' she muttered apologetically.

In answer, Shahir bent down. Closing one deft hand into the shining fall of her silvery blonde hair, he circled her luscious pink mouth with his until her lips parted and allowed him to delve deep in an expert and provocative foray. Wildly disconcerted by that sensual exploration, Kirsten felt her body quicken with startling urgency. The rosy tips of her breasts pinched tight into a distended and tender fullness that made her whimper low in her throat in disconcertion. Coming down beside her on the bed, Shahir tasted her lips slowly and hungrily, and then lifted his dark head.

'If only we were free to take advantage of being alone…but we're not. The sweetest pleasures are always forbidden.' A wicked smile slashed his lean, savagely handsome features with a wildness that shocked her as much as it excited her. 'But the knowledge that you desire me as much as I desire you helps me to be patient.'

Ludicrously unprepared for his confrontation, which had come out of nowhere at her, Kirsten quivered with outrage and uncertainty. 'But that's not true!'

Assured brown fingers smoothed over the prominent thrust of her pouting breasts beneath the fine silk, teasing at the stiff and straining crests she would have hidden from him had she only had the opportunity. With a moan of shame she flushed to the roots of her hair and shut her eyes tight, even though she was guiltily conscious that she was revelling in the achingly sweet tingling of her sensitive flesh.

'Your body knows me—and the truth. Were it possible I would lie with you now and give you all the pleasure and excitement that you could handle,' Shahir murmured huskily. 'But the present need for restraint will make those delights all the more intense when the time comes.'

'This is supposed to be a fake marriage!' Kirsten framed in shaken protest.

'That was your idea. Is it also your wish? What benefit would such an arrangement offer to either of us? I don't do fake,' Shahir enumerated with precision. 'You are my wife, whom I would protect with my life, and soon you will be the mother of my child. I want nothing false or pretend in our marriage. Did I mention that there will be a second wedding held for us in Dhemen?'

She stared back at him, her eyes clinging to his lean strong face, to the fierce resolve etched there. 'No…you didn't.'

'Perhaps by then you too will know what you want. Even were we able to share a bed now I would prefer to honour you by restraining my ardour until you are considered truly mine by all my family,' he admitted levelly.

'Will your family accept me?' she asked in sudden apprehension.

'Of course,' he said gently. 'For the sake of appearances a polite fiction has been coined. According to that story, we married in secret last year because my father disapproved of our match and withheld his consent for an official wedding. The imminent birth of our child can in that way be viewed as having softened the King's heart into accepting the wife I chose for myself, and nobody loses face.'

Kirsten veiled her eyes, for she was thinking that he had *not* chosen her. Sexual attraction had overruled self-discipline, and the price of succumbing to temptation had been high. But possibly he had paid the highest price, because he did not love her as she loved him and she would never be the wife he would have chosen for himself.

'That soft shade of green suits you to perfection,' he remarked huskily. 'Your hair looks like white-gold against it.'

'I didn't even say thank you for your gifts… Thank you—you picked beautiful things.'

'It was nothing. I only suggested the colours.' Honesty bade him admit it, and a faint darkening of colour emphasised the stunning angle of his proud cheekbones. 'I was lost when it came to styles, although I mentioned what I thought you would like to the manageress.'

Kirsten was watching him in fascination. 'Haven't you bought anything like this before?'

He frowned at the idea. 'No…but if I didn't take care of it, who else was there to do it?'

Kirsten dropped her head to conceal the smile creeping

over her lips. Evidently he had made a special effort on her behalf, and shopping for such intimate apparel had rather embarrassed him. She was delighted to discover that she was the very first woman he had bought lingerie for. Maybe he wasn't quite as much of a womaniser as she had imagined…

'Ah!' she gasped abruptly, pressing her palm to the side of her tummy as the baby chose that instant to kick with vigour.

'The baby?' His spectacular golden eyes shimmered and he moved closer and extended a lean, bronzed hand. 'May I?'

Her hesitation was brief. 'Yes…'

He spread gentle fingers to the firm swell of her belly and laughed out loud with satisfaction. His wonder and pride were reflected in his eloquent gaze. 'What joy you are bringing me,' he murmured, with a sincerity that touched her deep.

Shahir might not love her, but on the other hand he certainly didn't seem to feel trapped by her pregnancy, she reflected with satisfaction. His genuine pleasure at the prospect of fatherhood meant a great deal to her. He definitely wanted their unborn child, and was prepared to celebrate his or her arrival rather than simply accept it as an inevitable event. Furthermore, although she currently had as much shape as a barrel and could not see her feet, remarkably Shahir still seemed to find her attractive. Those were very strong positives to build on, Kirsten told herself dizzily.

Yet for all that she was married to a man who still firmly believed she was a thief.

That unwelcome recollection hit her like a bucket of icy water. With difficulty she suppressed her hurt and resentment on that score. Although it mortified her to acknowledge the fact, she felt that Shahir had barely known her as a person before he had swept her into bed at Strathcraig, and he had misjudged her accordingly. Now they were finally getting to know each other, and forming a real relationship with bonds that were new and fragile. And she did not want to damage those bonds by staging a confrontation too soon. After all, what evidence of her innocence could she offer him? She had none. But when Shahir had a better understanding of her she would reopen the subject of her supposed dishonesty, and insist that he hear her out with a more open mind, she decided tautly.

The next morning she was having breakfast when a sizeable bundle of magazines and books arrived. She smiled at yet another demonstration of his thoughtfulness. Without thinking about nausea or appetite, or indeed noticing the presence or lack of either, she somehow managed to happily work her way through a bowl of cereal, a whole buttered croissant and two cups of hot chocolate.

Over the couple of weeks that followed Shahir spent all of his free time with her, but even though she would not have objected he did not make any attempt to kiss her again.

Like Squeak, she found herself yawning and nodding off to sleep with very little warning.

Shahir cancelled his business trips abroad, and tried not to travel too far out of reach, and as her due date drew closer she felt more secure when he was around. The consultant had already warned her that the baby was too large for her narrow pelvis and would have to be delivered by Caesarean section.

In the end, she went into labour a fortnight early. It was mid-morning, and Shahir was on the other side of

London. She had already been admitted to the clinic when he arrived there.

'You will be absolutely fine…you will feel no pain,' he whispered urgently, holding her hand a little too tightly for comfort. 'I have discussed it fully with the surgical team. There is to be no pain…not even a twinge. I could not bear to see you suffer.'

Below his bronzed skin he was pale as death and tense as a steel girder. He seemed much more afraid for her than she was for herself. She was already suffering slight contractions, and she did not think it was possible to give birth without enduring some level of discomfort, but evidently nobody had dared to tell him that. Worried that even a moan from her might utterly unnerve him, she embraced a stoic silence until the medication kicked in.

Shahir was struggling not to betray his fear for her, and he was praying. He knew his own family history too well to assume that nothing would go wrong. Even the best medical attention could not guarantee a happy conclusion to every birth. His own mother had been young and healthy, but she had died soon after his birth from a seizure. His father had never really recovered from the loss of the wife he had adored.

Within half an hour their little boy was delivered, with an amazing lack of fuss.

Shahir touched a reverent fingertip to their son's tiny starfish hand and swallowed convulsively, the fierce tension he had endured slowly dissipating.

'He is…he is truly precious,' he breathed thickly, his dark golden gaze shimmering with emotion. 'We are blessed indeed. In a few weeks, when you are well enough to travel, we will take him home to Dhemen and show him to my people.'

CHAPTER EIGHT

WHEN the jet landed in Dhemen, Kirsten lifted her son Tazeem out of his travelling bassinet the instant she was free to undo her seat belt. Cradling his warm little body with tender care, she dropped a kiss on his satin-smooth cheek.

'Who is the most beautiful little boy in the world?' she whispered.

Tazeem opened big dark brown eyes that promised to be a mirror match of his handsome father's and studied her with the unflinching regard that was equally reminiscent of his genes. He was a good-natured baby, but he had a strong will as well and could complain bitterly if given cause. She smiled down at him, noting the warm colour in his cheeks and the clearness of his eyes with satisfaction.

For the first few weeks after his premature birth, Tazeem had demonstrated a dismaying tendency to pick up every stray infection going. Shahir and Kirsten had begun to worry that their child's early arrival in the world had undermined his health. When the little boy overcame those initial setbacks and went from strength to strength his parents had been hugely relieved. Even so, their natural disquiet had disrupted their plans to travel.

Kirsten had ended up staying with Tazeem in London while Shahir flew round the world dealing with all the business concerns that had had to take a back seat while Kirsten was unwell. Tazeem was now seven weeks old, and it was three weeks since Kirsten had seen his father.

As a result of what felt like very serious deprivation, Kirsten's eyes were sparkling with anticipation. She could hardly wait to see Shahir again. He had been wonderfully kind and supportive after Tazeem's birth, especially as it had taken time for her to recover from surgery. And having said that he would honour her by not consummating their marriage until after their second wedding had taken place, he had adhered so rigidly to that decision that he had not even kissed her.

In truth it had been hard for Kirsten not to feel rejected, and even harder for her to overcome the suspicion that Shahir was not unduly taxed by his restraint because he no longer found her much of a temptation. Indeed, it seemed to her that she was continually faced with the humiliating reality that a shotgun wedding such as theirs carried no promise of love or even desire—only the far more prosaic assurance that their child's needs had taken precedence over their own.

Passing her infant son over to the caring attentions of his nurse, Kirsten rose with a rueful sigh from her comfortable seat and prepared to leave the jet. Long before landing she had taken the chance to freshen up, and had changed into the blue suit she had picked with care for her arrival in the kingdom of Dhemen. She had read every book about her husband's country that she could lay her hands on. Certain colours were considered auspicious, and blue was one of them.

Hearing Shahir's rich dark drawl, she realised that the cabin door was already open and that her husband must have come to collect her off the jet. Delighted by what she assumed to be his impatience to see her, she hurried down the aisle to greet him. 'Shahir…'

Brilliant dark as ebony eyes assailed hers and he smiled, his sculpted mouth curving with megawatt charm.

Her heart went on a rollercoaster ride. 'You have been missed,' he murmured, clasping her hand in greeting and then stepping back from her again with a formality that took her by surprise.

'Tazeem…' Shahir paused to look down at his son and laughed softly, 'He looks happy—and so he should be now that he is finally coming home.'

Feeling rather hurt by his cool, calm welcome, Kirsten bent to glance out of the nearest window. She was aghast when she saw the serried ranks of people standing out in the baking sun. 'Oh, my goodness, what's going on? Who are they waiting for?'

'You and Tazeem. Are you ready? It would be most discourteous to keep our well-wishers hanging around in this heat.'

'Waiting for me and Tazeem?' Dismay made her voice strike a shrill note. 'My goodness…'

'All you have to do is smile. You're a bride, and already the mother of the second in line to the throne. You are also incredibly beautiful. All of those facts will ensure that you are very popular,' Shahir pointed out bracingly, while he edged her with gentle determination towards the exit.

The sunlight almost blinded her and the heat closed round her like a velvet cocoon. A band struck up a rousing musical arrangement. Before she could carry on down the steps, Shahir closed a staying hand round hers.

'Don't move. Keep your head up,' he instructed, half under his breath. 'That's our national anthem.'

Embarrassed pink suffused her fine skin.

At the foot of the steps a few minutes later, Shahir exchanged salutes with a man in a military uniform. The crowds behind the barriers bowed and cheered and applauded, but did so in a very restrained and respectful way. Shahir guided her straight into the welcome shade of an elaborate marquee, where she was ushered towards the seats raised on a dais.

'Don't sit down until I do,' Shahir warned her in an undertone, belatedly appreciating that she would have to be taught royal protocol—and fast.

It was dawning on him that he had been thoughtless in not equipping her better for the challenge of this rarefied world in which he lived. The many privileges of royal status came at the cost of an equal number of restrictions. When his wife appeared in public she would be expected to demonstrate an impeccable grasp of etiquette and the old-fashioned formality that was the hallmark of his family.

An adorable little girl presented Kirsten with a beautiful bouquet of flowers. Kirsten's generous smile lit up her face and she thanked the child in Arabic, grateful that she had taken the time to learn a few basic words.

'I'm impressed,' Shahir admitted.

'Don't be,' she said shyly. 'I bought a tourist vocabulary book and I've only managed to learn about fifty words.'

A court ministerial advisor gave a rather lengthy speech of welcome with great enthusiasm. Then an impossibly long white limousine with a Dhemeni flag on the bonnet pulled up, and at Shahir's covert signal they stood up and left the dais. The band immediately began to play a classical piece that was familiar to her.

'In your honour, the musicians have selected a piece by an English composer,' Shahir explained.

She was touched. 'It's called "Chanson de Matin." It was a favourite of my mother's.'

For an instant he was surprised, until he recalled that

her mother had taught music. 'I didn't realise you were so knowledgeable.'

'I was still quite young when my father decided to get rid of the family television. Mum used music to keep Daniel and I occupied in the evenings. We were quite happy without a TV. Then Dad decided we were enjoying music too much and he sold the piano.'

His fine ebony brows pleated. 'It must have been grim.'

'It hurt Mum the most, and I promised myself that one day I would have a piano of my own and I would play it all day!' Kirsten confided with a rueful laugh. 'I'd be pretty rusty at the keyboard now.'

His dark golden eyes had a sombre light. 'I don't think that would matter.'

The interior of the air-conditioned limo was blissfully cool, and Kirsten stretched out her long slender legs and relaxed with a contented little sigh.

Shahir studied her delicate profile with keen masculine appreciation. Her wilful independent streak was matched by a surprising level of sensitivity. The more he found out about her, the more he wanted to know. Like an exquisite painting, she never lost her appeal. And the plain tailored suit she wore was the perfect choice for a woman of such stunning beauty. In so many ways, he acknowledged, she continually exceeded his expectations.

But no sooner had that thought occurred to him than he remembered the theft of the pendant. His proud bone structure hardened, and distaste filled him before he could suppress it. He removed his attention from her. Once again he reminded himself that she had made an appalling mistake in fraught circumstances, and that he had to find it within himself to understand and forgive.

'My word!' Kirsten sat bolt upright, her eyes rounding

in astonishment when she saw the giant advertising hoarding on the outskirts of the city. Unbelievable as it seemed to her, it carried a huge picture of her face and Shahir's. 'I don't believe what I'm seeing. What's that for?'

'It is announcing our wedding, which will be a public holiday. All of Dhemen will be celebrating with us,' Shahir proffered coolly.

She swallowed hard and wondered why he was being so distant with her. Was he wishing he did not have to go through another wedding with her? Was it the ultimate horror to be forced to marry the wrong woman twice over? Or was she simply being over-sensitive? It was not his fault that she suffered from such low self-esteem, she told herself uncomfortably.

The capital city, Jabil, was composed of wide thoroughfares shaded by mature trees. The busy streets were softened by enticing glimpses of lush green parks. Contemporary buildings sat side by side with ancient domed mosques and rambling villas, and there was a definite air of prosperity to the upmarket shops and hotels. The people wore both European and Arab dress, and many of them stopped to look and wave as the royal motorcade rolled past complete with outriders on motorcycles.

'We are to have a traditional wedding,' Shahir breathed tautly, suspecting that culture shock was about to engulf his European bride. 'The festivities begin tonight and will not end until late tomorrow. We will not meet again until the ceremony takes place.'

Kirsten was thoroughly dismayed at the prospect of being parted from him again so soon. 'Does it have to be like that? I mean, why can't we be together?'

The note of panic in her soft voice tugged at his self-assurance until it broke through his defensive barriers. Dark golden eyes intent on her, he closed a lean bronzed hand over hers. 'It is the way it has been done for centuries, and we have broken quite enough rules already in our courtship. As it is, the usual three days of festivities are being compressed into one and a half to suit my father's schedule.'

'But I don't know anybody…' She could hear her voice wobbling and she was ashamed of the tears gathering.

Shahir reached for her other hand as well. 'But there are many English speakers in my family, and they will be very kind to you,' he swore. 'My relatives are very relieved that I have finally found myself a wife.'

The level of his conviction soothed her. 'Relieved?' she queried.

'Apparently my father didn't put any pressure on me to marry because he believed that was the best way to encourage me to take a bride.' His darkly handsome features were wry. 'But I was in no hurry, and my indifference had become a source of concern.'

Curiosity about Faria stabbed at her. How many people were aware that he loved another woman? Had the awareness that his son could not have the woman he really wanted lain behind his royal parent's willingness to be patient?

'Why was the King so worried?'

Amusement gleamed in his stunning eyes. 'As you will learn, my father is a great pessimist. He thought that even after I married it might take years for me to father a child. He even considered the idea that I or my bride might prove incapable of that feat. It is safe to say that he looked at every negative possibility to such an extent that you and Tazeem together make a really winning package.'

She stretched her lips into a forced smile and hid the fact that once again she felt hurt and mortified. Naturally the need and ability to provide a royal son and heir was hugely important in a feudal kingdom with a hereditary line of rulership. Shahir was only being honest about the fact that as far as his father was concerned her greatest gift was her proven aptitude in the fertility stakes. Certainly it was true that she had fallen pregnant easily.

My goodness—had he told his father just *how* easily? Inwardly she absolutely cringed.

'How much did you tell your father about how we met and…er…stuff?'

'I told him the truth.'

Kirsten tensed in consternation. 'So you told him… What did you tell him?'

His imperious black brows pleated as though he considered that a strange question. 'That I had seduced a virgin…what else?'

'But that information wasn't for sharing!' Kirsten launched at him aghast, her face hot as fire. 'That was between us, and private.'

'Not in this case.' His lean strong face betrayed not a trace of regret. 'For your sake I needed to be sure that my father put any blame he wished to bestow on my shoulders, where it belonged. And he did.'

Kirsten breathed in deep and tried to master her embarrassment.

The motorcade was already moving swiftly along the highway that led out of the city. Ahead lay the Ahmet Palace, the private home of the Dhemeni royal family since the seventh century. High fortress walls studded with towers surrounded the vast complex which was spread across a hill. That much alone the books had told her, but no further details had been given. On either side of the road stretched a rolling landscape of sand dunes that disappeared into the distance—terracotta in colour on the shaded side, glistening gold in the harsh sunlight of late afternoon.

They passed through a vast medieval gateway, but even as her curious eyes were widening to absorb the great domed entrance of the nearest building, and the red carpet awaiting their arrival, another daunting thought was occurring to her.

'You didn't tell your father about the theft thing, did you?'

Beneath her scrutiny, Shahir froze to carved ice. 'I presume you are joking? My father believes you to be a woman of irreproachable good character and virtue.'

Anger and pain coalesced inside Kirsten and flared up in a spirited venting of all her pent-up emotions. Green eyes bright as the heart of a fire, she rounded on him. 'Shahir, I've kept quiet about this for far too long, and I think I've been really stupid. I thought that as you got to know me you might start doubting my guilt without me having to plead my own case. For goodness' sake, don't you know anything about me yet? I did not steal that pendant—nor did I put greedy hands on that woman's stupid brooch! Isn't it about time that you accepted that I'm telling you the truth?'

'Please don't shout at me!' Shahir grated.

'Maybe I'm shouting because you're as stubborn as a rock and you just make up your mind about things and won't listen to any other version!' she condemned heatedly. 'But this is my reputation we're talking about, and I've never stolen anything in my life.'

'This is not the time for this, and I do not respond to the aggressive approach.'

'Well, I'm not being humble about it!' Kirsten informed him in a fiery interruption. 'The rumour at Strathcraig is that Lady Pamela set me up because she saw that you were attracted to me. Unfortunately I don't have the slightest idea why the witness lied and said she saw me put the pendant in my locker. But the point is you're my husband. Instead of hammering on about how honourable you are, and how you would protect me with your life, you should get out there and *prove* that I can depend on you—clear my name!'

Shahir was livid with a dark fury as volatile as volcanic lava. How dared she question his honour? How dared she scorn his protection? And as for the theft—how could she possibly believe that he wanted to accept that she was a thief? But the case against her was watertight and left no room for doubt. Had it been otherwise he would have moved heaven and earth to clear her name.

Yet for the first time he was being presented with the possibility that there might have been a deliberate conspiracy aimed at discrediting Kirsten. That risk had not occurred to him. How likely was it, though? He had suspected that Pamela Anstruther had noticed that he had a degree of interest in Kirsten. Could the other woman have come to view Kirsten as a rival and set out to plot her downfall?

Even furious as he was, Shahir knew he would have to check out that angle. But surely it was a fanciful idea?

The passenger door beside him sprang open. He stepped out of the limo. The Court Chamberlain bowed low. Tazeem was borne out of the limousine behind with reverent hands and extended to his father with great care.

Recognising the solemnity of the occasion, Shahir accepted his infant son and waited for Kirsten to emerge.

Kirsten was trembling. Words had exploded from her like uncontrolled missiles and she was in shock in the aftermath of that complete loss of temper. She had suppressed her feelings about the theft for too long because she had been afraid to reopen the subject with Shahir. Unfortunately all that hurt and resentment had broken through at a moment when her nerves were already on edge.

A slim brunette in her late twenties, with gentle dark eyes and creamy skin, moved forward. A long line of servants were bowing their heads at their approach.

Shahir murmured, 'My sister, Jahan…'

Jahan greeted her with a warm smile. 'You are very welcome to your new home. We are all very excited to be celebrating a wedding in the family again.'

A cluster of people eager to see Tazeem now surrounded Shahir.

'My brother will take your son to meet His Majesty the King. You will meet our father at the wedding,' Jahan imparted. 'Will you come this way now?'

Still shaken up after the blistering verbal attack she had launched on Shahir, Kirsten glanced anxiously in her royal husband's direction. For a split second he met her gaze in a head-on collision as physically disturbing as a crash. Her heartbeat jumped and her tummy muscles clenched tight with nerves. His lean, darkly handsome features were as impassive as ever, but she knew as surely as if he had spoken that cold anger still divided him from her with the efficacy of a solid sheet of ice.

At that moment she would have given just about anything to get just five minutes alone with him. Having waited too long to broach the thorny topic of her supposed dishonesty, she had gone overboard and attacked when she should have reasoned and explained. With a sinking heart she realised that in her distress she had been downright offensive. But unhappily, Jahan was urging her to follow her, and there was no way that Kirsten could have any private speech with Shahir.

'This evening you are to have a surprise,' Jahan announced with satisfaction as they crossed a huge echoing stone hall floored with worn marble and entered a passage that appeared to lead into a more modern part of the palace. 'A happy surprise, I hope. Shahir has been very busy on your behalf.'

Kirsten had no idea what Shahir's sister was talking about. Although she kept a polite smile of interest on her face she was still too upset by the argument she had had with Shahir to concentrate. 'A surprise?'

'To tell you about it would spoil it.' Jahan paused outside a door. 'Would you like to wait in here for Tazeem to be brought back to you?'

Surprised that she was being left to her own devices, Kirsten opened the door. 'Will he be long?'

'Half an hour at most….'

Jahan seemed to be waiting for something to happen. Her brow indenting, Kirsten entered the room, and then came to a surprised halt when she saw the tall broad male standing by the window. His hair was the same unusual shade of pale blond as her own. He too looked anxious. Her throat tightened and she stared, almost afraid to credit the powerful sense of recognition she was experiencing, for his features had been familiar to her from childhood on.

'Daniel…?' she whispered uncertainly, for when her brother had left home he had been a painfully thin teenager and this was a man.

'Yeah…it's me.' Her brother's voice was gruff with restrained emotion.

It was the telling glimmer of moisture in his eyes that convinced her that he was real, and she raced across the room and flung herself at him with a sob of happiness and welcome.

CHAPTER NINE

IT WAS some time before either Kirsten or Daniel paused long enough between questions to draw breath. After all, brother and sister had five years of news to catch up on. But, first and foremost, Kirsten could not be persuaded to talk about her own life until Daniel had explained how Shahir had managed to trace him.

'I haven't yet met your husband, but we've talked on the phone. Shahir hired investigators to go and ask questions of just about everybody who ever knew me. That helped to build up a profile of me, and one of my schoolteachers mentioned that at one stage I'd been hoping to go to university to do marine biology—'

'Until Dad said you had to work on the farm,' Kirsten recalled heavily.

'Maybe he was right about me just wanting to be a lazy student,' Daniel teased. 'I'm studying for a doctorate now. The detective agency found me by checking out the universities. I've been working abroad on a research project, so they only caught up with me the day before yesterday, and this is as soon as I could get here.'

Slowly Kristin shook her head, fighting back tears. 'I just can't quite believe you *are* here.'

He compressed his mouth ruefully. 'I should have come home to see that you were OK a long time ago.'

'Dad wouldn't have let you into the house.'

'He wouldn't even let me speak to you on the phone, so I gave up ringing.'

'I didn't know you'd phoned,' Kirsten muttered with a painful sense of loss. 'I wish I had.'

'I heard about Mum's death a year after it happened through an old school mate,' he confided heavily. 'I just couldn't handle the fact that I would never see her again because I hadn't been man enough to confront Dad. I felt so guilty.'

'No…you mustn't feel that way. Mum missed you, but she wanted you to have a life of your own. If you had got into a real fight with Dad it would have destroyed her.'

Daniel nodded, too choked up by grief for his late mother to respond.

It was at that point that a knock on the door heralded Tazeem's return. Now enjoying the well-sprung comfort of a magnificent pram wheeled by an English nanny accompanied by two nurses, Tazeem was fast asleep and amusingly unconcerned by the amount of attention he was receiving.

Talk of the promise of the future took over from the hurts and disappointments that Kirsten and Daniel had shared in the past, and Daniel cradled his nephew and grinned. 'I'm actually holding a future king…'

Refreshing mint tea and tiny sweet cakes were brought in and served, and an hour later Kirsten shared an evening meal with her brother in the luxurious suite of rooms allotted for her use. Squeak was waiting there to greet her, and enjoyed a most enthusiastic reunion with his former playmate, Daniel. The little dog would not settle with them, though. He kept on going to the door, sitting down there and sighing heavily.

'What's the matter with him?' her brother asked.

'He's nuts about Shahir,' Kirsten confided with a rueful grin. 'He must know he's around somewhere.'

After the meal, Daniel went off to meet Shahir and join the male wedding party while Kirsten was taken to meet a whole array of Shahir's female relatives. There was one more sister, an array of great-aunts, aunts, and innumerable cousins—and that was not counting those who were related only by marriage to her husband. Tazeem was hugely admired, and Kirsten listened without success for any spoken reference to a woman with the name of Faria.

As she clambered into her comfortable bed at the end of that busy day, her mind was spinning with a myriad of colourful impressions. But all she could actually think about was Shahir, and the reality that there were still hours and hours to be got through before she could see him again. She wondered anxiously if he was still furious with her.

The next day began for her at what felt like the crack of dawn. A delicious breakfast was brought to her in bed, but she had not even finished eating before Jahan came to collect her and escort her to another, older part of the palace.

'The bride receives every possible beauty procedure,' Jahan explained earnestly. 'We want you to relax and enjoy the preparations. It should be a lot of fun.'

The Ahmet Palace was an ancient building like a huge labyrinth. From the outside it resembled a desert fortress, but within the high stone walls it was a complex composed of airy pavilions and tranquil courtyards punctuated with delicate minarets and beautiful gardens. Buildings were linked by stone staircases and roofed walkways.

A little nervous of what might be part and parcel of the bridal preparations, Kirsten watched Tazeem being taken off to the nursery. Maids came to help her undress, and she was so shy at removing her clothes in front of them that they giggled and put up a screen to preserve her modesty. Wrapped in a capacious towel and accompanied by Jahan, she emerged from behind its cover. They entered a great domed and tiled steam room.

'My word…' she sighed, examining her surroundings with wide eyes full of curiosity. 'How old is this place?'

'It was once part of the old harem,' Jahan informed her.

'It's like something out of a film,' Kirsten carolled. 'Jahan…if I wanted to speak to Shahir how would I go about it?'

'You could speak to him on the phone.'

Kirsten nodded at that obvious answer, and wished she had come up with the idea for herself the night before. Working out what she would say, however, was a bigger challenge. How could she ever thank Shahir sufficiently for going to so much trouble to reunite her with her brother? She had not asked him to do that. It had not even crossed her mind that it might be within his power to do that. Yet, without any prompting from her, Shahir had recognised how much it would mean to her to have her brother back in her life.

She sat in the hot, steamy atmosphere mulling over his perception and generosity until a film of perspiration shone on her skin. Two sturdy middle-aged women appeared, divested her of her towel and with great seriousness proceeded to cover her from neck to toe in a substance that resembled green mud.

'It is marvellous for the skin,' Jahan assured her.

Imagining what Shahir would think if he saw her looking like a swamp monster, Kirsten finally started to relax and giggle. When the mud was scrubbed off, she felt as if her whole body was tingling with cleanliness. In yet another room her hair was anointed with a herbal preparation, and the palace beautician arrived with her assistant to administer a facial, shape her eyebrows and carry out a remarkable number of other procedures—all of which were new to Kirsten's experience.

A buffet lunch was served in a big reception room furnished with plenty of opulent sofas, and one by one the other women she had met the evening before began to filter in. Someone put on some music and the gathering began to turn into a light-hearted party.

'You must lie down and have a nap now. The bride has a very long day to get through.' Jahan showed her into a bedroom overlooking a quiet courtyard.

Kirsten was glad of the privacy, for she had finally decided what she should say to Shahir. She used the mobile phone he had given her to send him a text that was just one word long.

Sorry.

The phone was brought to Shahir while he was having a massage. He read the text and his charismatic smile put to flight his usual gravity. He didn't text. He might know how to read them, but he didn't *do* texts. He dismissed the masseur and rang his wife.

'Kirsten…?'

'I was upset, but I shouldn't have shouted.'

'Your anger had conviction. I will do as you ask. I will have discreet enquiries made concerning the allegations that were made against you.' Voicing the decision which he had reached in the early hours of the morning, Shahir stretched his long, powerful limbs and shifted into a more comfortable position on the couch. 'If I have misjudged you, you are entitled to feel angry. As my wife, it is your right to expect my support.'

Overjoyed that he was finally willing to consider that she might have been framed for the theft at Strathcraig, Kirsten felt a great weight slide off her shoulders. Even so, she could not help saying, 'But I want you to believe in me, Shahir…not just make enquiries because it's your duty to do that like you do everything else.'

Shahir suppressed a groan, for he did not know how to tell her that his whole life was governed by duty—first to the crown of Dhemen and secondly to his family. 'This is our wedding day,' he reminded her. 'I am not thinking of my duty at this moment.'

Kirsten closed her eyes and listened dreamily to the rich dark timbre of his voice. 'What are you thinking of?'

'Lying with you tonight,' he admitted with husky intimacy.

Disconcerted though she was by that candid response, she felt a twist of heat curl low in her pelvis. 'I'm surprised,' she could not resist admitting. 'After all, you're the man who hasn't even kissed me since before Tazeem was born.'

Shahir was startled by that complaint. 'I was showing you respect!'

'Do you still feel *that* guilty about what we did that day at the castle?' Kirsten whispered ruefully, marvelling at how much easier it was to say things on the phone that she would not have dared to say to him face to face.

'No…I think about what we shared far too often,' Shahir confided thickly. 'I remember every second of our passion…'

Her heartbeat accelerated and she blushed. 'That's good.'

'No, it's frustrating. But tonight is my reward for almost a year of cold showers. My reward and your pleasure.'

Her green eyes opened wide. 'Almost a year?' she parroted in astonishment. 'Are you saying—I mean…well, that there hasn't been anyone else?'

'Only you since we first met.'

She squeezed the mobile phone so hard she was vaguely surprised it didn't smash into smithereens. 'I like that. Oh, my goodness—I haven't even thanked you for finding Daniel yet! That was the most wonderful present ever.'

'It was nothing. I have to go,' he told her apologetically. 'My father is waiting.'

Kirsten set aside the phone and stared dizzily into space. Shahir had not made love with anyone since he had swept her off to bed at the castle. Her eyes shone. That thought made her feel very special. Had he desisted from sex out of guilt? She thought about that and decided that in some circumstances guilt was good—especially the kind of guilt that kept Shahir from straying into the beds of other women. For the first time he felt like hers, because he had not touched another woman since first meeting her on the hill above the glen.

When she wakened from her nap she felt as she were in a dream as all the activity of which she was the centre began again, with renewed enthusiasm. Her hair was washed and rinsed until the water ran clear. She bathed in a scented bath and lay down to have perfumed oils rubbed into her skin. While her hair was styled, her nails were manicured, and swirling designs in henna that symbolised good luck and health were skilfully painted on her hands and feet. A make-up artist attended to her face, while her companions chattered and enthused and commented at embarrassing length about how handsome, how virile, how *everything* Shahir was.

When it was time for her to dress, another screen was erected for her with much laughter. She rolled on sheer hold-up stockings edged with lace and donned a long fine silk chemise that felt sensuously soft against her skin. No other lingerie was offered to her. Amazing shoes ornamented with glittering stones were brought for her inspection and slipped on to her feet. Finally she was helped into a fabulously ornate embroidered and beaded robe in royal blue.

'You look amazing.' Jahan drew her out from behind the screen so that all the women could see her, and there was a spontaneous burst of appreciative comment and hand clapping.

Kirsten was transfixed by her unfamiliar reflection in a mirror nearby. She looked incredibly exotic.

She was encouraged to walk round an incense burner three times for good luck.

'The bridal gifts.' Jahan presented her with several boxes. 'We are all eager to see what Shahir has given you.'

'I didn't know there were to be gifts. I didn't give your brother anything,' Kirsten lamented.

'You gave Prince Shahir a son,' an older woman piped up in astonishment. 'A son in the first year of marriage. He has been blessed enough.'

Kirsten gazed in shock at the delicately worked gold crown that emerged from the first box. It was light, and not over-large, but it was definitely a crown and not a tiara. Jahan lifted it with reverence and placed it on Kirsten's head. 'This has not been used since Shahir's mother, Bisma, died. You are honoured, for only our father, the King, could have offered it to you.'

There was an emerald necklace that flashed green fire, and it had been matched to drop earrings and a bracelet of fantastic design. Kirsten had never seen such fabulous jewellery, or dreamt that she might own it.

'The emerald set was made especially for you. The goldsmith and the designer worked day and night to finish them in time,' Jahan confided. 'You must be so happy that you have my brother's love.'

Kirsten veiled her gaze. 'Yes…'

'My mother was a second wife and less fortunate.' The other woman sighed. 'Shahir's mother was the King's first wife. She died of a seizure when Shahir was born and my father almost went mad with grief. He was urged by the people to marry again and have more sons. I was born, then my sister, and then Raza. My father could not love my mother as he felt she deserved and she was unhappy. In the end they divorced.'

'That's very sad,' Kirsten remarked, with a hollow feeling of threat in her tummy. She was trying not to wonder if some day Shahir would also decide that he was making her unhappy.

Jahan turned aside to speak to someone, and then turned back to Kirsten. 'Faria says it is time for us to go to the audience hall.'

Faria says. That was all Kirsten heard. Her green eyes lodged on the piquant face of the young woman. She was gorgeous, if a little sullen in expression. She had eyes that were the alluring shape of almonds, honey skin and a wealth of tumbling black curls. Kirsten felt huge and clumsy next to her, for the other woman was much smaller and yet surprisingly curvaceous in shape.

'You've gone white…don't be nervous,' Jahan whispered gently.

For goodness' sake, how common was that name? Faria? What reason did she have to believe that the Faria whom Shahir loved belonged to the privileged circle of those invited to attend the royal wedding? Faria might well live in another country, thousands and thousands of miles away, Kirsten told herself in urgent consolation.

The crown, she discovered, was heavier than it had initially seemed. She had to keep her back straight as an arrow and hold her head high to prevent it from slipping.

The audience hall was thronged with people. She exchanged a warm smile with her brother. Only when the crowds parted did she see Shahir. His brilliant dark eyes were sombre, his lean, bronzed features stunningly handsome below the crown he wore as if to the manner born. In his scarlet and black military uniform, with a sword hanging by his side, he was magnificent. As she drew level he reached for her hand, and the words of the marriage service were spoken in Arabic and then in English.

Shahir slid a gold ring that bore a crest on to the forefinger of her right hand. 'Now it is time for you to meet my father.'

King Hafiz received them in the privacy of an anteroom. He was a tall, sparely built bearded man, with astute dark eyes and a rather gloomy aspect. He did not speak English and Shahir acted as an interpreter. He bestowed his blessing on his son and daughter-in-law as both father and ruler. He raised Kirsten up from her deep curtsey and kissed her solemnly on either cheek, and told her through Shahir that she was so beautiful his son would only have had to look at her once to love her and see her smile to know that she had a true heart. He also came very near to smiling when he forecast that Tazeem would be the joy of his old age.

The festivities moved to a chamber where twin thrones

on a raised dais awaited the bride and groom. Jasmine blossoms were scattered round her feet and Kirsten was given a drink composed of honey and rose water. Traditional folk dances were performed. Poems were read. A lute player sang plaintive songs.

'Now, before we eat, you may change into something more appropriate…' Shahir informed her.

'Do I get to take off the crown?'

Vibrant amusement lit his eyes. 'Yes.'

'I know it's an honour to wear one, but it's hurting my neck.'

In a room down the corridor she was helped out of her ceremonial robe and shoes. She was astonished when a glorious white wedding dress was brought to her. The gown was a neat fit at breast and waist, accentuating her slender figure. A simple circlet of pearls was set on her head.

From the instant she reappeared and began moving down the room towards him Shahir's smouldering dark golden eyes were welded to her. A heady pink lit her cheeks and her mouth ran dry.

'You look amazing…you look as I dreamt you would look,' he confessed in an appreciative aside.

The wedding banquet was served, but she had no appetite for food. After the meal she was formally introduced to courtiers and officials. She saw Faria with a man who appeared to be her husband, and it looked very much as though the couple were having a fight. At least Faria had a tight mouth and seemed to be talking through gritted teeth while her companion seemed to be trying to placate her.

'That couple over there…who are they?' Kirsten finally asked Shahir.

His bold, classic profile tensed. 'My foster-sister and her husband.'

'What do you mean...*foster*-sister?'

'For several months her mother was my nurse after my own mother died in childbirth. In our society that relationship is viewed as the same as one formed by blood.'

Feeling as if she had hit the bullseye, Kirsten fixed her attention elsewhere. Her throat ached, for his tension and his every word had confirmed her suspicions. The exotic brunette *was* Faria, the woman he loved and could not have. Another man's wife and his foster-sister. She felt gutted, and her eyes were stinging like mad.

Raza strolled up and bent his dark head towards them. 'Have you been watching Faria? Do you remember how she always seemed to be all sweetness and light? What a shrew she's turned out to be!' he remarked with an exaggerated shudder. 'Poor Najim. He's an easygoing chap, and very clever, but he made a bad choice there. Watching Faria make a fool of him in public is enough to keep me single for ever!'

Kirsten's dulled eyes took on a sparkle of renewed animation. There was nothing appealing about a shrew, was there? She did not dare to look at Shahir lest she reveal her less than charitable feelings. Instead she gave Raza a big sunny smile.

'May I dance with the most beautiful bride ever to have entered this family?' Raza asked her winningly, down on one knee, hand clasped to his heart in melodramatic fashion.

As Kirsten laughed in appreciation of his sense of humour, Shahir rose upright in one powerful movement. 'Perhaps...after she has danced with me.'

His dark golden gaze shimmered over her flawless face and he extended a lean brown hand to lead her on to the floor. Suddenly she was very conscious of his raw masculinity and she lowered her eyes.

'I know what is on your mind,' Shahir murmured quietly. 'We will discuss it—but not here. We'll be leaving soon.'

Kirsten did not know how to dance in a formal way. She tripped over his feet and tried to head off in the wrong direction. The experience was sheer purgatory for her. Worse still, she was tormented by the conviction that he must have seen her staring at Faria. Had her interest been that obvious to him? Could he know what she had been thinking? The jealousy? The hatred? The evil thoughts? She really didn't want Shahir to have an accurate take on what went on in her mind

'You are a possessive husband,' Raza told his elder brother with lively amusement as the bridal couple left the floor. 'But on your wedding day I will forgive you.'

Rose petals and rice were scattered in front of Shahir and Kirsten as they walked out of the palace and got into a white limo adorned with streamers and flags.

'Now for the embarrassing stuff,' Shahir groaned, flashing her a rueful smile that made her heart jump inside her. 'Wave to the crowds as we pass.'

'Where are we going?'

'We're flying to my grandfather's palace at Zurak. Tazeem will join us tomorrow. But I do not wish to wait until we reach Zurak to say what I need to say to you.'

Kirsten stiffened and stole an apprehensive glance at him.

It was not a conversation Shahir wanted to have, but he knew he could not avoid the subject, for silence would encourage division. He breathed in deep. 'A long time ago I told you that I loved another woman.'

Kirsten shrugged both shoulders with overstated nonchalance while still waving and angling a fixed smile out at the crowds of spectators waiting for the royal motorcade to pass by. She behaved as though the issue of his loving another woman was of as much interest to her as watching paint dry. 'So?'

'As you now appear to be aware, I was referring to my foster-sister, Faria.'

Her wooden pretence of composure cracked and her pale head swivelled, green eyes flashing defensively. 'Am I that obvious?'

His dense black lashes screened his gaze. 'No. I am attuned to your mood now.'

The royal couple waved, and the silence stretched like an elastic band being yanked to breaking point.

'Don't keep me in suspense,' Kirsten breathed between clenched teeth.

'I do not find it easy to talk about feelings,' Shahir confessed in a driven undertone. 'But I do know that I should never have told you that I loved Faria.'

'Well…how were you to know that you were going to end up married to a woman with a memory like an elephant's?' Kirsten muttered waspishly, and it was awful because she could feel the tears gathering up behind her eyes like a dam ready to break.

'That is not the reason why I should not have made that statement. Since that day I have come to appreciate that I was mistaken about what I believed I felt,' Shahir disclosed tautly, his accent fracturing his words. 'I am not in love with her. I have never been in love with her. It was…I now see…no more than a foolish fancy.'

'Really?' Kirsten prompted chokily, thinking that he really had to think she was the stupidest woman in Dhemen to be telling her such a story on their wedding day.

Yet she understood what he was doing. When he had admitted that he loved Faria he had never dreamt that Kirsten would one day become his wife. Naturally he now wished he had kept quiet, and was keen to cover his tracks. Some dark secrets were better left buried. And how could she blame him for trying to hoodwink her? Recognising how jealous and insecure his bride was feeling, he was attempting to defuse the situation in the only way he could. He had told her a little white lie, the way well-meaning people lied to children sooner than reveal the cruel truth.

'You need never think of the matter again,' Shahir asserted with conviction.

'I won't.' At least not around him, she thought tragically.

A helicopter ferried them to the palace at Zurak. She gazed in wonder at the picturesque stone building. Surrounded on all sides by desert, the palace sat in the middle of a lush oasis of trees and greenery like a mirage.

'When my ancestors were nomads they stayed here in the heat of summer. My grandfather met my grandmother when she drew water from the well for him. It was love at first sight for them both. His father asked her father for her hand in marriage and that was that.' Shahir laughed and linked his fingers firmly with hers. 'Life was very much simpler in those days.'

'As long as you didn't have to draw the water from the well,' Kirsten could not resist pointing out.

'In all the great poems of the East men are portrayed as the more romantic sex,' Shahir informed her without skipping a beat. 'From the first moment I saw you, you were never out of my mind.'

That was lust, not love, she almost told him morosely. Did he think she had forgotten that every time he had touched her he had regretted it? Didn't he realise she still remembered that he had proposed marriage out of guilt at having taken her virginity? But their lives had moved on and they were married now. Furthermore, he was clever and he was practical. He wanted their marriage to be a success and naturally he was trying to make her feel good. Romance and compliments were part of the show, she reasoned.

She asked herself if that really mattered. Although he did not love her, she loved him, and she too wanted their relationship to work.

A fountain was playing in the centre of the tiled entrance hall. It was deserted. He pulled her gently round to face him and kissed her slow and deep, until she was dizzy with longing. She discovered that she no longer wanted to think about the fact that he was laying sensible foundations for a successful royal marriage.

Hand in hand, they walked up a wide marble staircase. Their footsteps echoed in the hot still air and the silence was magical after the noise and bustle of their wedding celebrations.

He thrust wide the door of a room at the end of the long gallery, and swept her up into his arms to carry her over the threshold. 'You look amazing in that dress...like you belong in a fairytale.'

He kicked shut the door in his wake and strolled almost indolently across the huge room to deposit her on a big four-poster bed. Silk and lace frothed round her in a highly feminine tangle of fabric.

'Oh, my goodness,' she gasped, tipping her head back to survey the map of the heavens painted on the vaulted ceiling far above.

'A bed with a view.' In the act of unbuttoning his military jacket, Shahir came down on the bed on one knee to claim her lush pink lips again, with a hunger that jolted her right down to her toes. 'But it will be morning before you have the time to admire it.'

'Is that a promise?' she asked breathlessly.

He unclasped the sword and set it aside with care before removing his jacket. 'Come here…'

Entrapped by the scorching gold of his scrutiny, she slid off the bed and approached him. He lifted the pearl circlet from her hair, gently turned her round and unzipped her gown. The dress tumbled round her knees and he lifted her free of the folds, hauling her back into the hard muscular heat of his masculine frame. The fine silk shift pulled taut over the pouting fullness of her unbound breasts and clung to skin that felt smooth and sensuous.

'You're so perfect, Your Serene Highness…' He sighed, his expert hands roaming over the pert mounds, massaging the rosy crowns into a swollen sensitivity that drew a breathless moan from her parted lips. Her head angled back, her silvery blonde hair falling like a sheet of polished silk across his shoulder. His mouth blazed a roving trail from her delicate jawbone to the pulse-point below her ear that made her jerk in response.

'Your Serene Highness…?' Kirsten echoed weakly, incomprehension gripping her at his form of address.

'My princess…my beautiful princess.' Shahir bent her forward to undo the tiny fasteners on the shift. 'The title comes courtesy of my father.'

The shift was being peeled down over the womanly curve of her hips and she could hardly breathe for anticipation, never mind carry on a sensible conversation. The pulse of desire throbbed an insistent beat between her thighs and her face was hot. 'I w-wasn't expecting it,' she stammered, shocked at the strength of what she was feeling.

'You deserve it—and more.' His rich drawl shimmied down her taut spine. 'You have gone through so much since I came into your life, *aziz*.'

'It wasn't all bad,' she confided unevenly.

'None of it should have been,' Shahir intoned, shedding his shirt.

Kirsten could not concentrate. Drawing her down on to the bed, he was caressing her lush little breasts with uninhibited masculine appreciation and skill. Her breath rasped back and forth in her throat as she struggled to stay in control. He lowered his proud dark head over the tormentingly tender tips that adorned the small ripe mounds and circled the stiff straining buds with the tip of his tongue. The onslaught of sensation was too much for her: her hips rose and she whimpered his name.

'Tonight…everything must be for your pleasure.' He straightened in one lithe movement and removed the remainder of his clothes.

Liquid heat danced over the delicate flesh at the heart of her. Even though she was taut with self-consciousness, and flushed with the shyness that even desire could not drive out, she couldn't drag her eyes from him.

'Why?' she whispered.

'The first time the pleasure was all mine.'

He had a stunning dark male beauty that mesmerised her. When she looked at him her heart pounded and she got butterflies in her tummy. His features were hard, sculpted and strong, brought to vibrant life by the dazzling dangerous gold of his eyes. He had the superb physique of an athlete. Lean muscle rippled below his bronzed skin, ebony curls delineating his powerful chest while a silky furrow of dark hair ran down in an intriguing line over his hard flat stomach. The bold thrust of his arousal ensnared her attention and filled her with sinful heat.

She was weak with longing when he came back to her, tasting her reddened mouth with hungry, marauding fervour. He worked his skilful passage down over her twisting, turning body, leaving a trail of fire wherever he lingered and parting her slender thighs. What he did next shocked her senseless, but before she could protest a wicked flood of unbearable sensation seized her and suddenly she had all the self-will of a remote controlled toy. Nothing could have prepared her for the sensual intensity of an experience that threatened to drive her out of her mind with an enjoyment so strong it came close to pain.

'Now…' Shahir framed with ragged force, pulling her beneath him when she could no longer stand the fierce need he had induced in her weak and unresisting body. With sure hands he tipped her up and plunged into the damp heated core of her with a harsh groan of wondering pleasure. 'It has never, ever been like this for me before…'

The raw passion of his possession sent such a shock wave of delight pulsing through her that she reached an instantaneous peak of ecstasy. The sweet violence of release gripped her in quivering spasms of joy until she was heavy and limp with satiation.

'Oh, Shahir…' she mumbled shakily.

In response he withdrew from her and turned her over, rearranging her on her knees.

'Shahir…?' she gasped in disconcertion.

He sank into her again, hard and fast, and she heard herself cry out with the intolerable pleasure of his entrance into her newly tender flesh. She had no thought after that. In fact wild excitement knocked every single thought out of her head. She abandoned herself to delight and more delight. Once more he drove her to the heights of an explosive climax, and with a cry of rapture she surrendered to the voluptuous waves of sweet pleasure that engulfed her.

When she recovered from that incredibly intense bout of passion Shahir was cradling her close. He had both arms wrapped round her while he scanned her delicate features with slumberous dark golden eyes full of appreciation. 'I will never let you out of my sight again, *aziz*. What a blessing it is that we found each other.'

Blissfully contented, and awash with love and security as Kirsten felt at that moment, she had, however, been disconcerted by one aspect of their lovemaking. She rested her cheek against a smooth brown muscular shoulder and murmured, 'You took precautions…'

'Of course…I won't run the risk of getting you pregnant again.'

Astonishment opened her green eyes to their fullest extent. 'But don't you want more children? I thought it sort of went with the territory,' she confided.

'Tazeem will have to be enough. Never again will I put you through birth…I could not do that to you,' Shahir admitted, a shudder of recollection rippling through the long lean body entwined with her softer curves. 'I found it very difficult to stand by while you were going through all that.'

A smile crept over Kirsten's full mouth. She snuggled closer to him. For weeks on end she had tormented herself with the belief that Shahir valued her mainly for her capacity to give him children. But he had just shown her how wrong she had been in that assumption. 'Is that because of what happened to your mother?' she whispered softly. 'Jahan mentioned how she had died.'

'It is true that my father has often spoken of that day

to me. Why not? It was the worst day of his life. But I wouldn't have discussed that tragedy while you were carrying our child,' Shahir countered. 'It would have disturbed you.'

He had been really worried about her, and yet he had kept his fears to himself rather than take the risk of frightening her with the story of his mother's sad demise. She was touched by his admission, and not for worlds would she have confided that she was just finding out that she had to be the most contrary woman alive on the planet. No sooner had Shahir assured her that Tazeem was to be their one and only child than she had decided that she wanted at least two more children. Once she'd realised that he valued her health more than her ability to have babies, her misgivings and sensitivity on that score had been vanquished for ever.

Shahir rolled her over and gazed down at her, inky black lashes low and sexy over striking dark golden eyes 'This is our wedding night…the talk is too serious.'

'But you're always serious.'

'Over the next few weeks you will learn that I have another side to my nature.'

'Weeks? How long have I got you for?' The instant that revealing question leapt off her tongue she wanted to cringe.

A wickedly attractive smile slashed his darkly handsome features. 'You have got me for at least six weeks…'

The pretence of cool could not contain her delight and she gasped, 'Six weeks? Honestly?'

'Honestly…and I intend for us to make full use of every priceless moment.' Matching words to action, Shahir captured her mouth with hungry urgency and let his tongue delve deep in an exploratory foray.

Tiny little darts of flame licked low in her pelvis. The

tender crests of her breasts tingled. Already she wanted to feel his hands on her again. Embarrassed though she was by her susceptibility, she couldn't resist him.

Reaching up to him in a helplessly encouraging movement, she let her fingers spear through the tousled depths of his black hair.

Shahir lifted his head again, his dark eyes reflective. 'You see, it will take every day of those weeks for you to learn royal etiquette and the history of our family…'

Kirsten blinked. 'I suppose…'

'And perhaps a little more Arabic.'

She nodded, seeing the solid sense of that as well.

Looking pensive, Shahir continued to study her. 'As my wife you should get to know the desert. The ability to ride a horse would be an advantage…and of course I could teach you to dance…'

Kirsten turned brick-red at that low reminder. 'It all sounds very educational.'

He unleashed his vibrant smile again. 'And the education will continue in private as well, while you teach me what you like,' he suggested huskily, letting a caressing hand curve to the swell of her hip as he brought her closer. 'And I teach you what I like…'

'But I might not have the energy to learn anything after all those lessons in etiquette, history and dancing.' Kirsten let her fingertips forge a provocative feminine trail down his taut flat stomach.

Shahir could not conceal his surprise or his instant fascination at that first show of boldness on her part. 'We'll make the time, *aziz*, ' he breathed unsteadily, hauling her to him with unsubtle force. 'Even if we have to stay here for ever!'

CHAPTER TEN

THE music Kirsten's nimble fingers coaxed from the piano keyboard in a rich flood of virtuoso notes flowed round the room and out into the corridor where the staff stood listening. The difficult technical passages of a Rachmaninoff prelude gave way to the fast upbeat rhythm of several Gershwin pieces, and finally to a dreamy waltz that soothed in the heat of midday when there was not a hint of a breeze in the air.

'If you hadn't married Shahir and become a besotted wife and mother, you might have become a great classical pianist,' her brother Daniel mused, reclining back in his seat in a lazy sprawl and sipping at a chilled lemon drink.

Kirsten laughed at the idea. Glazed doors had been folded back so that the room was open to the beautiful shaded courtyard beyond. Leaving the piano, she stepped over Squeak, who was snoozing in front of a whirling fan. She strolled out to sit down casually on a low wall beside Tazeem's pram. 'I'm not that good a player.'

'Oh, yes, you are. But you would have had to struggle to make a name for yourself in the music world, and you might never have got a lucky break. Instead you became a royal princess, with several palaces, legions of staff and a magnificent grand piano,' the young blond man quipped, watching her scoop his nephew out of the pram with loving maternal hands and proceed to cuddle him. 'There's no contest.'

'It's not all about what I've gained in material terms...I'm just happy,' Kirsten proclaimed a tad defensively as she dropped a kiss down on Tazeem's satin-smooth cheek.

'And you should be. Shahir spoils you rotten, I've got an open ticket to fly out here any weekend I want to see you—'

'Hasn't that been marvellous?' his sister interrupted with enthusiasm. 'We didn't have much time together at the wedding. But since then we've got to know each other again.'

'I must admit that it's no sacrifice to leave my student accommodation and enjoy three-course meals, a choice of swimming pools and servants on tap,' Daniel confided with engaging honesty. 'You are living an extraordinary life here.'

'Yes...' Kirsten gave him a dizzy smile.

'You wear diamonds one day, sapphires the next, and dazzling designer outfits you change every few hours. In fact you're better turned out than any Stepford Wife.'

Kirsten reddened and focused surprised eyes on him. 'I make an effort to look good. Is that a crime?'

Her sibling winced, looked as though he was about to speak, then apparently thought better of the idea and fell silent.

'What's wrong?' Kirsten prompted

'Well, I wasn't planning to comment, and maybe I should mind my own business...but sometimes it seems like you're trying so hard to be perfect at everything that you're stressing yourself out.'

It was such an astute comment that she paled and screened her eyes. 'Did Shahir say something to you?'

'Of course not.' Daniel fielded an instant rebuttal. 'Shahir would never dream of talking about you behind your back. Look, forget what I said. I don't know what I'm talking about.'

An hour later, he was on his way to the airport and a return flight to London. It had been his third visit in two months, and Kirsten had thoroughly enjoyed the time they had spent together. At the same time, however, Shahir's relatives had welcomed her warmly into *their* lives, and she had become particularly close to his sister, Jahan.

Shahir and Kirsten spent most weekends at Zurak, but weekdays were generally spent at the Ahmet, where they had the privacy of their own palace.

It was hard for her to believe that she had been living in Dhemen for two months on what felt like an extended honeymoon.

Those first few weeks of togetherness with Shahir at Zurak had been sheer, unadulterated bliss. The passion between them had burned hotter than hot, turning day into night and night into day. The wildness of the pleasure they had found in each other still shocked her. It was as though their desire was never fully assuaged. Shahir walked into a room and she wanted him. Sitting through a meal, getting through a polite conversation with visitors could be a private torment. Without the slightest encouragement she would find herself recalling the aromatic scent of his skin, the taste of him and the hard heat of his urgent body against hers, and occasionally it mortified her to be at the mercy of a hunger she could not control.

No onlooker would ever have guessed that Shahir was not in love with his wife, for he managed to act as though Kirsten was the centre of his world. He had shared so much more with her than a bed, she acknowledged, wanting to give honour where it was due. He had taken her into the desert to see the sun go down in crimson splendour, and there he had introduced her to the exquisite and unforgettable love poetry of Kahlil Gibran. He had also tried commendably hard not to laugh when she ran screaming from a lizard she had mistaken for a snake.

He rarely came home without a gift for her or Tazeem. It might be a single flower, a book, a toy for their son or an extravagant jewel, but he gave with immense generosity. He had told her about the harsh routine of the military school he had attended, and the rather disconcerting freedom that had been his when he'd later studied business at Harvard. She had begun to understand the forces and influences that had forged his reserve.

On a visit to a Beduoin encampment she had watched him take part in a sword dance and a camel race, and she had secretly savoured that glimpse of the wild side of his volatile temperament which he kept under such fierce control. They had spent the night in a tent bedecked with ancient rugs, and he had spread her out on the floor and made passionate love to her until dawn, masking her every moan with his mouth so that they would not be heard. In the morning she had watched him fly his peregrine falcon high and free, and he had told her that that was how she made him feel in bed.

She was madly in love with him, but she tried not to think too much about that. Such reflections tended to make her dwell on the fact that he was not in love with her. She tried not to remember that dreadfully stilted exchange on their wedding day, when he had tried to lay her fears about Faria to rest. She was willing to believe that he had never spoken a word of forbidden love to his gorgeous foster-sister. And she thought it was equally likely that Faria had no idea of how Shahir felt about her. But Kirsten was constantly aware that the man she loved had given his heart to another woman, and no matter how happy she was that knowledge was like a raw place on her soul that would not heal.

Somehow her brother had sensed that kernel of insecurity buried deep down inside her. She *did* strive to be the perfect wife. She took great care of her appearance and, although her cheeks warmed at this reflection, she knew she had been a fast learner in the bedroom. As she had a husband who was currently suffering considerable ribbing from his family for flying back from London just to spend two hours with her before leaving again, she was fairly certain she was meeting the right targets in that area of their relationship. She was equally diligent with lessons in Arabic and etiquette, and already knew more about the history of Shahir's family than he did.

'Kirsten…?' Shahir appeared in the doorway.

Her green eyes lit up. She flew down the length of the grand reception room and flung herself at him. He caught her up in his arms, but instead of kissing her as he usually did he set her gently and carefully back from him. Lean strong face grave, he rested his hands on her slim shoulders and surveyed her with strained dark golden eyes.

'What's wrong?' she pressed, a sliver of unease fingering down her spine.

'Pamela Anstruther is here in person to plead her case with you. Do you wish to see her?'

'Pamela…*Lady Pamela*?' Her smooth brow divided. 'Plead her case? What are you talking about?'

Shahir straightened to his full commanding height. 'I was planning to tell you tonight that the allegation of theft that was laid against you at Strathcraig has finally been disproved.'

Her lashes fluttered wide, her astonishment palpable. 'Has it?'

'Unfortunately neither of the two women who accused

you had anything to gain from admitting the truth. Both had committed a criminal offence. That is why it has taken such a long time to sort out this matter,' Shahir explained heavily.

'But you kept on trying?' Kirsten was impressed by the commitment he had brought to the challenge of refuting the charges made against her.

'Yes, of course I did. Unfortunately the continual round of interviews and questions carried out by my personal staff did not appear to be bearing fruit.'

'But they were still working on it all the same. I was afraid to ask you what was happening in case you'd given up,' Kirsten confided in a rush.

His clear eyes met hers levelly. 'I would not have done that.'

'How has the theft charge been disproved?'

'I understand that the assistant housekeeper, Morag Stevens, finally confessed yesterday that she had lied. She accepted a financial bribe from Pamela Anstruther to plant the pendant in your locker and act as a false witness against you.'

Kirsten could not hide her disgust. 'So why did Morag confess after all this time?'

'Pamela was afraid that Morag would crack under the pressure of the questions being asked. In an attempt to frighten Morag into continuing to keep quiet Pamela made the mistake of threatening her. Morag panicked and admitted everything she had done to the housekeeper.'

'So my name has been cleared?' Kirsten nodded to herself with satisfaction even as she frowned in puzzlement. 'But I don't understand why Lady Pamela would come all the way to Dhemen to see me.'

Beneath his bronzed complexion, Shahir seemed very pale. 'The woman is facing prosecution. I have already interviewed her. Our meeting was brief. I see no reason why she should escape punishment. Perhaps she hopes to awaken your pity. Remember that she had none for you.'

More troubled by his bleak attitude than by Pamela's arrival at the Ahmet Palace, Kirsten shook her head as though to clear it. 'To be honest, I'm in shock at all this.'

'You don't have to see her. Such a person is beneath your notice.'

'I would like to hear what she has to say for herself.' Kirsten's chin came up at a determined angle. 'But I really don't want her to enter our home.'

'It will not be necessary for her to do so.'

Shahir escorted her to a large building situated nearest the entrance to the Ahmet complex. It housed the offices of the senior courtiers, the administrative block, and the reception rooms used for formal public occasions. When he would have accompanied her into a small audience hall, she informed him that she would prefer to see Pamela alone.

'As you wish…then I will leave you.'

His formality offended her. She was on a high: her name had been cleared, her reputation cleansed, her innocence of theft proven. But Shahir, infuriatingly, was behaving as though someone had died.

As Kirsten passed by a tall gilded mirror, she realised what a staggering change Lady Pamela would now see in her. Her eloquent mouth quirked. Pearls glistened in her ears and round her throat. Her turquoise and pink wrap top, matching tiered skirt and fine pink leather pumps were the very latest in designer style.

Two of the élite palace guards were stationed in the hall where Pamela was waiting. Kirsten gave them a nod of dismissal. The brunette looked worn and tired, and her dress was badly creased.

'Your Serene Highness…' Pamela performed a low and very creditable curtsey without hesitation. 'Thank you for seeing me.'

'I just want to know why you did it.'

Pamela Anstruther fixed incredulous china-blue eyes on her. 'Because Prince Shahir was in love with you, of course…why else?'

Kirsten was paralysed to the spot by that retort. 'I beg your pardon?'

Pamela's mouth took on a resentful curve. 'I was mad for him too. I hated you for getting in the way.'

'You were jealous?'

'I saw the Prince with you twice—in the limo the day he offered you a lift, and the day I invited him for tea. The way he looked at you was really quite nauseating,' the brunette contended with a bitter laugh. 'He couldn't hide it. You were just a farm girl, but I could practically hear the wedding bells ringing. It was like you had cast a spell on him—and yet you were so naive that you didn't even *see* the power you had.'

'If you disliked me so much why did you ask me to help you with the party preparations?'

Pamela heaved a weary sigh. 'Right from the start I planned to have you accused of stealing. I wanted you out of the castle and away from him. But I didn't want to harm you personally—'

'Really?' Kirsten cut in very dryly.

'Really,' Pamela insisted. 'It was simply a case of needs must. I had no hope of getting anywhere with the Prince while you were around.'

'So you decided to frame me for theft? You ensured that I found that brooch while Shahir was in the next room and that was your first step towards setting me up to be accused of stealing, wasn't it?'

'I'm not denying what I did. I bribed silly little Morag to lie and stick the pendant in your locker. But I had no luck, did I? You're years younger than I am, and perfectly beautiful. Your Prince was obsessed with you and he married you all the same. And Morag got cold feet and dropped us both in it.' Pamela Anstruther settled defiant blue eyes on Kirsten. 'I'm ruined anyway. I'll have to sell up and leave the glen. I can't live there now that everyone knows what I did to you. I'm getting the cold shoulder everywhere.'

'That's not my fault.'

'No, but do I really deserve to be dragged into court and prosecuted into the bargain? After all, it's pretty obvious that Prince Shahir would have married you even if you had murdered someone!' Pamela pointed out sourly. 'I'm sorry I ever tangled with the pair of you. I'm sorry that I had you accused of something you didn't do and that you lost your job. But I do feel the need to point out that it doesn't seem to have harmed your social prospects much.'

Kirsten treated the other woman to a cool appraisal, and it took the self-discipline that Shahir had patiently taught her to prevent her from succumbing to an inappropriate desire to laugh. 'I believe I've heard enough. Go back to the UK. I'll think over what you've said, but I'm not making any promises.'

Without another word, her mind buzzing with feverish thoughts, Kirsten left the audience chamber and walked briskly back to the huge rambling palace that had been designated as her home and Shahir's. A palace within a palace, it rejoiced in its own high walls and the seclusion and the wonderful steam room she had enjoyed on her wedding day.

All Kirsten could really think about was Pamela's unswerving conviction that Shahir loved his wife. She was also starting to appreciate why Shahir had been under so much strain when he had last spoken to her: he would be devastated by the realisation that he had misjudged her. He set himself such impossibly high standards and tore himself up over every error. Hadn't she already learned that he was his own fiercest critic?

She heard her royal husband's voice before she saw him. Wondering who he was talking to, she tiptoed over to the door of his study and peered in.

'I blew it,' Shahir was saying morosely. 'I always blow it with her. I say the wrong thing…I do the wrong thing. How am I supposed to tell her that I didn't really care if she was a thief any more? That doesn't sound right, does it? It sounds crazy, but that's how it was. I had stopped thinking about it.'

His confessor loosed a sympathetic sigh as his floppy ears were stroked. Short stubby tail wagging gently, the little dog curled up at Shahir's feet and lay down to sleep.

'You should be talking to me, not Squeak,' Kirsten declared.

Shahir leapt upright in surprise and swung round in a fluid arc. A dark line of colour scored his proud, angular cheekbones. 'I didn't expect you to return this quickly.'

'Pamela is so self-obsessed she's not good company,' Kirsten quipped, moving in a restive prowl round the room, because she was so nervous that she could not stay still. 'I've decided that I don't want charges pressed against her or Morag. Presumably Morag Stevens has been sacked?'

'Of course.'

'Let that be enough, then. I just want the whole thing dropped and forgotten about now.'

'But you were deliberately singled out to suffer Pamela

Anstruther's malicious attacks on your reputation. What those women did was criminal.'

'I was the victim, but you were the cause. No, believe me, I'm not blaming you for being so fanciable that Pamela Anstruther was willing to break the law to discredit me in your eyes.' Reluctant amusement shone in Kirsten's gaze as Shahir slung her a disconcerted look. 'But what she did does seem to have been girlie warfare of the nastiest kind—and that's what it was all about. Of course I expect she was after your money as well as—'

'I imagine so,' Shahir slotted in, before she could elaborate on what else he might have to offer in the fanciable department. 'You are choosing to take a strangely light-hearted view of this affair.'

'Affair? Did you ever…with Pamela, I mean?' Kirsten suddenly prompted in horror, mentally crossing her fingers and praying that he had not.

Shahir spread two lean brown hands wide, his shock and embarrassment at finding himself the target of so intimate a question patent. 'Of course not.'

'But maybe you were just a little tempted by her before I came along?'

'Her manner was so encouraging that I may have considered the possibility once or twice.' His even white teeth were visibly gritted as he forced out that admission. 'But I maintained a formal distance with her and ultimately her boldness offended me.'

'Thank you for telling me that,' Kirsten murmured gently. 'I can now see how Pamela might have thought she had a chance with you and that I spoilt it.'

'That would be nonsense, and it should not influence your opinion of what she did to you.'

'You're not a woman, Shahir. You don't understand.'

But he was *so* honest. Kirsten marvelled at how honest

he was. She wanted to apologise for getting so personal, but she was impressed that he would tell the truth even when to do so affronted his fierce pride. Now she wondered how she had ever dared to doubt his word.

Lean strong face bleak, Shahir straightened his shoulders like a soldier facing up to a firing squad. 'You must allow me to offer you my profound regret for not having had faith in you when you were accused of stealing. I—'

'That's fine—it's OK. Pamela's clever, and that stunt she pulled with the brooch really did make me look very guilty.'

'Please let me say what I must,' Shahir incised.

Kirsten fell silent, frustration filling her—for she had wanted to discuss something that was much more important to her.

'I am ashamed that you came to me for help and I would not believe that you were telling me the truth. I did let you down,' he asserted, not quite levelly. 'That will live with me until the day I die.'

I know it will,' she muttered helplessly, wishing he didn't take everything quite so much to heart. 'But you are only human.'

Strained dark golden eyes sought and held hers. 'You left home without money or proper support. Any one of a number of appalling fates might have become yours. Throughout the seven months it took for me to find you I was haunted by fear for your wellbeing.'

Kirsten nodded thoughtfully. 'Even before you knew I was pregnant?'

'Yes…and that discovery made my betrayal of your trust all the more unforgivable,' he reasoned grittily.

Kirsten lifted her head high, green eyes full of resolve. 'I forgive you.'

Shahir frowned. 'But you cannot—'

'If I say I forgive you, I forgive you!'

'Yes, but—'

'Is *my* forgiveness *mine* to give or not?' Kirsten suddenly shot at him in exasperation.

Shahir paled and compressed his beautiful mouth into an austere line. 'Of course it is yours to give.'

'Then you're just going to have to live with being forgiven for thinking you were married to a thief.' Studying his darkly handsome features, Kirsten felt her heartbeat accelerate, and tried not to smile because he was being so very serious. 'We didn't know each other when Tazeem was conceived. That was the real problem. We had all that physical attraction going for us and complicating things, but we were still almost strangers.'

Shahir looked pensive. 'I had not thought of it from that angle. You are right. Trust takes time to build. But I had never known a hunger such as you awakened in me,' he confided, half under his breath. 'It was like a fire that burned out my common sense and control. I saw you and I was lost. I fought it and the fire kept on blazing up, destroying all my good intentions.'

'I didn't help you stick to your good intentions when I lied and said I wasn't a virgin. Don't keep on talking as if only one of us was in charge of events.'

A rueful laugh was wrenched from Shahir. 'I was not in charge at all. With hindsight I see that when Pamela suggested you were not as innocent as you seemed I wanted to believe it because it made you seem more within reach.'

Temper sparking, Kirsten exclaimed, 'What did that witch say about me?'

'Foolish insinuations which I know to be untrue—for you were pure until I took advantage of you,' Shahir stated soothingly.

Feeling that her being taken advantage of was not a direction she wanted their dialogue to travel in, Kirsten changed the subject to the one that had been on her mind from the minute she'd rushed to find him. 'On our wedding day you told me you didn't love Faria…'

His imperious dark brows rose in surprise. 'I don't.'

'But, you see, I didn't believe you. I assumed you were just saying that to cover up the truth and keep me happy.'

He viewed her with candid bewilderment. 'I would not have deceived you.'

Excitement was beginning to nip at Kirsten. He had been telling the truth when he'd said he no longer loved Faria!

Shahir grimaced. 'Perhaps I was not very convincing when I tried to explain about Faria, but I was most embarrassed. To reach my age and to realise that I had never been in love—'

'Never?' she whispered in wonderment.

'It wasn't until I met you that I realised that the emotions you inspired far surpassed anything I had ever felt for Faria. I then felt very foolish. I had mistaken a moment of admiration, a daydream, for the real thing.'

Kirsten reached hurriedly for his hands and tugged him closer, fingers curving into his and clinging like mad. 'So you were saying…?' she encouraged.

Anxious dark golden eyes gazed down into hers and his hands tightened in the hold of hers. 'I think I may have fixed on the dream of Faria, who was conveniently out of reach, as an excuse to avoid the threat of having to marry when I didn't want to.'

Kirsten shifted enticingly closer, freeing one hand to slide it up over a broad shoulder. 'It really doesn't matter. What does matter is that when you took me into the desert and read all that gorgeous love poetry to me you were being romantic.'

'What else?'

'Because you *felt* romantic—not because being romantic was what you thought of as a duty on your honeymoon.'

Shahir looked indisputably lost as he attempted to work out that statement.

'I've been so stupid… Of course, if you'd just *said*.' Kirsten gave his tie a little admonitory tug as she began to unknot it. 'Just said you loved me, then I would have known and I would have told you how I feel about you.'

Shahir trailed loose his tie and unbuttoned his collar with rare clumsiness. 'So I just say…I love you?' he breathed unevenly.

'And I say… Fancy that? I love you too. I've been in love with you ever since you swooped up on that dangerous motorbike and almost ran Squeak over.'

They stared at each other, absorbing their respective expressions. A joyful smile had illuminated her face and a glow of happiness had banished his gravity and tension.

'I think that must have been when it happened to me too. I never knew a happy moment after that until we were safely married,' Shahir confided. 'But how can you love me when I have made so many mistakes?'

'Stop arguing about it…you're loved,' Kirsten told him.

'I thought you were only marrying me because you were pregnant.'

'And I thought that was the only reason you asked me.'

'You could not have believed that the first time I proposed at the castle,' Shahir pointed out. 'At that stage it hadn't occurred to either of us that you might have conceived.'

'No, but I thought you were proposing out of guilt.'

He closed his arms round her and crushed her to him in a fierce embrace. 'There was some guilt, I admit,' he told her huskily. 'But much more love and desire was involved. Regrettably, I didn't understand my own heart that day—and the accusation of theft against you shocked me and divided us. Had that not occurred I would have realised within days that you were the woman I wanted to share the rest of my life with. Instead I let you down—'

'No…no…no. No more of that,' Kirsten scolded, resting an admonitory forefinger to his beautifully shaped mouth.

He pressed his lips to the centre of her palm and then lowered his head to savour her lush mouth with reverent appreciation. 'I love you so much it hurts,' he admitted gruffly. 'Never again do I want to relive those months of searching and fearing that I would never see you again.'

Her hands slid below his jacket and across his lean, muscular chest. With a ragged groan of response he devoured her mouth again. Kisses interspersed with passionate declarations of devotion followed, until matters became so heated that Shahir swept Kirsten off to the privacy of their bedroom…

Eighteen months later, Kirsten bustled round the spacious nursery at Strathcraig Castle until Tazeem finally and reluctantly dropped off to sleep. Her toddler's boundless reserves of energy never failed to amaze her, and he had enjoyed a very sociable day. Now, with his black lashes resting on his cheeks like silk fans, he looked like an angel. That idea made her grin, for he could be as naughty as any other child and she had to learn to be firm with him.

Earlier that day Shahir and Kirsten had thrown a huge Christmas party for the tenants, the staff and their neighbours, and a very good time had been had by all. King Hafiz, who had become a regular visitor at his son and daughter-in-law's Scottish castle, had laughed uproariously at the antics of the clowns hired to entertain the children. And even the latest additions to Shahir and Kirsten's family circle had managed to stay awake later than usual.

But now their infant son, Amir, and their daughter, Bisma, were slumbering in perfect peace in their adjoining cots. These twins had been a surprise package, for their arrival had not been planned.

In fact Kirsten had not even got round to tackling Shahir about his fear of her undergoing childbirth again before she had realised that she was already pregnant again. She had discovered that spontaneous passion in the steam room could have consequences—quite delightful consequences, she reflected, regarding her eight-week-old twins with fond maternal pride.

Amir and Bisma had been born without surgical intervention. Shahir had still looked rather faint once or twice during the proceedings, but had held up valiantly to the challenge.

Indeed, the past year and a half of married life had been blissfully happy for Kirsten. Secure in her husband's love and admiration, she made occasional appearances in support of various charitable enterprises in Dhemen, and she was now much too busy and much too content to worry about trying to be the perfect wife all the time.

Her brother Daniel had achieved his doctorate, and was currently employed on a conservation project in the

Arabian Gulf. He was able to visit his sister in Dhemen as often as he liked.

There had, however, been a less happy conclusion to Kirsten's attempt to mend fences with her father. Her letters had been returned unopened, and six months earlier Angus Ross had passed away suddenly after suffering a heart attack. Daniel and Kirsten had attended the funeral and paid their last respects with sadness, but also with acceptance that they had done what they could to re-establish contact with the older man. Perhaps it was for that reason that Kirsten had increasingly come to rely on and appreciate the love, kindness and support she had found within Shahir's family.

'We have two nannies and a host of other helpful staff,' Shahir remarked from the threshold of the room, Squeak trotting at his heels. 'But where do I still find you?'

'The same place I often find you at the end of the day. Has the King retired for the night?' Kirsten asked as she accompanied her tall, handsome husband along the passage to their bedroom.

'Yes, and I've booked the clowns for his birthday this summer. I haven't seen my father enjoy himself that much in years. I know who to thank for that too.' Shahir gave her a warmly appreciative smile. 'My royal parent has never liked traveling, but you have organised his suite here exactly as his rooms are at home and he seems very relaxed.'

'I'm glad.'

Curving a possessive arm round her slender back, Shahir slowly welded her soft, yielding curves to his lean, muscular frame and murmured huskily, 'I really love being married to you. '

'Do you?' A highly provocative and feminine smile tilted her mouth.

The answering glitter of his stunning dark golden eyes made her mouth run dry. 'I'm crazy about you.'

As Shahir splayed his fingers to the swell of her hip, to ease her into even closer contact, Kirsten stretched up her arms to link them round his neck. 'I love you too…so much.'

He bent his proud dark head and circled her lush pink lips with his own. She quivered in wild response. He kissed her breathless. He told her how happy she made him. He told her that without her and the children his life would have no meaning.

Kirsten listened starry-eyed while Squeak yawned, and yawned again. He had seen it all before, and he headed off to his cosy basket in the room next door and snuggled down to sleep.

The Sheikh's Disobedient Bride

JANE PORTER

Jane Porter grew up on a diet of Mills & Boon® romances, reading late at night under the covers so her mother wouldn't see! She wrote her first book at age eight and spent many of her school and college years living abroad, immersing herself in other cultures and continuing to read voraciously. Now Jane has settled down in rugged Seattle, Washington, with her gorgeous husband and two sons. Jane loves to hear from her readers. You can write to her at PO Box 524, Bellevue, WA 98009, USA. Or visit her website at www.janeporter.com

For Lee Hyatt and all readers who
love sheikh stories

CHAPTER ONE

TALLY heard the guttural shouts seconds before the gunfire. Dropping to her stomach, she hugged her camera and struggled to protect her head.

"Soussi al-Kebir," her guide screamed as he ran from her.

Soussi al-Kebir? Tally pressed her forearm to her face, struggling to make sense of the words with the little Arabic she knew.

Soussi were Berbers from the south, those that lived close to the desert. And al-Kebir was big or great. But *Soussi al-Kebir?*

More gunfire rang in the small town square, the rat-a-tat of machine gunfire and the hard clattering of horses' hooves.

Was this an ambush? Robbery? What?

Heart racing, Tally hugged the cobblestones closer, her camera gripped tightly in the crook of her arm, certain any moment a whizzing bullet would hit her.

Not far from her a man screamed and fell. She heard him hit the ground, the heavy thud of body against stone. Moments later red liquid ran toward her, inches from her face and she recoiled, lifting her head to avoid the blood.

It was then a shadow stretched long above her, the shadow enormous, blocking the intense Barakan sun.

Fear melted Tally's heart. She wanted to squeeze her eyes shut but fear wouldn't let her. She wanted to be brave and bold, but fear wouldn't let her. Instead she huddled there, eyes riveted to the shadow and the foot frighteningly close to her head.

The foot was big and covered in pale suede. The soft leather boot the type desert tribesmen wore, they were made of the softest, most supple leather to protect from the heat of the sand and yet light to make walking in the soft surface easier. White fabric brushed the top of his boot. It was the hem of his robe.

Soussi, she thought, putting it together. The huge shadow. The suede boot. *Soussi al-Kebir.* Chief of the Desert.

Hands encircled Tally's upper arms and she was hauled to her feet. The same hands ripped her camera away from her even as a dark rough fabric jerked down over her head, turning day to night.

Tally screamed as everything went black, but it wasn't the dark fabric that upset her. It was the loss of her camera. Her camera and camera bag were her world, her livelihood, her identity. Without her camera and film, she had no way to pay her bills. No way to survive.

"Give me back my camera!" she demanded, voice muffled by the coarse fabric.

"Quiet!" A harsh male voice commanded.

Suddenly she was lifted, tossed high onto the back of a horse and someone leaped behind her, settling onto the blanket and seizing the reins. Heels kicked at the horse's flanks and they were off, galloping away from the town's medina, down the narrow cobbled street into the desert beyond.

Panicked, Tally struggled in the saddle, battling to pull the fabric off her head but it'd been pulled low and it was tied somehow, anchored around her shoulders.

"Ash bhiti?" She choked in broken Barakan Arabic. *What do you want?*

The only response was an arm pulling her closer, holding her more firmly, the arm thickly muscled, very hard, drawing her against an even thicker, harder torso.

"I have money," she added frantically, growing hotter by the second inside the dark fabric. "I'll give you money. Everything I have. Just go with me to my hotel—"

"Shhal?" he grunted, interrupting her. *How much?*

"Nearly five hundred American dollars."

He said nothing and Tally tried not to squirm even though the fabric was oppressive, suffocating. She had to stay calm, strike a bargain. "I can get more."

"Shhal?" he repeated. He wanted to know how much more she could get.

It was at that point Tally realized she was dealing with a mercenary. "A thousand dollars. Maybe two thousand."

"Not enough," he dismissed, and the arm around her tightened yet again.

"What do you want then?"

"For you to be quiet."

"I—"

"Enough!"

Fear made Tally silent. Fear made her hold her breath, air bottled inside. She'd read about kidnappings in the Middle East. So now instead of fighting further, she told herself not to scream, or thrash. She wouldn't do anything to provoke him, or his men, into doing something that would later be regretted.

Instead she told herself that if she stayed calm, she'd get out of this. If she stayed calm, things might turn out okay.

Not every hostage was punished. Some were released.

That's what she wanted. That's what she'd work to do.

Cooperate. Prove herself trustworthy. Get set free.

To help stay focused, she went over her day, thinking about the way it began, and it began like any other day. She'd loaded her camera with film, put a loose scarf over her head and set out to take her pictures.

She never traveled alone, had learned the value of hiring escorts and guides, bodyguards and translators when necessary. She knew how to slip a few coins into the right hands to get what she wanted.

In remote parts of the world, her native guides and escorts allowed her access to places she normally couldn't visit—temples, mosques, holy cemeteries, inaccessible mountain towns. She'd been warned that being a female would put her in danger, but on the contrary, people were curious and realized quickly she wasn't threatening. Even the most difficult situations she'd encountered were smoothed by slipping a few more coins into a few more hands. It wasn't bribery. It was gratitude. And who couldn't use money?

She'd thought this desert town was no different from the others she'd visited and this morning when she crouched by the medina's well, she'd heard only the bray of donkeys and bleating of goats and sheep. It was market day and the medina was already crowded, shoppers out early to beat the scorching heat.

There'd been no danger. No warning of anything bad to come.

With her camera poised, she'd watched a group of children dart between stalls as veiled women shopped and elderly men smoked. She'd smiled at the antics of the boys, who were tormenting the giggling girls, and she'd just focused her lens when shouts and gunfire filled the square.

Tally wasn't a war correspondent, had never worked for any of the big papers that splashed war all over the front pages, but she'd been in dangerous situations more than once. She knew to duck and cover, and she did the moment she heard the gunfire. Duck and cover was something all children learned on the West Coast in America, earthquakes a distinct possibility for anyone living on one of the myriad of fault lines.

As she lay next to the well, she'd tried to avoid the bright red liquid running between cobblestones and that's when the desert bandit seized her.

If she hadn't looked, maybe the bandit wouldn't have noticed her…

If she hadn't moved maybe she'd be safe in town instead of being dragged into the middle of the desert.

Inside the stifling black fabric Tally struggled to breathe. She was beginning to panic despite her efforts to remain calm. Her heart already beat faster. Air came in shallow gasps.

She could feel it coming on. Her asthma. She was going to have an asthma attack.

Tally coughed, and coughed again.

The dust choked her. She couldn't see, could barely breathe, her throat squeezing closed in protest at the thick clouds of dust and swirling sand kicked up by the wind and the horse's pounding hooves.

Eyes wet with tears, Tally opened her mouth wider, gasping for breath after breath. She was panicking, knew she was panicking and panicking never helped, certainly not her asthma but it was all beyond her, the heat, the jostle of the saddle, the wind, the dust.

Reaching up, out, her hand flailed for contact, grappling with air before landing against the bandit's side. He was warm, hard, too hard, but he was the only one who could help her now. She clung convulsively to the fabric of his robe, tugged on it, hand twisting as frantically as her lungs squeezed.

One, two, she tugged violently on the fabric, her hand twisting in, out, pulling down, against the body, anything to express her panic, her desperation.

Can't breathe…

Can't breathe…

Can't…

Tair felt the hand grappling with his shirt, felt the wild frantic motion and then felt her go slack, hand falling away limply.

He whistled to his men even as he reined his horse, drawing to a dramatic pawing stop.

Tair threw the fabric covering off the foreign woman captured in the town square.

She was limp and nearly blue.

He lifted her up in one arm, turned her cheek toward him, listened for air and heard nothing.

Had he killed her?

Tipping her head back, he covered her mouth with his own, pinched her nose closed, blowing air into her lungs, forcing warm air where there had been none.

His men circled him on their horses forming a protective barrier, although they should be safe here. This was his land. His people. His home. But things happened. They knew. He knew.

He felt their silence now, the stillness, the awareness. They wouldn't judge him, they wouldn't dream of it. He was their lord, their leader, but no one wanted a death on his hands. Especially not a foreign woman.

Much less a young foreign woman.

Not when Ouaha still fought for full independence. Not when politics and power hung in delicate balance.

He covered her mouth again, forcing air through her once more, narrowed gaze fixed on her chest, watching her small rib cage rise. Come on, he silently willed, come on, Woman, breathe.

Breathe.

And he forced another breath into her, and another silent command. You will breathe. You will live.

You will.

She sputtered. Coughed. Her lashes fluttered, lifted, eyes opening.

Grimly Tair stared down into her face, the pallor giving way to the slightest hint of pink.

Alhumdulillah, he silently muttered. Thanks be to God. He might not be a good man, or a nice man, but he didn't enjoy killing women.

Her eyes were the palest brown-green, not one color or the other and although her expression was cloudy, unfocused, the color itself was remarkable, the color of a forest glen at dawn, the forest he once knew as a boy when visiting his mother's people in England.

Her brows suddenly pulled, her entire face tightening, constricting. She wheezed. And wheezed again, lips pursing, eyes fixed on him, widening, eyes filled with alarm.

Her hand lifted, touched her mouth, fingers curving as if to make a shape. Again she put her hand to her mouth, fingers squeezing. "Haler."

He shook his head, impatient, not understanding, seeing the pink in her skin fade, the pallor return. She wasn't getting air. She wasn't breathing again.

Her eyes, wide, frightened, held his and her fear cut him. She was hurt and in pain and he was doing this to her.

"What do you need?" he demanded, switching to English even as he lightly slapped her cheek, trying to get her to focus, communicate. What was wrong? Why couldn't she breathe?

Her fingers merely curled, reminding him of the letter C from the Western alphabet as she gasped, and he blocked out her frantic gasps of air studying her fingers instead. And then suddenly he knew. Asthma.

"You have asthma," he said. He was gratified to see her nod. "Where is your inhaler?"

"Cam-ra."

He lifted a hand, gestured, signaling he wanted it. The bag was handed over immediately.

Tair unzipped the top, rifled through, found the inhaler in a small interior side pocket and shook it before putting it to her mouth. Her hand reached up, released the aerosol, letting it flood her lungs.

Still holding her in the crook of his arm he watched her take another hit, saw her chest rise and fall more slowly, naturally, saw that she was breathing more deeply and he felt a measure of relief. She lived. He hadn't killed her. Good.

Hard to explain a dead Western woman to the authorities.

Minutes later she stirred again.

Tally didn't know at exactly what moment she realized she was lying in the barbarian's arms, her legs over his, her body in his lap, but once she knew where she was, and how he held her, she jerked upright.

She wrenched free, attempted to jump from the horse but instead fell to the ground, tumbling in a heap at everyone's feet.

She groaned inwardly, thinking she was getting too old for dramatic leaps and falls. Tally rose, straightening her white cotton shirt and brushing her khaki trousers smooth. "Who are you?" she demanded.

The man on the horse adjusted his headcovering, shifting the dark fabric to conceal all of his face but his eyes and bridge of nose. Face covered, he just looked at her, as did the others, and there were about a half dozen of them altogether.

"What do you want with me?" she persisted.

"We will talk later."

"I want to talk now."

He shrugged. "You can talk but I will not answer."

Tally inhaled, felt the hot still air slide into her lungs. She couldn't believe this was happening. It made no sense. Nothing about this made sense. She'd been kidnapped from the medina, taken right from the market by a group of masked men. But why? Who were they?

Her gaze settled on the soft suede boot in front of her, the color light, cream, just slightly darker than the white robe. Her gaze rose, lifting from the pale suede boot which covered from foot to calf, up over his knee, to the horse's ornate saddle and bridle. Both were made from pounded silver, heavily decorated with bits of onyx and blue stone, finished with colorful woolen tassels. The bridle's decorative leather curved protectively around the neck, nearly covered the ears, shielding the eyes. More silver and leatherwork ran across the front of the horse to match the saddle.

Tally's gaze lifted higher, moving from horse to man. He, in comparison, was dressed simply. White pants and robe, and a dark headcloth that wrapped around the neck, covered the head, and cloaked his face from nose to throat.

His eyes she could see. And they were dark, fixed, penetrating, nearly as strong as the bridge of his nose.

"Who are you?" she asked.

"We will talk later," he said, and turning slightly in his silver and gold embroidered blanket that served as a saddle, gestured to his men. "We go."

"No."

"No?"

"You nearly killed me!" Her voice was deep, raspier than usual.

He shrugged. "Fortunately I also saved you."

"And you what? Expect thanks?"

"Indeed. If it weren't for me, you would have died."

"If it weren't for you, I'd still be in town. Safe."

"It's a moot point. You're here now." He shifted on the embroidered blanket, reins loose in his palm as his gaze swept the barren landscape. "And this is where you want to stay? In the middle of the desert, on your own?"

Tally glanced right, left, saw only sand and pale dunes, the world a stunning ivory and gold vista in every direction. "We're just hours from the nearest town."

"Hours by horse." His head cocked and he studied her curiously, black eyebrows flat above intense eyes. "Do you have a horse?"

She felt her spine stiffen, her teeth clamping tight in the back of her jaw. "Not unless you kidnapped one for me."

"I'm afraid I did not."

"Right. Well, then, no horse."

He leaned down, out of his saddle so that his face loomed above hers. "I guess you'll be coming with me." And before she could protest, he swept her into his arm and deposited her on the saddle in front of him, back onto his lap from where she'd only just escaped.

Tally grunted as she dropped onto his lap. Damn. His lap was big, hard, just like the rest of him. Soussi al-Kebir. Chief of the Desert, indeed. "What group are you part of?" she asked, unable to remain silent despite her best intentions. She needed to know the worst.

"Group?" her captor grunted, even as he resettled her more firmly into his lap, his left arm slung around her, holding her against his hips.

She squirmed inwardly at the contact. "Who are you with?"

"With?"

If ever there was a time to be sensitive—diplomatic—this was it. But it wasn't easy finding the right words, or the right tone. "You must be part of a group, a tribe maybe?"

She felt him exhale. "You talk too much," he said exasperatedly even as he urged his horse into a canter. "Practice silence."

They rode the rest of the day in virtual silence, traveling deep into the desert, racing across the sand for what seemed like hours. Tally had given up sneaking glances at her watch. Time no longer mattered. They weren't close to anybody or anyplace that could help her. There was no one here to intercede on her behalf. The only thing she could do was stay alert, try to keep her wits about her, see if she couldn't find a way out.

Just before twilight they slowed, horses trotting as they reached the bandits' camp city, an oasis of tents and camels in what seemed to be the middle of nowhere.

At the camp, the men dismounted quickly. Tally's bandit jumped from his horse but when he reached for her, Tally squirmed away and dismounted without his help. She'd had enough of his company and wanted nothing more to do with him. But of course her captor had other plans for her.

"Come," he said, snapping his fingers. "Follow me."

He led her past a group of men sitting on the ground, and then past another group of men cleaning guns. She gave the second group of men a long, hard look. Guns were not good. This situation was not good.

Her bandit stopped walking, gestured to a tent on his left. "You'll go there," he said.

She looked at the tent and then the tribesman. "It's a tent."

"Of course it's a tent," he answered impatiently. "This is where we live."

She looked back to the tent, the fear returning, squeezing her insides, making it hard to breathe. "Is this a temporary stopping point?"

"Temporary, how? What are you asking?"

"Are we traveling on tomorrow?"

"No."

"Then what are we doing here?"

"Stopping." He gestured to the tent. "Go inside. Dinner will be brought to you."

Tally faced the tattered goatskin tent. It was hideous. Stained, patched, and worn. She'd been traveling in Northern Africa and the Middle East for six months now and she'd never seen such a rough encampment before. This was not a friendly camp. This was not a nomadic tribe, either. There were no children here, no women, no elderly people. Just men, and they were heavily armed.

Tally didn't know who they were and she wasn't sure she wanted to find out, either. Survival was paramount in her mind at this point.

She turned to look at her captor. He was tall, and hard and very indifferent. She suppressed a wave of emotion. No tears, no distress, no sign of weakness, she reminded herself. "How long will you keep me here?"

"How long will you stay alive?"

A lump filled her throat and she bit her lip, hot, exhausted, grimy. "Do you intend to…kill…me?"

His dark eyes narrowed, and a muscle pulled in his jaw, tightening the weathered skin across his prominent cheekbones. He had a strong nose, broad forehead and no sympathy or tenderness in his expression. "Do you *want* to die?"

What a question! "No."

"Then go inside the tent."

But she didn't move. She couldn't. She'd stiffened, her limbs weighted with a curious mixture of fear and dread. While she hated how he snapped his fingers as he ordered her about, it was the cold shivery dread feeling in her belly that made her feel worse.

She hated the dread because it made her feel as if nothing would ever be okay again.

"What do I call you?" she asked, nearly choking on her tongue, a tongue that now felt heavy and numb in her mouth. Tally had been in many dangerous situations but this was by far the worst.

He stared down at her for a long, tense moment. As the silence stretched, Tally looked past him, spotted a group of bearded men still meticulously cleaning their guns.

"Do you have a name?" Her voice sounded faint between them.

"Seeing as you're from the West, you can call me Tair."

"Tair?" she repeated puzzled.

He saw her brow crease with bewilderment but didn't bother to explain his name, seeing no point in telling her that his real name was something altogether different, that he'd been born Zein el-Tayer, and that he was the firstborn of his father's three sons and the only son still alive. He'd survived the border wars and the past ten years of tensions and skirmishes due to a lethal combination of skill and luck.

In Arabic, Zein or Zain meant "good", but no one called him Zein even if it was his first name because he wasn't good. Everyone in Baraka and Ouaha knew who he was, what he was, and that was danger. Destruction.

Tair wasn't a good man, would never be a good man and maybe that was all his captive needed to know.

"You'll be fine if you do what you're told," he added shortly, thinking he'd already spent far more time conversing than he liked. Talking irked him, it wasted time. Too many words filled the air, cluttering space, confusing the mind. Far better to act. Far better to do what needed to be done.

Like he'd done today.

He'd removed the threat from town, away from his people. He'd keep the woman isolated, too, until he understood what she was doing in his land, and who—or what—had brought her here in the first place.

Single women—and single women with cameras—didn't just happen upon Ouaha. If Western women visited Ouaha, which didn't happen very often, they were part of a tour, something that had been organized by a trusted source, and their itinerary was publicized, known.

"How did you get to Ouaha?" he asked abruptly, studying her wan face. She looked tired, but there was nothing defeatist in her expression. Rather she looked fierce. Furious. A wild animal cornered.

"Airplane to Atiq, and then jeep and camel from there."

"But someone planned your itinerary."

"I planned it myself. Why?"

The flare of heat in her eyes matched the defiant note in her voice. If she was afraid or worried, she gave no outward appearance. No, she looked ready for battle and that fascinated him. But it wasn't just her expression that intrigued him. It was her face. Strong through the brow, cheekbone and jaw, and yet surprisingly soft at the mouth with full, rose pink lips. Her gaze was direct, focused, not at all shy.

She had the look of a woman who knew her mind, a woman who wasn't easily influenced or deceived, which made him wonder about her appearance in Ouaha.

"I'm the one to ask the questions. You're the one to answer.

Go now to your tent. I shall speak with you later." Tair turned and walked away, but not before he saw her jaw drop and the blaze of fury in her eyes.

This woman didn't like being told what to do. His lips curved as he returned to his men. She'd learn soon to mask her true feelings or she'd simply continue playing into his hand.

CHAPTER TWO

TALLY watched the bandit—Tair, he'd said his name was—walk away. She noticed he hadn't even waited for her to respond. He'd ordered her in and then just walked away knowing she had no choice but to obey.

She clutched the tent flap, and stared at his retreating back, watching his white robe flow behind him.

Tally swore silently. Think, she told herself, do something. *But what?*

She caught the eye of one of the men cleaning guns and his expression was so disapproving that Tally shivered, and swiftly stepped into the tent.

But once inside, Tally didn't know what she was supposed to do. The tent was crude. There were few furnishings—just a low futonlike bed, a blanket of sorts, a small chest and a couple of pillows on the bed—and nothing remotely decorative. No wardrobe for clothes (not that she had any!), no chair, no mirror, nothing.

It would have been so easy to panic, but Tally resisted falling apart. There was little point in giving way to hysterics. No one even knew she was gone. No one would know she was missing. As far as her family knew, she'd been missing for years.

Sighing, she rubbed her brow, feeling the grit of sand and dust at her temple, against her scalp. Riding across the desert had been an illuminating experience. She could have sworn she ate more sand and dust than what they'd traveled over thanks to the horses' flying hooves.

Loosening her ponytail, Tally pulled the elastic from her hair and dragged her fingers through her hair, working the kinks free. What was going to happen now?

What was she supposed to do? Run? Steal a horse? Make vague threats about human rights and government relations?

Lifting the weight of her hair from her neck, she let her nape cool. She felt hot and sticky all over. Hot, sticky and afraid.

Why was she here? Were they going to ransom her? Punish her? What?

What did they want with her?

Reluctantly Tally pictured Tair, the bandit who'd taken her from town, and her stomach did a dramatic free fall all the way to her toes. Tair wasn't like the others. He was bigger, harder, fiercer. The way he'd held her as they rode today had been possessive, the very way his arm curved around her, his hand against her stomach sent shockwaves of alarm through her. It was as if he'd laid claim to her, a statement of ownership.

But she wasn't his. She'd never be his.

Her stomach did another nosedive and goose bumps covered her arms. Irritably she rubbed at her arms, trying to ignore the crazy adrenaline ricocheting through her.

He hadn't let her die in the desert. When she'd had her asthma attack he'd forced air into her lungs and then found her inhaler. He obviously didn't want her dead. But then what did he want from her? And would anyone back in Seattle care if she never returned?

Don't be a pessimist, she rebuked herself severely. *You're a freelance photographer, and maybe you've never deliberately photographed war, but you knew that life in the desert wasn't without violence.*

For a moment Tally felt calmer, stronger, at least she did until her tent flap snapped open and a dark shadow filled the opening.

Tally's stomach jumped, her heart plummeted. God help her. The bandit was back.

Dropping her hair, she smoothed her white cotton shirt over the waistband of her khaki slacks and watched as he entered her tent. He had to stoop to get through the covered opening. Once inside he glanced casually around, as if taking stock.

Tally swallowed hard, hands knotted at her sides. "Can you tell me why I'm here?" she asked, trying to sound conversational, not confrontational.

The tent flap swished behind him, allowing in bits of the twilight. He'd changed, and his outer robe hung open over a loose shirt and fitted pants. "You've interesting friends," he said, after a long tense pause.

"I don't understand. What friends are you talking about?"

"The friends you've been traveling with."

Her forehead furrowed. "I'm on my own. I've traveled with no one."

"You had men with you this morning."

"Ah." Her expression cleared. Comprehension, as well as relief swept over her. "Those men worked for me. They're Barakan. One was my translator. The other a guide."

He said nothing so she pushed on, praying she sounded confident, reasonable. "I hired them in Atiq and they knew I wanted to visit the kasbahs on the other side of the Atlas Mountains."

"How much did they pay you?"

Tally felt a prickle behind her eyes, pain that reminded her of the migraines she used to get when she was in college. "They didn't pay me. I paid them. As I said, I hired them. Their names were given to me by the hotel and they came highly recommended."

"And did they do what you wanted?"

"Yes. Until this morning there'd been no problem."

He regarded her for a long silent moment. "Why did you want to come to Ouaha?"

"Is that where I am?"

"Don't act so surprised."

"I am surprised. I hadn't realized we'd left Baraka. There was no border crossing—"

"A desert separates the countries, Woman."

She flinched at the "woman" but didn't contradict him. Instead she took a breath, suppressing her aggravation. "There was no plan to come to Ouaha. I merely told my guides what I wanted and they set the course knowing I needed to be in Casablanca by the first of October."

"Why the first of October?"

"My visa for Baraka ends and I need to be in Morocco by then."

His thickly fringed eyes narrowed, his angular jaw thickening yet again. "And so what exactly are you doing here, so far from your home?" His voice had dropped, and it was low, low and deadly.

"Nothing. Just sightseeing."

"With rebels as your guides?"

Her pulse quickened yet again. She pressed her palms together, the skin damp, sticky. "I don't know their politics. We never discussed—"

"But you paid them."

"Yes. I needed them. This part of the world is remote, and often inaccessible for women. I needed experienced guides."

"You're sure they didn't pay you?"

Tally would have laughed if the situation weren't so precarious. "For what?"

He slowly crouched down in front of the bed until he was eye to eye with her. His dark gaze met hers, held, the set of his mouth anything but gentle. "Why don't you tell me."

His eyes were so dark, and the expression so intense that Tally felt her heart stutter, not just with fear, but awareness. She knew men and was comfortable with men but Tair wasn't like men she'd ever known. There was an untamed element to him, a primitive maleness that made her feel increasingly small, fragile, female. And she didn't like feeling small or fragile, she just wasn't. Life had toughened her. She didn't frighten easily.

Swallowing, Tally gathered her courage. "I have no idea what you want from me. I'm just a tourist—"

"Not just a tourist. You've spent two weeks with those men. Two weeks photographing, documenting." His voice dropped even lower, deeper, and the husky ominous pitch slid down Tally's spine.

"We'll try this one more time," he said slowly, quietly, "and I warn you, I'm not a patient man but I'm trying. So don't test me. Understand?"

She nodded, because she did understand, and she also understood that things weren't going well and if they didn't come to some kind of agreement relatively soon, she would be in even greater danger. "Yes."

"Now tell me about the men you were traveling with."

"I know very little about them. They were quiet. They kept to themselves quite a bit. I thought they were good men."

"You've been with them two weeks and this is all you can tell me?"

How did he know she'd been traveling for two weeks with the men? He'd either been told, or he'd been watching her. Either way she'd been followed. "I'm sorry," she said, picking her words with care. If ever there was a time for diplomacy, this was it. "We didn't speak much. They're men. I was a foreign woman. There were cultural differences."

"Cultural differences."

She flushed, locked her fingers together. "I wish I could tell you more. I hadn't thought I was doing anything wrong. I've always wanted to visit Baraka—"

"But you're not in Baraka anymore. This is Ouaha. An independent territory, and this is my country, and these are my people and you entered my country with Barakan rebels. Men who have brought violence and destruction to my people."

She shook her head. "I don't know what you're talking about. I arrived in Atiq, hired these men as escorts, and yes, I have been traveling with them but that's because I'm a tourist, and traveling alone. I needed local guides and they came highly recommended."

"What about your pictures?" he asked, eyes narrowing.

She paled. "What about them?"

"You were taking pictures for them, weren't you?"

"No. They were for me. I didn't work for those men. Those men worked for me. The pictures are for me."

"Why do you want photographs of a nation so far from your own?"

For a moment Tally didn't know how to answer. His question had rendered her speechless. Why would she be interested in something so far from her home? Had he no desire to see the world, know something of places foreign to him? Finally she found her voice. "Because I'm curious."

"Curious about what?"

"Everything. Food, culture, language, lifestyle. I'm fascinated by people, by the differences among us, as well as what we have in common, too."

He snorted, a deep, rough sound of contempt. "We've nothing in common."

She couldn't hide her own flash of disdain, her jaw tightening, temper flaring. This is one of the reasons she traveled, as well as one of the reasons she'd left home. She'd abhorred ignorance and control. "Perhaps not. But instead of me staying home and sitting in my living room twiddling my thumbs, I've decided to go out and discover the truth for myself."

"Women belong at home."

"Maybe in your opinion—"

"Yes. In my culture women have a vital role taking care of

the children, watching over the family, making sure her husband is fed and rested. Comfortable."

"And when does she get to be fed and rested? When is she comfortable?"

"She is comfortable when her family is healthy and at peace."

"Huh!" Tally scoffed scornfully. "Why do I get the feeling that never happens?"

He swore something in Arabic she couldn't catch but from his tone she knew it wasn't kind. She'd angered him. She felt his hostility rolling off him in waves. She also felt his ambivalence. He couldn't decided what to do with her and Tally bit her lip, knowing she'd pushed him too hard, said too much. She'd never been a big talker but she'd certainly said quite a bit since arriving here.

"I'm sorry," she said, struggling to be conciliatory. "I'm just a curious person by nature, and I'm here in Baraka—"

"Ouaha."

"Ouaha," she amended, not really knowing anything about the territory but anxious to move on, "because I'm curious about your part of the world. I don't want to be ignorant."

"So you're just a tourist."

He was testing her, she thought, probing for the truth and her insides knotted, twisting with apprehension. No, she wasn't just a tourist. She was a professional photographer but right now she didn't think that would go over real well. He already mistrusted her. Would his opinion change when she told him she was in his country taking pictures for a book on children? "Yes, a tourist," she echoed.

"And that's the truth?"

She regarded him steadily even as she scrambled to consider all the angles. It wasn't a complete lie. She was a tourist, and she did love travel and discovering faraway places. Why did he have to know about her work? Why couldn't she just be a traveler with a camera?

Tally held his gaze. "Yes," she said, proud that her voice didn't wobble in the slightest.

"We'll see, won't we?" he answered even as a voice sounded from outside the tent.

Her bandit shouted back and the tent flap suddenly lifted and a man entered carrying her camera. The man handed her camera to Tair and then left without once ever looking at her.

As the bandit handled her camera, pulling it from the leather case and turning it over, Tally's legs went weak. She had a sudden desire to sit. But she didn't dare move and instead she watched as he pushed buttons, turned the camera on and off, zoomed the telephoto lens out before bringing it back.

It made her nervous, watching him play with her camera. It was a good camera but not the most expensive on the market. However the pictures were important and the memory disk was full. She'd planned on putting in a new disk today, after she left the market.

"Tell me what you're looking for," she said now, careful to keep her voice calm, "and I'll show you."

He ignored her. Instead he opened the cover and then slid open the memory card slot. She watched as he tapped the small blue memory card, popping it out. Tally dug her nails into her hands. The card was tiny, looked like nothing, and yet it was everything to her. Her work, her life, her future.

"That's more or less the film," she said. "It's a digital camera which means it uses a memory card instead of 35 millimeter film."

He held the blue card up, twisting it one way and then the other.

Her heart was in her throat. It was as if he held her whole life in his hands. "I know it's very small, but it holds hundreds of photos."

"Are there hundreds of photos here?"

Reluctantly she nodded.

"Do you have other cards?" he asked.

Tally chewed on the inside of her cheek. She didn't want to tell him that she had months of work on the memory cards, hundreds and hundreds of photos she hadn't managed to download to her editors in New York or save to CD-ROM yet. Everything she'd done since April was on the memory cards in the camera bag and her hotel room. "Yes."

"Where are they?"

Oh God. He wasn't going to take them from her, was he? He wasn't going to destroy her work? "Why?"

He shrugged. "They're just pictures. You don't need them. It's not why you're here. You're a tourist. You're here for the experience, not photographs."

She exhaled so hard and sharp it hurt. Her eyes burned. She fought to remain calm. "But the photos are important. They help me remember where I've been and what I've seen."

"You seem anxious," he said, slipping the memory card back into the camera and clicking the card-slot door closed.

She was anxious. She was trembling. "Can I please have my camera back?"

"Maybe. When I'm finished. But you'll get it back without the memory card."

"The camera won't work without it."

"You can always buy new ones."

"But I'll lose everything I've done."

"They sell postcards in town. Buy those on your way home." He turned to leave but she rushed toward him.

"Please," she cried, stopping herself from touching him, knowing instinctively that that would be bad. She was already in trouble. She couldn't risk offending him more than she already had. "Please don't erase my photos. I'll show them to you. I'll explain the camera to you—"

"I haven't time," he interrupted turning to walk away. "Dinner will be brought to you soon. I'll see you tomorrow."

"Tomorrow." Tally's heart raced, fueled by fear and fury. It was a maddening combination and her hands shook from the adrenaline of it. "You're going to leave me here until tomorrow? And then what happens? Will you give me my camera back then, and the film?"

"Dinner will be brought soon," he repeated tonelessly.

But Tally wouldn't simply be dismissed. She didn't understand what any of this was about. She'd paid her guides good money and yet when the shots rang out in the medina this morning, the men had just left her. They ran. Well, both ran. One was shot. She shivered in remembrance. "What is it that you want with me?"

"We'll talk after I've gone through your pictures."

"You won't delete anything, will you?"

"It depends."

"On *what?*"

"What I find." His dark head nodded. "Good night."

Tally threw herself on her low bed, buried her face in the pillow and howled with rage. He could not do this! He could not!

She couldn't accept it. Wouldn't. What he did was wrong, and unjust.

In his tent, Tair slouched low in his chair, closed his eyes, doing his best to shut out the American woman ranting in the tent not far from his.

She needed to accept her fate more gracefully. Surrender with dignity. He was almost tempted to tell her so, too, but she might perceive it as some hard won victory and he wouldn't get her the satisfaction.

First she'd yield.

Then he'd show mercy.

Not the other way around.

Besides, his father had kidnapped his wife—Tair's own mother—and his father was a good man. Decent. Fair. Well, fair enough.

Eventually the American woman would realize that Tair was just as decent, if not fair.

* * *

Tally ended up crying herself to sleep. She didn't remember falling asleep, just weeping and punching her pillow. But now it was morning and opening her eyes, she stretched.

Her eyes still burned from the tears and it took a moment for her to focus. Tiredly her gaze settled on the small chest at the side of the bed. Oh God. She was still here. The tent. The encampment. Tair's world.

It wasn't just a bad dream. It was a bad reality.

Groaning Tally stretched an arm down, reached for the pillow that had fallen from her bed and bunched it under her cheek.

Okay. Last night she'd fallen apart. Today was strategy. Today she'd get her camera and film back. It was hers, after all, not his.

Already dressed in her thin cotton khaki slacks and white shirt, Tally left her tent in search of answers. Like who the hell was in charge of Ouaha.

Stalking out of her tent, she felt the intense desert sun pour over her, blinding her, scorching her almost immediately from head to toe. It was hot. A blistering heat, a heat unlike anything she'd ever known, either, and she'd been in some hot places before. The Brazilian jungle. The Outback in January. Marfa, Texas in July.

"Lady!" An elderly Berber man rushed toward her. He was thin, slight and stooped but he moved quickly. "Lady!" he repeated urgently, gesturing to the tent flap.

Tally felt the corner of her mouth lift in a faint, dry smile. She was supposed to go back inside the tent, sit and wait like a good little girl, wasn't she?

The corner of her mouth lifted in an even drier smile. Too bad she wasn't a good little girl anymore.

The old Berber turned and ran, and Tally suspected he'd gone in search of Tair. Good. She wanted to see him.

But as Tally passed one tent, she spotted on a chest outside another tent a leather case that looked suspiciously like her camera bag. Tally glanced around, no one was near by, everyone busy with tasks elsewhere and took several steps closer.

It was her camera bag and it was partially unzipped. She could see her camera tucked inside.

Tally sucked in a breath. The camera was so damn close. She had to get it back. At the very least, she had to get the memory card out before the bandit destroyed any photos.

Crouching down next to the chest, Tally pulled her camera from the bag, opened the card slot, popped the memory card out, closed the slot, dropped the camera back into the bag and stood up to return to her tent.

But suddenly the old Berber was in front of her, a long cotton gown draped over his arm.

Tally didn't know what he was saying but once he unfurled the robe she knew he wanted her to cover up.

"No, thank you," she said, shaking her head. "I'm fine. I'm just going back to my tent now anyway."

But he insisted and the more he insisted the faster Tally tried to walk, but he wouldn't stop talking and he was drawing attention to them.

Cheeks burning, Tally finally took the robe and tugged it over her head. "Thank you," she said stiffly. "Now if I can just go back to my tent?"

But the old man was still talking and gesticulating and Tally clutched the small memory card tighter, her palm beginning to grow damp. She had to get the card hidden before Tair appeared.

Finally she managed to escape, slipping beneath the flap of her tent and diving onto her bed. She was shaking all over. Shaking with fear, shaking with relief. But she had the memory card back. That was the important thing.

But where to hide it? She still hadn't decided when she heard voices outside her tent. She was out of time. Hastily Tally tucked the memory card under her shirt, inside her bra just as the tent flap flipped over and Tair's long shadow stretched over the floor, his powerful frame silhouetted by the bright morning sun.

"You lied to me and you stole from me," his deep voice rasped. "If you were a man I'd cut your tongue out and you'd lose a hand."

Tally wrapped her arms around her knees, hugging them for protection.

"Where is the memory card?" he demanded.

Tally hugged her knees even tighter. "What are you talking about?"

"You know perfectly well."

"I don't."

He said nothing now, just stared at her, his expression hard, unforgiving, brooding. His eyes were dark like coffee and a deep line seemed permanently etched between his black eyebrows.

He finally spoke. "I saw you. I was watching."

Tally shuddered. She felt his anger and scorn, it was also there in his eyes and the mocking tilt of his lips but she wouldn't let him know it bothered her. And she wouldn't act afraid, or acknowledge that she was stuck here. Stranded and powerless.

"I want it," he added softly. "Now."

"It's mine!" she answered fiercely, even as she bowed her head. She couldn't give him the memory card, she couldn't. It was hers, all she had of the past few weeks.

"Before you tell me no again," he added even more quietly, "before you tell me another lie, know that in my world thieves lose hands. Liars lose tongues. Think for a moment. Decide if your photos are worth it."

Tally couldn't look at him now. All thoughts of being tough and strong were crumbling. "Please," she whispered. "Please let me keep the card. You can have the camera."

"That's an odd thing for a tourist to say."

Slowly Tally lifted her head, swallowing around the lump of fear.

"You told me you were just a tourist," he added, his dark eyes boring into her, staring so hard, so intently she felt as if he were seeing inside her, all the way to her heart. "You lie. You steal. What else do you do?"

She shook her head, terrified.

"Perhaps you aid the insurgents. Those who want to be rid of us. Those that take our land from us."

"I help no one—"

"Why should I believe you?"

"Because I'm not political. Yes, I'm a photographer, but I'm not political, I take no sides, I do not even know the history of these border wars you talk about."

"Prove it."

She looked at him for a long unblinking moment. "How?"

"Give me the memory card back. I will look at the photos. I shall see for myself if you tell the truth."

She couldn't look away from his dark eyes, or his hard features, each strong, defined—nose, jaw, cheekbone, brow bone. "What if you don't like my work?"

He shrugged. "I'll erase it."

Tears filled her eyes and she hated herself for being weak and emotional but she was in agony. Those photos were months of work, work in nearly unbearable heat, work in wretched conditions, work where she'd sacrificed comfort and her own health to get just the right shots. "Please don't erase my work. I've weeks and weeks of shots on that memory card. I haven't downloaded anything in ages since I've been traveling."

He was still, very still and his hard gaze reproving. "Why did you lie to me?"

She searched his face, searched for a sign of compassion or comprehension. "I didn't think you'd understand."

He stared down at her, expression shuttered, and when he spoke his voice was cold. "No. I don't understand." Then he walked out and for a moment Tally did nothing and then leaping from the bed, she chased after him.

"Wait," she shouted, running to catch up with him. "Wait, please. Please!" She caught his sleeve, tugged on it. Her legs were shaking, her heart pounding and her mouth tasted sandy and dry.

Reaching into her bra, Tally pulled out the memory card and with a trembling hand gave it to him. "Take it. Look at the photos. See what I've done, see my work for yourself. If certain pictures offend you, then erase those, but I beg you, please don't delete everything. Please leave me something." Her voice cracked, broke. "I've spent months here, months in the desert, months away from my family. Please don't take it all from me."

Silently he accepted the memory card, his large hand wrapping around the small disk. Tally met his gaze, and blinking back tears she held it, looked him square in the eye, looked without pretense or pride. She was asking him to be fair, that's all she wanted. For him to be fair.

Legs still shaking, she walked back to her tent, and dropped weakly onto the low bed.

This wasn't good. So not good.

This is exactly what her mother always warned her about. This was what her friends had predicted. This was what her editor cautioned every time Tally set out on a new expedition. But she'd been a photographer for years and although she'd been in some tight spots, she'd never had serious trouble. She'd been doing so well traveling on her own until now. But this…this…was bad.

CHAPTER THREE

TALLY wasn't alone long. Almost immediately her captor returned with her camera and bag. He dropped them on to the bed next to her and she grabbed them, held the camera and case to her as though they were her last lifeline to the outer world.

"Why?" she stammered, looking up at him.

He shrugged. "You said the camera wouldn't work without the memory card."

For a moment she didn't see where he was going with this, and then she understood. Even as she searched her camera bag she knew all the memory cards were gone. He'd kept them. Her pleasure in having the camera returned dimmed. "I shouldn't have given you it back," she said bitterly. "I should have protected my pictures."

"It didn't matter if you gave it back to me or not. The card you took from the camera was blank. It was a new memory card. I switched the cards before I left the camera out."

Tally shoved a hand through her hair, pushing it off her face. She was so hot she wanted to scream. Throw things. Pick a fight. "You didn't. You're bluffing."

"Bluffing?" His gaze locked with hers. "Is that what I think you just said."

Her heart pounding, she held his gaze, showing him once and for all she wouldn't be intimidated. "Yes. That's what I said. Bluffing."

"I don't bluff, and what I did was test you." His dark eyes burned. "You failed."

"I'm not surprised," she flashed. "And just a little FYI, it's hard to feel sympathy for you, or your causes, when you so blatantly disregard other people's needs and feelings."

"You have no idea who or what you're dealing with, do you?"

She did, actually. He was a bandit and a kidnapper and it wouldn't be wise to push him too far but she was so angry now she wasn't thinking straight. "You don't test people."

"Of course you do. It's smart. It's strategy. One must know others strengths and weaknesses."

"And you think you know mine?"

"I know you're not to be trusted." His lips compressed, and he looked hard, knowing, controlled. "But then, few people can be."

She looked away, eyes burning and for some reason this last trickery hurt more than anything. He'd manipulated her all along. Played her. But it wasn't just what he'd done, it was his attitude that hurt. "You have a terrible way of looking at life."

"It's practical. It keeps me, and my people, alive."

A voice spoke from outside and then the tent flap was pushed aside and the elderly man from last night appeared with a large breakfast tray heaped with fresh and dried fruits, a mound of round, flat flour-dusted breads, and steaming cups of mint tea. The man disappeared as soon as he placed the tray on the carpet in front of the bed.

Her captor motioned to the carpet. "You'll join me," he said, and it wasn't a question or invitation but an order.

"I'm not hungry." She was still seething over the loss of all her photos. So much work. It was a loss of devastating proportions.

"You need to eat," he answered with a snap of his fingers. He jabbed downward to the ground, pointing at the carpet.

"I've never met a ruder Berber man," she muttered under

her breath but she knew he heard—and understood—from the look he gave her.

He took one of the small flat breads. "There are worse."

She watched him eat, eyes burning, head throbbing. She did need to eat, as well as drink, but she was afraid of getting sick, and at the moment her nervous system felt as though it were in overdrive. "What do I have to do to get my pictures back?"

"I don't wish to discuss this topic anymore."

"It's important—"

"Not anymore. You're not taking pictures here."

"So what will I do while I'm here?"

He looked at her for a long, tense moment, his expression blank, dark eyes guarded, shadowed. "Nothing."

"Nothing?"

His broad shoulders shifted carelessly. "I'm not going to make you do anything. I'm perfectly content now that I have your film to wait."

"Wait for what?"

"The truth. It will emerge. It always does."

"Maybe, but it could take a long time."

"Indeed. And if that is the case, you'll get to enjoy desert life for an indefinite period of time."

"Indefinite."

"Unless you care to tell me the truth now, Woman?"

"I've told you the truth and my name isn't Woman, it's Tally."

"I've never heard the name Tally before. That's not a name." A glint of light touched his dark eyes, something secret and perverse and then the corner of his mouth nearly lifted, the closest thing she'd seen to a smile yet. "I shall call you Woman."

She didn't know if it was his words, his tone or that perverse light in his eyes but it annoyed her almost beyond reason. "I won't answer to it."

"You will."

"I won't."

"You will." And more fire flashed in his eyes. "Even if it takes days. Weeks." He hesitated, and his dark gaze slid over her, the first openly assessing look he'd given her, one that examined, weighed, understood. "Years."

Heat stormed her cheeks. The same heat that flooded her veins. "*Not* years."

"You will answer to me one day, Woman. You might not like the idea, but it's true. The sooner you accept it, the sooner life will become easier for you."

She wanted to throw something at him, anything. The cups of tea. The tray. A pillow. He was so damn smug. So horribly arrogant. "I take it then I call you Man?"

His faint smile faded. "You are very impertinent for a woman." Silent, he regarded her. "You may call me Tair," he said after a moment.

"Why do you get a name and I get Woman?"

"Because I brought you here, which makes you my responsibility, and therefore my woman."

"That doesn't make sense."

"It does to me and that's all that matters since this is my tribe and you are mine."

"Will you please stop calling me your woman? I'm not your woman. I'm no one's woman, and I wasn't spying on you or whatever you think I was doing in El Saroush's medina," she said, referring to the border town's old square where he'd kidnapped her. "Why would I spy on you? I don't even know who you are, and what point would there be spying on a group of bedraggled men riding through town on horseback? I may be an American," and she drawled the word for his benefit, "but I do have standards."

He nearly hissed. "Bedraggled men?"

She crossed her arms, chin titled rebelliously. "Even your horses are bedraggled."

"They're not," he contradicted, incensed. "Our horses are

some of the finest Arabians in North Africa. We breed them ourselves."

"They're dirty. You're all dirty—"

"You should see yourself."

"I'd bathe if you let me! I'd love some clean clothes, too, but somehow I don't think you kidnapped a change of clothes for me."

"I'll get a knife," he muttered, "get rid of your damn tongue now."

She should be afraid, she should, but somehow she wasn't. He might be huge, and fierce and intimidating but he didn't seem cruel, or like a man who impulsively cut out tongues. "The point is that I didn't even notice you in town. I was interested only in the children playing. And all I want to do is be allowed to continue on to Casablanca."

"Why Casablanca?"

"It's the next stop on my itinerary."

His expression turned speculative. "You've friends there?"

"No. I'm on my own."

"Casablanca's a rebel stronghold."

Tally sighed. "You're rather obsessive about this whole terrorist thing, aren't you?"

He studied her for a long moment before leaning forward to take her face in his hand. He lifted her chin this way and then that. "You are what, thirty years old? Older?"

She tried to pull away but couldn't. Her pulse jumped, skin burning. She didn't like him touching her. He made her feel odd, prickly things. Things she had no business feeling. "I just turned thirty," she answered faintly.

"You wear no ring," he said, still examining her face. "Did your husband die?"

"I've never been married."

"Never?"

"I don't want a husband."

He let her go then and his dense black lashes dropped, concealing his expression. He was silent, assessing her, and the situation. "You're not a virgin, are you?"

His tone had changed and she didn't know if it was shock, or respect but either way it irritated her. Her life, her past, her relationships, and most of all, her sexuality were her business and no one else's. Least of all a barbaric desert tribesman. "I'm thirty, not thirteen. Of course I've had relationships—and experience—but I choose to remain single. I prefer being single. This way I can travel. Explore. Do what I want to do."

Tair continued to study her as though she were alien and fascinating in a strange sort of way.

Tally wasn't sure she liked the look on his face. His expression made her nervous. Made her feel painfully vulnerable.

"Your parents—they're still alive?" he asked.

She nodded, neck stiff, body rigid. She really didn't know where he was going with this and didn't want to find out.

"They don't worry about you?" he persisted.

"No." She caught his eye, flushed. "Maybe a little. But they're used to my lifestyle now. They know this is who I am, what I do. Besides, they have other kids who supply them with grandchildren and the like."

Tair refilled his cup of tea from the small glazed pot. "I shall find you a husband."

"What?"

He nodded matter of factly before sipping his tea. "You need a husband. It is the way it should be. I shall find you one. You will be glad."

"No." Her head spun, little spots danced before her eyes. He wrong, absolutely wrong and she couldn't even get the protest out. Instead she sucked in one desperate breath after another.

"Women are like fruit," he said picking up a date, gently squeezing it. "Women need husbands and children or they dry up."

Dry up? He didn't just say that. He didn't say that while

squeezing a little date, did he? My God. This was a nightmare. This was worse than anything she could have ever imagined, and she'd imagined some pretty awful endings. Kidnapped, her photos stripped from her and now what? Married to a desert barbarian? "Let me go home. Please correct this before it turns out badly."

"I will make sure you have the right husband. Do not worry." His lips curved and she saw teeth, straight white teeth and thought this must be his idea of a smile. "Now eat. Berber men like women with meat on their bones. Curves. Not stringy like you."

Tally went hot and cold. She felt wild, panicked. She couldn't be here, couldn't stay here. This was all wrong. Wrong, wrong, wrong.

Tair sighed, frowned. "You must at least drink the tea. You're dehydrated. I can see it in your eyes and skin."

Tally wasn't a crier but she was close to tears now. How was she going to do this? Would she escape?

"You don't like tea?" he persisted, the strain on his patience showing. "Would you prefer water?"

"Is it bottled water?"

His black brows tugged together. "It's well water."

"But not processed?" She'd only just gotten off of weeks of wretched antibiotics, antibiotics that were proved to be just as hard on her stomach as the parasite and food poisoning. Just remembering the forty-eight hours in the Atiq hospital made her stomach cramp. "You see I can't drink water that isn't purified. I've had problems—"

"You are without a doubt the most delicate, finicky female I've ever met."

"I'm not finicky and not overly delicate—"

"Asthma, heat stroke, stomach ailments, dehydration—"

"I didn't ask to be kidnapped! This was your idea not mine. If you don't like that I'm so delicate, next time do more research before you kidnap a woman!"

He shook his head, expression grim. "You are not going to make it easy for me to find you a husband. Men do not like mulish wives."

Mulish. Mulish, was she? Tally nearly laughed. That was rich, coming from him. "You know, you have a very good vocabulary for a desert bandit."

"I like to read between making raids on towns." He snapped his fingers. "Now drink. None of my men will marry a woman if she's nearly dead."

"I don't want your men."

"How you love to argue."

"I have my own opinions and point of view, and contrary to what you might think, I'm not normally difficult. You just happen to bring out the worst in me." She glared at him. "Until yesterday, I hadn't had an asthma attack in years. The attack was thanks to you nearly suffocating me in that horrible bag of yours. I can't believe you did that. It was terrible. Awful. I couldn't breathe."

"So I noticed." His brow lowered, his expression dark. "But you were quiet at least."

She covered her face with her hands, breathing in carefully, deliberately, doing her best to block out the smell of the mint tea, the peculiar sandalwood scent and smoke of Tair's skin, and the intense heat already shimmering all around them. She couldn't do another day in the desert. Not like this. Not with this man.

She was near tears and cracking. "Can you please go? Can you please just leave me alone?"

He didn't answer. He was so quiet that after a minute Tally was certain he'd gone but when she lifted her head she saw him there, still seated across from her. He didn't look the least bit sympathetic, either. If anything, his jaw jutted harder, his mouth pursed in a now familiar look of judgment and condescension.

"Drink your tea," he said wearily. "This is the desert, and

the heat is quite deceptive. You need to stay hydrated or you won't live long enough to take another picture, much less visit Casablanca." His dark eyes gleamed as he pushed a cup toward her face. "Which is overrated, if you ask me."

Her eyebrows arched. Was that a joke? Was that flat tone and deadpan expression his idea of a joke? "I don't trust the water," she retorted, pushing the cup away. "And yes, I am thirsty, and I will drink. But it must be bottled water."

"Bottled water?"

She ignored his incredulous tone. He didn't understand the difficulties she'd had these past four weeks. She'd never had a cast iron stomach but it'd become particularly finicky lately ever since she picked up parasites from local water just outside Atiq. The parasites had her practically sleeping in the bathroom and she had no interest repeating that experience again. "Yes, bottled water. You sell it in the stores."

A small muscle popped in his jaw as he gave her a ferocious look, one that revealed the depth of his irritation and aggravation. "And you see stores near by?"

"No, but there were stores back in El Saroush."

"Are you suggesting I send someone back for bottled water?"

"I'm suggesting you send someone back with me."

He sighed heavily and pressed two fingers to his temple. "You have the most tedious refrain."

Her lips compressed. He might not realize it, but she was just as irritated and frustrated as he was. "I've only just begun."

"I should just cut out your tongue."

"You wouldn't want to do that," she flashed. "My new husband might not like it."

"That's true," he answered. "He might miss it, and it could lower your bride price. So, keep your tongue and drink your tea. Or I shall pour it down your throat."

The cup was pushed toward her face again and this time Tally took it. "If I drink the tea, you'll leave?"

His dark gaze met hers and held. The corner of his mouth lifted, a faint wry acknowledgment of the battle between them. "Yes."

And yet still she hesitated. "And if I die out here of dysentery, will you at least promise me a Christian burial?"

The corner of his mouth twitched. "I can't promise that, but I will take your ashes to Casablanca."

Tally wasn't sure if she should be reassured or troubled by his faint smile. He wasn't a particularly smiley-kind of guy. "Fine, I'll drink it. But then you go." Quickly she downed the now lukewarm tea, scrunching her nose and mouth at the bitter taste but at the same time grateful for the liquid. Her throat had been parched and one cup wasn't going to be enough, but it was a start. "There. Done."

He rose, but didn't leave immediately. Instead he stood above her, gazing down at her. "By the way, we may be bedraggled barbarians and bandits, but all our water is boiled. Any water we cook with or drink is always boiled. You might get parasites in town, but you won't get any parasites from me."

And smiling—smiling!—Tair walked out. As he left the tent, Tally grabbed a pillow, pressed it to her face and screamed in vexation.

He couldn't keep her here! He couldn't. And he couldn't be serious about finding a husband for her. My God. That was just the worst.

She gripped the pillow hard. But what if he never returned her to town? What if he just kept her here? What if he were serious about marrying her off?

She shuddered, appalled.

Her lack of communication with her world back in the States made her situation doubly frightening.

The fact was, there was no one who'd even think to worry if she disappeared from the face of the earth.

Raised in a tiny town at the base of the Cascade Mountains in Washington, Tally had lived at home far longer than she'd ever meant to stay but once she'd left North Bend, she'd gone far away.

Her mother sometimes joked that the only time she heard from Tally was the annual Christmas cards Tally sent documenting her travels. One Christmas card was a misty hand-tinted shot of ancient Machu Picchu high in the mountains of Peru. Another year it was the sun rising in Antarctica. Last year's card was a child born with AIDS in sub-Sahara Africa.

Once Paolo was the one who would have cared. It was Paolo who taught her to rock climb and sail, Paolo who'd taught her to face her fears and not be afraid. But Paolo wasn't around anymore and since losing him all those years ago Tally had never tried to replace him.

Love hadn't ever come easily for Tally and one broken heart was more than enough. And not that she would have married Paolo, but if she'd wanted a husband—and that was a huge *if*—it would have been him. And only him. But with him gone, marriage was out of the question.

Tossing aside the pillow, Tally forced herself to eat even as she struggled to remember who she last spoke with, whom she'd written, and the last e-mails she'd sent from the Internet café in Atiq a month ago.

Did anyone even know she was still in Northern Africa? Her editor might, but they hadn't communicated in weeks.

No, keeping in touch wasn't her forte. While she loved taking pictures, she didn't like writing and most of her e-mails were brief one-liners. *In Israel, went diving in the Red Sea.* Or, *Arrived in Pakistan, took a bus through Harappa, have never been so hot in my entire life.*

Tally now stared glumly at the breakfast tray. She was going to pay for her laissez-faire attitude, wasn't she?

The older man was outside her tent again, calling to her, saying something she didn't understand as he spoke with an accent or in a dialect she'd never heard before. But before she could answer, he'd entered the tent, carrying a relatively large copper tub. He placed the tub on the carpet, indicated that he'd go and return and when he returned he had help. Three men carried pitchers of water.

A bath.

So something she'd said to Tair had sunk in. Thrilled, Tally watched as the elderly man filled the tub with the pitchers of steaming water and left behind a soft soap and towel. The bath wasn't particularly deep, and not exactly hot, but it was warm water and she had a bar of soap, a soap that reminded her of olive oil and citrus. She washed her hair, soaped up and down and by the time she rinsed off, the water was cold but she felt marvelous. Marvelous until she realized she had nothing but her dirty clothes to put back on.

Regretfully Tally dressed in her clothes, combed her fingers through her hair, pulling the wet strands back from her face and then looked around the tent. She was sick of the tent. She'd been here for not even a day and she already hated it.

So enough of the tent. She was heading out to explore the camp.

From the moment she pushed the goatskin flap up and exited her tent, stepping into the startling bright sunlight, Tally became aware of the eyes of the men in camp on her. It was obvious they didn't approve of her wandering around but no one made a move toward her. No one spoke to her and no one detained her. They pretty much let her do as she pleased.

The camp was actually bigger than it first appeared. There were over a dozen tents, and several large open ones with scattered rugs and pillows and Tally guessed these were the places the men gathered to eat and socialize.

A mangy three-legged dog hopped around after her and Tally considered discouraging the dog but then decided she liked the company. And it was her first friend.

Crouching down, Tally scratched under the dog's chin and

then behind one ear. "If I had my camera working, I'd take a picture of you." The dog wagged its tail that looked half gnawed. "Poor dog. You look just as bad as this camp does."

And the camp did look bad. She'd never seen anything like this place. It was poor. Stark. Depressing. And once again she thought she'd give anything to have one of the memory cards back because she'd love to photograph the camp. The stained tents with the backdrop of sand dunes and kneeling camels would make amazing pictures.

Suddenly she heard a now familiar voice—the old Berber man—and he was running toward her with long cotton fabric draped over his arm.

Tally didn't know what he was saying but once he unfurled one of the strips of fabric and she saw it was a robe she knew he wanted her to cover up.

"No, thank you," she said, shaking her hands and head. "I'm fine."

But he insisted and the more he insisted the more adamant Tally was that she wouldn't wear the black robe and head covering. "No," she said more firmly, even as she began to wonder just where Tair was. She'd walked the circumference of the camp twice without spotting him once.

"Tair," she said to the old man. "Where is he?"

The old man stared at her uncomprehendingly. Then he lifted the robe, shook it. She knew what he wanted but he didn't understand what she did.

"Tair," Tally repeated and this time she stood on her toes, lifted her hand high above her head to indicate Tair's immense height. *"Tair."*

The elderly man only looked more puzzled and Tally wanted to pull her hair out in mad chunks. This was a nightmare. A nightmare. She couldn't stay here, couldn't be left here, couldn't. Wouldn't.

"Tair," she said more loudly, firmly, extending her arms to show width, size.

The old man just looked at her with absolute incomprehension.

It was at that moment she spotted the horse. The horse was saddled, bridled and unattended.

Unattended.

She could just go.

It wasn't logical, nothing rational about her plan. She was just going to go and she didn't know anything other than to go, just go, and let the chips fall where they may.

She climbed up, onto the blanket that served as the saddle and taking the reins she kicked at the horse, urging him to go.

The horse gave her a funny sideways glance before stretching out in an easy canter. They rode across the pale creamy sand at a quick clip, Tally's heart racing at the same speed they were traveling.

This was crazy, foolish, dangerous. But she didn't turn back and didn't slow. She felt as if she were running for her very life. Or make that, running from her very life.

She wouldn't be trapped again. She wouldn't let others control her life or her destiny.

She'd had years of answering to others, years of giving up her own hopes, years of waiting and she couldn't wait any more.

With the dazzling sun shining in her eyes and the heat exploding all around them, Tally tried to get a better grip, the blanket style saddle unfamiliar. Part of her brain told her to slow down and another part was just wild—frenzied—and she simply kept going at that reckless, breakneck speed.

Maybe if she'd had a different past, a different experience with life, she could sit in the camp and wait. But she wasn't good at waiting, not when she felt as though she'd spent her whole life waiting.

Tally wasn't an only child. In fact, she was far from an only, being the eldest in a family of five children. She'd been responsible for so much. She'd been responsible for well, virtually everything.

From an early age Tally walked her younger brothers and sisters to and from school, fed and clothed them when their mother had to return to work after their father's back injury put him virtually to bed for the rest of his life. Tally oversaw homework, meals, shopping, laundry, cleaning. If one of the youngest needed a parent for Open House or Back to School Night it was Tally who showed up more often than Mom.

As a teenager Tally used to dream about leaving home, about the day she'd pack everything into her car and just go—flee the pressure and responsibilities—but by the time she graduated from high school her mother's health was in decline and Tally knew she couldn't go. Couldn't walk away from the younger ones who wanted her, or her parents who needed her.

Instead of escaping in real life, she escaped in her mind, using books and movies, theater and photography to go places she couldn't go in person. The Amazon? She was there! Everest? She climbed it! Egypt? On the next camel. Paris? Bring on the Eiffel Tower.

It wasn't until the youngest one, her brother Jude, started high school that she allowed herself to dream of actually going away. But when fifteen-year-old Jude turned sixteen and earned his driver's license and made Varsity on the football team she realized the baby Deavers was old enough, big enough and strong enough to take care of himself.

Her parents begged her not to go, pleaded that they still needed her but Tally was nearly twenty-six, had never been anywhere, had done nothing for the past ten years but take care of everyone else and she was going to go now. She'd have her turn. Even if it killed her.

And staring at the huge expanse of desert with sand and sand and more sand Tally realized her need for her turn might just kill her, too.

What the hell was she doing in Baraka—or Ouaha, or wherever she was at the moment—anyway?

Tally didn't know if she slipped, or the horse stumbled, but one moment she was on the horse, and the next, she'd somehow lost her balance and was falling. Tally tumbled to the ground even as the horse continued on.

The fall knocked the air from her but the burning sand quickly roused her.

Gasping, she dragged herself to her feet, wincing at the pain in her side. Oh, that hurt.

Eyes damp, she lifted a trembling hand and brushed the grains of sand from her cheek and collar. For a moment she felt a surge of panic, but just as quickly she smothered it. She wasn't going to panic. She was going to be strong. Tears wouldn't help. Just determination. And lots of resolve.

Gathering her resolve, Tally set off, heading in the same direction the horse had gone. It was relatively easy following the horse's hoofprints.

Ignoring the blistering sun, she walked on. This is what she'd done the past five years, she reminded herself. Ever since she left home she'd been living with a knapsack slung on her back, traveling to the most remote corners of the world, photographing the children time seemed to have forgotten.

Tally had never really examined why she'd become a children's photographer. Yes, it was the first work she'd gotten in Seattle, but why babies and toddlers? Why leggy little girls and wide-eyed boys torn between childhood and adolescent?

And with the glimpse of swirling sand darkening the horizon Tally realized it wasn't by accident. She photographed the faces of children to learn her own.

There'd been no real childhood for her. No time to indulge in play. No fantasy and fancy, no dress up, no costumes, no baton lessons or classes of gymnastics and ballet. No ice skating—*where would the money come from, honey? Besides we need you here.*

A lump filled Tally's throat but she didn't dwell on the emotion, not when the horizon seemed to turn black before her very eyes.

Just moments ago the horizon had looked dark, muddy with swirling sand but it wasn't muddy anymore. It looked eerie, frightening.

Her steps faltered. With her heart in her throat she realized she was walking straight into a sandstorm.

CHAPTER FOUR

TALLY turned, looked behind her, wondering where she could go, how she could protect herself. But there was nowhere to go. And as she watched, the cloud and wind of sand grew, stretching from her feet far overhead as if even the sky was made of beige and brown. The pale sun disappeared and the afternoon grew ominously still.

Goose bumps covered Tally's arms and lifted the hair at her nape. She felt the danger, felt the heaviness in the sky, the weighty silence of impending doom. The sandstorm was growing, building, billowing like a sci-fi monster come to life.

There was no sound anywhere. No sound of anything but the stillness of the desert and yet to Tally it was like a roar, a scream. The sand monster breathes, she thought, wrapping her arms around her upper body, fingers pressing tightly against her skin as the blackness sailed toward her.

I'm going to perish here. This is where it ends. And I don't even have my camera.

She tried to laugh at her feeble humor in the face of abject terror but her laugh was a hiccup and her gaze clung sickeningly to the huge black whirling wall of sand very nearly on her now.

This is it. This is all. This is how it ends.

And then from nowhere came the sound of hooves, fast furious thudding hooves and turning Tally saw a blur of horse and man as Tair on his flying black horse raced toward her, leaning low on his stallion's back and with one arm he scooped her up, lifting her onto his saddle in front of him. And he never slowed, not even to grab her, or settle her. Instead he pushed her low against the horse's neck and he dropped his body over hers urging his stallion on, and they were running for their lives, running against sand and storm and monsters shaped from the vengeful desert wind.

They were riding toward a rock that protruded from the land, something Tally had seen only from afar and had never thought twice about but now that they were closer she could see crevices in the rock, openings like little caves and Tair rode there now. The wind storm with its pelting sand began to bite at their skin, sharp cuts and stings and Tally covered her mouth and nose to keep from sucking the sand in.

"Get in," Tair shouted above the storm's roar. He half-dropped, half-tossed her toward the cleft in the rock and as terrified as she was of scorpions and snakes she knew they were a safer option.

Tally crawled swiftly in, and Tair followed, dragging his horse's head in after him, holding the reins tightly so his stallion couldn't escape.

With the sharp rock pressed to her back and Tair pressed to her front Tally closed her eyes and listened to the howling storm outside.

If Tair hadn't come…

If Tair hadn't gone in search of her…

And her eyes burned, and despite her tightly closed lids she could feel small hot tears prick and sting, could feel her throat squeeze.

This was not the way she liked to live life.

This was not her life.

She was going to have adventures, yes, and she'd see the world, but it'd be her way. In her time. She'd explore and venture out but she wouldn't have to rely on anyone.

Wouldn't be dependent on anyone.

Wouldn't need anything from anyone, either.

Tair's horse shook his head unhappily several times, shifting from foot to foot as the howling outside became a shrieking crescendo.

"Your horse is unhappy," she said, feeling the stallion's discomfort, knowing the pelting sand must be biting through his hide.

"He's not the only one unhappy," Tair said tersely.

It was dark in the cavern, and yet tilting her head back she could just make out Tair's hard features but they didn't appear harsh as much as set. Fixed. Determined.

She swallowed, painfully aware of him and the press of their bodies. He rested his weight on his arms, tried to keep his body from crushing hers and yet even without him touching her, she could imagine how his hands would feel against her skin, could see his fingertips trail slowly down her spine.

Oh, it'd be hot.

It'd burn her up.

Tally felt desire curl in her belly and heat wash through every limb. Her body shook and she wondered if Tair could feel it.

Balling her hands into fists, she tried to intellectualize what she was feeling, dissect the attraction and rationalize it was fear, adrenaline. These things happened. Paolo had even said that many men and women fell in love with each other in the midst of dangerous situations, something about raised hormones and chemical surges.

It's the danger, she told herself, feeling the tension between her and Tair. It's the storm and the noise, the pelting sand and the intense heat inside the cave making everything extreme. I'm not attracted to him. Can't be.

"How did you sleep last night?" Tair asked, raising his voice to be heard over the howling sand devil.

She stiffened beneath him. "Like hell, and you know it."

His mouth curved and with one hand he lazily pushed her thick hair back from her face. "You put on quite a show last night. Everyone could hear you. My men were most fascinated."

Tally jumped at the brush of his fingers, so sensitive that just that fleeting touch made her tremble. "I'm glad I could provide them with some entertainment."

His smile broadened. He'd shaven this morning and his jaw was clean, a hard polished bronze, which accented the height of his cheekbone and his strong aristocratic nose. "Your future husband will have his hands full with you."

She averted her face, stared at the rough sandstone wall. "I'm not interested."

The horse shifted, moved forward, nudging Tair and his body pressed against hers. Tally shivered at the press of his hips and chest.

"I am sure we will find one man here who can manage you. Clearly it will take a special man—"

"I'm not amused," she answered breathlessly, feeling trapped, panicked. He was so solid, and yet warm and it confused her. The same way her attraction confused her. She couldn't want him. It was illogical. Everything about this was crazy. He was a man wedded to the desert while she craved freedom, freedom and adventure.

Freedom. And this, she thought, stricken as his body touched hers in every place it shouldn't, wasn't freedom.

She couldn't live in his world here and to even be tempted by him, to even be tempted to want someone like him spoke of disaster.

With an unsteady hand she pressed her fingers to her brow and closed her eyes, willing herself to ignore him. Forget him. The cave might be small and his body might be torturing hers but she'd been in more dangerous situations than this. She could survive this. She just had to stay calm.

And then the horse shifted again and Tair's right knee went forward, sliding between her own and she felt his warm hard thigh slide against her, felt the heat and sinewy strength against her where she was so sensitive, where every nerve ending screamed for increased sensation and it was shocking. Disturbing. Arousing.

She opened her mouth to gasp, her mind protesting the intimacy even as her body wanted more but the sound was swallowed by the wild roar outside.

Inwardly she cursed the desert and its oppressive heat as well as the wretched Berber tribesman who took her.

Wildly, she looked up, caught Tair's eye.

The wretched man was smiling. "Perhaps with the right man you will grow to like it here with us," he said, voice low, taunting. "Perhaps you will never want to go back to America."

Tally couldn't answer. Never return? Live here in his encampment? With a shake of her head, she turned her face away, squeezed her eyes shut and tried to think of other places, other people.

She wouldn't remain here. Wouldn't belong to a Berber. Never. Ever.

Ever.

Tally didn't know how long they lay there, huddled in the crevice, the air so hot, stifling that sweat dribbled down her neck, between her breasts, her skin damp, the air stagnant and old.

But finally the noise outside faded and the stallion shook his head again, pulling at the reins and this time Tair loosened his grip allowing his horse to slowly back up. Tally got a glimpse of blue sky. The storm had passed.

They climbed from the cave, and Tally slowly straightened, limbs achy and tight. Tair tossed her onto the saddle and jumped behind her and with a shake of the bridle let the horse run, and they were off, cantering toward the encampment.

"Are your men all right?" Tally finally dared to ask as she spotted tents ahead, sand piled high against the sides. "The sandstorm won't have hurt them?"

"They're fine," he said curtly, reining his horse in. "You're the one in danger."

Men surged around them as they dismounted and Tair brusquely answered several of the men even as he hauled her through the crowd to his tent.

In his tent he thrust her down onto the low chair that faced a simple desk.

"Have you lost your mind?" he roared, planting himself before her, hands on his hips. "What do you think you were doing?"

Tally clenched her hands in her lap. "Running away!"

"It was stupid."

"Keeping me here is worse."

"No. Keeping you here is keeping you safe. And I won't have you running off, putting yourself in danger, making my men chase after you. It's time you learned to stay put. Act like a woman your age."

"Why do you keep bringing up my age?"

"Because you're not a child. You're a woman of childbearing age—"

"Leave my age out of it!"

"I can't."

"Why not? It's none of your business. Nothing I do is any of your business."

"You're wrong about that. Everything you do in my country is my business." He pulled up a second low stool and sat down directly in front of her, but even sitting he was a full head and shoulders taller, and even sitting he towered over her. "And where were you going anyway?"

She tried to rock back on her chair hating his close proximity. With his dark hair coated with grit and sand, and sand in his black eyebrows he looked wild. Instead of a pirate on a ship, he was a pirate of the desert. "To get help," she answered coldly.

"Help?"

"Police, or protection—"

"Protection from who?" he roared.

"You!"

He threw up his hands. "I protect you. I saved you from the rebels. I saved you from violent people."

"I'm sorry, Tair, but you're the only dangerous man I've met in Northern Africa!"

He made a rough sound of disgust. "And just who is going to give you this protection from me?"

"The government of Ouaha."

"The government," he repeated, giving her a look she couldn't decipher even as he shook his head. "I am the government."

She didn't like the look in his eye or the smugness at his mouth. "You're chief of the desert."

"Yes."

"But surely there is someone else higher than you…someone with more authority."

He just looked at her.

Tally's heart and stomach seemed to be in direct collision and it made her very very nauseous. "Isn't there a sultan of Ouaha? A king? Someone higher than a sheikh?"

If he heard the panic in her voice he gave no indication. "There is one that holds the title Sultan of Ouaha, but he isn't one of our people. He is a Berber sheikh from Baraka and he and his family have befriended Ouaha, but they have no power here."

"But you do answer to him?"

"I answer to no one."

Reason, not emotion, reason, not emotion she chanted to herself but it wasn't helping. "But if I went to him, this Sultan who is Barakan, he would help me, wouldn't he? He would free me. He wouldn't allow you to keep me, an American woman, hostage here."

"First, you will not be able to speak to Sheikh Nuri as he lives in London and you don't have the means to get there.

And second, even if you should speak to him, he wouldn't go against my wishes. We have fought too many wars together, protected each other's backs too many times. He trusts my judgment. I trust his."

"So how long do you intend to keep me here?"

Tair shrugged. "Forever?"

"You're going to feed and clothe me forever? Very generous of you."

He shrugged again. "Not that generous. You might not live very long. The desert is a dangerous place."

"A threat?"

"I don't threaten. No need. My word here is law. Anything I want, I get."

"Must feel pretty wonderful."

The corner of his mouth lifted ever so slightly and yet his gaze remained just as flat, hard, unfriendly. "It's not a boast. Just a fact."

"So what exactly do you do? What are the job descriptions of a sheikh?"

"Think of it as a mini-kingdom."

"And you are the king?"

"Exactly. I make the final decisions. And now I decide its time for you to bathe and return to your tent where you will behave the way a woman should."

Alone in his tent, Tair bathed, soaping up and washing his hair before toweling off and changing into clean trousers and a loose overshirt. He slicked his wet hair back from his brow.

He was going to have to do something about the American. After what happened today there was talk in the camp, a great deal of talk, and most of it was about her.

Tair didn't like the talk, or the speculation about the kind of woman she was, or how she'd be in bed. In his culture men didn't discuss women—unless they were foreign women and then the assumption was that they were up for grabs.

Tair folded back the cuffs on his shirt and then stood to watch the setting sun paint the desert shades of crimson and gold.

In his culture women married young to protect their reputations. If a woman remained single too long no one would believe she'd remained a virgin, and in Ouaha, a woman's virginity—her purity—was her greatest asset.

Tair realized Tally wasn't of his culture, and he was familiar with her Western thought and education, but she was here now, living among his people, his men. He had to do what was right. To protect her. To ensure no one exploited her. And he knew just how to solve the problem.

Tally paced her tent in an absolute temper. She wouldn't bathe. Wouldn't change. Wouldn't do anything she was told. She'd do what she wanted to do, and only what she wanted to do. Period.

Back and forth she went over the old carpet, footsteps muffled by the soft handwoven wool.

He could say he'd lock her up. He could threaten isolation. Starvation. Fine. It'd make a great book someday. She'd become a bestseller. Maybe she'd even win a big literary prize.

Tally glared at the tent opening where the flap had been tied back, in case she tried to run away. *In case.* Huh. How about, for *when* she ran away again.

Now she glared at the undulating sand dunes in the distance and the men crouched in a circle by the black fire pit.

She didn't care if Tair was sheikh, or king, or emperor of the whole damn desert. He'd hate keeping her here. She'd be a horrible captive. She'd make his life miserable. He had to know it.

Furiously, restlessly, she kicked at the carpet covering the sand. My God she was going crazy here. But better to be angry than helpless.

Anger was a much better emotion than fear, than doubt. Years ago she'd made a vow—with Paolo's help, of course—

to face every fear with action. And confronting her fears had worked. Look at all the things she'd done: climbed treacherous mountains, kayaked in shark-infested seas, learned to fly solo. All because she'd once been afraid of danger. And change.

Now look at her. Captive in the desert, held hostage by Sheikh Tair el-Tayer, or whatever he called himself.

If only she could stay calm, really calm, not just on the outside but on the inside. Unfortunately, on the inside right now she was a hellcat, all anger and hissing sound and claws. But sometimes anger wasn't a bad thing. Sometimes, anger protected, empowered. Anger got things done.

Tally exhaled slowly. Okay, maybe in this case anger wasn't going to accomplish anything. Maybe anger was just going to make life worse.

She dropped onto her low bed, flung her arms over her head, stared up at the roof of her tent. He had to let her go. Send her back. He had to.

Minutes crept by. Endlessly long minutes. Tally yawned. Wiggled. Shrugged her shoulders, stretching.

The sun still wasn't down yet. The night would be endless. She'd be alone and going crazy again.

If only he'd just give her one memory card. Let her do something. Let her photograph the sky, the dunes, the sunsets. She needed activity, needed to keep her mind occupied. If she didn't find a way to stay busy she'd lose it for certain.

She was bored. And worse, lonely. Tally hated being lonely, hated that awful empty feeling she got inside.

Even Tair's horrible company would be better right now than no company.

She slammed her fists on either side of her, hitting the bed's mattress hard. She couldn't do this. Couldn't handle this. She was bored and mad and ready to explode.

"You should try meditation." Tair's deep voice, tinged with amusement, broke the stillness.

Tally sat up swiftly. "Meditation?"

"It'd help," he added kindly, the fading sunset behind him shot with lavender and purple streaks.

She hated the sudden leap inside her, a funny twitchy feeling in her chest, matched by a flutter in her stomach. Disgusting, she thought. She *was* glad to see him. "Help how?"

He smiled idly, as if enjoying her temper. "You're the least peaceful person I've ever met."

How could he enjoy her misery? What kind of man was he? "I don't want to be peaceful, Sheikh Tair. I *want* to leave."

"But you're not going to leave so you might as well learn to relax." He entered the tent, spotted the tub of water and stack of soap and towels that hadn't been touched. "You haven't bathed."

"I wasn't in the mood."

"You like being dirty?"

Tally was just about to make another comment on the squalor of his encampment but decided better of it at the last moment. "If you'll give me some privacy, I'll bathe now."

"I'll give you five minutes—"

"Why so little?"

"Because dinner is on the way and tonight I'm having dinner with you."

Tally took a very fast bath, not just because she only had five minutes to bathe and change, but because the water had cooled and a chilly bath wasn't her idea of fun.

Dressed, Tally was just combing her damp hair when Tair's elderly servant arrived with dinner.

Tally sat down across from Tair in her tent, the lantern tonight replaced with three fat flickering candles. The meal was simple, stew and a couscous and some flat bread, but she was hungry and ate virtually everything.

She looked up to find Tair watching her and his expression with its hard features, and firm proud mouth, softened with a half smile. "It's good to see you eat," he said.

"That's right. You think I'm stringy."

He had the grace to make a face, laughing at himself. "You didn't like that."

"No, I didn't."

He laughed softly now. "You are so feisty. Everything is a battle with you."

"I just have opinions of my own."

"So I've noticed." But he wasn't angry. He sounded almost…indulgent.

Their gazes locked, and she felt her face burn and darken, as a rush of heat swept through her cheeks. Impulsively she leaned forward, over the small table with the flickering candles. "Can we try this again?" she asked. "Can we try to start over?"

Tair leaned back, reclining against the pillows behind him. "Why would we want to start over?"

"Get a fresh start. Things haven't gone well and I thought it'd behoove us both—"

"Behoove?" he interrupted, dark eyes gleaming, and a single black eyebrow rising to mock her. "I haven't heard that word in years. Didn't realize it was still part of the English language."

Tally felt her jaw clench. How quickly he could kill her good moods. "I don't see why it shouldn't be used. It's a wonderful word."

"Indeed, it is."

Her hand squeezed the cup of mint tea she'd been holding. Why did she think she enjoyed his company? Why had she even missed him earlier?

"The point," she said carefully, trying to sidestep her profound—and growing—resentment, "is that we haven't gotten off on the best footing and I think it'd be good if we tried again. Started over. Formed new first impressions."

"Why?"

She couldn't seem to escape the intensity in his expression, his dark eyes fierce, demanding, insistent. And while he wasn't touching her, she felt the heat again grow between them, matching the heat growing within her.

"I don't understand you," she said, swallowing hard, trying to calm her racing heart. She'd never win an argument with Tair by getting emotional. He was reason, and logic. "I don't understand anything about you."

"What do you need to understand?"

Helplessly Tally searched his face. "I've told you I'm a photographer. I've told you I work for no one but myself. You've even had the chance to see my photos but it doesn't seem to matter to you. You refuse to help me and only you can."

"But I have helped you," he answered calmly. "I will always help you."

"How?" she demanded, genuinely perplexed. This was probably a cultural thing, some distance between East and West, but he had to realize she wasn't one of his women. She'd never be a Berber woman.

"And for that matter," he continued, not bothering to answer her question but finish making his point, "why would we want to start over, or try to form new impressions, when what we know might be true?"

"But maybe it isn't the truth. Maybe you have some idea of me that I'm not—"

"I don't think so."

Her brow creased. Her head had begun to throb again. Amazing how he could give her a headache in just minutes.

The problem with Tair, she thought, was that he was too confident. Too sure of himself, and comfortable with his power.

It didn't help that he was so powerfully shaped, either, as if cut from the desert rock and ravines—solid, invincible. He wasn't just tall, he was broad, strong, big in the way warriors were big. He dwarfed the tent, ate up space with his endless legs and broad shoulders. His wrists and hands were just as immense, his skin a golden-bronze from sun. But it was his hair that gave him the look of the barbarian. His hair was thick, jet-black, and long. His hair ought to be cut or at least tied back from his face but he didn't bother with it, although his jaw was smoother than it had been. Normally it was shadowed with a day's growth of beard but he must have shaved again since morning.

"Tair," she said, and her voice was soft, almost pleading. "I'm not whatever you think I am."

"And what do I think you are?"

"A spy!" Tally flashed, livid all over again.

Tair chuckled softly, dark hair falling forward, shadowing his face. "You object?"

"Of course I'm not a spy. Why would I be a spy? My camera's nice, but it isn't even that high-tech!" She continued to frown at him, hating him, even as she found him horribly, alarmingly attractive. If only she didn't find tall, dark, handsome appealing. If only Paolo had been blonde, frail. But no, Paolo had been her type, too. Brazilian, rugged, muscular, handsome.

But Tair, he put a whole new spin on rugged and muscular.

He put a whole new spin on everything.

"Why do you have such an excellent vocabulary?" she asked, exasperated. It amazed her that at times his English was better than hers. "You speak English flawlessly."

"You pick up things along the way," he answered, shifting a little and then placing one pale suede boot on top of the other. "But tell me more about these first impressions. Why do you think they're wrong?"

He'd changed the subject, she noticed, deliberately focusing the attention away from him back on her. He certainly didn't reveal much about himself and yet there was lots she'd like to know. Like—was he married? Did he have children? How long had he been sheikh? "You want me to divulge all these things about myself but you won't say anything about you."

"I already know me. I don't know you."

"But I don't know you."

"Good. It's better off that way." He grinned, flashing white straight teeth. "How long have you been a photographer?"

She gave up trying to deflect his questioning. At least when talking he wasn't making threats. "About seven years now."

"How did you get into it?"

"I liked photography in high school—worked on the yearbook—but dropped it in college. Then in my early twenties I got a job working in a photo studio at the mall. Lots of family portraits and naked babies lying on sheepskin rugs, but I enjoyed setting up the shots, liked the photography aspect. One thing led to another and here I am."

"In Northern Africa."

She smiled fleetingly. He sounded almost amused and she realized yet again that he wasn't entirely without humor. "Working at the Factoria Mall got boring, as well as claustrophobic. I hated being cooped up inside a big building. I like being outside. Free to roam."

"You had a lot of freedom then as a child?"

Tally suddenly thought of her childhood and her mood instantly changed. She didn't like remembering her childhood, or her home. She didn't want to think about a place that had trapped her, confined her, limiting her opportunities and choices. "No," she answered firmly, and her voice sounded sharper than she intended.

Tally saw his eyebrows lift and she grimaced, gentled her tone. "I was the oldest in a big family. I didn't have a lot of freedom. Just a lot of responsibility."

"So tell me about your family."

But Tally didn't want to talk about her family. Her family had been poor, and poor wasn't interesting or glamorous, but it had taught good lessons. Like, poor tasted hungry. Poor felt weary. Poor smelled fearful. Poor heard despair.

Poor wasn't what Tally wanted to be ever again. Not poor, not helpless, not dependent, not trapped. And maybe she'd never be rich doing her freelance photography, but she always managed to pay her bills and take care of herself.

So no, she didn't like to think about her family or the past, not when it depressed her. Far better to just look forward, set out on fresh adventures, tackle new challenges.

"I was raised in Washington State," she said, deftly side-stepping his question, "between the Cascade Mountains and the Puget Sound. It's rainy and green. No matter where you are you get views of these staggering mountains—Mount Baker, Rainier and St. Helens. The mountains, some extinct volcanoes, are interspersed with lakes and rivers. It's beautiful. Dramatic."

"So why leave it?"

"Because that's where I was raised, but it doesn't feel like my home anymore—"

"Why?" He interrupted, not satisfied with her answer.

"Because."

"Because why?"

She sighed, exasperated. "I need…I want…" She shook her head, irritated by his persistence and her inability to articulate an answer. "Change. I need change."

CHAPTER FIVE

HIS gaze narrowed, resting on her critically. “But if things were good there?”

Her lips compressed. He was being deliberately provocative. “They weren’t, they haven’t been good there in years. So I travel. Okay?”

“You still live with your family when you’re in Washington?”

“No way.” Tally shuddered. “Absolutely not. I have a loft in Seattle. Pioneer Square. It’s the historic district. Lots of artists and photographers have galleries there.”

“Do you have a gallery?”

“I used to.”

“And…?”

“I sold it to come here.” She smiled to hide the uneasiness inside of her. Even though she’d begun to find some critical, as well as commercial success as a photographer in downtown Seattle, studio work wasn’t her passion. Anyone could stage a scene, get the lighting just right. She needed greater challenges and bigger risks.

Paolo had said she needed the challenges and risks because she was always running away from herself—a statement that had annoyed her tremendously—but there was truth in it. She hadn’t been happy at home. She was still trying to understand what happy meant. Happy seemed to be a very hard concept at times.

"I want the memory cards back," she said huskily, looking up, tears in her eyes, blurring her vision. "I want them back, and I know what you've told me, but I don't accept it. There's no way I'll let you keep them or let you delete my work. I've spent weeks in Egypt, Morocco and Baraka photographing children. I'm not about to lose months of work because you disapprove."

She drew a quick breath and reached up to swipe away tears before they could fall. "And if you don't give them to me, when I get out of here, I will tell everyone what you did. I will put it in every magazine, and on every Internet site. I will do endless interviews and send thousands of e-mails. How you kidnapped me, held me hostage, threatened me, intimidated me, took my film—"

"Do you know that our people frown on the use of representational images?"

His quiet question silenced her. He leaned forward, dark gaze intense. "And this problem we have with images extends to photographs. Most of our people have an aversion to cameras, and photographs."

"But no one's had a problem with me taking pictures," she said in a small voice.

"Are you sure? Or have you had to bribe your way into getting the shots you wanted? Money to this person, money to that person?"

Tally swallowed. "My work isn't exploitative—"

"You photograph children and teenagers."

"It's a book about childhood, and the rites and passages of childhood."

"What makes you think you can come here and photograph our children? Families here don't even have photographs of their children. The few photographs we have are formal portraits and those usually commemorate a special occasion."

"I didn't realize. However—" She pushed hair from her face, shoving it behind her ear. "Tair, I understand your resistance to me including the children from the village in my book, but there are nearly three hundred shots on that card. They're not all *your* children and I've spent more than a year on this book. I must finish my book. I need to complete it."

He said nothing. He simply looked at her and the silence grew long, stretching tautly between them.

"Why don't you say anything?" she demanded.

"There's nothing to say."

"But there is. You can tell me when you'll return the cards to me. You can tell me you've changed your mind. You can tell me I'll soon be able to continue my work—"

"But that's not true, so how can I say it?"

"You can't really mean to keep me here!" The threat of tears was real and imminent. Tally closed her eyes, pressed the palms of her hands to her face. All her feelings of good will toward him disappeared. "I don't want this," she protested huskily. "I don't want to be here. I don't want any of this."

"But sometimes what we don't want, is exactly what we need."

"I will keep running away!"

"And I will keep bringing you back."

"Why?"

"Maybe because I want you for me."

Tair's words hit her like ice water thrown in her face. She jerked upright, gasped, blinked, mouth opening and closing in shock and confusion. *He* wanted *her?*

Tair rose slowly, unfolding himself with a deliberate grace and Tally watched him rise, heart in mouth as she realized he was going to reach for her. Her pulse raced, her hands grew damp, her fingers curling into fists even as a strange desire filled her.

She couldn't do this. It was wrong. Everything about it was wrong. "Please go," she choked, voice strangled as she jumped up, taking a panicked step backward. "Please leave now."

But he didn't go. And Tally scooted past him so they circled each other. She was on his side of the table now and she stumbled over one of the cushions he'd been leaning against.

As she kicked aside the cushion, Tally saw a flash of silver and it took her a moment to realize it was a knife. An ornate dagger. His. He must have accidentally dropped it.

The knife wasn't particularly big, the handle jeweled, almost too pretty for a knife, but the blade glinted silver, sharp. She looked at Tair and then down at the knife. It could help her. Save her.

She put her foot on top of the knife, hiding it. It gave her courage. "I don't know what you want from me," she said huskily. "In fact, I don't think you even know what you want from me. Admit you made a mistake and send me back now before it's too late."

"It wasn't a mistake," he answered, arms folding over his chest, eyes narrowing. In the flickering candlelight he looked huge, calm, unflappable.

"But it is. I'm not an object to be caught, trapped, possessed. This isn't my home and I won't live here…although I might die here."

"The way you're going about it, yes, you might. But you could also have a good life here."

"Never." She wouldn't live here, and yes, maybe she would die here, but it was because she had no other choice.

But she wasn't there yet. She still had options. At the very least, she had one option. Fight. Struggle. Survival.

Survival being the only thing important to her at this point.

Veins laced with adrenaline, Tally bent down, grabbed the knife and held it behind her.

"You look so uncomfortable standing there," he said. "Does your arm have a kink in it?"

Hand sweating, she shifted her grip on the dagger's handle. This could go badly, very badly. But she had to try. Had to force the situation somehow. Anything but sit, wait, allow herself to be swamped by despair. Despondency. Passivity.

She'd climbed mountains, scoured the face of granite cliffs. She'd competed in triathlons. Marathons. Could bike, hike, run, sail, surf. If he thought she'd meekly give herself up, hand over her dreams, her goals, her vision for herself—he was wrong. Her eyes burned. Her chest ached. She'd never cut anyone before, never hurt anyone. But she'd hurt him. If she had to.

And she had to.

She had to make him understand she was serious. Had to make him pay attention.

And what if he died?

Her heart did a painful thump, almost as if it were breaking, falling, tumbling into her gut. Well then, she told herself, ignoring the horrible free-fall plummet, he'd die. It's not as though he didn't create this nightmare. This situation was his doing. She was a visitor in his country and he took her, violated her security, stole her security, and now held her captive.

If he had to die, then maybe he had to die.

She swallowed miserably. Hopefully he wouldn't have to die. Hopefully he'd be smart and realize this was going to end badly for both of them.

"No, my arm doesn't have a kink in it," she answered flatly. "I'm armed."

"Armed?" He nearly smiled. "Oh, I see. You found my knife."

So he knew he'd dropped his knife. She brought her arm around, held up the knife, the blade at an angle. Paolo had showed her how to hold a knife, use a knife. He'd taught her the rudiments of weaponry. "Don't move," she warned.

He closed the distance between them, stepping around the table to haul her against him. "Or what?"

Hand shaking, she pressed the tip of the blade to his chest. "I'll kill you," she choked, fire and ice flooding her limbs. "Make one more move and I swear, I'll kill you."

Tair didn't even blink. He simply looked down at her, his expression long suffering. "Put that away."

"No."

"You'll hurt someone."

"Yes. You."

He grabbed her wrist so suddenly she didn't even see him move. But now he held her hand in his and with a swift wrench on her wrist, forced the knife from her hand. Her fingers opened in pain and with a whimper she watched the knife bounce to the carpet.

He let her go and she immediately went to her knees, grabbed the knife and came back at him.

Tair sighed and ripped open his robe. "If you insist," he drawled, now unbuttoning his shirt, "let me at least make this easier for you by giving you the correct target."

The knife in her hand wobbled as she stared at his chest, the bronze skin scarred over dense honed muscle. She looked at the scar tissue that stretched from his sternum toward his left nipple. "Someone's tried this before," she said faintly.

"You're not the first, no." He waited, looked at her. "Give it a shot. The skin's tough but you might be able to do it."

Tally couldn't look away from the thick scarring, the seams marring his beautiful skin. Fresh tears filled her eyes and with a groan of despair she gave him the knife. "Go," she said. "Just go. Get out of here."

Tair had played it cool in the her tent, but once he'd left his temper surged and he yanked off his robe and tugged on the shirt, freeing it from his trousers and then opening it to the chest, letting the night air cool his skin.

Savage, that's how he felt tonight. A savage on fire. A savage burning from the inside out.

Standing at the edge of camp, facing the endless desert illuminated only by the moon overhead, Tair could see the sandstorm from earlier, and then the sky once they'd returned, the sky seemed to bleed tonight as the sun set, orange weeping into red against bruised violet. He'd seen the sandstorm on the horizon. He'd seen the clouds gather, the dark brown turning black as the storm touched down, wreaking havoc with the wild whipping winds that decimated everything in its path.

He hadn't thought he'd reach the woman in time.

He hadn't thought he'd save her.

He blew out a breath, the air a harsh exhale. He'd told his men to turn back. Told them to return to camp and safety and he alone went ahead for her.

He wasn't afraid to die. He knew he'd die eventually, it was just a matter of time, but he feared for her. She wasn't of his people, didn't know the desert as he did. She would have suffered alone and he couldn't allow that. If she were to perish he should at least be there with her. No woman should die afraid and alone. It was wrong. Went against every belief he had, every conviction he held.

No, the American didn't understand his world. His world was primitive and it fit him. Here justice—and death—came swiftly. In the desert, justice was meted out by a fierce and unwavering hand. If not nature's, then his.

After all, this was his country, his people, his land, his desert, his sun. His father had ruled before him and his father before that, and back it went, on and on, generation after generation.

Tair knew what the American woman said, knew in her world what he did was criminal, knew in her world he had no right. But she wasn't in her world, she was in his, and here what he did was allowed. Permissible. Just.

She'd get used to his world. Sooner or later.

Tally couldn't sleep that night. Every time she drifted off, some thought, some terror brought her back awake again.

The fact that she found Tair attractive—in any size, shape or form—horrified her. He wasn't a good man, nor kind, nor gentle, nor sophisticated. He might have the title of sheikh, but underneath it all he was a kidnapper, a bully and a thief. But knowing that, accepting that, she still couldn't hurt him.

This is why she couldn't stay. This is why she had to go. She was losing her mind, losing perspective. She couldn't allow a desert barbarian to confuse her. And she was confused. Very.

Just before dawn, Tally left her bed. She'd leave while everyone still slept. She'd go on foot, but she'd take the dried fruit she'd been saving from her meals, and the dried bread, and the jug of water from her bedside chest and go before camp woke.

The sun was just breaking on the horizon when she left her tent. The camp's three-legged dog stirred from his place by the now cold fire and bounded toward her. Before he could bark, Tally broke off a piece of bread, tossed it at him, and the mutt, pouncing on the bread, was quite happy to eat not bark, allowing Tally to leave camp undisturbed.

"She's left, sir. Again." It was Tair's elderly Berber servant standing at the entrance of Tair's tent, his head bowed.

"I'm sorry," the servant added apologetically, his head drooping even lower in disgrace. "She must have left early, when the camp was still sleeping."

Tair briefly closed his eyes and pressed two fingers to the bridge of his nose. "Footprints?"

"Yes. West, toward the wadi, sir."

Tair bit back his oath of impatience and irritation. This Tally was proving to be a great deal of trouble for just one woman. "Thank you," he said, remaining at his desk where he'd been drafting a document that would eventually be sent to the royal palace in Atiq, to the attention of Malik Nuri, the Sultan of Baraka.

The servant hesitated. "Do you want me to send someone after her?"

"No."

And the elderly man hesitated even longer—a testament to his inherent goodness. "It wouldn't be any trouble. We have men to spare at the moment—"

"Not necessary. But thank you." Tair didn't even look up.

His man murmured acknowledgment and exited, letting the tent flap fall behind him and it wasn't until Tair was alone that he glanced up, forehead furrowing with aggravation.

Tally lacked sense even a child would have. Rushing blindly into the desert. Running off with no chance of escape. She must have a death wish. She had to know she couldn't—wouldn't—survive even twenty-four hours in the desert unprotected.

Sighing, he leaned back in his chair and stared across the tent to the cushions scattered on the floor.

The whole point of kidnapping a woman and making her yours was that one had effectively bypassed pretense and any ridiculous notions of romance.

Tair didn't do romance. He didn't woo or court. He didn't have time, and even if he did, he wouldn't anyway. Wooing was for men who lacked confidence in their ability to make a woman adapt, conform, behave. And that had never been Tair's problem. Women—for better or worse—liked him. Loved him. He didn't always love back but that was his fault. He didn't love, didn't know how to love, not the way women wanted to be loved and yet he'd accepted this flaw in his personality, realizing he had strengths that compensated for his deficiencies.

He was loyal. He was strong. He understood and respected commitment.

He was also wealthy enough, and although scarred—he'd fought in just one too many battles—he wasn't completely deformed and women so far hadn't minded the wounds. In fact, women—who would ever understand them?—seemed to like the scars. Made them protective.

Tair snorted to himself. Women made no sense but that was nothing new.

Maybe he'd just have to tie Tally up. She'd hate it but maybe that's what he needed to do. Tie her to the pole in the center of his tent, keep her tethered like one of the baby goats that tended to wander off if not kept safely roped.

And then picking up his pen, Tair returned to his work, determined to finish his letter before setting off in search of the woman he had decided would be his. Even if she hadn't accepted it yet.

So this was how she was going to die. An awful, horrible death. Suffocation by sand.

Tally had always feared drowning in the ocean but this would be just as bad. Sliding beneath the surface, buried in a sea of sand. Sand in her eyes, her nose, her mouth. Sand filling her lungs.

Tortured by the thought, Tally struggled, grappling upward but the movement worked against her and she dropped lower, sliding down instead of up. She'd heard that fighting quicksand was a death sentence, but this wasn't real quicksand, was it? She'd never heard of desert quicksand but one moment she'd been walking and the next the world beneath her gave away.

Shock caused her to kick her legs and down she went lower, the sand completely enclosing the lower half of her body. She'd slipped further down in the hour she'd been trapped.

Don't panic, she told herself, even as she flailed again, and the flailing just pulled her down deeper, faster.

Come on, Tal, get control. This won't be pleasant. No need to rush blindly into this. Try at least to savor your last hour of life.

The realization that she was trapped and unable to free herself finally hit home and some of the desperate fight left her. No reason to hurry death along. And she wasn't sinking anymore. For a moment she just rested there, ribs buried, legs gone, but her arms were still free and she could breathe. That was something.

A big something.

Now all she had to do was stay relaxed and think.

Think.

There's got to be a way out.

But turning her head, she could see nothing to grab, nothing secure to hold. No way to pull herself out.

She drew a deep breath and felt the sand give and she slipped, not far, just a couple inches, but that was far enough.

To die in quicksand.

No one died in quicksand. People couldn't die in quicksand. And desert quicksand? Didn't exist. That was just movie stuff.

And yet she was trapped and it was sand.

Tally felt the slow slip of sand and knew she was sinking again, still slowly, steadily, sliding though to where? What lay beneath the sand? A hole? More ground? A cave? Why had the sand beneath her given way?

Tally shuddered imagining the very end and her shudder speeded the slipping sand. Or maybe it was her weight—and gravity—pulling her faster now but she continued to drop, lower, much lower, the weight of the sand on her chest, pressing hot and hard against her lungs.

Her pulse quickened and adrenaline coursed through her. Hell, hell, hell.

She didn't want to go this way. Didn't want to go at all, but certainly not this way. And the more she knew she didn't want to suffocate in sand, the harder she thrashed the lower she slipped.

God, don't let me die this way!

"Stop fighting," a familiar voice said from behind her.

"Tair?" Hot tears surged to her eyes. Relief flooded through her. She tried to turn to see him and just sank deeper.

"You've got to stop moving," he said, walking around the side of the sandpit, keeping a careful distance between them.

The sand was up to her armpits and weighing heavy on her chest. "Can you get me out?"

"Yes. After we talk."

Tally instinctively kicked, feeling the sand creep through the armholes of her shirt, sliding against her bare skin. "Talk now? Tair, I can hardly breathe!"

"Then don't talk, listen to me." He crouched down, arms resting on his knees, white robe billowing. "I'm losing patience, Tally. This is the second day in a row I've had to save your skin and it's getting old."

"You're giving me a lecture now?"

"You're making life harder for everyone. You need to accept your fate more gracefully—"

"Accept being kidnapped?" Her voice rose in an indignant howl. "No. Never! This is not my fate. My fate isn't to be trapped in the desert forever with you."

"You're right," he answered mildly. "It seems your fate is to die today in quicksand."

"Tair!"

"It's one or the other, Woman. Make up your mind. I haven't all day." He leaned back, took a seat on the sand. "Actually, you haven't all day. But why beat the point to death? It's your life, not mine."

"Stop threatening me and just get me out."

"Tsk tsk," he chided her. "So rude. Is that the way to ask for help?"

"You know I want your help."

"You don't appreciate all the things I do for you."

"Do for me?" Her voice rose as she slipped lower, sand engulfing her all the way to her shoulders. "Tair, I'm going to go under. Get me out now."

"Ask nicely."

"This is a game to you!"

"I wouldn't call it a game, but it is interesting. Will the American ask for help or will she sink all the way under?"

"Tair."

"Ask for help, Tally."

She felt wild, panicked. "You're not being fair."

"Life's not fair." His dark gaze met hers and held. "Learn to ask for help, Tally."

"I did. I asked you to get me out."

"It wasn't very polite."

She could feel the sand on her neck, feel it press relentlessly, feel the slippery cool grains everywhere and her head spun, dizzy. "I hate you."

He sighed. "Why are you so stubborn?"

"Why are you?" Tears filled her eyes and she couldn't even brush them away. "You know I can't get out of here without your help but you're making me beg and that's cruel—"

"Refusing to ask for help is worse. That's a death wish, and stupid."

"What word do you want? What is it you want to hear? Tair, you're so marvelous. Or Tair, you're my man. What is it you want?"

The edge of his mouth tugged. "That's quite gratifying, Woman, but I was actually just looking for please."

Tair rose in one fluid motion, white robes swirling and going to his horse, he withdrew a rope, tied it to his stallion's saddle and returned to her side.

He stretched out on the sand, and inched his way toward her and tossed the looped rope around her shoulders, and tugged, the loop tightened lasso-like and he had her secure.

Whistling to his horse, the stallion began to back up and with Tair guiding the rope, he managed to drag Tally free of the sand.

"Thank you," Tally choked, tears streaming and she rubbed one cheek and then the other, her face streaked with tears and sand.

"You're welcome." He whistled again to the stallion and the horse trotted over. Swinging into his saddle, he leaned down, held an arm out to Tally. "Let's go home."

Tally froze. She didn't put her hand in his. "But that's the problem, Tair. It's not my home."

"Here we go again," he muttered beneath his breath.

"It's not."

"I don't want to do this now. The sand is still unstable from yesterday's storm. There are probably more sand traps out here. If you really want me to leave you here, fine. But I'm going home."

Tally sagged, exhausted, forlorn. "I don't want to be left here."

"Then you're accepting my protection?"

Fresh tears burned her eyes but she wouldn't let them fall. "No." She turned, stared out across the desert that had become a treacherous prison and she wondered when and how this would end. Worn out, worn down she couldn't keep running away but how to give up her world? Her life? Her dreams? Because she knew once she said yes, there would be no going back.

Tair swore softly and with a scoop of his arm lifted Tally up, settling her in his saddle in front of him. His arm was hard around her, holding her completely immobile. "This is getting familiar," he said, dragging her even closer.

Tally shivered at the feel of his chest against her back, his body hard, solid, warm.

It wasn't a particularly long ride back to camp and as they arrived, Tair's men looked away, their heads turned, gazes respectfully fixed elsewhere as Tair wrestled with what they must think a truly demented woman. Well let them think she was mad. Because she wasn't going to go back without a fight. She wasn't going to just accept whatever sentence Tair handed out.

They were back. The men spilled from his camp, watching as Tair reined his horse to a stop but none actually looked at her.

Not a good sign, Tally thought, defensively. "You can't keep me here," she whispered. "I will take off first chance I can. I will continue to go—"

"You've nearly died in a sandstorm, spent a frightening afternoon in a sandpit. What do you want to happen now?"

"I don't know, but I'm beginning to think being eaten by a snake is preferable to staying here with you."

"Now come," Tair said, sliding off the horse and yanking her down behind him, "that's unfair. You haven't even been bedded by me yet. You might actually like being my woman."

"Never."

He clucked disapprovingly, and walked toward his tent, strides long, determined, his hold on her wrist just as hard. "The least you could do is withhold judgment until I've had you."

He tossed aside the curtainlike flap and pulled her inside. The flap snapped closed. "Which I intend to do—" he broke off as his gaze swept over her, up and down "—as soon as you bathe. You, my dear woman, reek."

"Reek?" Her voice rose and yet she threw her shoulders back, puffed her chest out. "Well, that's just lovely considering you've kept me in rank tents, eating tough goat meat and drinking warm goat's milk for days. You've no proper bath, no shampoo, no lotions, no scented oils. Nothing. I thought sheikhs lived in beautiful palaces filled with sunken tiled baths and gorgeous mosaic arches. But no. I have to get kidnapped by a sheikh who lives like a peasant with nothing but a half dozen ancient tents to his name."

Tair's jaw jutted. "You've forgotten my horse."

"I have." Her chest rose and fell with each rapid breath. "But one horse doesn't make a kingdom, Sheikh al Tayer—"

"It's el-Tayer. You're in Northern Africa not the Middle East."

She gestured impatiently. "The point is, where's Aladdin when you need him? Where's my genie to make everything beautiful? Because you might be a sheikh, *el-Tayer,* but this isn't my fantasy. Not even close."

"Enough," Tair ground out, dragging her toward him. "This may not be your idea of paradise, but I've had it with the running away, and pulling knives, and putting your life in danger. It's stopping. Now. Understand me?"

But he didn't give her a chance to answer. Instead he pulled her into his arms, fitting her against his body so that her softness curved against his hardness, her hips cradling his, her thighs caught between his own, her breasts crushed to his chest.

Heat flared in her cheeks, heat and awareness as well as shame. She wanted him, wanted this contact with him and yet everything about him was lethal, destructive. "Let me go," she begged.

His hand wound through her hair, forming a rope of the thick brown strands. "No."

She tried to push away from him but couldn't, not when he held her so securely. His head lowered, and fire flashed in his dark eyes. She felt her knees start to buckle as she realized that he was going to kiss her—whether she wanted him to or not.

His mouth covered hers hard, a fierce kiss of possession. She stiffened at the touch of his mouth on hers, stiffened from shock as well as pleasure. His lips made her own mouth feel hot, sensitive, alive and she shivered as his lips moved over hers, drawing a response.

He was warm and his beard rough and yet his lips were cool, firm, teasing. They teased her now and her lips parted beneath his, allowing him in and she arched helplessly against his heat, her lower body tingling as desire coiled in her belly, tight and hungry.

She wanted him. Oh God she wanted him and yet going to bed—making love—wasn't an option. She had to know that. She had to be smart enough to know she couldn't ever give herself to this man. And even knowing that, she couldn't end the kiss, couldn't break free.

It was Tair who finally lifted his head, his hands slipping from her hair to frame her face. "Tell me, when is this foolish, dangerous behavior going to end?"

CHAPTER SIX

TALLY could barely draw a breath, her heart pounding fast and furious, her pulse unsteady.

She heard his question but couldn't speak, not when her brain was too busy analyzing everything happening. Like the way he held her face, and the way his fingers curved to fit her jawbone and the almost tender way he plucked a hair from her eye and smoothed it back from her face.

She fought to steady her breathing.

"This must stop," he continued. "You're putting not just your life at risk, but mine as well as my men."

"Then let me go."

"That's not an option—"

"Why not?"

"Because you're mine now," he answered simply.

Tair's answer cut through her haze of emotion and sensation. She pushed his hands away and took one step back, and then another. She was his.

He said she was his…

She'd never been anyone's. Not even Paolo's, not even when she gave her body to him. Paolo hadn't been the marrying kind and she knew there'd be no settling down with him, no house, no children, nothing like that.

But Tair. Tair. He was so different. He was so strong, so intense, so possessive. From the moment he'd hauled her onto his horse he'd acted as though she were his and there were times it infuriated her and then times it did something to her, touched her, undid her.

She hadn't really felt like anyone's in so long.

Tally put a hand to her temple, tried to clear her head. "I'll keep running away, Tair."

"And go where, Woman?" He rarely raised his voice but it was loud now. "You're in the middle of the Sahara Desert. Doesn't that mean anything? Or maybe you truly have a death wish, and if that's the case, tell me now and I'll stop rushing after you."

All fuzziness in her head disappeared, all tenderness and ambivalence vanishing in the face of his insensitivity and arrogance. "Rushing?" she spluttered. *"Rushing?* I wouldn't say you rush. It seems to me you enjoy waiting until the last possible moment to do the big rescue."

"I can't drop everything every time you decide it's time to run away again."

"Drop *everything?* Sheikh Tair, forgive me, but no one here does anything but drink tea and play dice."

"It's not dice and we don't just drink tea. My men all have specific jobs they do."

"That's right. They have guns to clean." She clapped a hand to her forehead. "Silly me. How could I forget?"

"Every time I set off, my men accompanied me until I sent them back. Every time I left camp to look for you we took risks and if you don't appreciate me, you better damn well appreciate my men."

Tears filled her eyes and furiously she rubbed them away. "You keep acting as though I should be grateful you kidnapped me from the medina. But I didn't ask to have my life turned upside down. I didn't ask for any of this, not even your protection!"

"But that's not true. You came to our world, we didn't go to yours."

And that, Tally thought, shoulders slumping, was a most excellent point.

She walked away from him, a fist pressed to her mouth as she realized for the first time how this all must seem to him. He wasn't Western, he wasn't anything like the men in her world, and the rules here were so different. If as he said, she was traveling with dangerous men, he'd done what he'd thought was right, behaved fairly, protectively.

She focused on one of the wool pillows lying on the low bed. It was a beautiful pattern, handwoven. "How could you leave me in the quicksand so long?" Her voice broke and a lump filled her throat. "I could have died."

Tair didn't immediately answer and she closed her eyes as the silence stretched. Then she felt his hand touch her back, his palm warm, firm.

"Is that what this is really about?" he asked. "That I made you ask for help?"

She wiped away one tear and then another. "Maybe."

He put his hands on her shoulders and slowly turned her around. "All you had to do was ask for help. It was your impulsiveness that got you into trouble in the first place. You ran off. You were just lucky I decided to go search for you."

Lucky, huh? Tally sniffed. "If I'd been lucky I wouldn't have been in the medina when you were. If I were lucky you would have kidnapped some other poor Western woman. That's my definition of luck."

He shrugged, but in his eyes was a glimmer of a smile. "Perhaps it's a cultural difference, but to be given the gift of life—not just once, but twice—that's good fortune."

"You're speaking of the two times you saved me."

"Three now."

She stared up into his hard, arrogant features. Big nose, dark eyes, fierce mouth. And strangely—beautiful. God, she hated him. And wanted him. And hated herself for still finding him so attractive, despite everything that had taken place between them. "I don't know that you saved me three times," she answered, striving to sound cool. "The first time you'd almost killed me so I don't know if that counts."

The corners of his mouth tugged. "To show you I am a fair man, I am willing to compromise and will agree that according to your definition, I've only saved your life twice."

Tally hid her own reluctant smile, cleared her throat. "Since we're trying to be accurate, I think it should be mentioned that your rescue today would have been more heroic if you hadn't waited until I nearly slid all the way under."

He sighed and yet the heavy sigh was contradicted by the warmth in his eyes. "I've never met a woman that demands so much and expresses so little gratitude."

"We're talking about my life, Sheikh Tair!"

"Then ask for help, Woman. Don't wait until the grains of sand fill your nose. Ask for help while you still have air to speak with."

And then his head dropped and he covered her mouth with his once again, his lips coaxing and she didn't need much encouragement. Her mouth loved the feel of his, her body wanted him and her arms slid up around his neck as she kissed him back.

They were interrupted by a shout outside the tent, the voice raised in alarm.

Tair pulled away and turned to leave but not before he pressed a swift kiss to her brow. "I shall return for dinner. Wait for me."

Tally watched from her tent as men gathered around Tair in the deepening twilight. He was gesturing, speaking, giving orders. Some men began to saddle up while others packed bags. They were going somewhere and they had guns.

She felt her stomach flip and fall and she grabbed at the tent, held on. She wanted to rush out, confront Tair, ask what was happening but didn't dare, not after the day they'd just had.

Instead she stood in the shadows and watched as Tair,

leading twenty-some men, set off on their horses at a full speed gallop.

Tally had taken a bath, dressed in the simple black robe that Tair's elderly servant supplied, and with candles lit in her tent, tried to pass the time until Tair returned but he was gone a long time and the hours passed slowly.

Her stomach growled late in the night and finally the elderly Berber brought her food and even though she was hungry, Tally refused. "I'm waiting for Tair," she said to the old man.

"Ash?" he asked. What?

"I'm waiting for Tair."

The old man stared at her uncomprehendingly.

"Tair," Tally repeated and this time she stood on her toes, lifted her hand high above her head to indicate Tair's immense height. *"Tair."*

The elderly man only looked more puzzled and Tally wanted to pull her hair out in mad chunks. This was a nightmare. A nightmare. How could Tair think she could possibly stay here, the only woman—and a Western woman at that—in this camp? He was out of his mind.

"Tair," Tally said more loudly.

The old man just looked at her with absolute incomprehension.

"He doesn't have a clue as to what you're saying," an amused voice said behind her and Tally spun around.

"How long have you been standing there?" she demanded, exhaling a huffy puff even as she pushed her long hair back from her face.

"Long enough to enjoy your pantomime."

"Very funny." But it was, she knew and she smiled reluctantly. "So you're back. Did you get the bad guys?"

His lips curved but the smile didn't touch his eyes. "Most of them."

She felt his mood then and it was somber, heavy, and Tally

wondered just what had taken place out there in the desert tonight. "Hungry?" she asked more gently.

He nodded. "Let me just wash. I'll be right back." He returned shortly, jaw clean shaven, his hair wet, combed back from his face, the thick shoulder-length strands a glossy black in the soft yellow candlelight.

"You look…nice," Tally said awkwardly, shyly.

Tair laughed. "You sound so surprised."

"No, I…um, no." Blushing she moved to the table laden with trays and bowls, more food than Tally had seen in a long time. "No," she repeated and knelt on one side of the table. "Let's eat."

Over dinner she asked him why the older man didn't understand her when she asked for him.

"No one here knows me as Tair," he answered, dipping a hunk of the bread in the stew.

"Then what do they call you?"

"Sheikh Zein el-Tayer. Or Soussi al-Kebir."

Chief of the Soussi Desert. Tally bit her lip, thinking how odd it was that his name which had been so strange was now so familiar. "How does Tair come from Tayer?"

He grimaced. "Good question. It's pronounced like the English word for tire, and it shouldn't be hard to say but when I attended boarding school in England, the headmaster could never say my name quite right and pretty soon all the boys were calling me Tair."

"An English boarding school? That explains some things. So, did it bother you they couldn't get your name right?"

"No. A name's a name. There are other things more pressing."

"Like?"

"Politics. Survival." He hesitated and when Tally said nothing he continued. "You don't know our history, or our culture so I can't expect you to understand the turmoil in this region, but politics have given us a violent legacy. We've fought to maintain our independence but it's not been without great personal cost."

She didn't know if it was his expression, or his tone, but she knew somehow, sensed it maybe, that he'd suffered. Personally suffered. It wasn't just his people's conflict but his own. "Those scars," she said hesitantly, indicating his torso where his robe covered the thickened tissue crisscrossing his chest, "are they a result of this violent legacy?"

"Yes."

She looked at him closely, really looked at him and she saw lines in his face, creases at his eyes, grooves near his mouth and the hollows beneath his high cheekbones. "You've been to war?"

"I live the war."

She didn't know what that meant. It was such a vague, cryptic thing to say. Part of her wanted to know what he meant and another part of her didn't. He was frightening, too frightening, his body a canvas of cuts and wounds, his strength formidable, his courage incomparable. She'd never met anyone who could do what he could do. She'd never thought it possible that a man could do what Tair did.

But there was a dark side, too. He wasn't a good man, couldn't by any stretch of the imagination be called thoughtful, kind, or compassionate. "How do you live war?"

"You attack. Steal. Injure. Kill."

"I see." And she did, too well. She could picture him doing all of the above, and remorselessly, as well. "You've killed in self-defense?"

"If you want to call it that."

Again she hesitated. "And if I don't?"

"It's what it is."

He met her questioning look with a slow, mocking smile. "Revenge," he added quietly. "A settling of scores."

"Revenge for what?"

"Taking what was mine."

"Yours as in money…land…?"

"As in women and children."

Tally swallowed, put down her bread and dusted her fingers off. "You've been married?"

"Yes."

She didn't know what to say next. For some reason she couldn't bring herself to ask about his wife. She knew men in Baraka and Ouaha often had several wives but Tally didn't want to imagine Tair with wives, couldn't stand to think he had another woman somewhere, one that belonged to him legally, morally.

She shifted uncomfortably, appetite gone. Happiness fading.

"What's wrong?" he asked, watching her.

Tally shook her head. It would be too ridiculous to tell him.

"Did I ever tell you that my father kidnapped my mother?" Tair asked conversationally, before taking another bite.

She looked up, brows pulling. "No."

"Mmmm." He swallowed, took a drink from his cup. "You asked me before why my English was so good and it's because my mother was English. She was a schoolteacher. She was teaching for the International School in Atiq when my father saw her, kidnapped her, took her to his kasbah and made her his."

"Did your mother hate your father for what he did?"

Tair's mouth quirked. "No. She loved him. They were still quite together when my father died." He turned his cup on the table, ran his finger over the glazed pottery. "My mother never returned to Britain. She stayed here in Ouaha and then only recently has moved to Baraka. She has a home in Atiq." He half smiled. "She's in her sixties and she's teaching again."

"Your mother has gone back to work?" Tally was torn between admiration and concern.

"She wanted to. She loved teaching and she missed my father and my brothers. Atiq's a better place for her now." He broke off another hunk of bread. "You'll have to meet her. She's almost as feisty as you."

Tally heard the warmth in his voice and looking up, her eyes met his. The expression in his eyes was nearly as warm as his voice.

Her heart beat double-time. Butterflies filled her middle. She remembered the kiss from earlier. Remembered the feel of his mouth and his hands on her skin.

Still half smiling, Tair asked, "Your father didn't kidnap your mother?"

Tally's mind flashed to the cramped trailer, and the trailer park, she'd grown up in and cringed inwardly. He might as well have, she thought, thinking about her father who couldn't ever keep a job thanks to his drinking and her mother who juggled several but never particularly well. Her past seemed to be a horrible lesson in mediocrity. Everything she'd learned had been, don't do this if you want to succeed. "No. No kidnapping involved."

She felt his dark gaze move leisurely across her features, studying, analyzing.

"There's that expression again," he said. "You get that look every time you talk about your family. It's so hard, so judgmental. I thought perhaps the first time it was my imagination but you do it every time you speak of them. That look of disappointment. Disapproval."

She felt the muscles pull in her jaw, the jaw itself flexing and he was right. There was no point in contradicting him. "My life hasn't been like yours," she finally said when the silence dragged too long. Tair wasn't very good at filling silences and while she wasn't particularly fond of chatter, she'd rather talk than sit awkwardly silent with Tair watching her.

And he did watch her. He watched her always, watched her with intense speculation. A snake in the desert. A hawk in the sky. He was simply biding his time. Waiting.

Waiting.

Tally ground her teeth, tension making her shoulders, head, jaw ache. "I wasn't raised with money. We didn't have any.

We didn't even go to college. At least, not away, not to the good ones, the expensive ones. My younger sister, Mandy, got an athletic scholarship to Washington State University and one of my brothers went to University of Washington while another went to school in California—but that's because they played sports. I didn't."

"So what did you do?"

She looked at him from beneath her eyelashes, her teeth clicking as she bit down once and again. Goddamn him. She hated his stupid questions. Stupid annoying questions. Stupid annoying facts. He was a sheikh and she was a poor church mouse.

From a trailer park.

From North Bend.

From a place that got more rain and cloud than sun.

She sighed, rubbed her neck, stretched a little. Her head hurt, filled with strange pain and she'd thought it was tension, but wasn't so sure anymore. "I went to Bellevue City College." She swallowed, her mouth suddenly dry, her tongue feeling thick, numb at the tip. "Took courses there and then went to work."

"I've heard of Bellevue. Home of Microsoft, and Bill Gates, yes?"

"More or less." She closed her eyes, woozy. Tally drew a deep breath and then another. Maybe it was just remembering the past that made her nauseous. Maybe it was the hurt that lingered all these years later.

Why tell him the truth about her past? Why did he need to know her real world? There was no reason he should have all the details.

She swallowed with difficulty, her throat thickening. Wouldn't it be better to just pretend she was someone she wasn't? Wouldn't it make more sense to go with the rich and fashionably chic world of Bellevue instead of the damp misty town at the base of the Cascade mountain range? Pretend she shopped at Bellevue Square instead of North Bend's outlet stores? Pretend she had money to spend in the first place…?

"You didn't play sports?" Tair asked, persisting with his line of questioning.

His voice seemed to come from far away. She looked at him, forced herself to focus. "No. Not really." Her forehead furrowed as she looked at a spot on the low table between them. "Well, I did, in high school. Volleyball." She suddenly smiled, a wry remembrance. She'd been good, too. Really good. Not the tallest, but dang, she'd been fast, and aggressive. Tally had gone after every ball…

"I used to love volleyball. And softball. But volleyball was my sport." Her head cocked and she seemed to be looking back, listening to voices in the past and her smile faded. "I used to spend hours working with my sister Mandy." She hesitated, choosing her words more slowly. "I was glad Mandy got the scholarship. Mandy was good. At least one of us got a chance to go to college. Play in college, and not just any school, but a good school. A big name school.

Tair's dark eyes rested on her face, his expression perfectly blank. "But you were good, too."

Tally briefly nodded. She nearly smiled but it was too much effort. "Yes."

"Why didn't you get a scholarship then?"

She looked off to the side again, looking back to a past that had been more pain than pleasure. "I was the oldest."

"And?"

"Needed at home."

Tair's black eyebrows pulled. "So you were awarded a scholarship?"

To UCLA. A great school with a great program. And she couldn't go, couldn't take it. "My parents—" She broke off, swallowed, shoulders shifting in that same uneasy shrug. If only she felt better. If only her head didn't hurt so. "Dad—" She broke off, tried again, "Dad wasn't well and Mom was working full-time. Someone had to watch the younger ones."

"And that someone was you."

It took Tally a long moment to speak. "The oldest."

"And a girl."

Her tight, pained smile grew even tighter, more painful. "I guess being a girl has its drawbacks in every culture."

So that was it, Tair thought, leaning back, absorbing the revelation. This wasn't just about him and her—this was bigger, greater. This was about gender. Identity. Discrimination.

Tally leaned forward against the table. She felt increasingly woozy and weak.

Something was wrong.

Her head swam and her stomach cramped. Her insides felt as though boiling oil had been poured through her. Pain filled her, wrenching her insides, surging through her veins. She nearly crumpled forward, her hand knocking her bowl aside.

"Woman," Tair said.

She could barely focus, unable to get beyond the fire twisting her insides into two. But his voice was strong, commanding.

Tally looked at Tair, stricken, bewildered. Something was very wrong. Something she'd eaten. Drunk.

"Tally?"

There were two of him. Now three. She blinked, eyes heavy, hot with pain, the same fire consuming her belly. "What have you done?" she choked, before slipping sideways to the floor.

CHAPTER SEVEN

TAIR didn't waste any time sending for a doctor. This wasn't ordinary food poisoning. It was deliberate, and whatever had been slipped into Tally's food—or drink—could be fatal, toxic.

Tair did what he could until the doctor arrived. He followed the simple universal antidote his mother had used with them: two parts wood charcoal, one part magnesia milk and one part of very strong tea. He gave her two tablespoons of the mixture in a little bit of water. He didn't know what she'd ingested, but knew that if the poison was metallic or alkaline, the tannic acid in the tea would neutralize it. If the poison was acid, the magnesia would neutralize it. And the wood charcoal even in a very little dose can absorb strong quantities of toxin.

With his servant's help, he got the antidote in her, before inducing vomiting. After she'd thrown up, he gave her another dose of the antidote and then pumped as many liquids as he could get down her throat—not an easy feat considering she was oblivious to everything except the nightmare of pain that had swallowed her whole.

Even as he fought to save her, he pieced together the situation, needing to know who, what, where, how as quickly as he could. This wasn't an accident. Someone had deliberately doctored her food and drink. But which of his men would do it, and why?

The doctor arrived at dawn, less than seven hours after

Tally had been poisoned, arriving precisely the same time Tair discovered it was Ashraf who committed the crime.

Tair had Ashraf isolated and monitored but Tair couldn't deal personally with him until after the doctor had seen Tally.

"The Devil's Herb," the doctor said, naming the toxic herb he suspected she'd ingested after checking her pulse, her eyes, and her tongue, as he prepared an injection.

Tair lifted the glass vial, checking the medicine the doctor was about to administer.

"It's the fastest, best antidote for the central toxic effects."

Tair nodded, still studying the bottle. The Devil's Herb—belladonna—was extremely toxic, often fatal, death usually resulting from asphyxiation but the universal antidote seemed to have helped Tally. Now he just wanted to know she'd be okay.

"She'll be sick for quite a while," the doctor concluded, finishing administering the injection. "You'll find that she's restless, agitated. She'll experience varying degrees of hallucinations, delirium, tremors, but she should get through."

Should, Tair silently repeated, leaving Tally in the doctor's care while he went to deal with Ashraf.

Tair gave Ashraf an opportunity to explain what he'd done and why, and Ashraf was all too happy to talk and Tair listened to Ashraf without interrupting him.

This was about *sehour,* Ashraf said, witchcraft. Tair hid his disgust as Ashraf talked. He couldn't believe it. Not just poison, but witchcraft. His people were superstitious. But Ashraf was not at all repentant.

"I did not give her poison," Ashraf said. "It's a *potion,* a potion to drive her and the evil eye away. She will bring destruction on all of us if we don't. She must go."

"What have you been smoking?" Tair demanded shortly, stunned that it was Ashraf who had done this. Ashraf had served him well for years.

"She's not Aisha Qandisha," Tair added, referring to the

mythical figure many of the people in the countryside believed existed.

Aisha Qandisha was reportedly a beautiful, seductive woman with the legs of a goat and she lived in riverbeds, in flames, and sandstorms. She is said to appear to men in dreams, enchanting them, enslaving them and children always fear her but Tally wasn't a mythical figure, and he'd seen her legs—and they were far from goatlike.

But Ashraf had his own ideas and shook his head. "The sehirra gave me something to put in the Western woman's food and drink. The sehirra said the woman will curse us, and she was right. She has brought trouble here."

"She's not right—"

"Look how the she writhes. She's sick—"

"Because you poisoned her," Tair thundered, cutting Ashraf short. "You poisoned her food and drink and she writhes with physical pain, not with some mystical spirit. You gave her poisonous herbs to kill her and you are lucky that I do not give you some of the same."

"Ah! But see, you've just proven my point. Look what this woman has already done to us. Look at the evil she's brought on us. You're going to kill me and she what…will live here with you? How is that justice? How is keeping her and losing me right? Will she protect you as I have? Will she watch your back? No. She is bad and I tell you now, I warn you, brother to brother, man to man, not to keep her. She is a danger to all."

Tair let his other men take Ashraf away then.

Ashraf was wrong, Tair thought, watching the bound Ashraf settle onto his horse. Tair wasn't going to kill Ashraf, and Tally wasn't going to bring destruction on them. But things were getting complicated. As well as interesting.

Tally was sick, very sick, that much she understood, everything coming at her in a blur of heat and haze. She saw as if underwater, the world blurry and shapes shimmering toward her and then away. Even the voices she heard were like voices beneath the water, blah blah blah, strange tones and all jumbled sound. She tried to focus, tried to make sense of the noise and blur but it was too hard, too much effort and closing her eyes she gave up, returning instead to the bliss of sleep.

Tair stood over her bed, watching his woman sleep. The fever had finally broken. She was no longer thrashing so violently—thank Allah—but it'd been a difficult several days, days where he wondered over and over if he should air evacuate her to the hospital in Atiq but the doctor he'd sent for assured him she'd eventually respond to the treatment, and she had.

But there had been a night where Tair had doubted the doctor, threatening the physician with bodily harm if anything happened to his woman.

His woman.

A muscle in Tair's cheek pulled, a grim acknowledgment of a truth he was still coming to grips with. Somehow through the sandstorms and quicksand, knives and asthma attacks, he'd come to see her as his.

His responsibility. His duty. His fate. Whatever that meant.

And now that she was out of danger he'd have to break the news to her. She wouldn't like what he had to tell her. Not the first bit—she'd been poisoned. Or the second part—the culprit had been discovered and punished. Or the third—and he'd come to a decision.

It was time. To bring her home, introduce her to his people, make her his. He wasn't sure if they'd accept her but he had to find out now, before it was too late.

Two days later, Tally stared at Tair uncomprehendingly after he broke the news. "We're going to your home? To meet your people," she repeated slowly. "But I thought this was your home, and these your people."

"This is just a military outpost."

"An outpost!"

"One of three strategic positions that protect our people and territory."

Tally struggled to sit up, her body still weak. Shaky. "You've kept me in a military outpost instead of your home because…?"

"I didn't know if I could trust you."

"And now you can?"

"Yes."

"Why? Because I survived being poisoned by the belladonna flower?"

Tair grimaced. "No. Because I've been through your photos. All five hundred of them. And you were right. They're all of children." He paused, looked chagrined. "They're good, too."

Tally put a hand to her head, touched her forehead as if checking the temperature. "I'm hallucinating. Dreaming. Right?"

"No. You're sitting up and your eyes are open. You're quite awake."

Tally slowly lay back down again, and closed her eyes. "You liked my photos."

"Yes."

"And that's why I'm going to your real home?"

"I know you're not a spy."

She pushed up on one elbow. "Then maybe instead of dragging me across the desert to another horrible place I don't want to go, why don't you let me return to town? I'd love to have my things back. I miss my clothes more than you know."

"You'll like my home."

"Tair."

"It's pleasant there."

"Tair."

"It's already decided. Conserve your strength for the trip."

Tally's eyes fluttered closed, even as it crossed her mind that she rather liked the fever and delirium better than this wretched return to reality. Tair had no intention of ever returning her to Baraka, did he? If he had his way she'd live in Ouaha forever, wouldn't she?

"I'll have to kill you," she said dully, filled with weary resignation. "It won't be easy, but it must be done."

The tent was silent and for a long moment Tally held her breath, waiting for his response. And then it came. He laughed softly. "Good luck."

Two more days passed before Tair announced that they would be leaving in the morning. "I know you aren't completely recovered—"

"I'm fine," she interrupted, cutting him short.

"—so you will travel with me, on my horse," he continued as though she'd never spoken. "It will be a long day, we'll leave early, but we shall reach Bur Juman before dusk."

"Bur Juman?"

"Home."

Tally blinked, confused. "I thought this was your home."

Tair's hard features shifted, his firm mouth easing into a faint mocking smile. "This was a test."

"A test?"

He shrugged nonchalantly. "Now you will see where I live."

Tair was right. It was a long day traveling, and sitting so close to Tair on his horse made her even more restless than her fevers and delirium. The constant motion of the horse shifted her back and forth against Tair until every nerve ending felt rubbed raw.

Just when Tally didn't think she could handle another moment of such intimate contact, something took shape on the horizon. It wasn't cloud or wind. Wasn't a sandstorm or anything sinister. It was a mountain.

"Is that where we're going?" Tally asked, turning to look at Tair.

"Just wait," he answered.

It was a long wait. Another hour or more of riding but the

mountain grew larger and little by little Tally could see that the mountain was actually a mammoth rock jutting from the earth.

Tair and his men rode toward the rock, and then around the base of the rock and where there was a narrow ravine, they nudged their horses forward.

"Where are we going?" Tally whispered, awed by the sheer size of the rock soaring above them.

"You'll see."

And then she did.

Tally leaned forward on the horse, craning her head to get a better look.

This, she thought awed, was more like it.

This was a secret world Westerners were rarely permitted to see, a fantasy world carved from desert and wind, storm and age.

Tally tried to hide her excitement as the mountain opened up before her eyes. Tair's home appeared to be carved from rock—right from the mountain itself.

There were rooms marked by windows, shutters and iron grillwork, and then there were terraces, balconies, patios and stairs everywhere. Wooden staircases, ladders, wide stone steps, curving stone staircases. It was a fantasy world that was also home. Incredible. Like Swiss Family Robinson but only better because it was real. And she was here.

She felt Tair's gaze rest on her, felt his hard, male amusement.

"You like it," he said.

She shrugged indifferently. "It's…interesting."

"You should learn to lie better. Especially if you're going to lie as often as you do."

Tally pressed the tip of her tongue to the back of her teeth, pressing hard enough to feel the seam between her teeth and the little ridges high near her gums. "Why hasn't anyone put a poisonous snake in your bed yet?" she asked sweetly.

"They've tried."

She snorted, part laughter, part exasperation. "Just how many times have people tried to kill you?"

He crossed his arms, half-closed his eyes, counting. "Ten. Fifteen. Something like that."

"Come on. I'm being serious."

"You're right. It's higher than that. Probably closer to twenty. But I try not to dwell on negative things."

Tally shot him a look of disbelief before seeing the smile in his eyes. It was amazing how he could do that. His face was rigid—marble-like—and yet his eyes were so fierce and alive. And lately those beautifully alive eyes had been smiling.

"I'm so not surprised," she teased as gates were opened and men appeared to take the horses.

Tair greeted those who'd come to welcome him and then turned back to Tally. "Are you tired? Do you need to sit?"

"I've been sitting for hours."

"Yes, well, you're a weak sickly woman—" he broke off with a grunt as Tally's elbow made contact with his ribs.

"I wasn't that sickly until I was poisoned."

"And the asthma?"

"You don't want another one of these, do you?" she asked, pointing to her elbow.

"Indeed not. It's a dangerous weapon. One you actually know how to use." He led her to a wide stone staircase. They took the steps slowly and Tair talked as they climbed.

"This is Bur Juman." His voice was toneless and yet she heard his pride, as well as possession. "It was my father's home, and his father's home before that. For one hundred years my family and our people have lived here."

"Bur Juman," he said, pausing at the top of the staircase, "means Pearl on the Other Side."

Tally immediately got the significance of the name. Pearl on the other side. This beautiful retreat of sun drenched stone patios and terraces was a world away from the dangerous desert they'd left, a world dominated by barbarians much like Tair.

And yet here, this was a world of beauty, of women, of jewelry and ornamentation. The women were all hennaed, draped in gold, gold bracelets, necklaces, earrings, gold everywhere. Even the air around the women smelled sweet, perfumed by some indefinable Arabic scent that she'd caught whiffs of in town but here the fragrance permeated the very air, rivaling even the cloying sweetness of lemon and orange blossoms.

Pearl on the other side. Yes, definitely and Tally felt almost overwhelmed by the sensual beauty of it, ensnared by mystery and that which was new, different, exotic.

It was even harder to fathom coming as she and Tair had from the Spartan conditions of the desert camp. The encampment had been eerily desolate, deprived of women, softness, comfort of any sort. There were the men, the animals—goats, horses, the one scrawny dog that followed Tair everywhere—but no families, no children, no cry of babies or murmur of elders talking.

"Your men," she said, comparing the encampment to this stunning city cut from the cliffs, "this is their real home, isn't it?"

Tair turned, looked at her. For a moment he didn't speak, then just when she thought he wouldn't answer, he said, "My men choose to live apart from their families part of each year to better protect them. It's a choice they make. I've never insisted or dictated. They do it because they know they must."

"You rotate the men?"

"Regularly. It is hard on them—on the wives and children, too—when they are gone. But this is life on the border.

"Thirsty?" he asked.

Tally nodded. "Very."

"We'll have tea in my orange garden," he said, gesturing up one gently curving staircase carved from the peach colored stone of the mountain. "There's a private room and bath off the garden. Your attending girl will be waiting for you there."

A private room? A bath? A garden? Tally felt like she'd died and gone to heaven. She nearly clapped her hands. "This is wonderful here. Really lovely. Now if I could only have my camera back with the film," she concluded wistfully.

"You can," Tair said. "I'll have both brought to you later tonight."

Tally spun to face him. "Are you serious? You're giving me my camera and all the pictures back?"

"Yes."

"I can take pictures again…pictures here?"

He nodded gravely. "Yes."

Tally nearly hugged him. "That's fantastic, absolutely fantastic. You don't know how happy you've made me. Thank you." She beamed, impulsively touched his arm. "Thank you."

"My pleasure."

She rocked back on her heels. "So you believe me now. You know I'm a photographer, and trustworthy."

"Tally—"

"I'd love to take pictures here. But if you don't want me to photograph the children, I understand. And even if you don't want me to photograph the children, I'll still send you copies of the photos I take when I'm home—"

"Tally."

His curt tone cut through her bubble of happiness. She broke off, looked at him, saw the shadows in his eyes and the fierce lines in his face. He looked like the old Tair, the one who was more monster than man. "What?"

"This is home now."

She stared at him not understanding. She tried to hang on to her smile but it wobbled, disappeared. "You said that about the camp, Tair."

He didn't answer.

Tally's mouth dried. She swallowed quickly. "You said you trusted me. You said you knew I was a photographer, and you liked my photos. You said they were good."

"They are."

"Then what do you mean this is home. Tell me what you mean by that."

"I mean, this is where you'll live now. This is your home now, here at Bur Juman, with me."

"No. You can't mean it. You can't." The words burst from Tally in an impassioned frenzy. "You might say you're a brutal, vengeful, violent man, but I don't see it. Your men adore you—"

"Please don't say my men and adore in the same sentence. It makes me extremely uncomfortable."

"The point is, you know your men care about you."

"You're confusing affection and respect. My men don't care about me. They fear me. Two significantly different things."

"And why would they fear you?"

"They know the facts."

Tair sighed inwardly as he saw Tally's expression harden. He was familiar with women's emotional tendencies, understood they valued connection and relationships over logic and accomplishment, but this one, this woman, defied logic altogether.

He'd kidnapped her from the medina. He'd dragged her across the desert. He was holding her against her will and fully intended to keep her here. What about those actions symbolized tenderness or kindness? Where was the empathy? The compassion?

"Do not think you can change me," he said tersely, irritated to even be having this conversation. He was not a conversational man. Tally should know that by now. She should know him by now. "Do not imagine you can somehow shape me into a better, kinder version of me. It will not happen."

"I've no desire to change you. The only thing I want is to get out of here. Go home."

"Which I'm not going to allow you to do."

"So, let me get this straight. You've no intention of becoming the least bit likable, and I've got to spend forever here, too?"

Tair nearly smiled. Finally she sounded properly horrified. Now this was conversation he liked. "Yes. Exactly. I will not change. I will never be likable. And you will never be returned to your people."

A small muscle jumped in her jaw, near her ear. Her expression subtly tensed. "You mean, I won't be returned until I agree to erase all the camera's memory."

Tair didn't reply immediately, too intent on studying her eyes, where the sunlight shone, reflecting glints of green and gray and brown. He loved the color of her eyes. They reminded him of the part of Europe he loved, the old forests and cool woodland glens, the river beds filled with polished pebbles against banks softened by violets and ferns. In her eyes he remembered swimming in sun dappled ponds and hiding inside hollowed tree stumps. He could smell the water, the sticky sap of trees, the softness of moss growing on the far side of trees.

He remembered his mother.

He remembered the boy.

He remembered innocence.

"If I give you all the disks now, let you erase them, destroy them, you will let me go." Tally's voice was firm but he heard the whisper of uncertainty. Suddenly she wasn't so sure. Suddenly she doubted him. Again.

As she should.

His gaze dropped from her eyes, over the satin cream and rose of her fine Western skin to her mouth. Her lips were full, wide, the color a dark-dusty pink which he'd thought initially was makeup, but knew now it was just the color of her skin.

Pink and cream, rose and ivory.

The color of his woman.

His woman. And he knew without a doubt what he'd suspected earlier. He'd never intended to return her, never planned to let her go back.

She was his woman. She was going to be his wife.

They'd been together long enough. It was a longer courtship than he'd had with his first wife.

It was time to make their relationship official. Time to announce that the foreigner would soon be his bride.

"Tair." Her tone was increasingly urgent. "I'll do it. Get my camera and memory cards now. Let's just do it. Destroy them and be done with it."

"No."

"No?"

He shrugged, increasingly comfortable. Easy now that he'd made his decision, or more correctly, recognized the decision he'd made when he first spotted Tally in the square. It was kismet, he understood now. Fate. He'd seen her and knew without understanding why, that he had to have her. She was supposed to be his. "You'll stay here with me."

"I won't, Tair, and you know me. I'll run."

He shrugged again, unruffled. "And I'll come find you."

Her head turned and she looked at him from the corner of her eye. "Don't do this," she said softly, the warning clear enough in her voice.

"It's already done. You're here. We're together. I shall announce our marriage—"

"Marriage?"

"You shall be my second wife."

"And your first?"

"Dead."

Her mouth opened, closed and she put fingertips to her forehead where everything seemed fuzzy. Heatstroke. That's what it was. She was suffering heatstroke. "I will never marry you."

"There's no real ceremony. Nothing you have to do—"

"That's not the point."

"—so I say the words, announce it to my people, and it is done. You are my wife."

"Your wife."

"It is not such a very big step. Everyone already knows you

are mine. We are merely making official what is widely assumed. That you are my woman."

Tally honestly thought she was going to faint.

If only she could faint. If only she could slide to the floor and not have to listen to another word. But maybe in her dead faint he'd wave his hand over her and do his hocus-pocus wedding ceremony and then she'd really truly be in trouble then.

No, she couldn't faint. She had to stay calm and find a way out of here. Marry Tair? Be a sheikh's bride? Never.

CHAPTER EIGHT

THEY didn't end up having tea, at least, not together. Tally was too upset and Tair wasn't in the mood to coddle her. It'd be so much more convenient if she knew who he was. If she understood his power. His name. His reputation.

His reputation.

Leaving his stables where he'd checked that all the horses had been properly seen to, Tair slowly ran his thumb across his jaw, rubbing slowly, thoughtfully over the squared chin.

Tally didn't know his reputation but she should. She should know the kind of man he was. She should know what he'd done, what he'd do, without the least bit of remorse.

He was proud of his nature, comfortable being the warrior. The aggressor.

Bandit. King. Thief. King.

His lips pressed as he inhaled, nostrils pinching.

He'd lived too long to be timid, suffered too much to be gentle, risked too much to be sympathetic. Perhaps there were other men in his tribe, future leaders who'd be more temperate—just—but that was not him.

He wasn't kind, or generous. Neither patient nor sensitive.

He stole. He demanded. He insisted. And that was the way it was. He was also a man who had vowed to protect Tally now she was his.

And his Tally would be wise to accept the truth, and facts, fast.

* * *

Exhausted from the trip, Tally had hoped she'd fall into bed and sleep one of those deep dreamless sleeps but no, sleep wouldn't come and she spent hours tossing and turning in her bedroom high in Tair's personal tower.

Rolling over onto her back, she punched her pillow behind her head and took a deep breath, trying to calm herself.

It wasn't that getting married or being a wife was so distasteful. It was the way Tair did everything. It was his highhandedness, his authority, his insensitivity. It was the fact that he *insisted* it be done.

First of all, marriage wasn't a solution. Tally had lived enough years to know that love and relationships were important, but marriage was more of a problem then a solution. Marriage meant compromise, loss, sacrifice, and maybe someday she'd be ready to settle down, scale back her aspirations, give up some dreams but she wasn't there yet. Wasn't ready. There was still so much she needed to see, so much she wanted to do. Tally knew she had it in her to be a good mother—someday.

Someday. As in five, ten years from now.

Impulsively Tally left her bed. She knew where Tair's room was. His room was just doors from hers, on the same floor. Slipping a silk robe over her nightgown she went there now.

Tally knocked softly. "Tair?"

He called for her to enter.

His lamp was on and he was stretched out on his bed, shirtless, reading the first of an enormous stack of newspapers. His room was considerably cooler than hers with the tall glass paned doors open to the night.

"Can't sleep," she said nervously, glancing at his thickly muscled chest, and the scars over his heart, before looking away. The scars troubled her. Made her afraid for him somehow. "Am I bothering you?"

"No," he said, folding the paper he was reading in half, watching her approach.

She moved round the side of the bed. There were no chairs near the bed, just two nightstands heaped with books and more books. She glanced at the spines of one stack of books. The titles were all different, most foreign and it was like viewing the entries in an international film festival—French, English, Arabic, Italian.

Tally picked up a book from his nightstand, studied the cover. *Theory of Economics: Supply and Demand in Agrarian Society.* "Nice, light reading," she noted, returning the book to top of the stack. "Are they all like this?"

"There's a comfortable mix of history, politics and economics."

She bit her lip, wondered how on earth to start. The beginning, yes, but what was the beginning?

"Something's on your mind," he said.

"Yes." She suddenly wasn't sure she could do this after all.

"So tell me what's on your mind." He set the paper aside. "Or let me guess. You're angry about the wedding plans. You don't want to marry me. And you've no intention of staying here and spending the rest of your life at Bur Juman. How's that?"

"Pretty good."

He patted the side of his bed. "Sit."

Tally sat on the foot of the bed, taking a seat as far from him as she could. "So you know why I can't do this."

His gaze met hers. "I know why you can't leave." His gaze never wavered. "Tally, you know too much about us."

"Too much?"

"You have seen where we live, and work. You have seen the most private aspects of our lives. I can not send you back now. I can not risk my people's safety."

"I'm no risk. Surely you can see for yourself. You are a leader. You must be able to read people. You must be able to see the truth. I am not a dangerous person. I'm a good person."

"But even good can turn to bad."

"Not me. If I'd gone bad, I would have been years ago. But

I've always done the right thing, the good thing. I love art, and nature, books and adventure, and more than anything peace."

Tair's cheek pulled, a grim hint of a smile. "Are you sure you're not a politician?"

Tally made a soft sound of protest. "I know this much—you wouldn't have saved me three times if I was a bad person. You risked your own life three times for me. That means something."

Tair didn't move, just his lashes lowered, and yet he seemed harder, tougher. "Maybe here you pose no threat, but if I send you back to Baraka…" His voice drifted off.

He seemed to think he'd conveyed something very important, something earth shattering but she didn't have a clue as to what it was. "How does it change in Baraka?"

"In the wrong hands, you would be dangerous."

He was just confusing her. "I don't understand what you mean about the wrong hands?"

"I have enemies, *laeela.* We have enemies and I work very hard to protect my people. The women, the elderly, the children."

"But I would never hurt them—"

"Of course you wouldn't. But the problem isn't your camera or the photos anymore. It's you. Your mind. Your memory. The pictures in your head. In the wrong hands, with enough pressure—coercion—you could reveal things that would cause us all great harm."

Tally turned away, went to the window where night cloaked Tair's walled mountain city. Earlier the sunset had painted the city red and pink before fading to violet but now it was dark and she could only see dim murky shapes.

Pressing her hand to her cheek, her palm felt so hot against her skin, her cheek cold, cold, cold like the rest of her. "I can not live here forever," she whispered. "I can not stay here. This would be death for me. This would be nothing short of prison."

She didn't hear him leave the bed but suddenly his hands

were on her shoulders. Firm, but not heavy, steady, but without pressure. "You do not know the meaning of death, then," he said nearly as quietly. "Bur Juman is not death. Even prison is not death. Death is death. Death is death and nothing else."

She felt her eyes burn, her throat ache as if swelling closed. "My life is spent traveling. I live in hotels. I never stay in the same place long, never spend more than a week in the same city. I just can't live another type of life anymore."

His hands fell away. "Maybe it is time you stayed in one place."

"No!" She faced him, turning swiftly, passionately, her insides hot, as if on fire. "I am not ready to stay put. I am not ready to give up my life, or my work."

"But you're not a child anymore. You're a woman. Thirty-one. It is time for you to have children. You must have babies before you are too old."

Tally nearly choked on her own tongue, words strangling inside her throat. "I have only just started my career. Everything is still so new. I refuse to end my life here!"

"Marrying me, having children is not ending your life. It's a beginning. A beginning at Bur Juman. A beginning with me."

And that, she thought, pulling away from him, was no beginning at all. "We barely like each other," she flashed, facing him.

"It's not necessary."

"Not necessary? You're talking about marriage."

"Wives don't need to like their husbands. They just need to obey."

Tally spun on her heel, clapped her hands on top of her head and walked the length of the room. This was ridiculous, the most ridiculous conversation she'd had yet, and she'd had many ridiculous conversations with Sheikh Tair lately, but this, oh, this took the cake.

Good God. Marry Tair? Live forever in his desert? Not just have his children but *obey* him?

Tally almost laughed, hysteria building. "You do not know me well, do you?" she spluttered, hands still on top of her head, fingers locked down against her scalp. It was that or let her panic spill out. "I am not the stay home and have babies kind of woman. I climb and run and swim and—" she broke off, dragged in air "—*not* have babies. And *not* obey." She looked at him, trying to make him understand. "I don't obey."

His eyebrows lifted and his lips pursed. "Not very well, no."

"Not at all." She exhaled again. "So save us both endless frustration and disappointment. Get me to the next big city and put me on an international flight home. I won't even stop to buy postcards. I'll just go. I'm out of here. I won't even look back—"

"Bur Juman is a beautiful place to live."

"For Berbers or Bedouin, or whatever you are."

His lips pinched. "I have much to teach you."

"But I don't want to be taught. I've had enough lessons from you, and my family, and everyone else who thinks they know what's best for me. But no one knows what's best for me but me."

Tair sighed deeply. Silence stretched between them, heavy and heavier. Tally's fingers knotted into her palms and silently she prayed, prayed he'd come to his senses and do what was right, do what he needed to do.

"Yes," he said at last, "it is going to be a very hard marriage. And I'm afraid, a very long life."

He joined her for breakfast on the stone terrace that adjoined her room. "Sabah-ul-kher," he greeted, taking the low stool across from her and reaching for one of the tangerines and then one of the pomegranate sections. "How did you sleep?"

Tally gave him a baleful look. "Not particularly well, thank you."

"You might want to take a rest later today. You're still on the weak side—"

"Tair—"

"My delicate little flower." His dark eyes flashed with amusement.

Tally marveled at the pleasure he derived from her misery. "Why are you so happy? You're like a different man now you're back in your palace."

He peeled the tangerine, bit into one bright orange wedge and offered her a piece. Tally shook her head. Tair ate another, wiped his hands and asked, "Do you have a preference for your robe for the wedding?"

He was serious about this. He was moving ahead with plans for a wedding. "You can't make me marry you. You can't."

"I can, actually. I'm a sheikh. You're part of my harem—"

"I'm not."

"Harem doesn't mean a dancing girl, Tally Woman. It means part of one's household."

"So I'm like cutlery or dish towels, is that it?"

"More or less." His mouth curved, eyes glinting, baiting her. "You know, marrying me is in your best interest."

"No, Tair, it's not. It's in your best interest."

And then he did what he always did. That horrible, arrogant, infuriating shrug. "So it is."

Tair looked up as the serving girl brought him hot coffee. He thanked her and the girl flushed, pink with pleasure. Tally groaned inwardly. Everybody loved Tair but her.

He turned his attention back to her. "You haven't given me your preferences for your robe for the ceremony yet. Surely you'd like to select that yourself."

"I didn't realize your attractive robes came in a number of different colors and designs," Tally answered with mock sweetness. "So far I've only seen basic black and basic white."

"There is a lovely shade of blue."

"Navy."

He tipped his head. "See."

"So you're asking if I'd like to be married in black, white, or blue?"

A muscle popped in his jaw. "Yes."

"Hmph." She couldn't believe how much he irritated her, infuriated her, couldn't believe he really thought they could marry, spend time together, much less time in bed!

At thirty-one she was no simpering virgin, but she'd never managed to look at sex as recreational activity, either. Sport was sport, and sex was well, private. Intimate. Sex was making love. And how was she supposed to make love with a man she didn't even respect?

Tally lifted her chin, forced a tight smile. "Surprise me. It will make the wedding day such a delight."

Tair suddenly reached for her wrist, fingers encircling her slender bones and he pulled her up, to her feet, and then around the table toward him. "You're such a feisty bride to be."

She tugged hard, resisting. "Because you're so not the groom I ever wanted."

He dropped her into his lap. "Why?"

His thumb was slowly, lazily drawing circles on the inside of her wrist. It was annoying. Distracting. Disturbing. Little forks of sensation raced through her arm, licks of fire and ice that tingled from her arm to her middle, curling hotly in her belly. Damn him. He couldn't arouse her. She wouldn't let him arouse her. She had no wish to be aroused by Tair of the Desert. He was horrible. Uncivilized. Barbaric.

"You know why," she said gruffly.

"Because I'm a sheikh?"

She growled a protest. *"No.* It's not cultural, or religious—it's you. You. You stole me, kidnapped me, imprisoned me. Why would I want to marry you?" Then she shuddered, shivering not from distaste but the unnerving things his touch was doing to her. He shouldn't be able to make her feel anything. She didn't like him. Didn't admire him. Didn't want him.

But oh, and she shivered again, a ripple of helpless response as his thumb stroked over and over that little sensitive pulse point on her wrist. Problem was, that little sensitive spot seemed to be growing. Her whole arm had come alive, her skin flushed, her body tensing in protest.

Delicious protest.

Tally's brows pulled, flattened. Damn him. How could she ever respect him if he didn't even let her respect herself? A man that broke down her defenses with touch—with pleasure—well, that was just wrong.

They should talk. Converse. Even play a game of chess. But touch? So brutally unfair.

"And if I hadn't kidnapped you? You'd like me then?"

She couldn't meet his eye. "Maybe."

"Woman, I think not," he scoffed.

Woman. She clenched her teeth. Why did he still call her that? He knew she hated it. He knew she hated his chauvinistic attitude, but did he change? No. Would he ever change? *No.*

"You're right," she fumed. "Even if I'd met you at a cocktail party at the Barakan Embassy I wouldn't like you. It's not political. It's personal, completely personal. You're everything I don't like in a man. Hard, mean-spirited, bullying."

She paused for breath before continuing. "A man should never try to dominate a woman and yet that's all you do. Dominate and push me around."

He leaned toward her, closing the distance so that she felt the warmth of his skin, the tension crackling between them. "I've saved you, too."

His mouth was so close, his lips just there above hers and she felt a sharp lance of pain, and it surprised her, the cut and twist in her chest and belly. Wrenched, that's how she felt. Wrenched.

"You were the one that put me in danger," she protested, voice hoarse. "It's only fair you saved me."

"I didn't put you in danger." He head dipped, his lips just missing hers to brush her cheek and then lightly touch the corner of her mouth. "You put yourself in danger by behaving in an emotional, impulsive, irrational manner."

She wanted to jerk away, wanted to pull back and escape but the feel of his mouth against her skin was so seductive it confused her, held her, made her want more.

How could she still hate him and yet feel so good when he touched her? How could her mind reject him and yet her body came up with a totally different assessment?

"You are bad," she whispered, voice thick, deep, tinged with a longing she couldn't reconcile herself to.

"You must like bad." He touched her face, fingers lightly stroking one cheek as his lips brushed the other.

"No."

"Mmmm."

She squeezed her eyes shut as silver streaks of sensation raced up and down her spine. "I'm good," she insisted.

She felt rather than heard him laugh softly, felt the rise and fall of his chest, the muffled humor. "So you keep saying."

She was just about to protest when his hands moved, and he cupped her jaw between his palms, holding her face up to him.

The air caught in Tally's throat and she stared up at him wide-eyed. This was as fantastic as it was awful and like a deer caught in headlights, she waited, waited, spellbound for disaster to hit.

And it did.

His head dropped, his lips covered hers and in that instant his mouth touched hers, she exhaled, resistance disappearing as she gave in to his warmth and scent and skin.

His kiss was again right, absolutely right, and maybe she couldn't marry him, and maybe she wouldn't live with him, but God, he knew how to kiss her. His kiss was amazing. She'd hoped it was just the first kiss that she responded to, hoped that having kissed him once, she would have become immune to him. But no, no immunity here. If anything it was even better.

Tally felt his arm slide around her waist and pull her against him and it was so right. Exciting and yet comforting.

It made her think, imagine, that somehow in his arms she was home. That somehow right now, like this, she'd found the only place she needed to be.

And like that, cold reality intruded, and Tally pulled abruptly away.

She stared at him accusingly, seeing him through hazy eyes. *"No."*

"No what?"

"No to everything." And yet inexplicably tears burned the back of her eyes. "No, you can't have me. No, I won't stay. No, I won't marry you. No."

He looked at her a long level moment than shrugged. "So it's a blue robe you want for the ceremony."

"Tair."

But he wasn't listening. He was lifting her off his lap and now he was standing. "I shall see what we can do."

"Tair!"

But he was walking, heading out the door. He didn't stop, turn, didn't respond. No, he just kept walking, leaving her alone with the memory of a kiss that burned and burned and burned some more. And it wasn't just her lips burning. It was her heart.

CHAPTER NINE

THE women want you to join them for coffee this morning. Tair's voice echoed in her head as she made her way from her suite of rooms to the rooftop on the far tower of the walled city, that tower officially designated as the women's space.

Tally hesitantly entered through the high arched doorway, the stone columns supporting the fancifully carved arch. She heard a chorus of voices down a corridor and followed the sound of the voices into a large chamber lined with low benches and vibrant silk pillows and cushions.

Everyone stopped talking and turned to look at Tally when she appeared. Tally hadn't been sure if she'd truly be welcome but as she shyly entered the room the circle of women beamed at Tally. "*Ahlen-wa-sehlan,*" one after another cried. *Welcome, welcome!*

They bustled about, finding space for Tally among them on the cushions on the floor. Flustered at the attention, Tally sank onto one of the cushions and made a show of arranging her robes, and pulling back the veil on her head so that her long hair spilled down one shoulder.

Beautiful, one woman said, while another reached forward to touch Tally's hair.

"Salaam," Tally greeted, nodding at one and all, trying to ignore the flurry of nerves. There was no reason to be so fearful, she told herself. They wouldn't bite.

But they won't approve, either, she thought darkly, knowing that for a man like Sheikh el-Tayer, a man with such great power, a suitable marriage was one with a woman from his own people, a woman from his tribe.

The women were all still beaming at her, waiting, and Tally's smile wobbled a little. What if she never did leave? What if she couldn't escape?

Her forehead furrowed as she scanned the eager, open, curious faces of the women gathered. Her gaze lighted on one of the youngest women, visibly pregnant.

What if this place truly became home? Nodding, smiling, she accepted a small cup of Turkish coffee. Could she ever be happy here? Could these women become friends?

She didn't know. Tally bit the inside of her lip, fought the wave of confusion, realizing the only thing she was sure of was that these ladies deserved some place nicer than a rooftop and cemetery for socializing.

She kept coming back to anger. She couldn't get away from it. No matter what she did, no matter how she tried to occupy herself, the anger snuck in and colored everything.

Maybe Tair could be good company. Maybe they even had moments that were surreal—gorgeous, sensual, seductive—but in the end, they were just moments and reality barged in, reminding Tally about truth. Honor. Justice. Never mind respect.

The truth was men couldn't kidnap women. The truth was a man couldn't hold another human being hostage. The truth was she couldn't respect a man who refused to let her make decisions for herself...indeed, who forced his decisions on her.

This is why she couldn't like Tair, and wouldn't like Tair, and wouldn't calm down and wouldn't play nice, and wouldn't be the good girl and do as she was told.

She couldn't.

There had to be a line that one didn't cross. There had to be morals. Principles. Values. Tair was about neither.

Tair was about Tair.

She harrumphed beneath her breath, temper hot, spiking. It seemed to always be up lately, always heated about something.

Tair's effect on her world.

Tair should be kidnapped, she silently groused, scooting lower in bed, tipping her head back against the bright silk cushions, staring up at the dark carved bed canopy that had been lined with silk the color of orange marmalade.

The orange silk made her hungry and marmalade made her think of toast and toast made her think of tea and toast and tea made her wish she were back in her own apartment in Pioneer Square with her own kitchen and her own groceries. She hated relying on others, depending on others, hated not being able to do what she wanted when she wanted it.

Like now. She wanted food, a snack, wanted to wander out and about and not be sent to her room simply because it was late, and dark, and all good women went to their rooms now.

Tally reached for a crimson cushion, the corners heavily embroidered with gold and crimson beads and nearly tossed it across the room, but at the last second, didn't throw it. Clung to it.

Why couldn't she go get a snack? She knew the general vicinity of the kitchen. Why couldn't she get something because she was hungry?

Pushing the pillow aside, she slid off the bed, dragged a dark outer robe over her delicate teal gown and left her room in search of food and drink.

She didn't get far before a robed man noticed her. He didn't stop her though. Nor speak to her. He watched her, then stepped back and she continued on, walking down one hall and stairs to another floor where she encountered another man—Tair's guards?—and then another. Each time the men let her continue, none of them disturbing her, none of them saying a word, or giving her a look of reproof. Tally soon found out why.

Tair had been alerted—probably by the very first man she'd passed in the upper hallway—and was waiting for her downstairs.

"Running away?" he asked mildly.

"Hungry." She shot him a swift glance. "Is that allowed, my lord?"

"Oh, if only that were the case." He held out a hand, gestured for her to follow him. "But let me see if we can get someone to prepare something for you. Should only take a moment to wake one of the cooks."

"I don't want to wake the cooks—"

"Yet you're hungry."

"I know, but I can help myself. I like doing things myself."

"I'm afraid our kitchens aren't like yours in America. You'd find it difficult to get anything prepared."

"How about simple tea and toast?"

"I'll have the cook—"

"Forget it," Tally sighed, turning away and pushing a hand through her hair, lifting it off the back of her neck. She was hot. Hungry. Grouchy. Tonight the heat hadn't abated and she didn't want Tair's company and what she really wanted—was something comforting. Something that would calm her, relax her, make her feel like herself again.

"I'll just go back to my room," she said unenthusiastically, turning to retrace her steps and head back to her room on the third floor of the tower that wrapped around the mountain and gave expansive views of the desert valley beyond.

Tair fell into step beside her. "What's wrong?"

She grimaced. "What do you think is wrong? I'm hot, and hungry—I'm not used to eating goat and goat and goat—and I've no books, and nothing to write with, and no camera to play with." They were climbing the first staircase, their slippered feet silent on the worn stone steps. She lifted her hair off her neck again, exhaled a little, blowing the wisp of hair off her brow. "I'm bored. And trapped. And really really hot."

Tair's eyebrows lifted. "And you're hot."

"Yes."

"Hungry and hot."

"Yes."

"And tired?"

"No. Not tired. Just bored."

"Restless."

"Exactly." She paused on the second landing, her hand on the banister. "Tonight I just feel like a…" She glanced around, at the thick walls, and the iron bars on the lower windows. She shook her head. "A caged cat. And I hate feeling this way. I've spent too much time out—exploring—to feel comfortable all cooped up."

His lips twisted and for the first time in days his expression was almost sympathetic; something had changed in him. "You sound like one of my men who has been here at Bur Juman too long." His jaw shifted ruefully. "I have certain men who can only be here so long before they go stir-crazy."

"Stir-crazy," she echoed before shaking her head. "You know all the oddest expressions."

"My English education."

Tally lifted her head to search his face, trying to see past the wall he kept up, the wall that hid his thoughts and emotions from everyone around him. "You never talk about your education in England."

"I know." He gestured toward the next set of stairs. "Shall we?"

Resigned, Tally set up the next flight, torches flickering soft gold and orange light. She glanced at Tair once, and then again, wanting to push him for more information. She was fascinated by this side of him, the Western mother, the Western education, but he said so little *she* didn't really know what he knew. How he felt. And that brought her back to the wall he maintained, the wall that kept him so mysterious as well as aloof.

Tally hated the wall. Hated it so much she vowed to break

it down. She'd know him. She would. Even if it was the last thing she did.

On the third floor Tally turned toward her room when Tair's hand touched the small of her back. "Not yet," he said, his deep voice, so rough in the way he spoke his English, even deeper, rougher in the hollowed tunnels of the castle Tair called home. "I've something spectacular to show you."

Curiosity piqued, Tally followed.

Tair led her to the door of his room and when she balked at the entrance, he smiled mockingly down at her. "And just what do you think I'm going to show you? A part of my anatomy?"

Heat surged to her cheeks and she rolled her eyes. "No."

"It is spectacular," he added, his dark eyes glinting wickedly, "but it's not why I've brought you here. You won't get that lesson until our wedding day."

"Which will be never," she muttered beneath her breath.

"Not so," he corrected, "but for tonight, let's focus on this—" He pushed open his door, took her hand and led her through his room to the set of glass doors across the way.

Tally expected to go through the doors to a balcony much like hers, a balcony with a view of the desert and the endless vista of moonlit sand, but his room had French doors on both sides of the room and while one set of doors opened on the desert, there was another set that opened to a private patio—a huge patio, a virtual walled garden that shimmered in the moonlight. Shimmered.

It was a pool. A pool carved from the stone, a pool that must have been like something in Eden. So natural, so real, so…cool.

Tally felt immediate relief and she looked up at Tair who was watching her, smiling his faint knowing smile and then she looked back to the water. "You have your own pool."

"I am the sheikh."

Tally stood just inside the doorway staring at the glistening water. My God, this was like the VIP rooms at the elite hotels and clubs. This was the life she'd never known, a life she didn't think existed, a life carved from rock and on the surface arid, so dry, but in truth nothing like that. Tair's world was more seductive, more erotic than anything she'd found in Seattle or the Pacific Northwest. Tair's world was…indulgent.

And Tally, deprived of indulgences, found it horribly, shamefully attractive.

You won't be bought, Tally, she sternly reminded herself. You have better morals. Remember your scruples. Remember that high road, that's the one you decided to take.

But really, the high road was less interesting than what lay before her. The high road was hot and difficult, rough and lonely and God—what she wouldn't give to plunge into the pool and just float there, cool, calm, comfortable.

"Can I swim?" she asked, laying an impulsive hand on Tair's arm. "I don't have a suit but it's dark out and you won't see—" She broke off, remembered herself. Remembered him. "Unless you have a suit for me?"

"Not readily, no."

"So your lady friends don't keep suits here?" she asked, knowing she was being arch and unable to help it. She was curious after all.

"No." He closed the French doors, so that they were alone in his walled garden with the pool reflecting the very nearly full moon.

"They swim naked?" she persisted.

Tair moved toward her, took the outer robe in his hand and drew it off, over her head and dropped the dark fabric in a puddle at her feet. His gaze lowered, lingered, taking in the fullness of her curves beneath the thin silk of her aqua gown. "They swim naked."

Naked.

Tally sucked in air, heat flooding her limbs yet again.

The man had a way with words.

Trying to hide her flurry of nerves, Tally moved away from

him, walking to the edge of the pool. She crouched at the side, reached in, touched the water. Not hot like a spa, nor cold. Just perfect.

Staring toward the bottom she tried to make out the depth of the pool and she couldn't see the bottom, not easily. It wasn't a shallow pool. And it wasn't small. It was a pool one could swim in, exercise in.

Tally stood, dipped a toe into the water, the hem of her gown trailing in the water, too.

"You're getting your robe wet," he said, watching her from the shadows.

She smiled. "I don't have a suit."

"And so what are you going to do?"

Her smile stretched and she felt suddenly, surprisingly carefree. My God. She was here, she was okay, she was—and just like that, she dove into the pool, a shallow dive, not deep, just in case the pool was more shallow than she thought, but the water was perfect, so cool, so refreshing and Tally surfaced and turned over on her back and smiled up at the sky. She hadn't felt so free ever before.

"Look at all the stars." It was such a beautiful night. Stars and stars—galaxies of them.

Tair joined her at the pool, sat down on one of the low chairs at the pool's edge. "Better?"

"Yes." She turned over onto her stomach and kicked her feet to stay afloat. "This is bliss."

"Bliss?" His black eyebrows arched. "You're easily pleased."

"No. But this is amazing, you have to admit." She turned in a circle, gazed around the courtyard formed by mountain and castle, and the sole palm tree that arched above the pool in its small allotment of dirt. "You have a pool in the middle of a mountain."

"A man's got to do what a man's got to do."

Tally laughed. Not a fake laugh, not one of her tense

laughs, but a big belly laugh and the sound poured out, filling the moonlit, star filled night.

"I've never seen you so happy," Tair said after a moment, watching Tally slowly swim one length of the pool and then another.

"I feel free," she answered, turning easily onto her back to float, head back, eyes riveted on the indigo sky above, the heavens blue-black in places and fluorescent in others. So much sky. So many stars. So much life still ahead of her.

Her hands fluttered at her sides, small strokes to keep her floating.

As a kid in North Bend she used to sit in her backyard and stare up at the sky and make wishes and dream, and vow to get the life she'd never had, the life she'd always wanted, all the adventure, all the drama, all the great moments denied because she wasn't pretty and wasn't clever and her family was poor.

"When I was little I wanted to be a princess," she said, water lapping at her ears, making her voice sound hollow and far away. "I used to count the stars and make promises to myself. Someday I'd be beautiful. And someday I'd be famous. And someday I'd be rich." She sat up, her arms and legs circling, keeping her upright in the water. "I really thought if I could just be a princess—marry Prince Albert of Monaco or even one of Princess Diana's sons—I'd be happy."

Tair's dark gaze followed her in the night. "And you still think becoming a princess would help?"

She laughed softly. "No. I don't want to be a princess, but I still want a lot. I still want virtually everything."

Tair sat in a chair at the side of the pool and watched Tally float, her skin pale, pearl-like in the light of the moon.

She'd bewitched him. She with her hellcat ways, temper and tears. So full of fire, her spirit never seemed to break and the fact that she hadn't bowed to him—that, too—he welcomed, wanting a woman not a doormat. No matter how much he teased her.

He needed a woman like Tally, a woman to stand up to him, be honest with him, give her opinions. He'd been feared by so many, and women either adored him or ran in abject terror. He craved neither pedestal or absolute authority. A relationship was what he wanted, needed, a relationship with a woman like Tally.

Tally reminded him of a past he no longer knew, a past where he'd been fun, carefree, easy. When he was sent to England at six for school, it'd never crossed his mind that he'd return years later sheikh and leader. He'd never wanted to lead. It hadn't been his dream, or his vision. He'd loved sports. He'd loved studies. He'd loved fun.

Fun. The corner of his mouth lifted, his gaze resting on shimmering Tally. She made him want to join her, made him want to shed his robe and responsibility and just let go. Let go of power and duty long enough to live. Long enough to feel. Long enough to let go of the pain of the past and the man he had become.

But no. That couldn't be. Horrific things happened in life and Tair had to be prepared for every possibility, had to be aware, alert, vigilant.

Tair's first lesson in reality was his father's death. Summoned from the university in Cambridge, Tair came home to a changed world. A world where the West was bad, evil. A world where his father had been killed by a superpower sharpshooter. The jittery soldier had assumed Tair's father, Sheikh Hassem el-Tayer, was dangerous, a threat, and pulled a trigger too quickly. The foreign governments and their military offered perfunctory apologies but apologies don't bring men back from the dead.

As if the death of Tair's father wasn't hard enough, there were the border wars and the endless bloodshed, senseless bloodshed in Tair's estimation. Why should Arab be pitted against Arab? Why Berber against Bedouin? Tair had fought to remain impartial—fair—until the war came home while he was in Baraka on business.

The war shouldn't have come home. Ara should have listened to him. Ara should have obeyed. But no, his Ara had been proud, fierce, beautiful and so sure she could handle anything life threw at her.

Pain flickered through him, orange spots before his eyes and he curled the fingers of his right hand into a fist. All these years and he still remembered, all these years he felt the same shock and despair.

If Ara hadn't opened the gates for the others…if Ara had just done what he'd always told her to do. If she'd listened, if she'd been less brave…

Tair's hand opened and clenched again, and as he clenched his fist, the muscles corded all the way up his arm, tightening, squeezing.

He missed them. He'd missed his wife and son more than he could admit, more than he could bear.

Zaki in his arms, Zaki dying, Zaki's blood running, spilling, no way to save the child he'd loved from the moment of conception in his mother's womb.

Tair closed his eyes. *My son, I have never forgotten you. My son, I will never forget.*

"Tair."

The soft voice, warm, tender, whispered to him and for a moment he could have sworn it was Ara. Ara speaking.

"Tair. What are you thinking?"

But of course it wasn't Ara. Ara was dead.

He opened his eyes, and even though he knew Ara was gone, he half expected to see her standing there, Ara his brave heart, his courageous foolish dead wife.

"Tair." Tally had climbed from the pool and she was naked, wet, shivering. "You're so far away. What are you thinking?"

Tair looked at her, slender, bare, beautiful woman and he

held out a hand to her and she came to him as if it were the most natural thing in the world. And maybe it was.

Tally felt Tair fold her to him and seconds ago she'd been cold, and yet in his arms she felt warm, nearly as warm as he was. Instinctively she lifted her face, wanting his kiss, needing his kiss, sensing that just maybe he needed her kiss, too. Men were so complicated and simple—male, hard, arrogant, but then tender on the inside with their profound need for a woman's touch. For a woman's love.

Hot tears burned the back of her eyes and a lump filled her throat as she felt Tair draw her closer, fitting her naked body to his. She ought to feel self-conscious, ought to feel strange with him but there was nothing strange in being held in his arms, or being close against his heart. He with his wounds across his chest had been wounded in other ways, and she didn't know what those wounds were but they mattered to her.

He mattered to her.

Maybe more than her own freedom.

CHAPTER TEN

WITH her still pressed to him, Tair began walking backward, leading her away from the pool and into his room.

As he walked, he kissed the side of her neck, just beneath her earlobe, and then worked his way down all the way to her collarbone. Hot forks of sensation raced through her and she couldn't suppress the shivers of pleasure.

She knew where he was going, seeing his great bed with the silk coverlet from the corner of her eye. "Is this wise?" she whispered, forced to cling to him, her legs weak as he kissed the rise of her collarbone and then the small hollow at her throat.

"Yes," he murmured against her skin, "very wise. I'm losing my patience with waiting to make you mine."

His deep rough voice hummed and vibrated through her. Her head spun, dizzy from her shallow breathing and yet she couldn't slow her pulse, her heart beating too hard and fast. Tally felt wild with desire and excitement. How was it possible to feel so much? She was exquisitely aware of his hands, his mouth, his warmth and frantically sucked in air as he cupped her breasts, letting the weight of them fill his hands.

There was something so seductive and yet so gratifying in his touch. She recognized him at a level that couldn't be explained. But she knew him in some deep primal part of her, knew him as a man, and her man. And yes, she thought, arms wrapping around his neck, her skin alive, body rippling, she was his. His.

Tally pressed closer, impatiently unbuttoning his shirt to kiss the warm spice-scented skin that stretched across his chest, the warm fragrant skin just above the scars. She'd never been bold with men but Tair made her brave, Tair made her want to seize all the life she could and make it hers, including sex, if not love. And opening his shirt wider, she touched her lips to the scars marring his chest thinking this is where she wanted him to want her, carry her, here in his heart.

His horrible awful barbarian heart.

The heart she wanted more than anything.

He lifted his head to look down into her eyes. "You know you're mine. You know there's no leaving me. This is where you belong. You know this now."

His words rushed over her, through her, even as his voice hummed in her veins and skin. It was hard to think clearly, hard to think of anything at all but getting closer, eliminating the last bit of distance between them. She needed him, not just his mouth and mind, but his body, his powerful fearsome body with the corded tendons and rippling strength, the biceps and quadriceps, the roping of muscle beneath bronzed warrior skin.

"I claim you," he added, hands sliding down her back to clasp her buttocks, and hold her firm against his hips where his erection pressed thick and hard against her belly. "Don't think you can change this. Don't think you can run away now."

Her eyes closed as she felt his fingers grasp her bottom, the pressure of his hands on her tender skin. His hands were warm and they made her feel hot and madly empty. She wanted those hands on her everywhere, wanted those hands to take her, and even take her apart like a tower of children's building blocks and then put her back together again.

"You won't run away," he insisted, hands moving between her legs, touching her lightly, intimately.

She shuddered and nodded blindly. Nothing he said registered. Everything he said registered. He'd become all, primal and sexual and male. Her male. The one that made her shiver and shudder. The one that had set loose this firestorm of need. As he touched and stroked she arched, breasts crushed against his chest, hips swaying to a silent tattoo of hunger, a hunger she desperately needed him to appease. "Yes," she choked.

"Yes, what?" he demanded, bending her back over his arm to look at her, see her, the woman he would soon possess as only he could possess.

"I won't run away," she said, voice husky, feeling her breasts tighten at the rush of cool air, her nipples ruche, peak.

Tair couldn't fail to notice her response and his gaze dropped appreciatively, resting on the ripe swell of her rose-tipped breasts.

Tally had been eyed by men before, but it had never felt like this. This was ownership, a claiming that burned all the way to her soul.

His dark head dipped, thick black hair hiding his face as his mouth touched her breast and then her nipple, his lips parting to take the aching peak into his mouth, against his tongue and teeth. He tugged at the sensitive flesh and she moaned deep in her throat as he licked, bit, teased until she was trembling, her nerves taut, tauter. She was melting and craving and needing and shuddering Tally pressed herself closer.

She needed him. Needed to appease that hollow feel inside of her, her body hot, and yet increasingly empty.

They'd reached his bed and Tair pushed her down on his bed cool and smooth with luxurious silk coverings. Tally reached for the front of his shirt and pulled him down to her, on her.

"But I want to look," he said, drawing back.

"Yes, but I want to feel," she answered, cupping the back of his head and bringing his face to hers. Her eyes closed as his lips covered hers, the sensation again electric. His kiss felt unlike any kiss she'd ever known before.

Tair stroked the length of her and when she couldn't stand the coiled tension inside her any longer she tugged at his robe, and then his trousers wanting him naked.

Lashes lowered, Tally watched Tair strip, her breath catching in her throat as all the clothes came off and he was even harder, prouder, more gorgeous than she'd expected. He was all muscle and sun-tarnished skin, smooth, cut, fiercely made. She'd seen men with gym-toned bodies but Tair's was shaped by life and battle, desert, wind and sun and she knew then she loved him, knew she loved him in a way she hadn't thought possible.

He was the man she'd been searching for. He was the love she'd looked for all these years.

Stinging tears filled her eyes and she blinked them away before Tair could see.

"Come to me," she whispered, reaching up to take his hand.

Tair's eyes were dark, nearly black and the expression in them scorched her.

He was all fire and danger and she was running straight into the flames. She was tugging him down to her and as he settled over her, he parted her thighs with his own. She muffled a groan as he explored the indentation of her waist and then the flare of her hips and over her hip bones to her flat belly. Every place he touched grew hot, while her insides felt wicked, liquid, hungry for him. Ready.

But Tair wouldn't be rushed. He seemed to delight in her body, in the curves and shapes, the softness of her skin, the pale globes of her breasts, the shadow between her thighs. And as he explored, he paid attention to each of her soft gasps, remembering what she liked, how she responded so that he could play her as if she were an instrument and his alone to enjoy.

Tally felt mad with all the sensation. No one had ever touched her like this, making her want at so many levels, making her body feel both familiar and strange. She'd never thought she was passionate, or physical but as Tair cupped her full breasts, his thumbs grazing her nipples, all self-consciousness fell away. She'd do anything for him, anything with him. Somehow he'd found a way into her heart and now her body wanted him, to be joined with him, now and forever.

He entered her with a smooth, hard thrust, confidence in the way he took her, confidence in the way he moved in her and Tally wrapped her arms around him, her heart and mind and body wanting him like she'd never wanted anyone.

An expert lover, Tair took her to the highest pinnacle of pleasure, driving her to the point of no return and beyond until she shattered in a thousand iridescent pieces, falling apart in his arms, held safely by him in great arms against a hard, muscular chest.

With her body still trembling she laced her fingers through his and held on. If only this moment could last forever. If only she could feel this way always…

Heart thudding, Tally pressed her cheek to his chest just above his heart. She could feel the scar tissue from his wounds against her cheek even as his powerful heart beat a steady rhythm against her ear.

All she wanted now was to hold him, touch him, remember. Remember not just him, but the way it felt to be held like this. Closing her eyes, she tried to memorize every muscle, imprinting his warmth and strength and scent in the deepest part of her.

"You are a very complicated woman." Tair's voice rumbled from him and idly he lifted a heavy strand of hair back and drew it from her face. "And yet when I hold you like this, you are so simple. You make perfect sense."

"I could say the same for you."

He suddenly lifted her, moving her higher on his body, up into his arms so that he could better see her face. "You're beautiful. I'll always marvel at the way you were put together." He grasped her jaw, lifted her face, studying it in the candlelight. "This jaw, the nose, the cheekbones, such wide clear eyes. Such clear intelligent eyes. You must know your beauty. The effect you have on men."

"I've no effect on men."

"No effect? You've turned my life upside down, Woman. I've chased after you across the desert far too many times to count—"

"Two actually."

"How you love to have the last word."

"No more than you do."

"There you go again."

Smiling, she clasped his face and kissed him deeply, giving him her heart not with words but actions. He had to know how she felt about him. He had to know that she couldn't imagine not being here, not being his. "Maybe just a little of what you say is true," she whispered against his mouth.

He laughed softly, the sound of deep rumble in his chest. "So you've finally come to your senses."

Tally loved the feel of his chest against her own and the way her legs tangled with his. If this is life this is all she wanted. To be loved and held. Kept. Savored. Treasured. "I think you've taken my senses, that's what I think."

Laughter rumbled through him again and the sound was alien and yet right. Tair should laugh more, she thought. Tair deserved more happiness and turning her head, she found his hand and kissed his palm. "Make love to me again." Her gaze lifted, her eyes met his and her lips curved slightly. "Please."

Tally spent the night in his bed, sleeping close to his side, his arm around her waist holding her firmly against him. He was warm and hard and she found it difficult to sleep with his big body so close to hers but it was a wonderful strangeness, the kind of strangeness that brought comfort. Peace.

Peace.

And holding that warmth and peace in her heart she finally closed her eyes and fell asleep. Life was good and life could only get better.

* * *

Tally's feeling of goodwill did not last long. When she woke she discovered that Tair was gone, and not just out of the bed gone, but gone gone. He and a number of his men had left for El Saroush and wouldn't be back for days. Maybe a week. *A week!*

Back in her room, Tally paced the room, her bare feet silent on the thick wool and cashmere rug. Why hadn't he told her he was leaving? He'd had plenty of time last night to update her with his schedule. Or did he think she wouldn't be interested? That she had so many friends and interests here at Bur Juman that she wouldn't notice he'd left?

Furious, simply furious, Tally marched across the room, alternately balling her hands and flexing them, trying so hard to contain her temper when all she wanted to do was let out a scream.

He'd brought her so far, taken her from what she'd known, made love to her and then left. Left and left her here, behind, alone without him?

He was a beast, an absolute beast and she hated him. She did. It wasn't love she felt, it was hate. There was no way she was going to love a man who didn't talk to her, communicate with her. She refused to love a man who would just come and go and expect her to stay behind, happily waiting.

Wrong. He was wrong, wrong, wrong and considering he had an English mother and education he should know that Western women don't just wait for a man. They don't just sit around and drink tea and wait for life to come, wait for life to happen.

A flutter of pink-gold caught her eyes. The breeze was blowing through the open French doors, lifting the delicate pink-gold sheer curtains hanging inside and Tally watched the petal-pink and gold sheers swirl, the gold starbursts in the sheer curtains catching, reflecting the fading sunlight. It was beautiful, the bursts of gold and pink, beautiful in a way that filled her heart with pain.

She felt so much her chest ached. It actually ached and Tally put a hand to her mouth to hold back the sadness swamping her.

Oh, she didn't like feeling this way. Didn't like feeling left, forgotten.

Fighting tears she spun on her heel, and her silky robes flared out. Tally could feel the delicate fabric brush her bare calves but the wispy caress of fabric maddened her, just as the tender aching in her chest infuriated her. She didn't want to feel. Not if feeling hurt. Not if feeling made her feel worse.

This is why she'd left home. This is why she'd become an adventurer, explorer. Far better to risk life and limb than sit captive, passive, then sit with hurt and heartbreak.

Tally reached the wall and turned sharply to retrace her steps. Come on, Tal, she said to herself, trying to be reasonable not emotional. He won't be gone a week. He'll be back soon. He will.

But it didn't help. And it wasn't that she couldn't go two days, or even five days, without his blasted company—God knows it'd be a relief not to have to endure his sarcasm and mocking smiles—but he should have told her. He should have communicated with her. He should have told her himself.

If he'd cared, he would have.

If he cared…

Tally stopped pacing, arms going slack, heart squeezing. Maybe that was what was driving her mad. She wanted him to care. She wanted him to care and he didn't.

Oh God. It was true. He'd never said he'd cared. He'd said he wanted her. He'd said he'd possess her and claim her. He'd said many things about ownership but never once about love.

Her lower lip trembled and she bit into it ruthlessly. What did you expect, Tally girl? It's one thing to care about your neighbors, and have feelings of goodwill for those around you, and those less fortunate than you, but to fall for a Berber sheikh? For a man that would rather kidnap women than meet them on an online dating service?

Numbly Tally sat down on the carved chest in front of the window and stared blindly out at a horizon she didn't see. What she saw was herself. What she saw was heartache.

What she saw was loneliness and pain. Men like Tair didn't want to be close to other people, least of all women. Men like Tair didn't share feelings and communicate emotions, or needs or dreams. No, they made decisions. They took action. But they didn't let anyone get close. Didn't become vulnerable.

Tally knew about men like Tair because Paolo, her Brazilian lover and friend, had been the same.

And look where that got him. Dead. Falling off Everest in one of his daring adventures.

Exhaling hard, Tally blew out a stream of air, and with a shaking hand pushed a long strand of hair back from her eyes. She'd fallen so hard for him, too.

She'd fallen just the way Paolo had and just like Paolo she had no safety line, no rope or anchor. She was just going down.

Her fingers curled, her stomach knotting the same way. What had she done? What had she been thinking? How could she have let down her guard, allowed him into her heart? Hadn't she been hurt before? Hadn't Paolo's death taught her anything?

Good grief, if she was going to fall in love again, why couldn't she fall for a nice, sensitive man who'd treat her like a princess, someone who'd put *her* first?

Maybe because she wasn't comfortable with touchy-feely men. Maybe because men who kept her at arm's length made her work for their love, made her feel as if she had to earn their love. Like her father.

After all, isn't that why she'd stayed home as long as she did? Wanting to prove to her dad that she was loyal? Loving? Good?

That she—of all the kids—respected him most. Loved him best.

Tally bit her tongue, gave her head a faint shake. Couldn't be. Couldn't be. That wasn't the case, wasn't the scenario at all. She stayed home, gave up her UCLA scholarship because she was needed, not because she had to be Daddy's girl.

Goddamn it, she wasn't Daddy's girl.

She blinked, her eyes suddenly burning, her chest feeling just as hot, her throat filled with the same gritty emotion. It would have been pointless to give up her college scholarship, her chance to play volleyball at a top ranked school for her father's love. That would have been stupid. She wasn't his favorite, not even close. Mandy was his girl. And the boys, they were his, too. But not asthmatic Tally with her serious brown hair and serious brown eyes and serious tortoise frame glasses she wore until she got contact lenses her sophomore year of high school.

Serious Tally—even as a killer athlete—was never Dad's girl. Not even when she did everything exactly right.

Tally reached out, grasped a handful of the silk curtain, crushing the sheer panel in her palm. How pointless it had been to do everything right. How pointless to have given up her dreams to try to make his come true.

If only she'd been bad. If only she'd been more selfish. If only she'd learned to be tougher, harder sooner.

Her fingers tightened convulsively around the fabric, squishing it into a smaller ball of silk. Feelings weren't good. Feelings, she knew, couldn't be trusted.

Just like now.

Tally drew a deep breath, held the air bottled inside her lungs until the burning sensation left her eyes, until her throat ached for another breath, until she knew she'd gotten a handle on the tumultuous feelings.

Okay. Finally she exhaled and rose. Whatever she felt wasn't going to influence her decisions. She was still going to leave here. Still going to have the adventures she wanted, adventures for one, not two. She wasn't going to let anyone interfere with her dream for herself—least of all a desert bandit sheikh named Tair.

On the second day, eager to pass the time as well as put Tair from her mind, she agreed to visit the bath house with the ladies. She had a milk bath, which seemed odd, but the women convinced her it was good for her skin.

On the third day of Tair's absence Tally permitted the ladies to henna her hands, her wrists and the soles of feet. It was a lengthy process but it took up one day and part of the next. The women giggled as the designs took shape and Tally had to admit she liked it. It was like getting a dramatic tattoo, but this one would eventually wear off.

That third night lying in bed Tally lifted one hand up, letting the moonlight illuminate the intricate patterns on her palms. It was really beautiful and she was glad she'd had it done. Even if she hated Tair.

Smile fading, Tally finally drifted off to sleep.

Tally's mood took another dramatic turn when she woke to discover that Tair had returned in the night.

Leena, Tally's attendant, brought the news along with the breakfast tray to Tally on her patio adjacent to her room. "His lordship is back," Leena said, arranging the plate and cup and small pot of Turkish coffee. "He arrived with many men last night."

Tally's heart jumped. She felt a thrill of pleasure which quickly faded as she remembered how angry she was. She wasn't going to have this kind of relationship with a man. She wouldn't be a woman that just sat around and waited to be noticed. Waited to be remembered.

"That's nice," Tally said striving to sound indifferent even as she added sugar to her coffee. She wasn't going to get excited about his return. She wasn't. But as she carried the small cup to her lips her hand shook and the coffee was tasteless in her mouth.

Food was just as bad. Blah, bland, might as well be cotton or sawdust. And yet she forced herself to eat, forced herself to act nonchalant despite the wild beating of her heart.

She wasn't entirely surprised when his shadow stretched on her sun-drenched patio. His huge shadow seemed nearly as big as that first day she met him in El Saroush. What a huge horrible man.

She'd never love him. She wouldn't.

"Good morning," Tair greeted, pulling a chair out but not immediately sitting.

She didn't know what he expected. A kiss? A warm tender embrace? *Hmph.* He certainly wasn't getting it. "You're back," she said coolly, somehow managing to hide her flurry of hope, hurt and nerves.

The corner of his mouth tugged and he sat down. "I didn't die, no."

Tally forced herself to take another bite of her sweet roll but it was nearly impossible to get it down, swallowing suddenly a skill she hadn't mastered.

"Everything all right?" he asked, accepting a coffee from Leena.

"Just dandy."

His lashes dropped, concealing his expression but not before Tally saw the gleam in his eyes. He was laughing. At her.

She clenched her jaw, anger building. Who was he to laugh at her?

Tair suddenly looked up, into her eyes. "What's wrong? You're fit to be tied."

She was. She was having a fit if nothing else. A fit of madness for ever agreeing to go to bed with someone who had to be the most arrogant man on earth.

"You look beautiful," he added kindly. "Absolutely radiant. Have you been visiting our baths?"

She glared at him. "Yes."

"Milk baths?"

Her glare deepened. "Yes."

"That's wonderful."

"Why?"

He shrugged, and then reaching out, he took her hands in his, first one and then the other. She jumped at the touch, hot sparks shooting madly from her palm through her wrist and up her arm.

Tair turned her hands over and looking at her palms, one black eyebrow lifted.

"What?" Tally demanded, immediately defensive. She didn't know why he did that to her, didn't know why she cared what he thought. His opinion didn't matter. What he thought was of no consequence.

"Nothing," he answered but she heard the mocking note in his voice, his tone indicating that he knew something she didn't—and whatever that something was, she wouldn't like it.

"I think the women did a lovely job," she said, still sharp, still defensive.

"Yes, they did."

"It's an art form."

"Yes, it is."

"So why the smirk?"

His upper lip curled. "I'm not smirking."

"You are."

He shook his head, lips twitching.

Tally tugged on her hands but he wouldn't release her. "Tell me."

His broad shoulders shrugged and a small muscle pulled in his jaw, his lips battling the smile that wanted to be there. "It's just that the design on your hands says something."

Tally's heart dropped into her stomach and she knew, she knew, what he was going to say next and he was right—she wouldn't like it one bit.

He took her wrists in his hands, and lifted one hand up, and then the other, as if reading them. "You, *laeela,* belong to me." He lifted both her hands and turned her palms toward her. "See, it says so here."

She curled her fingers into fists. "It doesn't." But she knew it did. Knew now that was why the women giggled as they dyed her hands, and why Tair had smiled that smirking smile of his.

Tally swallowed around the lump of anger. "Show me where it says that."

With the tip of his finger he traced one of the intricate designs. "This," he said, "is the Arabic symbol for love—"

Tally flung her head back even as she tried to break free of Tair's clasp. "Love?"

He shrugged, not releasing her. "I'm just reading what it says."

Tally balled her hands so he couldn't read anymore. "I'll make sure I get this stain scrubbed off immediately."

"It'll take a couple weeks…even scrubbing hard."

"Weeks," she repeated stonily.

"Usually months."

"Months."

"It's to last for the duration of our honeymoon."

Honeymoon! "There's no honeymoon."

"Not until we're married, no. But we will have a honeymoon. It's custom—"

"I don't care if it's the damn law. But we're not having one as we're not getting married."

"We are. Sorry. The papers have all been drawn."

"Undraw them."

"Can't. It's as good as done. Give up, you won't win this one."

CHAPTER ELEVEN

"YOU'RE not serious," Tally whispered.

Tair's dark eyes narrowed "Afraid so." He paused. "Where did you think I went?" he asked mildly, leaning back, letting her go free.

Tally wasted no time dragging her chair backward, defiantly moving away. "I haven't a clue and as I'm sure it has nothing to do with me, I don't want to know."

"Actually it had everything to do with you. I went to get the Mullah from town." Tair smiled—always a dangerous sign. "The judge. He's the one that will marry us."

"And what do I get for marrying you?" she mocked.

He extended his hands. "My name. My home."

"Which I don't want."

"My protection."

"Which I don't want, either."

"But which you need." He contemplated her rebellious expression for a long pensive moment. "You seemed eager to marry me four nights ago. Why the change?"

Color surged to her cheeks as she remembered their passionate night together. Sex with him had been so intense, so explosive. "It was a mistake. A moment's madness."

"A moment's madness," he repeated thoughtfully.

"Yes. And we can't marry. I won't get married, not in these circumstances, not when we have so many differences."

"Which are?"

"Everything."

"Name one."

"Religion," she said, holding up a finger.

"Name two."

"Politics."

"Name three."

"Disparities about gender and culture."

He leaned back in his chair, eyes narrowing, jaw jutting. "So that's it?" he asked, chin lifting and in the sunlight she could see the bristles of his beard, the gleaming texture of his golden skin, the lines at his mouth and she had to fight the impulse to lean forward and kiss that mouth. Her mouth. Her man. She clenched her hands in her lap, sick at heart.

She wanted him to say the words she needed, wanted him to give her the tenderness she craved. She needed him to love her. Love her.

Tally left the table, exhaled in a rush as she crossed the small patio with its pots of jasmine and citrus. The air smelled like perfume and sunlight patterned the creamy stone pavers in shades of silver and gold.

Tair's voice followed. "This is not Seattle or Bellevue or wherever you're from. This is the desert, a different world with different laws and rules. You are mine to protect, and I will protect you, whether you want it or not."

Tally turned and took a furious, frustrated step in his direction. "You can't make me do this—"

"I can. I can even say the vows for you, make the promises. You don't even have to come to the ceremony—although it'd be nice to see you there tomorrow—and we'd still be joined as husband and wife."

"As your property."

"Let's just use the word wife."

Tally shook her head frantically. She knew he was being deliberately provocative, baiting her, tormenting her. She knew he was angry with her less than enthusiastic welcome but she wasn't going to bend and she wouldn't break. "It appalls me that you would force me to marry you. It appalls me that you'd be so barbaric and heartless."

"You're not that appalled. You know me well enough now to know that I don't say one thing and do another. If I say I've claimed you, I've claimed you and twenty-four hours apart, or seventy-two, wouldn't change anything. You are mine and tomorrow we make it legal."

He could fix this. He could make this right, or at least make it better. He knew how to soothe her, comfort. But he wouldn't. He'd be a brute. He'd be insensitive and unfeeling.

"I won't marry you out of duty. If I married you, it'd only be out of love."

"And you don't love me."

Her eyes burned, her heart on fire. Did he love her? Did he feel that way for her? Was he taking her out of pride? To prove a point? To show that he'd conquered her?

"No, I don't," she choked, eyes gritty, throat sore as she tried to swallow around the lump filling it, blocking air.

Expression dark, dangerous, lethal, Tair rose from his chair. "Your right hand says you do love me."

"My right hand has been hennaed by a gaggle of giggling older women. My right hand knows not what it says—"

"I think it does."

"Well I know it does not."

He shrugged, supremely indifferent. "Then perhaps you could tell your right hand—along with your heart—that maybe it should learn to like me, if not love me, as we're about to have forever together."

"Forever."

"Eternity."

"I get the concept," she snapped, glaring at him, her pulse racing far too fast for her own good. With her heart thumping this hard she couldn't think straight, couldn't get control of her emotions, couldn't find the right words to argue. But she knew she must. She knew she couldn't let this happen, knew that if Tair said he intended to marry her tomorrow then he intended to marry her tomorrow. Even his jests were true. Everything he said, he did. Which so did not bode well.

Not for the future. Much less now.

Be logical, she ordered herself now. Say something intelligent, something that makes sense.

"Why me?" she cried, settling on the most obvious argument. "I don't like you, you don't like me, we're completely different culturally. Our values clash, our interests don't align. Why not marry a woman who wants to be with you instead of one determined to keep running away?"

"You're here."

"So are one hundred other women!"

"You need me—"

"I don't—"

"You do, but since you won't accept that argument then here's another." He walked toward her, one step and another, closing the distance with his silent catlike strides that made him king of the desert. He didn't stop walking until he stood just in front of her.

Tally had to lift her chin and look up, way up, to meet his dark eyes. Her breath caught in her throat as his gaze met hers and she felt consumed by him, consumed by a heat she couldn't explain. All she knew was that when he looked at her she felt her insides melt, felt her bones dissolve.

Like now.

Hot, so hot, and the corner of his mouth lifted and he knew the effect he had, and he loved it.

"I want you as my wife because I like the way you look." He smiled a little as if he knew how she'd take the words, appreciating how offended she'd be.

"I also like the way you kiss," he drawled. "And I very much like the way you taste."

Tally's stomach flipped. She tried to look away, but his gaze was too intense and she felt caught, trapped in his smoldering eyes, his desire there, revealed for her. He was keeping nothing hidden now.

"There are few women," he added, "that taste like you. And if I am to have a wife, I want one that I can kiss and lick and eat."

Tally's stomach flipped again, so high, so fast she shook. "You have a horrible sense of humor."

His lips pulled and white wolf teeth flashed. "None whatsoever," he agreed. His dark gaze settled on her mouth, and he cocked his head, drinking her in, making her lips feel full, swollen.

Tally's belly clenched and she knotted her hands, a silent protest at his expert seduction. It wasn't fair that he could just look at her, study her, say a few words and she'd feel this way. Feel this hot and anxious, this tight and unsatisfied, muscles snapping, pulse racing, temper flaring. It wasn't fair that he created so much tension in her and that she'd want him to relieve it. Want him to satisfy her. Appease the hunger, satiate the ache.

"You don't marry a woman just because she kisses good."

"Of course you do."

"Tair—"

"Come, think like a man. If you kiss like that, God, can you imagine what a delight you'll be in bed?" He forced her head back and his mouth descended, his lips covering her, overwhelming her, lips ruthlessly parting hers to plunder the softness and sweetness inside.

Tally grabbed at Tair's robe, clutching the fabric with every bit of her strength. She didn't want to want him, didn't want to feel like this, didn't want to give in but as he shaped her body to him, she could only feel and feel how much she craved him.

His hands slid down her body, molding her curves, lingering on her breasts before setting fire to her spine and hips. His lips found that electric spot on her neck and she felt her legs nearly buckle beneath her. But he didn't let her fall. He just took his time with her, breaking down her defenses, weakening her resolve with expert touch.

Shuddering she buried her face against his chest as his palm pressed against her pelvic bone and then down over her mound, cupping the warmth of her. He didn't press into her, but then he didn't need to. It was obvious to both of them she wanted him and for Tair that was victory enough.

"You are mine," he said, lifting his head, his dark eyes burning with the same heat and desire that filled her. "Your body knows it even if your mind refuses."

"It's a physical thing," she flashed, even as she struggled to clear her head, all her senses shaken, her legs weak.

"Fine. I'll take whatever I can get." He started to walk away but turned at the doorway. "For your information, it was a ceremonial bath you took two days ago, and the henna party yesterday? Another prewedding ritual. Here in Ouaha the bride is always painted before the ceremony." His expression hardened, features grim. "You might not want to be a bride, and might not feel like marrying me but the Mullah is here and you've been prepared."

He inclined his head once. "I'll see you in a couple of hours."

Tally sagged, clutched the wall behind her. Couple of hours? *Hours?* "We're getting married *today?*"

"Yes. Leena has your dress." His granitelike jaw shifted, upper lip curling. "It's not black, blue or white."

Tair was right. The dress, part traditional caftan and part Western evening gown, was a lovely golden beige silk trimmed in velvet green and studded with silver and jewels along the dramatic velvet neckline.

The dress wasn't snug or revealing and yet the sumptuous fabric and ornamentation made it elegant and the color suited Tally's coloring, turning her eyes a darker shade of green and heightening the cream in her complexion.

Leena wanted to do Tally's eyes and makeup, and while kohl rimmed eyes and a pale face might be tradition in Ouaha, Tally didn't want the make up. She wanted to be herself. Needed to be herself. Besides, she didn't trust her eyes not to tear and the last thing she wanted was streaks of black on her cheeks.

Wrists laden with wide gold bracelets, and a gold headpiece that held a pale ivory silk veil, Tally was led to the formal reception room downstairs in the main building.

She sat while Tair and the Mullah discussed the marriage contract. Finally it was time to begin the actual exchanging of the vows.

The Mullah looked at Tair. "Are you Zein Hassim el-Tayer?"

"I am," Tair answered.

The Mullah turned now to Tally. "Are you Talitha Elizabeth Devers?" he asked slowly in broken English.

"No."

"She is, your Honor," Tair answered, giving Tally a sharp look.

"I'm not, your Honor," she answered giving Tair an equally disapproving look. "My name isn't Talitha, it's Tallis. Tallis Elizabeth Devers." She looked back at Tair, her eyebrows lifting as if to say, *so there.*

The Mullah didn't look pleased with the interruption but continued on with the ceremony. "Are you, Tallis Elizabeth Devers, being coerced into this marriage?" his voice was stern as he fixed Tally with his hard gaze.

"Yes," she answered at the same moment Tair spoke.

"No," Tair said.

The Mullah looked up from his paperwork, his reading glasses low on his nose.

"Yes," Tally repeated.

"Sheikh el-Tayer?" The Mullah asked Tair for clarification.

"No," Tair answered. "She said no, she's not."

"No," Tally said, frustration growing. "I didn't say no—"

"So it's no?" the Mullah said, looking at Tally now.

"Yes, it's no—" she broke off, shook her head. "What are you asking?"

"Do you wish to marry Sheikh Zein el-Tayer? Or are you being coerced?"

Color stormed her cheeks. "Yes."

"Yes, you want to marry him."

"Yes, I'm being coerced."

"Good. You wish to marry him. Yes." The Mullah nodded, shuffled his paperwork. "Let it be done."

And that was that. It was done. Tally had become Sheikh Tair's wife.

There was a huge celebratory party afterward, a banquet of gigantic proportions but Tally didn't have the heart—much less stomach—to eat, especially not after Tair told her they'd sit in separate sections during the banquet and celebrations.

Sit in separate sections? He still didn't get who she was, still didn't understand that he'd swept her into something so alien from her world that she still felt dizzy. Not just dizzy, but scared.

How could she live here, like this? Yes, she loved him but she didn't understand him or his culture. She wanted the hearth and home she knew growing up. Not exclusion. Not seclusion.

As the crowd surged around them after the ceremony, the men pulling Tair one way and the women pulling her another, Tally managed to slip away, leaving the banquet to run up the stairs for the sanctuary of her own room.

Fighting tears, she hiked up her long dress, tucking it into the waistband of her skirt and paced. Trapped, that's what she was. Trapped.

There was nowhere for her to go. No one to help her. She was truly alone.

And standing on her terrace, tears in her eyes, she heard the music rise from below, the one-string rababa violin mixing with the dalouka, or big drums.

Soon there would be singing and dancing. Tair had said his men, armed with swords and whips, would perform the war dance called the Al Ardha.

Tears falling, Tally looked out over the desert with its sand and more sand. How could she feel so much and none of it be easy? How could she love and still be unhappy? Where was the comfort? Where was the peace?

"What have you done to your gown?" Tair's quiet voice sounded behind her.

Tally dashed away the tears, lifted her shoulders in a shrug.

"Your legs are bare," he said.

She heard the disapproval in his voice and his censure just made the hurt worse, the wound deeper, the need for freedom more fierce.

Tally leaned forward to smell one of the miniature orange trees in one of the patio's glazed pots. "You said I could dress as I liked in private."

"Yes, in private, but this isn't private. It's a garden where many in my household could see you."

"Your household is all downstairs celebrating."

"Pull your gown down," he said sharply, losing patience.

Tally turned from the small tree. It galled her that this was her wedding day and she met his gaze directly without flinching. "No." And she forced a small competitive smile. "Thank you."

He showed his white teeth. "Please."

"I like my gown this way. I feel freer. Lighter."

"More exposed."

Tally felt a glimmer of a smile in her eyes. "Exactly."

"It's not proper."

"I don't really care about proper."

"You are my wife."

"Under protest."

"But nonetheless, my wife."

"I wish you wouldn't keep repeating yourself."

"And I wish you'd do as you're told."

Fire and fury in her heart, Tally looked at him, held his gaze, and as he watched, she deliberately yanked her skirts ever higher. Her right eyebrow arched as if to say, what now?

A small muscle pulled in his cheek. "Do you really want to fight?"

"I want you to accept that I'm not, nor ever will be, the kind of woman you want as a wife."

"It's too late to get out of the marriage. It's done. We're husband and wife. And as my wife, you must please me."

Her left eyebrow rose. "I think you've got the wrong woman, Tair."

"It's your duty, wife."

Tally walked toward him and once she'd reached him, she lifted her face to his and she took her skirts in both hands and pulled them even higher.

In the back of her mind she knew this was silly and she was behaving foolishly. She knew the issue was ridiculous and her behavior childish but Tair's arrogant high-handed manner made her see red. Everything he asked of her, everything he demanded went against her sense of self, grating her self-respect. She'd pushed herself to become her own person, to forge her own identity separate from anyone else and yet what he asked of her—demanded—seemed to negate that person.

"Tair, you might have married me, but you didn't buy me. You don't own me and can't control me. I don't have to wear your clothes the way you want me to. I can wear clothes the way I want just as I can keep my own name, my own personality, my own identity."

"You're not going to win, wife."

"But I'm sure going to fight, husband."

Tair leaned forward, closing the distance between them but instead of reaching for her with his hands he lowered his head little by little until his mouth was just inches from her.

He didn't move again, just stood there, his lips nearly

touching hers, and she felt her muscles tighten, her stomach squeezing, air bottling in her lungs.

She could smell the subtle spicy fragrance he wore, and feel the warmth of his skin and she remembered far too well how his mouth felt on hers, how her lower back prickled and her heart raced and the intense pleasure pain.

"You should have married a Berber girl," she whispered, trying to ignore the hot and cold ripples beneath her skin and the fierce coil of desire in her belly. She didn't have to have him. She didn't need to be touched by him. She didn't want anything he had to offer.

She didn't.

Then his head dropped and he closed the distance, and covered her lips with his.

White-hot lightning whipped through her. Her eyes fluttered closed and she sucked in air as her pulse quickened then slowed.

God, he was horrible. The kiss was so light, so gentle, so persuasive that she found herself leaning toward him, wanting more. He knew already how she liked to be kissed.

Take me, she thought. Take me here.

Tair lifted his head, dark eyes knowing, aware. "Come with me," he said, and kissing her once more he tugged her skirts down until all the fabric fell in long elegant folds covering her legs. "Tonight we shall finish this fight, but now, wife, isn't the time."

But that night after all the guests had gone and Tair had swept Tally in his arms and carried her to his bed, she didn't want to fight. She just wanted him—heart, mind, body and soul.

Their lovemaking was far from tender. Tair took her, possessed her, with a carnal intensity and Tally responded with the same fierce hunger. He made her furious and yet he also made her burn and hurt, wanting him, needing him, needing to be loved by him.

His fingers locked with hers and he held her arms over her

head as his body surged into her, his hips relentlessly driving and yet she wanted it, wanted him, and wrapping her legs around his waist she welcomed his body, welcomed the wild passion of him.

She fell asleep in his arms, damp, exhausted, and only partly satisfied. Her dreams were vivid and intense, dreams of women singing and drums beating and the heavy sweet smell of attar, the uniquely Arabic perfume she'd first smelled in Atiq and now here. And then in her dreams shrouded men with swords and whips stormed her room, taking Tair, dragging Tair far from her.

Tally woke with a start, heart racing, hands flying out to brace a fall.

But she wasn't falling. She was still in bed.

She reached out to touch the bed and instead her palm brushed warm skin and solid muscle. And heart still pounding she remembered. She was still here, at Bur Juman with Tair.

With Tair.

Putting her head back down, she left her hand on his chest and looked at him in the dark for a long moment, emotions fierce, intense, everything breaking loose. Everything stronger than she ever thought she'd know, feel. She loved him. The horrible man. Her horrible man. And she loved him more than she thought she could ever love anyone.

Tally's lashes slowly drifted down, and she exhaled softly, painfully. She was still here with Tair.

Thank God.

CHAPTER TWELVE

IT WAS the morning after the wedding and Tair was of course nowhere to be found while Leena was in Tally's bedroom with her putting away all the new clothes Tair had ordered for his new bride.

Leena was very excited about Tally's new wardrobe but Tally could hardly bring herself to look at the myriad of new gowns and robes. Instead she stood at the window, looking out at the desert and wanting to go, just go. Not to necessarily leave Tair, but to leave here, leave the confinement and the women's quarters and the world that kept her in long dresses and veils and away from action. Adventure.

She missed action and adventure. Wistfully she looked at the sand dunes and the shimmer of sun on the undulating hills.

From here, the room in her tower, the sand was beautiful. Mystical. From here, she even missed the sandstorm and sand pit and her asthma attack.

Tair had saved her each time. He'd come to the rescue, riding hard and fast on his white and gray stallion. He'd saved her.

Tally bit her lip, trying to ignore the ache in her chest. The ache was different from yesterday's anger. Her dream last night had frightened her, made her realize how little control she had. Not just over Tair, but Paolo, her family, her father. Life was slippery, nearly as slippery as those grains of quicksand.

"I like you, Madame," Leena said unexpectedly.

Tally turned from the window, smiled. She was touched. "I like you, too. You're very good to me. I appreciate it."

Leena smoothed one of the gorgeous silk sheaths that rested on her lap. She'd been putting each gown carefully into the enormous carved trunk. "I wish I could be like you. Fierce and brave. Strong."

Tally pushed a heavily jeweled hand through her hair, the myriad of gold bangles on her wrist jingling. "I'm not that brave," she answered, moving to sit on the edge of her bed. No, she wasn't brave. She actually felt like a coward. She felt afraid. Afraid for her, afraid for Tair. It was only a dream—not a foreshadowing—but it unnerved her, leaving her tender on the inside, tender and fragile. "I think I just like fighting with his lordship."

The girl's smile dimpled from behind the sheer veil. "Because you love him."

"I don't love him."

"He loves you."

"He doesn't."

The girl shrugged. "Then why does he permit you to speak to him as you do? No one else could address Sheikh el-Tayer that way. But when you open your mouth, he listens."

"Maybe it's because I'm Western."

"He's had other foreign women and he's not allowed any of them to speak to him as you do."

Tally's eyes widened. What did Leena mean, other Western women here? But she wasn't going to ask, couldn't ask Leena, wasn't right. But Tally couldn't stay quiet. "He used to entertain here frequently?"

"Not entertain, no, but there have been…" And Leena's voice drifted off and her shoulders shrugged. "Not a harem, no, but you must understand, he is a sheikh and he has had many women."

"*Western* women?"

"French. British." Leena's forehead furrowed. "One Canadian."

Tally nearly slipped off the bed. "They were here?"

"Yes, Madame."

"And they left?" Tally pressed her knuckles against the silk coverlet on the bed. "The Sheikh allowed them to leave?"

"Of course, Madame." Leena looked at her uncertainly. "But why wouldn't he?"

"I'm just going to have a word with my husband the Sheikh."

"And your husband is here." Tair gestured to Leena that she should go. He waited for the door to close. "What do you need to speak to me about?"

Tally sat on the bed and looked up at her husband, a man that towered over other men, a man with huge shoulders and a chiseled jaw and a stomach that was nothing but a ripple of hard, carved muscle.

This man was her husband. This man. A *sheikh.* And so what did that make her?

She stared at him so long and hard it hurt. If she was Tair's woman what did it make her? And then it hit her.

She was the Sheikh's captive bride.

Tally nearly smiled at the wretched state of affairs. One day into her marriage and she was already lost. How on earth was this going to work?

"What did you want to ask me, Woman?" Tair's deep voice cut through her fog of misery.

She chewed on her inner lip trying to think of a way to ask him about what Leena had told her without divulging that it was Leena who had told her. Tally didn't want Leena punished for gossiping. And maybe it was only gossip. Maybe Leena didn't really know the truth…maybe it wasn't the way it seemed…

"You've had other women here, at Bur Juman." Tally's gaze searched his autocratic face with its regal brow and nose and the jaw that could only belong to a man like Tair. Hard, fixed, immobile. "Is that true?"

He hesitated, and his gaze examined her just as closely as she'd studied him. "I could play dumb."

"You could."

"But I won't insult your intelligence."

"Thank you."

"There have been other women here."

Tally swallowed, surprised at how much it hurt, the idea of Tair with other women. Of course he had to have had other women. He knew exactly what to do with a woman—at least in the bedroom—and while part of his skill might be natural talent, the rest of it…the timing, the ability to hold back, the knowledge of a woman's most sensitive zones…that was education. "European women? Americans? Canadians?"

The corner of his mouth tugged but he wasn't smiling. "Someone's been talking."

"And they all were your lovers?"

His dark head inclined and his gaze narrowed, creases fanning from his eyes. He suddenly looked wise, and weary. "Yes."

"Where are they now?"

"Gone."

"Dead?"

He laughed shortly, not at all amused. "I've never hurt a woman. I'm a man, maybe not honorable, but not violent with women."

She nearly rolled her eyes. "So you let them leave after they visited you here?"

"Of course."

Of course. She felt her own lips curve, a tremulous smile of recognition that she'd caught him in a lie. A deliberate mistruth, one that had allowed him to manipulate her. Trap her. Her insides knotted, cramping. "You told me I couldn't leave here, you said I knew too much about your life, that I carried all the pictures in my head…" Her voice drifted off and she just looked at him, waiting for the explanation or apology, for the facts that would clear this horrible misunderstanding up.

Let him be heroic. Let him be good. Let him be true. At least, true to her.

Let him care enough about her to do what was best for her.

But Tair didn't answer and appeared indifferent. Blasé.

Why had she even begun this? Why care about the truth, whatever the truth was? She searched his dark eyes again. "You didn't have to keep me here, did you?"

For a minute she didn't think he was going to answer. She thought he'd pull the silent routine but he surprised her by smiling faintly. "No," he said. "I didn't have to keep you here. I could have let you go. I just didn't want you to."

"You lied to me."

"Tricked you, too."

She shook her head sadly, hurt, so hurt she could barely keep her heartbreak from showing. "Why?"

"All's fair in love and war."

"And you're a man of war," she said bitterly. "Soussi el-Kebir."

His expression was mocking. "The big man of the desert."

Tally rose, headed for the patio, needing air, space, relief. As she headed through the arched doorway Tair's voice followed her.

"Has Leena packed your travel bag? We leave for our honeymoon in the next hour."

"Honeymoon? You've got to be joking. I don't want to go anywhere with you."

"I know. But the plans have already been made and I'm not about to disappoint my mother."

Tally turned to face him. "We're going to Atiq?"

"My mother is anxious to meet my new wife."

"Does she know you forced me into marriage? Does she know that you kidnapped me and lied to me and tricked me into being your wife?"

Tair's jaw shifted. "Yes."

"And what did she say?"

Deep grooves formed on either side of his mouth. "That I'm just like my father."

An hour later they'd left the walled safety of Bur Juman behind riding on horseback for the distant city of Atiq. It would be a two-day journey. Tonight they'd overnight close to the border then in the morning switch the horses for four-wheel drive vehicles. At midday after they reached Fez, they'd leave the cars for Tair's private jet.

Living in such a rugged, untouched part of the world had its pluses, as well as minuses and it was only when Tair needed to make the trip to Baraka's capital city that the remoteness of Ouaha troubled him.

As they rode, Tair kept a close eye on Tally, making sure her horse never slowed or wandered. He knew his men were riding on all sides but he wouldn't take any chances with her safety. Or her state of mind.

She was angry, very angry and he didn't blame her. Everything she'd said was true. Everything he'd done had been manipulative. The problem was, in her world what he'd done was wrong. Immoral. But in his world, he'd been sly, clever. He'd found the woman he wanted and taken her, made her his. In his world this was good. Successful.

She was right about their worlds being different and he at least had the advantage of knowing her world having a mother who was English and years in English boarding school. Now his mother had never returned to England after marrying his father—another successful kidnapping story—but she was also a spirited woman, beautiful, educated, proud.

Tair's first wife, Ara, was Barakan—a chieftain's daughter—but she and Tair's mother were like two peas in a pod. They'd been close, Ara becoming the daughter his mother never had. Then the slaughter in the desert and all their lives changed.

It was then his mother moved to Atiq, giving up her beloved Bur Juman for the relative safety—and anonymity—of Baraka's largest city.

She lived close to the Nuri's palace, in a compound of her own but with excellent security. The Sultan Malik Nuri and his wife Nicolette included Tair's mother in many government and social events. Between her teaching and her friends at the palace, his mother lived a full life. But he knew his mother missed Ara and desperately grieved for the grandchild she lost. Zaki had been her only grandchild and it was hard on his mother—a good, kind and loving woman—to have lost so many of those she loved.

Tair hoped Tally would like his mother. He knew his mother would love Tally. He also knew that his mother hoped for more grandchildren.

Tair glanced at Tally who rode not far from him, her back tall, head high, eyes straight forward. She was so furious with him, barely speaking to him, answering in monosyllables.

That would change once he had her alone later, in his bed. She'd be far warmer and more eager to talk then.

They reached El Saroush just before nightfall and Tally gave his men orders. Some were to inspect the city palace maintained by the el-Tayer family for the past two hundred years. Others were to see to the horses. Others were to keep watch during the first part of the night.

Tair showed Tally where her room would be and told her that dinner would be served shortly. He encouraged her to explore the interior gardens where the purple and mauve jacarandas were in full bloom but not to leave the palace's high walls and impenetrable iron gates.

Tally was happy to wander through the walled courtyards and fragrant gardens. After riding all day she was tired and sore and she found the gardens, now illuminated at night by ancient torches, beautiful as well as inviting.

The assault happened so fast Tally wasn't even sure what had happened until it was all over. In one of the gardens she'd bent over a fountain to see the intricate mosaic in the bottom of the pool when a man grabbed her from behind, covered her mouth and nose and pressed something sharp against her ribs.

It was like the morning she'd been kidnapped by Tair—one moment she was fine, intent on taking pictures, and the next she was in danger. She bit the hand covering her mouth only to be rewarded with a forearm against her throat, pressing tight.

"You make a sound and you will die," a rough voice muttered in her ear. "Understand?"

He spoke English, excellent English. In fact, she recognized the voice and accent. "Sadiq?" she asked, realizing it was her translator. The man who'd spent two weeks with her traveling from Atiq to El Saroush.

"Be quiet and you won't get hurt," he said.

Tally nodded, wincing as the knife blade was pressed harder against her side. She could feel it nick, cut, but she wasn't afraid, not as afraid as she should be. Tair had said the men she'd traveled with were Barakan rebels, zealots who refused to recognize Ouaha as an independent territory. *"Ash bhiti?* What do you want?" she whispered, speaking the simple Arabic she'd learned, and calmed by the knowledge that Tair would help her. Tair would save her. He always did.

"How many are with him?"

"With who?" she asked, deliberately playing dumb because she knew this was about Tair. It had to be about Tair.

The forearm against her throat tightened, bruising. "Don't be stupid."

She wouldn't tell him anything. "I'm afraid I don't understand."

Her captor didn't like her response and he increased the pressure on her throat, ruthlessly punishing, squeezing, cutting off her air. Tally's head swam. Little spots danced before her eyes and just as her knees started to buckle everything went dark.

When Tally came round she was no longer in the palace garden by the fountain and pool. She was in a plain room somewhere, hands and feet tied, tethered to a chair. It was dark in the room and even though the shutters at the windows were closed, she knew it had to be dark outside. In the desert sunlight always penetrated the shutters and blinds but the room was eerily dark, almost black, and Tally felt fear. But also calm.

Tair would come. Tair would find her. Tair would save her before it was too late.

It was a long night but she did sleep for a while and when she woke again light outlined the square windows and poked through cracks and holes in the weathered wood shutters.

Tally glanced around the room and discovered she wasn't alone, either.

"So you're awake," the man said.

It was a different man than last night, and blinking Tally stared at him, wondering where the other one had gone, wondering what would happen next.

"How is your throat?" the man asked. "Sore?"

She swallowed, her gaze holding his and nodded.

"Sadiq wasn't to hurt you. He's been punished."

Tally just continued to hold his gaze and looking at him, she made a point of pulling on her hands, showing him she was tied, showing him she didn't like it.

"It's for your safety," he said almost apologetically. "This way you will be protected."

"From whom?" Tally finally spoke, her voice, rough, bruised, but her words were bitter and they betrayed her anger. "I certainly wouldn't hurt myself. So who would hurt me?"

He didn't answer her question, he merely shrugged and offered her an affable smile. "I am Imran. I want to help you." He extended his hands, demonstrating his friendliness, trustworthiness. "Tell me where you want to go. I will personally see you there."

"Tell me what you want first."

"Details about Sheikh el-Tayer's home. His travels. Future plans." Imran paused. "Things of that nature."

"I don't know any of that. He doesn't talk to me—"

"You're his wife, aren't you?"

"Yes but he's Sheikh el-Tayer. He doesn't confide in women."

Imran regarded her steadily, his gaze unwavering. "We just want him. We don't want to hurt you."

But they would hurt her. They'd do anything they could to get to Tair.

Tair was in trouble.

And she, somehow, unwittingly, was going to make it worse for him. Because she knew Tair and he would come after her. He wouldn't leave her, not behind, not even to save himself. Her Tair would risk himself to save her.

And she had to do the same. Something to help Tair, to protect him. "And if I help you, you'll send me home? You'll let me go?"

Imran smiled. "I'll take you to the airport myself," he answered.

Yes, she thought, in a body bag. Because now she knew just who and what she was dealing with. And Tair had been right. They were lawless men. Men who'd do anything to further their cause.

"We're returning to the desert late tomorrow," she said. "Going back to his home at Bur Juman."

"You know the way there?"

"But of course. I've spent the past few weeks there."

"You can show us?"

"Yes."

"I hope so. Because if anything goes wrong, if you're trying to be clever, you'll pay. We'll make you suffer."

Tair took a deep, sharp breath, lungs expanding to allow the searing blade of pain to slice between his ribs, up toward his heart. Up to his ugly blackened, badly scarred heart.

He was livid. Beyond livid. He was close to violence.

His men hadn't protected the palace or Tally. His men had fallen asleep on the job. Just as he had.

It killed him. Tally kidnapped. Taken. And he not being prepared. He felt worse than an amateur. He felt like a failure.

But he knew where she was, he knew who had taken her, knew that Tally's hired escort had been working in conjunction with Ashraf who had poisoned her.

It was hard to trust anyone. Much less himself.

Remorse and recriminations would have to wait. He could inflict his damage later. First he needed Tally safe.

In the house where Tally was being held hostage, the door to the upstairs bedroom suddenly burst open and Tair was there, scooping her into his arms.

"Hania?" he asked, cutting the robes that bound her hands and feet. *Are you well?*

She nodded, slumped a little with fatigue against his chest, gulping in great breaths of air. As Tair walked out of the chamber she spotted a crumpled body in the hallway next to her door. She shuddered and looked away, not wanting to know if he was alive or dead, not wanting anything but to leave this godforsaken place.

Her arm wrapped around his neck. "I didn't hear you outside."

"I am very quiet."

"Thank you."

He made a rough inarticulate sound that she didn't understand but she felt his chest vibrate and his hold on her tightened.

She knew he'd protect her. He'd protect her no matter what.

He loves me in his way, she thought. He loves me the way he knows how and it was enough. "I knew you'd come," she whispered, a lump forming in her throat.

"Did you?"

She nodded, insides knotting, emotions strange and strained. She never wanted to care for him; never expected him to care for her. Love between two people such as they complicated everything. It wasn't the tidy romantic love of Western culture—the love captured in movies and popular bestsellers. Love here in the desert was hard, fierce, sacrificial.

Love here wasn't safe. Love in Ouaha was dangerous, nearly as dangerous as Tair himself.

"Put me down," she said as they reached the street and were circled by Tair's men. "I can walk."

Tair put Tally down, let her walk.

They were in trouble. *He* was in trouble. He couldn't do this. Couldn't make this work. Not like this, not when he felt the way he did these past forty-eight hours, the worst hours he'd known since discovering the slaughtered bodies of his wife and tiny son. Feeling what he'd felt, going where he'd gone—into an endless abyss, a place of such darkness that he could only describe it as absolute rage and despair—and it wasn't a place he could handle, wasn't a place that allowed him to be.

He couldn't be *Soussi el-Kebir,* or Sheikh el-Tayer, not with Tally here.

The marauding Barakan rebels were cowards and villains and they didn't just pillage and burn. They'd slaughtered the elderly, the women, the children. Ara and Zaki had been among the dead in the terrible bloodbath seven years ago. But seven years seemed like nothing when he remembered his terror as he returned from Atiq riding through the night, riding with heaven and hell in his heart, only to arrive home and hold his five-year-old as Zaki died.

Tair wouldn't let himself think much more than that.

But he knew, he knew in his black scarred heart, that he couldn't go through that loss again, and he couldn't think, lead, guide—not with Tally here. It was one thing to have a mistress. Another to have a beloved wife.

And Tally was his—she'd been his from the start—and she made him afraid, made him worry, made him a man.

But he couldn't risk being an ordinary man. Mortal. He had to remain a monster. Frankenstein-like in his inability to give, or feel.

Tally. His woman.

He'd have to send her back, send her home. Not to his home, but hers, that loft space she rented in downtown Seattle's historic district.

He felt Tally slip her hand into his as they approached the waiting armored cars. His jaw hardened and he didn't look at her, didn't let himself think or feel. Once his mind was made up, he never changed it.

There'd be no reasoning with him, no pleading or emotional protests. He'd seen too much, known too much, lost too much to be moved by talk or tears.

He'd already battled death, grief, sorrow on his own and it'd taught him that strength came from loss. Power came from fear. Courage from the absence of hope.

A woman's tears didn't move him. Not if it meant he'd save her life. If not his own.

CHAPTER THIRTEEN

"TAIR," Tally whispered.

His fingers tightened around hers. *"Iya?"* Yes.

There was a brief pause. "Are you mad at me?"

"La." No.

"Okay."

But Tally wasn't reassured and as they passed through Tair's men, armed with swords and guns to enter the four-wheel drive vehicle, Tally flashed back to the dream she'd had on her wedding night. The dream of the robed men carrying swords and whips and how they'd taken Tair from her.

But Tair wasn't gone, she reminded herself as the doors closed and Tair personally locked them. Tair was here. Everything would be fine.

But on the way to Fez nothing was fine. For the first hour Tair barely looked at her and didn't speak. Tally looked at Tair and worried.

He could say that he wasn't angry with her, but he was definitely upset. "I'm sorry," she finally ventured. "I'm sorry about what happened—"

"It's not your fault."

But somehow she knew it was. She knew they'd used her to try to get to Tair and she knew Tair had had to come rescue her. Again. "I wasn't going to take them to Bur Juman. I wouldn't have—"

"They kill women, Tally."

Tally bit her tongue, waited for whatever else it was that Tair had to say. But what she thought he'd say and what he did say were two different things.

"This isn't working." His voice was hard and sharp. It was the voice of a stranger. "It's time for you to return to America."

Blood surged to her cheeks—hurt, shock, humiliation but she didn't flinch, not outwardly. "I don't understand."

His dark gaze was eerily cold, hard, ice in the desert as he stared into her eyes. "Then listen to me. I'm telling you. I don't want you here."

"Here." She pounced on the word as if it were the rope that Tair had thrown her the day she was sinking in the sand pit. "You don't want me here. But you do want me."

"No." His expression grew harder if it were possible, the dark eyes crackling with ice and storm. "I don't want you. I've—" and he took a quick fast breath "—tired of you."

Tally's upper lip twitched, an involuntary reflex. Pain. Panic. Disbelief. He didn't mean it. He couldn't mean it. She was his. *She was his.* She'd been his since that first day in the desert… "Tair." Her voice was but a whisper, husky, pleading.

"I will see you to Atiq. Make sure you board the correct flight. We go today."

"Today?" Her head was spinning. She couldn't follow him, couldn't see how she'd gone from a night in his bed, an endless night of endless exquisite lovemaking. A night without words, a night of just touch, a night where the caress of his fingers and lips meant more than words ever could and yet now…now…

"Tair." Tally couldn't even look at him, couldn't bear to see so much ice and disdain in his eyes, not in those beautiful eyes she loved, not in that fierce face of his that had always gentled when he looked at her. But it wasn't gentling now. There was nothing gentle about him anymore.

But Tally wasn't ready to quit. She didn't know how to quit, hadn't perfected giving up. "I don't believe you. I don't. You're just mad about something. I must have done something—"

"No, Tally, it's not something you've done. It's me. This is about me. I'm...bored."

Bored.

Tally nearly choked, air strangling in her throat. Her face felt strange. Her skin hot, so hot it was going to peel off her face. "I've never bored you," she retorted fiercely. "Never."

"Well, I'm bored now."

"You're not. Maybe you realized you couldn't handle me. Maybe that's what you're feeling, but it's not boredom."

He stared at her with cold, dead eyes. "You can protest all you want, but I know what I want, know what I feel—"

"You, feel? When did you start to feel?"

"—and I'm done. Finished. I need something else. Something you can't give."

It was like a knife in her chest, plunging through her breastbone into her lungs. She couldn't breathe, couldn't get air, couldn't get anything in or out of her chest. It felt like he was killing her, destroying her. Acid tears sprung to her eyes and her throat ached, as she took a step backward and then another. "You were the one that insisted we marry. You were the one that pushed. You—"

"I was impulsive. Wrong. The marriage will be annulled."

"Annulled."

"It will take some paperwork, maybe some money changing hands, but within a few weeks you will be single again."

She reached for the ornate trunk in Tair's room to steady herself, needing something to give her courage. Strength. "You can say that, but we made vows. Promises. Promises I fully intend to keep."

"You're not in America. This isn't Hollywood," he continued coldly, ruthlessly, "this doesn't have a happy ending. This is life. Reality. I was wrong to think you could live here, be here. I was wrong to think you were the right woman for me.

You're too different. Too—" and he broke off, searching for the right word, "Difficult."

Tally just looked at him, unable to find words or her voice.

"I don't want everything to be a fight," he continued mercilessly. "I have men to fight with. You don't behave like a woman. Instead of letting me be the master, you're always trying to take over, take charge and I'm tired of it. Bored. Better to end it now before things get complicated." He nodded at her flat belly, knowing she'd just had her period, knowing she wasn't pregnant and obviously not wanting to take another chance. "Pack whatever you need. Your cameras and memory cards will of course be returned to you."

That afternoon they traveled in silence through the crowded streets, past small neighborhoods and walled estates, palm trees shocking green against whitewashed buildings and the cobalt blue sky.

Arriving at the private airport used exclusively by royalty and the wealthiest of the wealthy, Tair walked Tally from the limousine to the jet on the tarmac.

He moved to take her elbow to help her up the stairs but Tally shook him off. If he was sending her away he didn't need to be so damn helpful.

He entered the jet with her, checked to make sure everything was okay before putting her small knapsack on the cream and red wool carpet.

Fighting tears, Tally stared at the carpet, thinking even her khaki knapsack looked forlorn.

"You'll be home before you know it," Tair said. "Soon this will just seem like a bad dream."

She shook her head. She couldn't speak, couldn't make a single sound.

Tair leaned forward to kiss her goodbye but she stepped back, moving away. If he didn't want her, he couldn't kiss her, either.

"It just wasn't mean to be," he said.

"You don't love me?" she asked, finally finding the words even though they were horrible to say.

He was silent and then the answer came. "No."

Tally turned away so she wouldn't have to watch him leave. But as the airplane door closed Tally felt as if her heart was being ripped apart.

He didn't love her.

Four words, four little words but words with the power to cut. Crush. Break her.

Like he just did.

Tally couldn't even cry, not then, not during the flight that went on and on. Not while the taxi took her from Boeing Field's executive airport home. Not while she struggled to unlock the door of her apartment.

But once the door shut, once she turned on the lights and looked around the place she hadn't been in nearly six months her control shattered.

He didn't love her. He'd never loved her. It was just a bad mistake.

The first week she was back she didn't think, couldn't think, couldn't even function. Tally spent more time in bed than out of it. More time with her face buried in her pillow crying her eyes out than functioning like a normal human being but she couldn't function. Couldn't eat. Couldn't sleep. Could only cry as if her heart were breaking. And it was breaking. It was shattering into little pieces of nothing.

He was horrible, hateful. How could he have sent her home like this?

How could he care so little that he'd just toss her aside? Throw her away as though she were garbage. Refuse.

It'd been so long since she'd been rejected like this, so long since she'd felt so bad about herself.

She thought he had cared. Maybe not deeply, forever love, but enough. Enough. Enough to keep her, love her, make her his.

Stop this, she told herself, stop thinking, feeling—just stop.

Eyes swollen from crying, Tally rolled from bed, desperate to put an end to the hurt, and the tears, and the heartbreak.

Despite her misery, she forced herself out to buy groceries. A day later she made herself watch a movie on cable television. On the weekend she went for a walk despite the black clouds overhead, walking for hours through rain; along the wharf and the piers where the ferries arrived and departed, silently sailing like giant wedding cakes on the dramatic Puget Sound. She walked to keep the tears from coming and it worked. As long as she kept moving, she was fine.

Ten days after returning she picked up her camera and went out to shoot whatever inspiration came.

But then on day seventeen Tally developed her memory cards of film and flipped through a couple hundred shots before coming across the last picture she took in Ouaha. It was the shot from the medina, near the well when the gunfire rang out and everyone ducked and covered as Tair and his men rode like hell's fire down the streets, taking Tally with them.

Tally studied the print for a long moment, seeing the children she'd been focusing on and yet there in the background was a horse pawing the air.

Tair.

Tair.

And just like that she was back in Ouaha, back in his home of sand and stone, back with the endless nights and the blistering heat.

Tally closed her eyes, and crumpled the photo in her hand. She wouldn't remember. Wouldn't go there. And instead of letting herself remember anymore, she e-mailed her editor and the senior editor she worked with letting them know she had prints she'd be sending. And then she got into her darkroom and began developing her black and white shots the old-fashioned way, taking time with processing, blowing up some shots, cropping others, printing on the special thick acid free paper she favored.

Her editors e-mailed her back promptly. They wanted to

see the pictures. They were eager to see where she'd gone, what she'd been doing these past four months in Northern Africa and the Middle East.

Tally buried herself in work, finding solace in long hours and a devotion to her art. It was at night, and on the weekends, that the lost sensation returned, that feeling she'd been drawn and quartered. Disemboweled.

It was at night and on weekends she didn't know what to do with herself, at night and weekends when she found it strange being home. After nearly a year on the road she realized she'd become a true nomad. She knew she'd had an apartment but forgot what it looked like, felt like, and for those first two months back in Seattle she felt like a stranger in her own place.

It wasn't even Seattle that felt so strange. It was—and Tally couldn't believe this—being alone.

Alone. She, the girl who'd decided she preferred being alone, didn't like being alone anymore.

Tair had done this to her. Tair. But that didn't mean she had to cry over him anymore. She was done crying, done grieving. She'd wasted too much time as it was on a man who didn't love her. Wouldn't love her.

Tally was just about to head out to photograph Alki Beach when a courier arrived with a package from Baraka. She sat on the bottom step of her staircase to open the brown padded envelope. And then the velvet box inside.

Emerald fire glinted at her. It was an emerald and diamond necklace, the kind of necklace only royalty and celebrities could wear. There was a small card nestled in the white satin lining. Tair.

Tair. Terrible, horrible hateful Tair.

Hands shaking, Tally snapped the lid down. Thanks, Tair, but no thanks. She wasn't going to be keeping this.

There was just one problem. No one would take the necklace back. With its twelve plus carats of diamonds and emeralds and the delicate platinum setting, no insurance company wanted to touch a necklace that was valued at over a quarter million dollars. Especially as the Sheikh's address was the middle of the Sahara desert.

And suddenly Tally was angry all over again. Instead of blocking out the memories, they all came rushing back, one after the other and they didn't fade. She remembered it all, remembered everything. The kidnapping from town. The asthma attack. The sandstorm. The quicksand. The knife. The poison.

Then Bur Juman and the first night they made love.

Tally swallowed hard around the lump filling her throat. She wasn't going to cry. She wouldn't cry.

But oh those battles.

She'd thought in the beginning that she'd hate him forever, thought she'd never like him, much less understand him, but that had changed. How that had changed…

Tally sank into the cushions of her couch, the old suede sofa more comfortable than attractive and the cushions gave way, swallowing her up even as she brushed away a stray tear.

To hell with him. She didn't need him. She didn't need another person in her life that didn't want her, or appreciate her. She'd spent way too many years throwing herself away, not valuing herself. She wouldn't do it again. Not anymore. Which is why she wouldn't cry for herself, or feel sorry for herself, or have one single regret much less one sad thought. He wasn't worth it.

He wasn't.

Not even if he was her husband and the horrible man she'd fallen in love with.

Tally grabbed a pillow and punched it and punched again.

If only he wasn't so impossible.

And so good-looking.

And smart.

And amazing in bed.

Howling her frustration, Tally threw the pillow up, up at

the industrial ceiling shot with massive metal trusses and beams. "I hate you, Tair," she roared at the ceiling as the pillow came down at her. She caught it neatly and tossed it again. "I will hate you forever!"

Damn him.

They shouldn't have ever had fun together. Much less really good sex. One could forget a man that was bad company, a man that was rude, crude, boorish. But sexy? Mysterious? Powerful? Interesting? Tender?

Stop thinking about him, she told herself. Stop thinking about the desert, and the starlit nights. Stop thinking about his smelly goatskin tents and the acrid smell of smoke and the fire burning late into the night. Put all thoughts of soft silk pillows and handwoven rugs and the perfume of roses and orange blossoms out of mind. Pretend you never slept curved against Tair's side, his arm around you, your cheek against his chest. Pretend you never listened to his heartbeat. Pretend you don't know every scar on his face and torso. Pretend you didn't lie awake some nights and worry about him, worry about his foolish courage, his lack of fear, his inability to protect himself as long as someone else is in danger…

Tally caught the pillow again and clutched it to her chest.

He'd never put himself first, not when others are in danger.

As she'd been in danger.

Tally felt the prickle start inside her, in her chest, and then her throat, working from the inside out until her forehead had the same tingling and her heart beat faster, harder, beat with a strange sense of awareness, an awareness that hadn't been there until a moment ago. But now that the thought was there it wasn't going away…

And she didn't know what to think.

Could Tair have sent her away, not because he didn't love her, but because he did?

Goose bumps covered her arms, the fine little hairs standing and everything inside her seemed to be turning inward, listening. Listening to her heart.

Listening to instinct, because wasn't that what Tair had taught her? Not to listen to the voice of fear, but the voice of calm inside her? The voice of strength?

He didn't not care for her.

He did.

He did.

She jumped up from the sofa, crossed the floor in long jerky strides, arms folded over her chest and tears hot and cold burned her eyes.

It hit her. Hit her so hard. Tair sent her away because he didn't want her hurt. He sent her away because he was afraid he couldn't protect her. He sent her away because he couldn't bear to have her hurt.

My God.

Why hadn't she seen it before? Understood?

Tally stopped at the loft window overlooking the street. It was a Sunday afternoon and traffic was light. No football game at the Seahawks stadium, no crowds, summer tourists gone. Just late afternoon sun breaking through the bank of clouds, splinters of long gold light and the green and yellow trolley traveling between all-brick buildings.

Here she was, safe in Seattle, just the way Tair wanted. But how was he? Where was he? What was he doing?

Tally stood at the window a long time, long enough to watch the clouds clear and the sun set, and the gold and red colors of autumn give way to burnt-orange and purple of dusk.

When it was dark, the sun gone, sunlight replaced by street lamps, Tally knew what she had to do. Knew where she had to go. Knew it wouldn't be easy but she was Tair's woman and she had to be where he was. It wasn't an option. She had no choice.

Two long flights, one terrifying helicopter landing, and a camel ride later, Tally had to admit that things were going badly.

She'd only been back in Ouaha twenty-four hours and she'd already been robbed, and left for dead. Not an auspicious return. Not exactly the homecoming she'd envisioned. She'd imagined well…not this.

And this was sand. Just lots and lots of sand. And this time Tair didn't even know she was back. Tair didn't know she'd decided to return. There'd be no daring rescue now.

Tally exhaled, and pulled a strand of hair from her eyelashes and tried to get more comfortable on her shirt which was protecting her from the burning grains of sand.

This was not the place to be.

She was parched, so thirsty she'd begun to see mirages in the sand. Dancing girls. Swaying palm trees. Robed warriors with swords and whips.

And guns. Or more accurately, one gun.

Tally blinked, looked up against the dazzling sun, head aching from the heat. A man stood in front of her, armed, fierce. Hideous. She frowned irritably, lifting a hand to block the sun and erase the mirage. "If you're not real, go away."

She heard a sigh, a very long drawn-out exasperated sigh. The kind of sigh only a man who is very long-suffering can make. "I'm real, and I'm not going away."

Tally tried to leap up but she wobbled and nearly fell, courtesy dehydration and a nasty case of sunstroke.

With a muttered oath, Tair lifted her in his arms, dropped her on his horse and climbed into the saddle behind her. They rode for an hour or more—Tally couldn't tell, didn't even really care—and then they arrived to the most pitiful desert camp Tally had ever seen.

"This place is still pathetic," she said as Tair swung her out of the saddle and onto the ground.

"We didn't have time to pick flowers or hang new gingham curtains," Tair said, circling Tally's wrist with his hand and pulling her after him.

Tally spotted Tair's old Berber servant and went to lift a hand in friendly greeting. Tair shot her a hard look. "Don't," he snapped. "I'm not in the mood."

Once in his tent, with Tally sitting on cushions on the carpeted floor Tair demanded an answer. Only he didn't put it quite that nicely. His request came out more like, "What the hell are you doing here?"

She could be offended. She ought to be offended. But she knew Tair better. "I brought you something," she said, reaching into her bra and pulling out the warm and very extravagant necklace.

Tair took the glittering emerald and diamond necklace from her. "You came all this way to return jewelry?"

"Yes."

"What's wrong with the postal service?"

Outside Tair's tent the men had begun to lay the fire for dinner and the little three-legged dog came hopping along. Tally looked at the licks of red and gold flames, the flea-bitten dog and Tair's dark, fierce scowling face.

"I wanted to be sure it'd reach you," she answered.

He made a rough inarticulate sound. "I take it you're not fond of emeralds?"

"It's a beautiful necklace but I'm not going to accept a gift like that. It's absurd. You send me away—reject me, break my heart—and then give me a necklace worth a quarter of a million dollars?"

The corner of his mouth curved. "How do you know its value?"

"I had it appraised." She stared him down. "And no, courier companies won't accept a $250,000 necklace, not if the address happens to be in the middle of the Sahara."

She snorted. "Can you imagine me trying to give directions? Tell your driver it's four hours east of El Saroush by horseback, or six if traveling by camel. Somewhere you'll encounter a riverbed and then you take a left at the wadi. Another hour later, you'll pass a cluster of palm trees. That's where you take a right. And then sometime in the next hour—or hour and a half depending on how fast you're traveling—you'll veer north and hope to find the rock fortress."

He smiled. "Your distances are off but the landmarks are good."

She hardened herself to his wretched barbarian charm. His smile wouldn't work on her this time, nor his offhand compliment. She knew him too well. Knew exactly how he operated. Bluster, power, intimidation, and sex appeal. A deadly combination if she'd ever heard one.

"The point is, *Tair,* you can't send *ex-wives* gifts like that and not expect them to fly off the handle."

"You do seem angry."

"I'm furious."

"But you're always furious."

"Because you're always trying to pull a fast one on me!"

"And how did I do that this time?"

"The necklace. You're trying to buy me. You were using emeralds to ease your guilt. You send me a necklace, tell me to have a good life, and you think I'm going to go—ooh! A lovely necklace. That's wonderful. My husband doesn't want me, and he won't love me, but he's sent me some really pretty jewels!"

Tair shifted on his haunches. "Are you telling me it didn't work?"

"I'm telling you—" She broke off, stared at him, shook her head in disbelief. "You're such a liar and manipulator and—" Tally didn't even try to finish the sentence. Instead she crept forward, clasped Tair's face in her hands and kissed him deeply.

It was a long time before she ended the kiss. His mouth on hers was too electric and she'd missed him too much. But finally she had to get some control, finish making her point, and reluctantly she sat back to study him again. "You love me."

"I don't."

"You do." She hesitated, hating the whispers of insecurity. *"Tair."*

"What?" he asked innocently.

But before she could answer he reached out and gently

plucked a hair from her eyes, and then another from her cheek. He smoothed the thick strands back from her face, his hand infinitely gentle as he touched her. "I do."

Tally sat very still, the air bottled in her lungs. She couldn't look away from his dark eyes and hard jaw and the strange expression on his face. It was torment. Agony. "What's wrong?"

"Everything."

"But I'm here, Tair."

"Yes, I know, and I can't handle it, Tally. I can't bear it if anything should happen to you. I can lose my arms, my legs, my life—but I can't lose you."

"You won't."

"I could."

"Tair, I'm stronger than I look. I haven't had an asthma attack since the day we met."

His jaw gentled. He nearly smiled but then the darkness returned to his eyes and his pain was there, in his face. "I'm afraid for you. Afraid for you every single day you're here."

"I don't understand, Tair—"

"Ara died here. My wife—and my son. I held Zaki as he died, I held him and couldn't save him, and I can't do that again. I can't. It would kill me and where would my people be?"

"Tair."

"I thought I could protect you, Tally, but when you were taken from the garden, when they held you hostage I couldn't do anything for you—"

"But you did, you found me, you rescued me."

He shook his head. His dark eyes were shadowed with pain and suffering. "I was sure there'd be blood. I could see it all happening, what they could do to you. I was sure I would be too late." His jaw tensed and he swallowed even as he reached out to lightly trace the curve of her cheekbone and then her upper lip that bowed. "You are too beautiful, Tally.

I would rather live far from you and know you live, than have you here and know you suffer."

"But I suffer when I'm away from you, Tair."

His eyes narrowed. A small muscle pulled in his cheek. "Death is worse."

"But away from you is death, too."

He turned his head, looked away, thick black lashes fringing his eyes, concealing the sheen of tears. "It isn't right to risk so much. It is selfish of me—"

"It's selfish of you to send me away when I love you and want to be with you. It's selfish of you to tell me I must be a coward and afraid. It's not my nature to be fearful. It's my nature to risk, and to want change."

"Tally." His voice broke.

"Tair, don't fear for me. And don't make decisions for me. I know the risks. I know what's at stake but I'd rather have a month with you than a lifetime without."

He reached up to shove hair back from his face. "That's ridiculous," he answered gruffly.

She leaned forward and reached out to catch the single tear on his lashes and wipe it away. "But romantic."

"And foolish."

"And exciting."

"You'll be the death of me," he muttered, even as he turned to her and lifted her face between his hands. He studied her face for an endless moment, his dark gaze searching her eyes, searching for truth, searching for the answer that seemed to elude him.

"I like exciting, Tair," she whispered.

The corner of his mouth reluctantly tugged. "You're impossible."

"But you like that, too."

He bent his head, touched his mouth to her forehead and then her cheekbone and finally her mouth. "You're beautiful."

His smile wasn't entirely steady. "You're exactly perfect, Tally."

"You called me Tally."

"I know. What was I thinking?"

She scooted toward him, practically climbing into his lap. "I don't know. But just keep me, Tair. That's all I ask. Keep me close to you."

"I thought you were a wandering woman. Someone who couldn't stay in one place long."

She blinked hard, blinked to keep the tears from falling. He undid her. He, barbarian that he was, made her heart hurt and hope in ways she'd never thought possible. "That was before I met you."

"You're a changed woman, are you?"

"Mmmmm."

"What's that?"

She tried to avoid his searching gaze but he wasn't letting her evade him. Tally sighed exasperatedly. "Maybe not that changed."

"So why can you stay here with me?"

"Because you're the ultimate challenge. You're Mount Everest and the Amazon put together. How could I tire of you? I'll never completely understand you but—" She broke off, took a quick, deep breath. "But I promise I'll always try."

Creases fanned from his eyes. His fierce features were inexplicably gentle, and the warmth in his eyes tangible. He stroked her cheekbone, and then the curve of her mouth, her soft pouting upper lip, the full lower lip and then down to her chin. "I love you. And I need you. I'm lost—" He broke off, struggled with the words, then forced himself to finish, "Without you. Come home."

She moved the rest of the way into his arms. "I have."

The Sultan's Virgin Bride

SARAH MORGAN

Sarah Morgan trained as a nurse and has since worked in a variety of health-related jobs. Married to a gorgeous businessman, who still makes her knees knock, she spends most of her time trying to keep up with their two little boys, but manages to sneak off occasionally to indulge her passion for writing romance. Sarah loves outdoor life and is an enthusiastic skier and walker. Whatever she is doing, her head is full of new characters and she is addicted to happy endings.

Sarah Morgan's new novel,
***Bought: Destitute yet Defiant*, will be available**
from Mills & Boon® Modern™ in March 2010.

For Nicola Cornick,
whose books I love and whose friendship I value

CHAPTER ONE

EVERYTHING *was in place.*

Like a predator he lay in wait, his powerful body still and his eyes alert and watchful.

Remote and unapproachable, Sultan Tariq bin Omar al-Sharma lounged silently in his chair and surveyed the ballroom from the best table in the room. The arrogant tilt of his proud head and the cynical glint in his cold dark eyes were sufficient to keep people at a respectful distance. As an additional precaution, bodyguards hovered in the background, ready to apprehend anyone brave or foolish enough to approach.

Tariq ignored them in the same way that he ignored the stares of everyone in the room, accepting the attention with the bored indifference of someone who had been the object of interest and speculation since birth.

He was the most eligible bachelor in the world, relentlessly pursued by scores of hopeful women. A man of strength and power, hard and tough and almost indecently handsome.

In a room filled with powerful, successful men, Tariq was the ultimate catch and the buzz of interest built to fever pitch. Women cast covetous glances in his direction, each one indulging in her own personal fantasy about being the one to draw his eye because to do so would be the romantic equivalent of winning the lottery.

Ordinarily he might have exploited that appeal to ruthless advantage, but tonight he was interested in only one woman.

And so far she hadn't arrived.

Nothing about his powerful, athletic frame suggested that his presence in the room stemmed from anything other than a desire to patronize a high profile charity ball. His handsome, aristocratic face was devoid of expression, giving no hint that this evening was the culmination of months of meticulous planning.

For him, tonight was all about business.

He needed control of the Tyndall Pipeline Corporation. The construction of the pipeline was essential to the successful future of Tazkash—crucial for the security and prosperity of his people. He needed to pump oil across the desert. The project was economically, environmentally and financially viable. Everything was in place.

But Harrison Tyndall, Chief Executive Officer, wasn't playing ball. He wasn't even willing to negotiate. And Tariq knew the reason why.

The girl.

Farrah Tyndall.

Daddy's baby. Spoiled little rich girl. Party girl. 'It' girl. The girl who'd always had everything she wanted.

Except him.

Tariq's hard mouth curved into a smile. She *could* have had him, he recalled. But she hadn't liked his terms.

And Harrison Tyndall hadn't liked them either. Weeks of delicate negotiation between the state of Tazkash and the Tyndall Pipeline Corporation had broken down and there had been no further communication on the subject for five long years.

It was a sorry state of affairs, Tariq mused silently, when the wishes of a woman dictated the flow of business.

Seated at his elbow, Hasim Akbar, his Minister for Oil Exports, cleared his throat respectfully. 'Perhaps I should walk around the room, Your Excellency. See if the Tyndall girl has arrived yet.'

'She hasn't arrived.' Tariq spoke in a lazy drawl, his fluent, perfectly accented English the product of the most expensive education money could buy. 'If she were here, I would know.'

Hasim tapped his fingers on the table, unable to conceal his mounting anxiety. 'Then she is *extremely* late.'

Tariq gave a faint smile. 'Of course she is extremely late. To be on time or even slightly late would be a wasted opportunity.'

He had no doubt that Farrah Tyndall was currently loitering in the wings somewhere, poised to make her entrance as dramatic as possible. After all, wasn't socializing the entire focus of her shallow, pampered existence? Having spent all day with her hairdresser and her stylist, she would be more than ready to display the fruits of their labour. Living up to her mother's reputation. Farrah Tyndall was just like every other woman he'd ever had dealings with. She cared about nothing more important than shoes, hair and the state of her nails.

'It is getting late. Maybe she's here somewhere,' Hasim suggested nervously, 'but we just haven't noticed her.'

'Clearly you've never seen a picture of Farrah Tyndall.' Tariq turned his head, a slightly cynical inflection to his tone as he surveyed the man next to him. 'If you had, then you would know that being noticed is the one thing she does really, *really* well.'

'She is beautiful?'

'Sublime.' Tariq's gaze slid back to the head of the staircase. 'Farrah Tyndall can light up a room with one smile from her perfectly painted mouth. If she were already here then the men in the room would be glued to the spot and staring.'

As he had stared on that first day, standing on the beach at the desert camp of Nazaar.

Her beauty was enough to blind a man. *Enough to blind him to her truly shallow nature.*

But it wasn't her beauty or her personality that interested him now. For the past few months his staff had been discreetly buying every available share in the Tyndall Pipeline Corporation. Control was finally within his reach. All he needed to take over the company and guarantee the pipeline project was a further twenty per cent.

And Farrah Tyndall owned twenty per cent.

Hasim was breathing rapidly. 'I still think this plan is impossible.'

Tariq gave a slow smile, totally unperturbed. 'The challenge and stimulation of business comes from making the impossible possible,' he observed, his long fingers toying idly with the stem of his glass, 'and to find a solution where there appears to be none.'

'But if you carry out your plan then you will have to *marry* her—'

Confronted by that unpalatable truth, Tariq's fingers tightened on the glass. Despite his outward display of indifference, his internal reaction to the prospect of marriage bordered on the allergic. 'Only in the short term,' he drawled and Hasim's expression transformed from mild concern to one of extreme anxiety.

'You are seriously considering invoking the ancient law that allows you to divorce after forty days and forty nights?'

'Everything my wife owns, and I do mean *everything*,' Tariq inserted with silken emphasis, 'becomes mine on marriage. I want those shares but I have no wish to stay married.'

The plan was perfect. Masterly.

Hasim fiddled nervously with the cloth of his suit. 'To the best of my knowledge, that particular divorce law has not been applied for centuries.'

'And most people have forgotten its existence, which is clearly to our advantage.'

'It is an insult to a bride and her family, Your Excellency.' Hasim's voice was hoarse and Tariq lifted an ebony brow.

'How is it possible to insult a woman who thinks only of partying and possessions?' His tone was sardonic. 'If you're expecting me to feel sorry for Farrah Tyndall then you're wasting your time.'

'But what if she doesn't come tonight? *Everything* depends on the girl.' The Minister shifted on his chair, beads of sweat standing out on his brow as the prolonged wait started to affect his nerves.

By contrast Tariq, who had nerves of steel and had never doubted his own abilities, sat relaxed and confident, his gaze still focused on the sweep of stairs that led down into the ballroom. 'She will come. Her father is patron of this charity and she's never been one to miss a good party. You can safely leave the girl to me, Hasim.'

And even as he said the words she appeared at the top of the staircase.

Poised like a princess, her golden hair piled high on her head in a style no doubt selected in order to display her long slender neck to greatest advantage, the dress a sheath of glittering gold falling from neck to ankles and hugging a body that was nothing short of female perfection.

Clearly he'd been right in his assumption that she'd spent the entire afternoon at the hairdresser and with her stylist, Tariq thought with cold objectivity, his expert gaze sliding slowly down her body.

Which meant that her priorities hadn't changed at all in the five years since they'd last met.

But there were changes, he noticed, as he watched the way she drifted down the stairs with the effortless grace of a dancer. She carried herself differently. No longer the leggy teenager who had appeared slightly awkward and self-conscious, she'd developed poise and sophistication. She'd grown into her stunning looks.

The girl he'd once known had become a woman.

Although he was careful to betray nothing, he felt everything inside him tighten in a vicious attack of lust. Desire, hot and fierce, gripped his lean, athletic frame and, for a moment, he was sorely tempted to drag her from the ballroom and make use of the nearest available flat surface.

Which just went to prove, he thought grimly, that the male libido was no judge of character and completely disconnected from the brain.

Irritated by the violence of his own response to her, he watched in brooding silence as she weaved between tables, pausing occasionally to meet and greet. Her smile was an intriguing mix of allure and innocence and she used it well, captivating her male audience with the gentle curve of her lips and the teasing flash of her eyes.

She was an accomplished flirt. A woman of exceptional beauty who knew exactly how to use the gifts that nature had bestowed upon her to best advantage. And she used each gift to its full as she worked the room, shining brighter than any star as she moved towards her table with a group of friends.

Her table was next to his. He knew that because his instructions to his staff had been quite specific and, like a jungle cat lying in wait for its prey, Tariq remained still, poised for her to notice him.

The tension inside him rose and anticipation thrummed in his veins.

Any moment now…

She exchanged a few words with a passing male, who laughed and kissed her hand. Then she dropped her tiny bag on the table and turned, the smile still on her lips.

And saw him.

The colour drained from her beautiful face and the bright smile died instantly like a vibrant flame doused by cold water.

Something vulnerable flared in the depths of her amazing green eyes and, for a brief moment, the woman vanished and he saw the girl again.

She looked like someone who had sustained a severe shock and then she dragged her gaze away from his, closed her fingers over the back of the chair to steady herself and took several deep breaths.

Observing the effect his presence had on her with arrogant masculine satisfaction, Tariq reflected on the fact that his task was going to be every bit as easy as he'd imagined it would be.

Simple.

He watched as she straightened her narrow shoulders and let her hands fall from the chair that she'd used for support. Her eyes blank of expression, she looked at him, inclined her head gracefully in his direction and then turned back to her friends, nothing in her demeanour suggesting that he was anything other than the most casual of acquaintances.

Playing it cool.

His gaze lingered on the soft swell of her breasts and he reflected that, although he had a personal rule of never mixing business with pleasure, he had no objection to indulging in pleasure once the business was over. And, although his marriage to the Tyndall heiress was business, the wedding night would most *definitely* be his pleasure.

Forty days and forty nights of pleasure, to be exact. With a clear mental vision of how he intended to pass his limited time as a married man, Tariq gave a slow smile of anticipation.

It appeared as though this business deal would not be anything like the arduous task that he'd initially imagined.

Marriage had suddenly taken on an appeal that had previously escaped him.

* * *

She had to get away.

Farrah stood in a dark corner of the terrace overlooking the manicured grounds. The rain had long since stopped and the August night was warm and muggy, but she was shivering like a whippet. She ran her hands up and down her arms in an attempt to warm herself but it made no difference. The chill was deep inside her. If there had been any way of leaving without her absence being noted she would have done so because to stay in the same room as Tariq bin Omar al-Sharma was nothing short of agony.

She hadn't even known he was in the country.

Had she known, she would have stayed at home, she would have gone abroad, *she would have dug a hole and hidden*—anything other than risk finding herself face to face with him. Especially with no warning. No chance to prepare herself mentally for the anguish of seeing him again.

One glance from those exotic dark eyes and she'd turned into a schoolgirl again. An awkward, wide-eyed, besotted teenager, weighed down by more insecurities than she could count.

She hadn't been good enough for him.

He'd taken her fragile, fledgling self-confidence and ground it into the dust. Misery and humiliation mingled inside her and she wanted to curl up in a dark corner and hide herself away until she was sure he'd flown back to Tazkash.

People always said that you could leave your past behind, but what were you supposed to do when your past had his own fleet of private planes and could follow you anywhere?

Dinner had proved a long drawn out ordeal, an exercise in restraint and endurance, as she'd talked and laughed in a determined attempt not to reveal her distress to her companions. And all the time she'd been aware of him.

Fate had seated her with her back to him and yet it had made no difference. She'd been able to feel the power of his presence. *Feel his dark gaze burning into her back.* And in the end, unable to sit a moment longer, she'd made her excuses and slipped outside.

It was odd, she thought dully, that however much you changed yourself on the outside, the inside stayed the same. No matter how glossy the outside, inside lay all the old insecurities. Inside she was still the same gawky, awkward, overweight girl who didn't look right, wasn't interested in the right things and was a massive disappointment to her glamorous mother.

Memories of her mother intensified her misery and she lifted a shaking hand to her throbbing head. It had been six years since her mother's death, but the desperate desire to please, *to make her mother proud*, still lingered. She felt herself unravelling and suddenly she knew how Cinderella must have felt as the clock struck midnight. If she didn't escape then all would be revealed. People might catch a glimpse of the real Farrah Tyndall and she owed it to her mother's memory not to let that happen. *She needed to go home, where she could be herself, without witnesses.*

She heard laughter from the ballroom and then footsteps, a purposeful masculine tread, and she stiffened her shoulders, trying to make clear from her body language that she sought neither company nor conversation.

'It's unlike you to miss a party, Farrah.'

His voice came from behind her, deep, silky and unmistakably male, and everything in her tensed in response.

Once she'd loved his voice. She'd found his smooth, mellifluous tones both exotic and seductive.

She'd found everything about him exotic and seductive.

They called him the Desert Prince and the name had stuck, despite the fact that he'd been the ruler of Tazkash for the past four years and was now Sultan. And, Prince or Sultan, Tariq bin Omar al-Sharma was a brilliant businessman. Fearless and aggressive, as Crown Prince he'd transformed the fortunes of a small, insignificant state and turned Tazkash into a major player in the world markets. As Sultan he'd earned the respect of politicians and business institutions.

He spoke and people listened.

Now the sound of his voice transported her to the very edge of a panic attack.

Part of her wanted to ignore him, wanted to deny him the satisfaction of knowing that she even remembered him, and part of her wanted to turn and hurt him. *Hurt him as much as he had hurt her with his cruel rejection.*

Fortunately she'd been taught that it was best never to reveal one's true feelings and her tutor in that lesson had been Tariq himself. He was a man who revealed nothing. She was ruled by her emotions and he was ruled by his mind.

She'd shown. He'd mocked. She'd learned.

Remembering the harsh lesson, she turned slowly, determined to behave as if his presence meant nothing more than an unwarranted disturbance. They were as different as it was possible for two people to be. And he'd made it painfully clear that she didn't belong in his world.

'Your Highness.' Her voice was stiff and ferociously polite and she was careful not to look directly at him. *To look into those eyes was to risk falling and she had no intention of falling*. A glance behind him told her that they were alone on the terrace although she saw a bulky shadow in the doorway, which she took to be that of a bodyguard. They were never far from him, a constant reminder of his wealth and importance. 'I find it warm in the ballroom.'

'And yet you are shivering.' With an economy of movement that was so much a part of the man, he stepped closer and panic shot through her.

Her throat dried and her fingers tightened around her jewelled evening bag, although why, she had no idea. The richest, most eligible man in the world was hardly likely to be planning to steal her possessions. And anyway, she thought dully, he'd already stolen the only part of herself she'd ever valued. *Her heart.*

Determined to send him on his way, she glanced up and immediately regretted the impulse.

His shockingly handsome face was both familiar and alien. When she'd known him, at the beginning at least, she'd always seen humour and warmth behind the cool exterior that he chose to present to the world. It hadn't taken her long to realise that she'd seen what she wanted to see. Looking at him now, she saw nothing that wasn't tough and hard.

'Let's not play games, Your Excellency.' She was proud of herself for keeping her voice steady. *For behaving with restraint.* 'We find ourselves at the same event and that is an unhappy coincidence for both of us, but that certainly doesn't mean we have to spend time together. We have no need to pretend a friendship that we both know does not exist.'

He looked spectacular in a formal dinner jacket, she thought absently. As spectacular as he did dressed in more traditional robes. And she knew him to be equally comfortable in either. Tariq moved between cultures with the ease and confidence that others less skilled and adaptable could only envy.

He was *totally* out of her league and the fact that she'd once believed that they could have a future together was a humiliating reminder of just how naïve and foolish she'd been.

An expensive dress and a slick hairstyle didn't make her wife material as he'd once cruelly pointed out.

Tariq had never met her mother, which was a shame, she thought miserably, because they would have had plenty in common, most notably the belief that she didn't fit into the glittering society they both frequented.

It didn't matter, she told herself firmly as she felt a sudden rush of insecurity. She had her own life now and it was a life that she loved. A life that suited her. She'd learned to do the glossy stuff because it was expected of her, but that was only a small part of her existence.

And it wasn't the part she cared about. *Wasn't the part that she considered important.*

But that was something she had no intention of sharing with Tariq. Her brief relationship with him had taught her that being open and honest just led to pain and anguish. *And she'd learned to protect herself.*

Music poured through the open doors, indicating that the dancing had begun. Farrah knew that in half an hour the fashion show would be starting. The fashion show in which she'd been persuaded to take part. But how could she? How could she walk down that catwalk, knowing that he was in the audience?

She'd call Henry, the family chauffeur. Ask him to come and get her.

The best way to protect herself right now was to leave.

Having planned her escape, she made to step past him but he caught her arm, long strong fingers closing over her bare flesh in a silent command.

'This conversation is not finished. I have not given you permission to leave.'

She almost laughed. For Tariq, the use of power was second nature. He'd been born to command and did so readily. At the tender age of eighteen she'd been dazzled by that power. Hypnotized by his particular brand of potent sexuality. *Mesmerized by the man.*

Even now, with his hard masculine body blocking her escape, she felt the hot, hot sizzle of excitement flare inside her. *And ignored it.*

'I don't need your permission, Tariq.' Her eyes flashed a challenge and anger rose inside her. *Anger at herself for responding to a man who had hurt her.* 'I live my life the way

I choose to live it and fortunately it no longer includes you. This was a chance meeting which we'd both do well to forget.'

And she *was* going to forget it, she vowed dizzily, as she struggled to control the throb of her heart and the slow, delicious curl of awareness in her stomach.

These feelings weren't real. *They weren't what mattered.*

'Do you really think that our meeting tonight has anything to do with chance?' He was standing so close to her that she could feel the heat of his body burning through the shimmering fabric of her gold dress and, even as she fought against it, she felt her limbs weaken in an instinctive feminine response to his blatant masculinity. Even though she was wearing impossibly high heels, his height and the width of his shoulders ensured that he dominated her physically. Being this close was both torment and temptation and she felt a helpless rush of wild excitement that she was powerless to quash. *And she knew, from the sudden harshness of his breathing, that he was feeling it too.*

It had always been that way between them.

From that first day at the beach.

From their first kiss at the Caves of Zatua, deep in the desert.

It was the reason why she'd made such a total fool of herself. She'd been blinded by a physical attraction so powerful and shattering that it transcended common sense and cultural differences.

For a moment she stood, frozen into stillness by the strength of his presence. There was something intensely sexual about him. Something raw and untamed. *Something primitively male*. She'd sensed it from the first moment of meeting him and she felt it again now as she stood, trapped by her own uncontrollable response to him. Her nipples hardened and thrust against the fabric of her dress and something dark and dangerous uncurled low in her stomach and spread through her body.

And then sounds of laughter from the ballroom broke the sensual spell that had stifled her ability to think and move.

With a flash of mortification, she stepped away from him and reminded herself of the lessons she'd learned in the wild desert land of Tazkash. She'd learned that a deep enduring love combined with wild, ferocious, untamed passion wasn't always enough.

She'd learned that he was ruthless and cynical and that their personalities and expectations just didn't match.

'You expect me to believe that you engineered this?' She threw her head back and laughed. 'Tariq, you were at such pains to be rid of me five years ago that I know that cannot possibly be true. I was unsuitable, remember? You were ashamed of me.'

Just as her mother had been ashamed of her.

'You were young.' His tone was cool. 'I've watched you with interest over the years.'

Her eyes widened in shock. 'Watched me?'

'Of course.' He gave a wry smile. 'You're rarely out of the press. Designers fight to have you wear their clothes on the red carpet. If you wear a dress, then it sells.'

And how sad was that? Farrah mused, producing a false smile designed to indicate that such an 'accolade' mattered to her. In truth, the thought that people regarded her—her—as a fashion icon was as ridiculous as it was laughable. Almost as laughable as the idea that Tariq had noticed and cared.

He was a man who negotiated peace settlements and billion dollar oil deals. It was hard to believe that he could be genuinely interested in something as superficial as the contents of her wardrobe, but she'd long since resigned herself to the fact that her priorities seemed to be different from those of almost everyone else on the planet. She cared about different things.

But, thanks to her mother, she'd learned to stay quiet about her real interests. Had learned to play the game she was expected to play and she played it now, lifting her chin, hiding behind the image she'd created for herself. She watched his eyes narrow as he studied her expression.

'You've developed poise, Farrah. And elegance.'

And duplicity. She was the master of pretence. Concealing her frustration behind another smile, she wondered why it was that everyone was so obsessed with how she looked on the outside. Didn't *anyone* care about the person behind the glitter? Wasn't anyone interested in who she really was?

Memories, painful and hurtful, twisted inside her.

For a short blissful time she'd thought Tariq was interested. *She'd thought he cared.* But she'd been wrong.

And his rejection had been the final spur for her to reinvent herself. To finally become the woman her mother had always wanted her to be. *At least for part of the time.* For the rest of the time she led an entirely different life. The life she wanted to lead. A life that few knew about.

A life she had absolutely no intention of sharing with Tariq.

'I'm glad you approve,' she said smoothly, stepping aside so that she could walk past him. 'And now I need to go and—'

'You're not going anywhere.' Without hesitation, he caught her round the waist and jerked her towards him. She lifted a hand in an instinctive gesture of defense, but it was too late. Her body had felt the hard brush of his thighs and responded instantly.

She shook her head to clear the clouds of dizziness and sucked in a lungful of air but even that was a mistake because the air contained the delicious, erotic scent of him and the clouds around her brain just grew denser.

Struggling to find the control that she was so proud of, she held herself rigid in his arms. 'Why would you suddenly seek me out? I can hardly believe you find yourself short of female company.'

'I'm not short of female company.'

His cool statement shouldn't have caused pain but it did and she dragged her eyes away from her involuntary study of his dark jaw.

'Then go and concentrate your attentions on someone who's interested,' she suggested, squashing down memories of past humiliation. 'I'm not. And I want you to let me go.'

The tension between them was overwhelming. 'If you're not interested,' he said silkily, 'why is your heart pounding against mine?'

Farrah decided that if there was anything worse than feeling this way, it was knowing that he was aware of her reaction. 'I don't like being held against my will,' she said frostily, a flash of anger in her eyes as she looked at him. 'And I don't like the way you use power and control to get your own way. I don't respond to bullying.'

'You think I'm bullying you?' His tone was lethally soft, his mouth only a breath away from hers. 'That's strange, because I let go of you the moment you requested that I do so, but you haven't moved an inch, Farrah. Your body is still against mine. Why is that? I wonder.'

She gave a soft gasp and stepped back, realising that he was telling the truth. He was no longer holding her.

'I think what holds us together is sexual chemistry,' he murmured, a self-satisfied look in his eyes as he lifted a hand to her flushed cheek, 'the way it always did. Which proves I was right to seek you out.'

From somewhere, she found her voice. 'Why would you

do that? What possible reason could you have for seeking me out?'

A man like Tariq did nothing on impulse. His schedule was punishing. Every moment of his day was planned in minute detail. Even when they'd been together, she'd had problems getting to see him. It was extremely unlikely that he would have been at an event like this without a purpose.

Was she that purpose? And if so, why? What did she have that he could possibly want?

There was a brief silence while he studied her beneath distractingly thick dark lashes. 'Five years is a long time. You were young and impulsive. You had no knowledge of my country or culture. It was, perhaps, inevitable that there would be problems between us. Misunderstandings.'

The injustice of his remarks stung her and her spine stiffened.

She'd been young, yes. A few weeks past her eighteenth birthday. Impulsive? Probably. But she'd also been ruthlessly manipulated by those around him, *those who professed to be close to him*. She'd been well and truly flattened by palace politics.

'I don't want to talk about the past and I'm not interested in your opinion, Tariq.' Her voice was flat. 'It was a long time ago and we've both moved on.'

'I don't think so.' His eyes, dark as night, slid down her slender frame and he reached out and lifted her right hand. 'You still wear my ring.'

The ring.

With something approaching horror her gaze slid to the sparkling dramatic stone. The ring had been the embodiment of all her girlish dreams and even when their relationship had fallen apart she hadn't been able to bring herself to take it off.

Cursing herself for being so sentimental, she snatched her hand away from his. The ring was exquisitely beautiful. A diamond so rare and perfect that she'd fallen in love with it on sight. *As she had with the man who had given it to her.* 'Actually, Tariq, I wear it to remind me that men bearing extravagant gifts are not to be trusted.'

An indulgent smile spread across his bronzed features. 'Fool yourself if you wish, *laeela*, but not me. Strong feelings are not so easily extinguished. There are some things that remain unaffected by the passage of time.'

Like pain, she thought dully.

'Just go, Tariq.' Her heart was beating frantically and the shivering started up again. 'If you want closure for what happened between us, then you have it. But go, and leave me alone to live my life.' She was fine, she told herself firmly. Really, she was absolutely fine.

'Closure. Such an American word.' He looked at her thoughtfully. 'You should not walk around in the night air, half undressed. You will catch a chill.'

Before she could anticipate his intention, he shrugged his shoulders out of his jacket and draped it around her bare shoulders.

Once again she was enveloped by the familiar masculine scent and her senses swam.

He leaned closer to her, his breath warm on her cheek. 'I did not come here to seek closure, Farrah. That is not the reason that I'm here tonight.' His voice was a soft, seductive purr and she flattened herself against the cold, hard stone of the balcony that skirted the terrace.

'Then why are you here? Can we get to the point so that I can go back into the ballroom?' He was standing too close to her. She felt stifled. Suffocated. And she didn't want to wear the jacket. It was too intimate. Too much a part of him.

But, before she could remove it, he closed in on her, the width of his shoulders ensuring that he was the focus of her gaze. She could no longer see the ballroom or the bodyguard.

She could no longer see the terrace. All she could see was glittering dark eyes and a hard, sensual mouth that knew how to drive a woman to distraction. And she'd forgotten about the jacket.

'Tariq—' His name was a plea on her lips and his own mouth curved slightly in acknowledgment of that plea. He could see everything, she thought desperately. He *knew* everything. Her thoughts. Her feelings. *The strange buzz in her body*. He had access to all of it.

'As I said, there are some things that the passage of time doesn't change. It is still there between us,' he said softly, lifting a hand and brushing her cheek gently with his fingers. 'That is good.'

His touch made her nerve endings tingle and her mind flickered to the rumours that abounded. It was said that there was nothing that Tariq al-Sharma didn't know about women. That he was a skilful lover. The best.

She'd never been given the opportunity to find out.

'There is nothing between us.' From somewhere deep inside her, she found her voice. 'You killed it, Tariq.'

His smile hovered somewhere between self satisfied and amused. 'Denial is useless when the body speaks so clearly.'

'You want my body to speak clearly? Fine.' Goaded by the expression on his face, she lifted a hand and slapped him hard across the cheek. From the darkness of the terrace bodyguards surged forward but Tariq halted their progress with a smooth lift of his hand, his eyes locked on hers in incredulous disbelief.

'You believe in living dangerously, *laeela*. But I forgive your reaction because I understand the depth of feeling that inspired such a move on your part.' The brief flare of anger in his dark eyes subsided, to be replaced by something slumbrous and infinitely more dangerous. 'There was always heat between us. And, despite what you may think, I don't want a meek, submissive wife.'

Coming to terms with the realization that not only had she just hit someone for the first time her life but she'd chosen to be violent with someone who could probably have her arrested, Farrah looked at him blankly, mortified that she'd lost control and shocked by her own uncharacteristic behaviour. 'Wife? You have a wife now?'

The possibility that he'd married someone in the five years since they'd met hadn't entered her head, but of course he would have married. Even a man as commitment phobic as Tariq couldn't avoid it for ever. It was his duty. Had she not recognized the pressures on him right from the start? Someone suitable and approved of by his wretched, interfering family. Why should she care? Why would it matter to her? She should pity the girl in question.

'I don't have a wife *yet*.' His tone was silky smooth. 'But you have led the conversation round to the reason for me being here this evening.'

'You're looking for a wife?' Her tone was faintly sarcastic. 'Then step back into the ballroom, Tariq. I'm sure they'll be queuing up.'

'They probably would be—' he gave a dismissive shrug '—but there's no need for me to look because the woman I intend to marry is standing in front of me.' He inclined his dark head and his mouth hovered close to hers. 'I've decided that I want you as my wife, Farrah. I have decided to marry you.'

CHAPTER TWO

FARRAH stood in shocked silence.

I want you as my wife...I have decided to marry you.

His words spun round and round in her head and when she finally spoke her voice was little more than a whisper. 'Is this some sort of sick joke?'

Once, to marry him had been her dream. And he knew it. Was he taunting her with her naïvety?

'As you well know, I have never found the prospect of marriage even remotely amusing.' Ebony brows locked in a frown. 'Why would you accuse me of joking?'

'Because you can't possibly be serious? We've had no contact for *five* years! And on the last occasion we were together—which, by the way, was when you told me that you could *never* marry a woman like me—' she supplied helpfully, 'you informed me that I was perfect mistress material but nothing else!'

Just saying the words aloud started her shivering again. You thought you'd recovered from something, she thought to herself as she tried to control her reaction, and then you realized that it had been there all along. Buried. *Waiting to be uncovered.*

People who said that time healed were lying. You made adjustments. You learned to live with things that you couldn't change. But that didn't mean that healing had taken place.

'Actually, I was wrong. Five years ago you were too young and innocent to be perfect mistress material.' Tariq studied her thoughtfully and he lifted a hand to touch her flushed cheek. 'The perfect mistress should be sexually experienced and emotionally detached. You were neither.'

The colour in her cheeks deepened and she pulled away from him. 'I'm not interested in your definition of the perfect mistress. It was a role I rejected, if you remember.'

He gave a slow smile. 'Oh, I remember. You were holding out for a much larger prize.'

'I made the mistake of thinking that our relationship meant something.'

'It did. We were good together,' he said smoothly. 'And, had you come to my bed, you would have experienced the true meaning of the word "pleasure."'

Her body heated with an explosive flash and she dragged her eyes away from the knowing gleam in his. 'Had I come to your bed, I would have been a total idiot and would have discovered the true meaning of the word "regret."'

He inhaled sharply. 'I made you an *extremely* generous offer.'

'Generous offer? Sorry, but I don't see what's generous about inviting someone to have sex with you.' She'd *loved* him, for goodness' sake. Passionately. Deeply. To the exclusion of all others. She'd believed he'd loved her. 'You're supposed to have a brilliant brain and a razor-sharp intellect but you know absolutely *nothing* about relationships or human emotions!'

'Being my "mistress" as you so quaintly call it, would have come with significant perks.'

'So basically you were offering me money in exchange for sex.' Her voice was filled with derision. 'There's a word for that, Tariq, and it isn't nice.'

His proud head lifted and the flash of his eyes was a

reminder that he wasn't accustomed to being challenged. 'A marriage was not possible between us at that time.'

'But now it is?' She couldn't keep the sarcasm out of her voice but he didn't react.

'Five years is a long time. You were very young. Much can be forgiven.'

'Maybe. But I'm not the one that needs forgiving here.' She was guilty of nothing more than being gullible and the injustice of the situation stung her deeply. She forgot he was the ruling Sultan of an oil rich state and one of the most eligible and influential men in the world. To Farrah, Tariq al-Sharma was just the man who had hurt her. She saw no further than that. Cared nothing for appearances or protocol. 'You were utterly ruthless, Tariq. When I refused your "generous offer", my father and I were forced to leave the country.'

His expression revealed nothing. 'In the circumstances, it was not appropriate for you to stay.'

She thought of the desert and the beaches. She thought of the golden temples and the dusty streets. She thought of the mysteries of the souk and she thought of those precious early morning walks on the beach, warmed by the hot, hot sun. She thought of the Caves of Zatua and the legend of Nadia and her Sultan. 'For a short time it was my home. I loved it. Leaving was hard.'

But not as hard as it had been to leave Tariq.

She'd felt as though a huge part of her had been left behind in the desert. The only part of her that mattered. She'd believed that he loved her and the discovery that his feelings had been no more than sexual had shattered her fragile self-confidence.

'If you truly loved my country then you will be only too happy to return.'

'I will never return.' For her, Tazkash was a place that

would always be linked with him. A place where there were too many painful memories. 'You're being ridiculous and I refuse even to have this conversation with you. I'm not one of your subjects or even one of your adoring women.' And there were plenty of those, she thought grimly. Women prepared to do just about anything to gain his attention.

'Once, Farrah Tyndall,' he said softly, the pad of his thumb brushing over the fullness of her lower lip, 'once, you begged me to marry you. You couldn't wait to climb into my bed. It was I who slowed the pace because you were so young. Once, you adored me.'

Her heart was thumping with rhythmic force against her chest. She didn't want to be reminded of just how open and honest she'd been with him about her feelings. Most women played it cool. At the age of eighteen, in love with a staggeringly sexy man, she hadn't understood the meaning of the word. How he must have laughed at her. 'That was before I discovered that princes work better in fairy tales. Before I discovered what a cold, unfeeling bastard you are.'

His head jerked back and his dark eyes narrowed in a warning. 'Be careful. I have always allowed you more leeway than most but no one speaks to me in such a way—'

'Which just goes to show what an unsuitable wife I would make. I thought you'd already made that discovery for yourself but it's good to remind you of that fact.' She shrugged her bare shoulders out of his jacket and handed it back to him. 'Thanks, but I don't need this. I prefer to go inside to warm up.'

He couldn't be serious about marrying her. Why would he be? She didn't understand what game he was playing, but she knew she didn't want to be a part of it.

Something flickered in his eyes. Something dangerous. 'You will come with me. Now.' It was an unmistakable command and she gave a slight shiver of reaction.

No one argued with Tariq—she should have remembered

that. His authority was absolute. Once, his status alone had been sufficient to render her tongue-tied, but not any more. She'd had plenty of time to reflect on what had happened between them. And she'd grown up.

'Why would I want to go anywhere with you?' She forced herself to speak lightly. Forced herself not to betray the effect he had on her. 'So that you can show me the way to paradise? I've been there once before, Tariq, and I think I must have taken a wrong turning because, frankly, it wasn't up to much. Excuse me, I'm going back inside.'

Long bronzed fingers caught her wrist in a steely grip. 'I wish to talk to you properly. In private.'

'But I don't wish to talk to you in private, or in public, come to that. Five minutes in your company has been enough to convince me that you haven't changed one bit so take my advice and quit while you're only slightly behind.'

His glance reflected barely contained frustration. 'You *will* come with me.'

'Why? Because you order it? I don't wish to go anywhere with you so what are you going to do? Kidnap me?'

His dark eyes were suddenly veiled. 'I hardly think such extreme measures will be required.'

She risked a glance at him and realized with a jolt that he was deadly serious. *He wanted her*. Why? She wondered desperately. Because she'd finally managed to reinvent herself? Because, on the surface at least, she'd turned into the woman her mother had always wanted her to be? 'Do you really think I'm going to walk back into your arms?'

'If you're honest about your feelings, then yes. It's still there. Farrah—' he used his superior strength to hold her fast when she would have run '—you can feel it and so can I. And I'm offering you what you've always wanted. Don't let a childish tantrum deprive you of your dream.'

Her heart thundered against her chest. 'Even for a sultan,

you are *insufferably* arrogant,' she gasped, trying to ignore the tiny shockwaves that gripped her body. 'And any dreams I might have had about you ended five years ago. You had your chance with me, Tariq, and you blew it. End of story.'

Far from being disconcerted, his eyes gleamed and she remembered too late that Tariq thrived on challenge. He was a man who hunted for obstacles just so that he could smash them down and prove his superiority.

'I am willing to play this your way for a while, Farrah, while you get used to the idea that we are going to be together again. But as my future wife you must abide by a certain code of behaviour. I understand you are to take part in the charity fashion show imminently.'

Farrah stared at him blankly. The fashion show? She'd forgotten all about the fashion show. The only thing on her mind since he'd walked on to the terrace had been escape. *From him and from her jumbled feelings*. His reminder of her commitment to the charity made her heart drop. She wasn't at all sure she could make it through another couple of hours, especially not in such a public way. Everyone would be looking at her. *Including Tariq.*

She opened her mouth to tell him that she was going to make her excuses but his eyes flashed dark and menacing, his ebony brows drawn together in a disapproving frown.

'I forbid you to take part.'

'You forbid—?' The word made her temper simmer and suddenly she struck on a foolproof way of removing him from her life again. After all, wasn't her 'inappropriate behaviour' one of the main reasons he'd cited for being unable to marry her? 'You don't want me to be in the fashion show, Tariq?' Suddenly she realized that appearing in the fashion show would be the perfect way of guaranteeing his rapid exit from her life.

'As my future wife, it would not be appropriate.'

'Good, that settles it, then,' she said sweetly as she twisted her arm free of his grip, 'because I intend to do the fashion show. So perhaps you'd better look elsewhere for the wife you so desperately need, Your Excellency.'

He inhaled sharply, disbelief flickering in his dark eyes. 'You persist in this ridiculous pretence that you're not interested. Do you understand what it is that I am proposing?'

'Proposing?' She tilted her head and her eyes sparkled with anger. 'Sorry, I didn't actually hear a proposal. I heard you ordering and forbidding and doing all the things that you're really, *really* good at. You're going to have to go and find someone else to command, Tariq, because I'm not interested.'

Without giving him a chance to respond, she walked past his bodyguards, back through the ballroom and into the room where they were frantically preparing for the fashion show. Her heart was thumping, her hands felt clammy and she felt physically sick as she joined the other girls who were modelling that evening.

His wife?

Why would he say such a thing?

Why on earth would he suddenly be talking about marrying her after five years of silence? What was going on? And why did her body still respond even though she knew what sort of man he was?

Like all addictive habits, she thought gloomily, you always wanted what was bad for you. And Tariq was extremely bad.

'Farrah, thank goodness!' Enzo Franconi, the famous Italian designer, embraced her with relief. 'We thought you'd gone home and I have the most *spectacular* dress for you to wear tonight. I predict that you will shine, you will positively dazzle, you will—'

'No dress.' Farrah's tone was grim as she slipped off her shoes and yanked the pins out of her hair. 'Are you showing any swimwear, Enzo?' Her hair fell smooth and sleek down her back while Enzo gaped in astonishment.

'Of course. But you never model swimwear. Always you refuse to dress in anything so revealing.'

Farrah's mind was on Tariq. On his proposal of marriage. *He couldn't have been serious.* It didn't make sense. 'Well, tonight I'm not refusing. I'll wear whatever you've got—but preferably the most shocking, daring thing in your collection.'

She didn't understand what the Desert Prince was doing here tonight. But there was one thing that she did know for sure. If she wore something revealing on the catwalk he wouldn't be bothering her again. A man as traditional and conservative as Tariq appreciated subtlety and dignity and she was determined to offer neither. She was going to drive him away by being as unsuitable as it was possible to be.

'I do have something—' Enzo waved a hand in a gesture as nervous as it was excited '—but you would *never* agree to wear it.'

'I'm sure it will be absolutely perfect.' *Perfect to send Tariq as far away from her as possible.* Once he had seen her making a display of herself in public he would march out of the room and she could get on with her life.

Enzo prowled around her, unable to believe his luck. 'On you—' he clapped his hands and an assistant came running to his side '—it will look sensational. I predict that men will faint.'

'Well, let's hope so,' Farrah said flatly, allowing Enzo's assistant to unzip her dress, 'and let's hope that one man in particular bangs his head hard when he hits the floor.'

'Who?' Enzo lifted a wisp of material in bright peacock blue from the rail next to him and then did a double take. 'Is that mud on your leg?'

'What?' She glanced down and blushed. 'Oh—sorry—' she scrubbed it clean with her finger and Enzo gave a soft smile.

'You have been helping those children in the riding school again—'

Farrah glanced around her nervously to see who might be listening. 'We had a little girl with cerebral palsy today,' she whispered. 'You should have seen her face when we put her on the horse, Enzo.' This man was her friend, she reminded herself, one of the few people who she could trust with the secret of her real life.

'Marvellous, *cara*.' Enzo sighed and shook his head as he watched her remove the final traces of mud. 'But did you have to bring the stables into the ballroom?'

'I was held up so I changed in the car.' Farrah gave a dismissive shrug and Enzo looked at her through narrowed eyes.

'So now tell me why you are suddenly wearing a swimming costume. It is about a man, obviously. You wish to make him jealous, no?'

'Jealous?' Staring at the costume on the hanger, she shook her head in disbelief, wondering how so little material actually attached itself to the body. 'No, I don't want to make him jealous. I want to make him run.'

She didn't want him in her life a second time.

Enzo frowned. 'Then take my advice and do not wear this costume. There is not a man alive who will run having seen you dressed in this. You will find yourself with the opposite problem.'

'You don't know this man. Give it to me.' Farrah held out a hand. 'I'll get changed behind the curtain.'

'Farrah, *tesoro*—' Enzo's tone was dry as he relinquished the garment '—if you need to get dressed behind a curtain, then that is *not* the costume for you.'

'If it serves its purpose then it will be fine.' Dressed only in her underwear, she walked in bare feet into the makeshift cubicle. 'Oh, and Enzo, ask someone to find me spectacular shoes. High heels. *Really* high heels.'

Enzo's eyes gleamed and he kissed the ends of his fingers in a gesture of approval. 'Almost, I feel sorry for this man.'

'I don't need you to feel sorry for him. I just need you to make me look shocking. I need to be unsuitable wife material.' She jerked the curtain across and her courage faltered. What the hell was she doing? Adrenaline surged through her body, fuelling her determination to go through with her plan. Before reason could take over and she could change her mind, she removed her underwear and wriggled into the costume. 'Enzo? Are you out there? This thing doesn't fit—'

The designer pulled back the curtain and sighed. 'Not like that—' He stepped forward and made several adjustments that had Farrah blushing. 'Better. Much better. And now this—' He flung a transparent filmy wrap over her shoulders and she looked at it with a frown.

'I don't want to cover up.'

'This covers nothing,' Enzo said dryly, his hands tweaking and coaxing the fabric until he was satisfied. 'It is designed to draw the eye. To tempt and tease.' He narrowed his gaze, nodded with approval and then snapped his fingers towards his assistant who was hovering at a discreet distance. 'Shoes?'

Farrah gave a wry smile as she slipped her feet into a pair of designer shoes with delicate straps and vertiginous heels. 'This is all going to be wasted if I fall off the shoes, break my neck and give myself two black eyes in the process.'

'Never.' Enzo frowned and stood back as the hairdresser took over. 'Leave it loose. Yes. Like that. She looks sensational. I predict that the costume will be this season's big seller.' He glanced at Farrah with a smile. 'You wear heels that high all the time. You will not fall.'

Farrah thought of the muddy riding boots in the back of the family limousine. 'Not all the time.'

Finally Enzo was satisfied and he stood back with a nod. 'It is perfect. You are perfect, and totally wasted in this life of yours.'

They shared a secret smile and impulsively Farrah leaned forward to give her friend a hug. 'You've helped me so much,' she whispered. 'You taught me how to dress, how to walk, how to—'

'Enough—' Enzo waved a hand to stop her but there was pleasure in his smile. 'I had good material to work with. You could be a model, *cara*.'

'No, thanks.' Farrah walked towards the entrance where the other girls were lining up and Enzo caught her arm.

'Not like that! You are walking as if you are angry and out for revenge and I taught you better than that! Your eyes spark and your mouth pouts. You look as though you're going to *kill* someone, not seduce them.'

Farrah wondered what he'd say if he knew how close to the truth he was. She was angry. *Angry and hurt*.

'This costume is about being a woman.' Enzo gave her a slow smile. 'Your eyes should say "look at me", your mouth should say "kiss me" and your walk should say—'

'Yes, all right,' Farrah interrupted him quickly. 'I think I get the message.' She sucked in a deep breath and tried to calm herself.

After all, wasn't that an even better way of displaying her anger to Tariq? For a man like him, displaying herself in such a public place would be enough to make him stalk towards the exit without a backward glance in her direction.

The music pulsed and she took her position near the entrance to the catwalk.

Tariq was in for a shock.

Still coming to terms with the fact that his first ever proposal of marriage had met with a decidedly unenthusiastic response, Tariq lounged in his seat in brooding silence, waiting for the fashion show to begin.

It was typical, he mused with growing tension, that she should refuse to turn down an opportunity to flaunt herself in public. It was one of the reasons that their relationship had floundered in the first place. He'd been able to see too much of the mother in the girl. The exact details of Sylvia Tyndall's early death had been kept out of the press, but her incessant wild partying had supported the rumours that her death had been linked with drugs or alcohol or possibly a mixture of the two.

If anything, Farrah appeared to have grown even more like her mother over the years.

His long fingers drummed a slow, steady rhythm on the table as he pondered their encounter on the terrace.

All traces of the innocent girl he'd met on the beach had gone. But why should that surprise him? The young girl who'd captivated him so completely had been nothing more than an illusion. At that particular point in his life he'd been jaded and unsettled and he'd been ensnared by her fresh, unspoiled enthusiasm for life. He'd enjoyed her sense of humour and unguarded response to him. She'd appeared to be refreshingly unaware of her own breathtaking beauty. He'd found her to be modest and even a little shy. Uninterested in material things or in glamorous social gatherings.

But events had proved him wrong on so many counts.

Everything had changed from the moment they'd moved from the desert to his palace.

Gone had been the respectable mode of dress and the caring attitude. In its place a woman who'd appeared to care for nothing except her appearance. A woman who'd gone to enormous efforts to shock those around her. A woman who'd wanted to do nothing but party.

In a sense that had made her easier to deal with because he'd been dealing with women like her for almost all of his life. Women who played games. Women who traded beauty for other, more tangible, benefits, from extravagant gifts to an excellent marriage.

He skimmed a glance over the women who were now strutting down the catwalk, but only to ensure that none of them was Farrah.

He knew her well enough to realize that his request that she abandon the fashion show would be met by defiance but, even so, her entrance, made even more dramatic by the use of spotlights and pumping rock music, took him by surprise.

Her golden hair flowed long and loose over her shoulders and was the only thing that kept the dramatic swimming costume even vaguely decent.

There was a collective murmur of appreciation from the men in the room and by his side Hasim Akbar made a strangled sound. In contrast, Tariq sat still, the flicker of a muscle in his cheek the only indication of his soaring stress levels.

The music pounded in a hypnotic rhythm that was unashamedly sexual and she started to walk in time to the beat, her movements graceful and seductive. It shouldn't have been possible to walk on the heels she was wearing but she made it look natural, as if she'd been born with high, slender spikes attached to her feet.

The swimsuit was cleverly cut to expose her long, long legs, her narrow waist and the tempting thrust of her breasts. A diaphanous wrap floated around her body, giving the illusion that she was walking through mist.

She was a vision of feminine perfection, every man's fantasy, and Tariq felt sharp claws of lust drag through his loins.

A temporary marriage came with definite benefits, he conceded. Not only would he gain ownership of the shares that were crucial for the future of his country, but he would have Farrah Tyndall naked and at his disposal for forty days and forty nights. As newly-weds he could justifiably keep her trapped in his bed and then he would divorce her before she had the opportunity to embarrass him the way she was embarrassing him now.

On the opposite side of the catwalk a man half rose to his feet, a look of naked longing in his eyes.

Devoured by ever increasing tension, Tariq discovered a hitherto untapped possessive streak deep within himself.

She was inviting male attention, he thought grimly, and she was doing it to taunt him. It was clear to him that she was still sulking over his rejection five years previously.

He lounged in his chair, simmering with ever increasing anger as he watched what he perceived to be a deliberate attempt to provoke him.

But, instead of making him stride from the room, her intentionally provocative display merely served to reconcile him finally to the concept of marriage.

He was determined to make her his.

He should have done it five years ago, he mused in brooding silence, but instead he'd respected her innocence. He'd valued her purity. Had taken his time, the better to savour the moment when he would finally make her his.

Clearly his restraint had been wasted since she appeared to place no such value on herself.

She reached the end of the catwalk, dropped a hip in a pose deliberately designed to inflame and finally she directed her gaze in his direction. Green eyes locked on his in blatant challenge.

Try and stop me, her gaze said, and Tariq rose to his feet in a fluid movement, determined to do exactly that.

Anger roared inside him like a wild, untamed beast and he stepped onto the catwalk, ignoring the astonished scramble of his security team as they attempted to intercept him.

Without uttering a word, he swung her into his arms and

strode out of the ballroom without glancing left or right. He was boiling and angry and he realized that he hadn't known the true meaning of the word *possessive* until that moment.

'Tariq—' Her voice was a shocked breathless pant as she pushed at his shoulders. 'What are you doing?'

Her words irritated him because they drew attention to the fact that for the first time in his life he'd acted without thought. *He didn't know what he was doing.* His actions had nothing to do with reason and everything to do with some dark, primitive need to remove her from the line of sight of every man in the room. If it had been within his power, he would have removed her from their minds and fantasies too, but the man in him knew that it was already too late for that. She'd ensured herself a place in every erotic dream.

The thought made him tighten his grip in raw, naked jealousy and she wriggled.

'Put me down!'

He was sorely tempted to do just that. Every part of him that mattered was in contact with smooth, warm female flesh—female flesh that squirmed in protest against certain vital parts of his body. Something dark and primitive broke loose and anger flared inside him.

Anger at her for deliberately provoking him.

Anger at himself for responding in such a predictable fashion.

Always, in her company, he found himself facing parts of himself that he didn't want to acknowledge, Tariq thought with grim honesty.

'You chose to invite attention, *laeela*—' he tried to ignore the low, throbbing ache that threatened to test his legendary self-control '—and now you have it.' He strode through the opulent foyer, through revolving doors and out to the street where his car awaited his return.

She weighed virtually nothing, he thought, as he all but

thrust her into the car and delivered instructions to his driver in a clipped, angry tone.

'Tariq, I'm not going with you—'

'Be silent!' Still seething, he shrugged out of his jacket for the second time that evening and dropped it into her lap. 'Put this on.'

'I don't—'

'Cover yourself!' The ferocity of his tone shocked even him so he could hardly blame her for shrinking back in her seat. Her reaction shamed him because whatever his faults, he had never struck a woman and never would. He was a man who prided himself on his self-control and yet at that precise moment he wanted to kill someone. 'You are barely dressed,' he said flatly, turning his head so that he didn't have to look at the confusion in her eyes. He didn't want to feel sympathy. *Didn't want to feel anything*. 'When we reach my home, my staff will find you something more suitable to wear.'

Preferably something that covered every inch of her.

She glared at him. 'You're behaving like a caveman.'

'If I were a caveman then I would have followed my baser instincts and stripped you naked in the ballroom when you all but begged me to do so,' he said silkily, 'and you would now be lying naked on one of those tables and your pleasure would be so great that you would be sobbing and begging for mercy.'

Her soft gasp of shock was at odds with her provocative appearance. 'I would never beg you for anything,' she said hoarsely, but her gaze held his for a fraction longer than necessary and his gaze hardened.

Experience told him that she was clearly not indifferent to him, no matter how much she would have liked that to be the case.

The attraction between them was as strong as ever and he was willing to overlook her less appealing traits in order to have her naked in his bed.

The marriage might be short lived, Tariq mused silently, but sexually it promised to be full-on and immensely satisfying.

'I don't want to go anywhere with you. Just drop me home, please.' Her tone was flat but she slipped her arms into the jacket and closed it around her. She was so slender that it would have been possible to fit two of her inside but she was also tall and the jacket did nothing to conceal the tempting length of her legs. Clearly aware of that fact, she pressed her knees together and slid her legs closer to the seat.

Tariq gave a predatory smile. 'It's a little late for modesty, don't you think?' For some reason the sight of her bare, beautiful legs served to reignite the anger that he'd only just managed to subdue. 'Charity balls have certainly taken an interesting turn since I was last in England. Is it suddenly a necessary requirement for the guests to reveal all?'

She didn't glance in his direction. 'It was all in a good cause.'

'If you're trying to persuade me that you really care about the charity then you're wasting your time. We both know that you just seize on any excuse to dress up and flaunt yourself in public.'

Like mother like daughter.

'That's right.' She turned her head towards him, her amazing green eyes glittering in the semi-darkness, her blond hair falling sleek and smooth over his jacket. 'I spend all day lying in bed resting so that I have enough energy to get myself through another night of drink-fuelled partying. Isn't that right, Tariq? Isn't that the person I am?'

She looked so innocent, he mused as his eyes rested on the tempting curve of her soft mouth. Nothing like a woman who'd turned flirting into an art form or a woman who was only interested in expanding the contents of her already bulging wardrobe.

'Don't try and provoke me,' he warned softly. 'Next time you wish to support a cause then let me know and I will write them a large cheque. It will save you the bother of stripping off.'

'I'll do as I please.' She lifted her chin and glared at him. 'Life is all about money to you, isn't it? All about power and influence. Well, I don't need your money and your power doesn't interest me. I don't need *anything* at all from you. The way I act, the way I behave, is nothing to do with you. You don't know me and you never did.' The words were thrown at him with careless indifference but he sensed the growing tension in her, saw her amazing green eyes darken as something live and dangerous snapped taut between them.

The car sped through the night, smooth and silent, the darkness of the interior ensuring their privacy and increasing the intimacy.

Suddenly stifled by it, Tariq lifted a hand and tugged at his tie, opening the top two buttons of his shirt with a deft movement of his lean, strong fingers. She followed the movement with her gaze, caught his eye for a single tense moment and then looked away. The silken fall of her hair concealed her face but only after he'd seen the colour pour into her cheeks.

The atmosphere was pulled tight with a sexual tension so powerful that the air throbbed and hummed.

And he knew she felt it too because he saw the rapid movement of her slender throat as she swallowed, saw her fingers clutch his jacket around her like a shield. In a self-conscious gesture she tried to tuck her legs away but there was nowhere to put them. Nowhere to hide.

'*Stop* looking at me, Tariq.' Her hoarse plea brought a faint smile to his lips and dampened some of the anger inside him.

Her almost childish plea confirmed his belief that she was suffering as much as he was. Evidently she wasn't as indifferent as she chose to appear.

'That outfit is an invitation to a man to look. It was designed entirely for that purpose,' he said smoothly, allowing his eyes to roam freely over her bare legs. 'Presumably you knew that when you chose to wear it.'

Her knuckles whitened as she clenched her hands in her lap. 'I wore it to annoy you!'

He gave a slow smile. 'Then you don't know much about men, *laeela*. In public, such an outfit would indeed annoy me but now we are in private my feelings are entirely different.'

'I'm not interested in your feelings.'

'No? We never found out, did we, *laeela*?' He leaned towards her and gently brushed her hair away from her face, revealing her exquisite profile. 'We never found out how we would be together. We dreamed and we danced around the edges of passion—those stolen meetings on the beach, kissing in the Caves of Zatua—all that foreplay—' His gaze dropped to her lips and lingered there. 'Five years. I have waited for five years to have that question answered.'

She turned her head then, her breathing rapid. 'Then I hope you're a patient man because you're going to be waiting for the rest of your life and still you won't find out. I'm not one of your toys, Tariq. I'm not yours to command. I'm not a fancy car you can buy or a jet you can fly. You can't just decide to have me.'

'Yes, I can. I have only to touch you and you will be mine.' He wound a strand of hair around his finger. 'And you want that every bit as much as I do.'

Her eyes stared into his, hypnotized. 'Not true,' she croaked. 'I don't want that. And your ego is sickening.'

'A ruler with no confidence in himself does not inspire the loyalty and devotion of his people,' he said huskily, moving his body closer to hers, 'and we both know that my ego is not the problem here. Your feelings are the problem. Or rather, your insistence on denying them. Despite what you say to the contrary, you're mentally undressing me and you're wondering how our bodies will move together when we're finally in bed. You're wondering how it will feel when I'm inside you.'

He watched the movement of her slender throat as she swallowed, saw the flash of shock in her eyes, the hint of excitement in those green depths. 'Stop it.' Her voice was a tortured whisper. 'I want you to stop it, now.'

His eyes gleamed dark with amusement. 'Do you think I was unaware of your feelings? At eighteen your sexual curiosity was hard to conceal. You hadn't learned to play games, *laeela.* Your eyes followed me everywhere and when I came near you, you felt an excitement so intense that you ceased to breathe.'

She blushed again. 'You are *so* arrogant.'

'I am honest.' He sat back in his seat, more than satisfied with her response. 'Which is more than you are. Five years ago I met the girl. Now I am eager to discover the woman. And this time we will not be flirting on the edge of passion, *laeela*, but plunging hard into its fiery depths.'

She really was astonishingly beautiful, he mused as he watched confusion flicker over her heart-shaped face as she registered his sexually explicit analogy. The prospect of marriage was growing more appealing by the minute. He was even starting to wonder whether forty days and forty nights would be long enough.

'I won't go with you, Tariq.'

'I hate to point out the obvious,' he said with gentle emphasis, 'but you *are* with me.'

'A mistake that I intend to rectify immediately.' She glanced out of the window and her eyes widened. She turned her head for an explanation, panic in her eyes. 'The airport? What are we doing at the airport?'

'As I said, I am taking you home. My home. We are going to Tazkash.' He leaned forward to speak to his driver and then turned back towards the woman who was trying to open the car door. 'Enough of playing games. I'm going to make you my wife, Farrah. And then I'm going to take you to my bed and keep you there for as long as it suits me.'

CHAPTER THREE

FARRAH sat in one of the soft leather seats inside his private jet, her slim body tense with panic as she struggled to find a way out of the current situation. She ignored the staff who discreetly provided for her every need and ignored Tariq who sprawled, relaxed and infuriatingly calm, in the seat next to her.

She was just *so* angry with him. He was high-handed, controlling, dictatorial— Her brain thumping with anger, she ran out of adjectives before she could compile a decent list.

But most of all she was furious with herself. *How* could she have got herself into this position?

How could she have forgotten what he was like?

He was arrogant and autocratic and used to dictating his desires to an audience of followers whose only purpose in life was to do his bidding.

It had been foolish of her to provoke him, she knew that now.

When he'd half flung her into the back of his limousine, she'd been so angry and churned up inside that all her emotions had been focused on him, rather than the situation. She'd given no thought whatsoever to where they were going.

When he'd said that he intended to take her to his home, she should have realized that he meant Tazkash. She should have remembered that he never played games and should have been instantly on the alert. When he'd said he intended to take her somewhere private to talk, she should have made her excuses and run, hidden.

Not taunted him.

Would she have climbed into a cage with a tiger and poked him with a stick? No, of course she wouldn't! And yet she'd as good as done exactly that with Tariq.

The more she told him that she wasn't interested, the more he seemed determined to make her his.

Why hadn't she remembered that no one ever won in a fight against the Desert Prince? How could they when he had so many weapons at his disposal? A sharp brain—astonishing mental agility had been her father's observation—and exceptional diplomatic skills. And if all else failed he had only to resort to power. He just gave an order and it was done. Instantly. Without question.

Which was how she now found herself sitting in his plane, forced to do his bidding.

She'd been so astonished to discover that their journey had taken them to the airport, so distracted by the growing tension between them, that she'd been urged up the steps and on to his waiting jet before she'd had time to formulate an escape plan.

The humiliation of walking on to the plane half naked had been intensified by the total absence of reaction on the part of his staff. It was obvious that they were accustomed to seeing Tariq arrive with a virtually naked woman in tow.

For some reason she couldn't identify, the knowledge infuriated her.

As did the way they'd bowed low and shown her into a spacious dressing room filled with a selection of clothes. They'd indicated that they were expected to help her to dress but she'd been stared at by enough people to last her a lifetime and rejected assistance in favour of privacy.

Clearly Tariq made a habit of transporting half-naked females, she'd thought angrily as she'd rummaged through the rails and settled on a silk trouser suit. It was high at the neck and long in the leg and, after the way he'd been looking at her in the car, that was all that mattered to her.

And now she was sitting next to him again, this time with a thin covering of silk to protect her legs from his masculine and blatantly sexual appraisal. It was dark outside and the dim lights of the cabin created an atmosphere of intimacy that made her thoroughly on edge.

She'd never wanted to see Tariq again.

And yet here she was. Closeted with him in the stifling intimacy of his private jet. Could anything be worse?

'Take me home, Tariq.' She turned her head to look at him, her voice cold. 'Take me home now.'

'I'm taking you to Tazkash. Your new home.'

'You can't just suddenly decide to marry someone.'

His smile was infuriatingly patient. 'Unlike some people, I don't have a problem with decision-making. I know what I want. Indecisiveness is not a trait that I value in others and even less so in myself.'

She tried another tack. 'My father will never allow it.'

'Your father is heavily involved in a project in Siberia and is currently out of contact,' he said smoothly. 'I understand that the project is extremely complex and taking all of his time. You are not currently his priority.'

She swallowed. Did he know everything? 'I can always reach my father.'

'And say what?' Tariq accepted two glasses from a stewardess and handed one to Farrah. 'That you are marrying me? He knows how much you wanted me. He would probably offer his congratulations.'

Farrah swallowed. 'You think you're such a matrimonial prize, don't you?'

Tariq smiled. 'I see the facts as they are. Dissembling and false modesty are a waste of time and not part of my nature.'

'Has it occurred to you that I don't want to marry you?'

'Why would it? Once, you could think of nothing else. Do you remember that first day that we met?' His voice was low and seductive. 'On the beach with the sun rising on the dunes behind us?'

She stared at him for a long moment and then turned her head away.

Oh, yes, she remembered.

It had been on that very first morning in Nazaar, the desert camp situated on the edge of the desert, bordered by sand and sea.

Her father had flown out to negotiate the terms of a major deal and she'd accompanied him. She'd been eighteen years old, still grieving for her mother, who had died six months previously, and still trying to be the daughter that her parents had always wanted.

She'd been walking on the beach, keen to explore her new home…

'You are an early riser, Miss Tyndall.'

The deep male voice came from directly behind her and she turned from her dreamy contemplation of the red gold dunes that rose upwards to hundreds of feet. Here, at Nazaar, the sea washed right up to the dunes, licking the edges of a desert that stretched far into the distance. It was a place designed for fantasy and dreaming, as was the man standing facing her. He stood well over six feet, his shoulders broad and muscular, his arms folded across his chest as he surveyed her with a masculine assurance that brought a soft gasp of awareness to her lips.

The subtle lift of an eyebrow was sufficient to tell her that her reaction had not gone unnoticed and she cursed herself for being so obvious. Any woman would have done the same, she told herself, struggling not to drool at the sight of the man watching her. Especially a woman who curled up in bed at night, dreaming of romance.

He was darkly exotic and staggeringly good-looking. From the proud angle of his nose and jaw to the fierce flash of his eyes, he was a man very much at home in the harshness of his surroundings. He was dressed in traditional robes, but they failed to conceal the athletic power of his physique or the width of his shoulders and the way he held himself suggested a confidence and sophistication that went far beyond that of a simple man of the desert.

An unfamiliar emotion sprang to life inside her and began to sizzle and burn.

Fear? Excitement? Perhaps a mixture of both—certainly this man was unlike any she'd met before.

An ebony brow lifted and he folded his arms across his chest, a glint of amusement in his dark eyes as he responded to her scrutiny. 'It is rude to stare, Miss Tyndall.'

'How do you know my name?' His gaze was disturbingly intent and she felt suddenly breathless and ridiculously self-conscious. 'I suppose a Western woman staying in Nazaar is unlikely to go unnoticed.' It was a place of business, her father had told her that. And in the oil rich state of Tazkash, business was the responsibility of men. Especially when it was royal business.

The hint of a smile touched his hard mouth. 'I think you are unlikely to go unnoticed in any part of the world, Miss Tyndall.'

It wasn't the compliment that made her skin prickle as much as the frankly sexual appraisal she read in the depths of those dark, dark eyes.

It wasn't the first time a man had shown interest in her, but it was the first time anyone had done so in such a blatant manner. Obviously his ego was well developed, she thought weakly as the wind picked up a strand of her hair and flung it across her face. She lifted a hand to anchor it behind her ear and discovered that she was shaking.

Still his gaze didn't waver. It was as if…as if he were making a decision about something. And she had the oddest feeling that the decision involved her in some way.

No, that was ridiculous.

Following her own preference, she was respectably and discreetly dressed but there was something about the look in his eyes that made her feel naked. Exposed. Vulnerable.

'So I'm not the only one who enjoys the beach early in the morning.' To disguise how unsettled she felt, she waved a hand and gave him a bright smile. 'It's fabulous here, isn't it? I can't believe that the sea meets the desert like this—it's like one giant beach—' She could hear herself chattering and cut herself off. She always talked too much when she was nervous. And the more she talked, the more likely she was to say the wrong thing.

His gaze didn't shift from her face. 'You like our country, Miss Tyndall?'

'Well, I haven't seen much of it,' she confided regretfully. 'My father is always too busy to accompany me. He spends the entire day in meetings with the Desert Prince.'

Something flickered in those dark, exotic eyes. 'You have met the Prince?'

'No. But that's probably just as well.' She gave a little shrug. 'I wouldn't know what to say to a prince. My father's afraid I'd say the wrong thing at the wrong time and cause offence. It's my special gift. I don't want to blow his deal out of the water so I'm keeping my head down and my mouth shut and restricting my explorations to a few walks on the beach.'

'That sounds tediously boring.' There was amusement in

his dark gaze. 'Perhaps the Prince would find it refreshing to be with a woman who speaks her mind.'

'Don't count on it,' Farrah said gloomily. 'My father always says it's my biggest failing. My mouth moves before my brain. I'm trying to learn to do it the other way round, but so far it's not working. Mental and verbal coordination aren't really my thing.'

He threw his head back and laughed. It was a rich masculine sound. 'Are you interested in seeing more of our country, Miss Tyndall?'

'Of course. But it isn't that simple, unfortunately.'

'Why not?'

She frowned slightly. 'Well, I can't just take off into the desert on my own.'

'I agree that to go alone would be foolhardy, but with company it would be a different matter.'

She stared at him. 'Is that possible?'

He angled his proud head as if the question were superfluous. 'Of course. Anything can be arranged if the desire is there. Is there anything in particular you wish to see?' His voice was deep and smooth and she wondered where he'd learned to speak such perfect English.

'I want to visit the Byzantine fort at Giga, but mostly—' she turned and looked out across the desert, her expression dreamy '—mostly I want to see the Caves of Zatua.'

She wanted to see the place where Nadia was said to have met her love.

'You are familiar with the legend of Zatua?'

Of course she was familiar with the legend. She preferred it to any fairy story she'd ever heard because it was so passionate, so heartbreaking and so *real.* She'd positively *ached* for Nadia and wanted to strangle the Sultan for his foolishness.

Thinking of it now, she stared at the rich, exotic colour of the dunes. She could imagine it all so clearly. 'A local girl fell madly in love with a man only to discover that he was actually the Sultan, who had been spending time incognito among her tribe. He loved her too, but her status was so far beneath his that they were forced to keep their relationship secret. So they met in the Caves of Zatua.' She turned back to him, her green eyes misty with emotion as she retold the story that had captivated her for so long. 'Then their meetings were discovered. The Sultan wasn't prepared to challenge the expectations of his people and marry her, so he ended the relationship. She was so devastated that she killed herself rather than be with another man.'

There was amusement in his dark gaze. 'I think the legend has been modified slightly over the years,' he said dryly. 'It would have been a fairly simple act on the part of the Sultan to have the girl brought into the Harem. I see no compelling reason why the relationship had to be played out in a dark cave. And no reason at all for her to end her life when she could have been his favourite. But the tourists like the story. It has a certain tragic romance about it that they find attractive.'

Farrah frowned at his dismissive tone. 'But Nadia loved him. She didn't want to be just his mistress. She wanted to be his wife. Perhaps she refused to enter the Harem.'

'To be the Sultan's mistress would have been considered a great honour,' he said smoothly, his eyes fixed on her face, 'and one which no woman would ever wish to turn down.'

'Good enough for bed but not to wed? Well, I don't think it's that big an honour! I mean the Harem is just about sex, isn't it, and—' Realizing what she'd said, she broke off and blushed, disturbed by the indulgent humour she saw in his gaze. 'All right, so maybe I'm getting a little carried away—'

'I am beginning to understand your father's concerns. Your mouth definitely moved before your brain on that occasion, Miss Tyndall.'

She chewed her lip and brushed her hair away from her face. 'It's just that I can't actually see the honour in just climbing into bed with someone until they get tired of you.' Was he shocked? He didn't look shocked, she thought. Just amused and perhaps a little thoughtful. 'Why would you do that if you were in love? It's insulting. A woman wants so much more than that.'

'He was the Sultan.' He lifted his dark head, the gesture both arrogant and dominant. 'He could never have married a woman whose status in life was so far beneath his. It would not have been possible. She would not have been suitable.'

'If they were in love then it shouldn't have mattered,' she said passionately, '*Nothing* should have mattered. He should have thrown away his kingdom for her if that was what it took for them to be together!'

'And what about his responsibility to his people?'

'Surely they would have wanted their Sultan to be happy?'

He stared at her for a long moment, the expression in his dark eyes veiled by thick, dark lashes. 'You make it sound very simple, Miss Tyndall.'

She flushed. 'It *should* have been simple. If he'd truly loved her, then he would have done anything to be with her.'

There was a long silence and then his eyes narrowed. 'How old are you?'

She stiffened, aware that she'd said far, far too much. 'I was eighteen last week, actually. But I don't see what that has to do with anything.' Should she apologize? Should she—

'You are very young and you have a naïve, romantic view of life. And of love.' He studied her at length and gave a smile and the unexpected charm of that smile made her heart leap into her throat. 'Let's hope you are never given cause to rethink your idealistic view of the world, Miss Tyndall.'

'Do you work with the prince? Do you know him well?'

There was an ironic gleam in his eyes. 'Well enough.'

And suddenly she knew who he was and closed her eyes in mortification. 'Oh, no—'

'You can stop worrying,' he said smoothly. 'Despite what you are thinking, you said nothing to embarrass either yourself or your father. I found your frankness unusually refreshing.'

Farrah stood still, feeling hideously self-conscious and more socially inept than usual. Since her mother's death she'd struggled to be more at ease in social situations, but she'd had no experience with royalty and suddenly she felt tongue-tied. 'You're here to negotiate the pipeline deal with my father,' she muttered as she searched for something meaningful to say. 'Your father, the Sultan, doesn't want the pipeline to be built. He wants things to stay as they've always been but the country needs to develop more wealth.'

'You appear to be an expert on the politics of Tazkash.'

Farrah bit her lip and remembered too late her mother's irritation whenever she'd overheard her talking about what she called 'serious subjects.'

Trying to redeem herself, she gave a vague smile. 'It would certainly be nice to see more of the scenery while I'm here,' she muttered, deliberately playing down her keen interest in history and architecture.

There was a brief pause. 'I would be honoured to act as your escort, Miss Tyndall,' he said gravely. 'It will be arranged.'

And just like that, it was.

A maid came to her tent just before dawn on the following morning and presented her with suitable clothing. Then she was escorted to a four-wheel drive vehicle.

Lounging in the driver's seat was the man she'd met on the beach. Only this time he was dressed casually in jeans and an open-necked shirt.

He greeted her with a smile and a faint bow of his glossy, dark head. 'Miss Tyndall. I trust you slept well.'

Actually she hadn't slept much at all and what little sleep she'd had, had been haunted by dreams of Nadia and her Sultan. For some reason the dream had been disturbingly explicit.

Pushing the memory aside, she climbed in next to him. 'Is it just the two of us? You're driving me yourself?'

'Why not?'

'I presumed a prince would be surrounded by bodyguards.'

His gaze lingered on hers for a moment and then he shifted the vehicle into gear and drove towards the road that led directly into the desert. 'Occasionally that is necessary, of course, but not for this trip. It is a two hour drive to the Fortress at Giga. We will have breakfast when we get there.'

She turned to him, excited at the prospect of visiting such a historic site, forgetting her resolve to be careful what she said. 'You give a lot of orders, don't you? A bit like my Dad. He suffers from a controlling personality too. I'm always telling him off for giving commands instead of making requests.'

'If business was conducted through a series of requests, not much would be achieved.'

'That's rubbish.' She frowned as she fastened her seat belt. 'Everyone knows that you get more from people if they buy into an idea. Giving orders simply turns people off.'

'Am I turning you off, Miss Tyndall?'

Something in his silky tone made her heart skip and dance and she resisted the urge to gulp loudly. 'I—you—I'm very pleased you're showing me round,' she finished weakly and he gave a slow smile.

'I'll try and remember to request rather than command and you need to keep that mouth of yours from misbehaving.' His gaze dropped from her eyes to her lips and she felt an almost agonizing pull deep inside her.

'I don't even know what to call you. Your Highness?'

His gaze lingered on her mouth and then he turned his attention back to the road. 'You can call me Tariq.'

And so her life changed.

Every morning she dressed quickly and hurried outside and into the four-wheel drive, eager to discover where he was taking her that day.

But by the end of the first week she'd stopped dreaming about Nadia and her Sultan and her nights were filled with hot, disturbingly erotic dreams about her own man from the desert. Tariq.

By the end of the month, she was in love.

They talked about everything and she forgot that she was trying to learn not to be so frank. Under that compelling dark gaze she revealed everything that she thought and felt. *Revealed everything about the person she was.*

And then, finally, he took her to the Caves of Zatua.

'It is a strange place to conduct a love affair, is it not?' His voice was husky in the semi-darkness as he led her deeper and deeper into the caves. 'One would imagine that they could have found somewhere more conducive to romance.'

'I think it's terribly romantic.' She stared up at the jagged rock and tried to imagine how Nadia must have felt. 'And it was the only place she could be with her Sultan without the people knowing.'

His dark eyes glittered with amusement. 'You have taken our legend to your heart, it would seem.'

'It's a sad story—' She stopped and looked around her, listening to the strange noises that were part of the cave. 'I wonder if she was ever scared? Waiting for her lover in this dark, empty place—'

'Are you scared, Miss Tyndall?' His voice was velvety smooth and she gave a shiver, aware of his powerful body close to hers.

'No.'

'Then why are you shaking?' His hand found hers in the semi-darkness and she swallowed nervously, although whether that was from the effects of her surroundings or the touch of his hand on hers, she wasn't sure. 'Do people ever get lost in here?'

'I don't know.' His smile flashed, teasing and dangerous. 'We could search for bodies if you like and then we will know.'

'Very funny, I'm sure.' The confined space and diffused light created an intimacy that was almost stifling in its intensity. She was aware of his strong grip on her hand, of the frantic beating of her heart and the dryness of her mouth. 'Do you think this is where they met?'

'Possibly. Can you imagine Nadia entwined in the arms of her Sultan?'

The image exploded in her brain with frightening clarity and she swallowed and stared at the dusty floor of the cave. *Oh, yes, she could imagine that.* 'You think it was here—?'

'Deep in the caves was the only place they could be assured of the privacy they needed. Here, they were totally alone.' His voice was a low seductive purr and she suddenly discovered that she'd stopped breathing. 'Here they were no longer a Sultan and his mistress, but a man and a woman.'

She swallowed. 'Nadia should have known that the Sultan would reject her.'

'He didn't reject her.' His mouth was close to her ear, his breath warm on her cheek. 'He offered her the role of his mistress.'

She couldn't breathe. 'It was an insult. True love deserves a better outlet than hot sex.'

'And yet the power of hot sex is not to be underestimated, would you not agree, Farrah?' He turned her to face him, his hands hard and demanding on her shoulders. 'The feelings between a man and a woman are sometimes so powerful that they transcend common sense. Those feelings become the only thing that matter.'

She stared up at him, his dark, compelling gaze holding

her captive. Shocked by the intensity of feelings that washed through her body, she felt suddenly dizzy and disorientated.

His mouth hovered tantalizingly close to hers and something hot and delicious uncurled low in her stomach. A frantic, breathless anticipation exploded inside her and her pulse started to race.

'Tariq—' She breathed his name and closed her eyes. She thought she heard him mutter, '*So be it,*' but she couldn't be certain because his mouth finally claimed hers and she lost the ability to think.

It was the kiss of her dreams.

His mouth was hot and demanding, the lean power of his body pressing against hers as he hauled her hard against him. She felt a tug at the back of her head and realized that he'd released her hair from the clip she'd used to restrain it.

He muttered something that she didn't understand and then sank his hands into her hair and held her head still while he explored her mouth in sensual, erotic detail. His fingers trailed lightly down her neck and then lower still, brushing lazily against the frantic jut of her nipple.

Desire stabbed through her, sharp and urgent, and still his mouth seduced hers, commanding her response. And she gave what he demanded. The world outside ceased to exist. She was cocooned in the heat of her own newly awakened desire, ready to give him everything. *All that she had and all that she was.*

Was this how Nadia had felt with her Sultan? She wondered dizzily.

Was this why she'd chosen death rather than a life without him?

Overwhelmed by emotion, she slid her arms round his neck. 'I love you.' She muttered the words against his clever, skilful mouth. 'This has been the best month of my life.'

He tensed and slowly lifted his head, his dark eyes scanning her face. 'You are very young, *laeela*, and extremely beautiful,' he said softly, lifting a hand and stroking his fingers through her hair, his expression thoughtful. 'You please me.'

Farrah tried to hide her disappointment. *You please me* wasn't exactly the same as *I love you*, but at least it was a start.

A shout from the entrance of the caves caught his attention. His wide shoulders stiffened with tension and there was a flash of annoyance in his dark eyes. 'Unfortunately it appears that we must return to Nazaar.' He turned back to her, his voice husky and intensely masculine. 'It is growing late and my presence is required elsewhere.'

'So? Can't you do your command thing and tell them all to go away?' She snuggled against him, wishing they could stay in the cave for ever.

There was a glimmer of humour in his gaze. 'Unfortunately not. There is a time for business and a time for pleasure. It is necessary to return now.'

She caught his arm. 'But will I see you again? What—'

'Trust me, *laeela.*' He touched a finger to her mouth. 'We will be together, that I promise you. And the pleasure will be all the greater for the wait.'

She didn't want to wait, but clearly she had no choice and she consoled herself with the fact that he obviously felt the same way that she did. He wanted them to be together.

He loved her too.

She dreamed all the way back to the desert camp and she was still dreaming when her father came to find her for dinner.

'I can't believe you didn't tell me, Farrah!' He glared at her and she struggled to concentrate on what he was saying.

'Tell you what?'

'That you have been spending every day with the Prince. Did you not think it worth mentioning?'

She hadn't mentioned it because she was afraid that her father might try and stop her.

'Prince Tariq bin Omar al-Sharma is totally out of your league,' her father said with a frown. 'You're not his type.'

Insecurity stabbed her but she ignored it. Her father hadn't been with them, she consoled herself. He hadn't seen what they'd shared. 'I love him. And he loves me, I *know* he does.'

'You're being naïve. Prince Tariq is the most eligible guy in the world. Women drop into his path.'

'And you're wondering what he could possibly see in me, aren't you?'

'The woman who finally captures the heart of the Desert Prince will be sophisticated and beautiful,' her father said wearily. 'I love you, Farrah. Just as you are. We both know that your mother tried to make you into something that you're not and you changed a lot about yourself in order to please her. But she's gone now. You can be who you really are.'

Farrah's eyes filled. 'Daddy—'

Her father shook his head, his eyes tired and empty. 'The shallow social scene isn't your thing, Farrah. And perhaps that's a good thing. It corrupted your mother. I'd hate to see it corrupt you too.'

'I'm not going to be corrupted and it isn't Tariq's thing either,' Farrah said urgently. Suddenly she needed her father to understand, needed him to give her hope. 'Tariq is interested in history and culture and things that matter.'

'He's the Crown Prince,' her father said dryly. 'He entertains world leaders. That matters too.'

Farrah thought of the month they'd spent together. Thought of their conversations, of the confidences they'd shared. 'I know he loves me.'

'Then you're a fool,' her father said quietly.

And her father had been right, Farrah thought numbly as she stared out of the window of the jet.

She *had* been a fool.

For a short, blissful, deluded time she'd managed to convince herself that Tariq loved her—*that he was going to ask her to marry him.* But marriage had never been on his mind.

Just like the Sultan and Nadia, he'd wanted their relationship to be kept a secret.

She was good enough to be his mistress, but not his wife.

The tender moments they'd spent together in the desert camp of Nazaar had been nothing more than a sophisticated seduction technique on his part. And at the age of eighteen, her brain full of romance and dreams, she'd fallen for it.

How naïve could a girl be?

But she knew better now, she reminded herself as she pressed herself back in her seat in an attempt to get as far away from him as possible.

She knew exactly what sort of man Tariq was and what sort of qualities he valued.

Obviously he'd studied her new sleek celebrity status and had decided that she was finally good enough to stand by his side. Ironically, she'd developed that side of herself in response to her mother's expectations and Tariq's own cruel rejection of her years earlier.

But only she knew that inside she hadn't changed at all. She was still the girl who preferred history and horses to house parties and hairdressers. But she had no intention of revealing herself to Tariq.

And, this time, she wasn't going to be blinded by the overwhelming sexual attraction that existed between them. No matter what the reaction of her body, she had no intention of making a fool of herself over him for a second time.

And no intention of letting him through the glittering web of deceit she'd spun to protect herself.

CHAPTER FOUR

THEY landed at dawn and transferred to a limousine for the ride through the desert.

Even though it had been five years, Farrah recognized the road immediately. 'We're going to Nazaar?' Nazaar, once an important trading post on the frankincense route.

Nazaar, the place where she'd fallen in love.

Tariq gave a faint smile. 'What better place to renew our relationship?'

She turned to face him, her expression exasperated. It had been a long night. She'd dozed on the plane but she was tired and cranky and he was the last man in the world she wanted to be with. 'I don't *want* to renew our relationship, Tariq. And I don't want to go there!' Nazaar held too many memories. It was the birthplace of all her hopes and dreams for the future.

A future that had disintegrated before her eyes.

She'd been hideously, embarrassingly naïve and open with him and she didn't want to be reminded of the fact.

'Nazaar is beautiful. You always said that you loved it.' Unperturbed by her outburst, there was a strange gleam in his eyes that she struggled to interpret.

'I did love it, but that doesn't mean I want to go there now. I want to go home.' She thought of her job at the stables—

the job few people even knew she had—and felt a pang of anxiety. She just hated the thought of letting them down. 'I have things that I need to do at home. Commitments.'

'More charity balls that require you to parade half-naked?' His gaze was sardonic. 'If you're worried about missing out on opportunities to dress up, then don't be. You can dress or undress for me as often as you please. I can assure you that I'll be a willing audience. And I know you'll be delighted to know that I've had an entire wardrobe flown over for your entertainment.'

Entertainment? She gaped at him and then reminded herself that the women that he usually mixed with would no doubt have embraced him at this point.

Women like her mother.

It was so unbelievably shallow that she wanted to roll her eyes. 'That sort of gesture may have been enough to guarantee you success with every other woman on the planet,' she said sweetly, 'but it doesn't work with me.'

'I don't think this is the time to explore each other's pasts,' he delivered smoothly and she flopped back against the seat, wondering what it took to deflate his ego.

'Well, that's a good thing,' she snapped, 'because I don't have a past. The good thing about having a brush with a guy like you early in life is that it tends to teach a girl a lesson that she never forgets.'

'If you're suggesting that you've lived the life of a nun since our last meeting then you're wasting your breath,' he drawled lazily. 'No one who saw you parading down the catwalk in that swimming costume would ever accuse you of sexual innocence, *laeela*.'

Realising that she was fast becoming a victim of her own deception, she frowned. 'Tariq—'

'Drop the conversation,' he ordered, a hint of menace in his dark gaze. 'I may be modern enough to accept that you have a past, but it doesn't mean I'm ready to talk about it.'

'There's nothing modern about you, Tariq,' she said flatly, 'You're well and truly stuck in the Stone Age. When it comes to women, the average camel is more advanced than you.'

'I see you still haven't succeeded in curbing your seemingly unquenchable need to verbalize every thought that enters your head,' he observed pleasantly and she gritted her teeth.

'Where I come from, women are allowed to speak.'

'They're allowed to speak where I come from too,' Tariq responded instantly, 'only those with sense learn to measure the impact of their words before they utter them. You might want to give it a try some time.'

'If you don't like the way I am then there's a simple solution,' she said flippantly. 'Turn round and drop me back at the airport.'

'I like the way you are.' There was amusement in his gaze and his tone was deceptively mild. 'If I didn't, then I wouldn't be marrying you.'

'You're *not* marrying me!' She turned to him, frustrated and goaded by his inability to listen to her. 'I don't know why you've suddenly decided that I'm "the one", but it isn't going to work, I can tell you that now. So you might as well turn this car around before I disrupt your life again.'

'Let's stop fighting.' Tariq slid an arm across the back of the seat, his long, strong fingers hovering within touching distance of her neck. 'I agree that we need time together before we get married. That is why we are going to Nazaar and not to my palace at Fallouk. It will give us time to get to know each other again without others interfering.'

'Again? You never knew me, Tariq. And I don't need a break with you! I don't want a break! I have things to do. I have to go to wo—' She broke off quickly, realizing just how much of herself she'd been about to reveal. She'd almost confessed that she had a job! But that was something she would *never* share with him. She was never revealing a single part of herself again! Why would she, when this man had hurt her *so* badly? She didn't care that he thought she was nothing more than a frivolous, empty-headed socialite. His opinion of her didn't matter. All that mattered was keeping herself safe from hurt.

'There are places that I need to be,' she muttered. 'I have a life back in England.'

He looked at her, a hint of amusement in his dark gaze. 'A life that will be outmatched by what I am offering? As my wife, you will have ample opportunity to indulge your passion for retail therapy and numerous social occasions that demand that you dress up and play princesses.'

'And that's all you want in a wife?' He obviously hadn't changed one bit, she thought, struggling to keep the contempt out of her expression. He still expected a woman to be decorative and nothing more.

Something flickered in his eyes but he turned his head away and gave a careless shrug of his broad shoulders. 'I need a queen and part of the role is entertaining. It's important to select someone who is up to the job.'

The *job*? She had to stop her jaw from dropping. How could he be so unromantic? 'And suddenly you've decided that I qualify?'

Her sarcasm appeared lost on him. 'You have learned how to conduct yourself in public.'

The less than subtle reminder that she'd done and said all the wrong things on the last occasion they'd been together brought colour to her cheeks.

'You were ashamed to display me in public.'

'Not any more. This time you'll be by my side when we return to Fallouk.'

She just heard one word.

Fallouk.

She stiffened and her eyes were suddenly wary. 'I don't want to go to Fallouk,' she said huskily. 'I hate Fallouk.'

'It is our capital city. I hardly need remind you that my main residence is there. Any time we spend at Nazaar can only be temporary.' The chill in his tone and the arrogant tilt of his head reminded her that Tariq bin Omar al-Sharma had been born a prince and would die a prince. Five years before, she'd thought she knew the man. *She'd fallen in love with the man she believed him to be*. But she'd been wrong.

So wrong.

'Your palace is full of politics and intrigue,' she said flatly, 'and frankly I've got better things to do with my time than walk around watching my back all the time.'

His eyes gleamed with amusement. 'I'd forgotten that you have a tendency towards drama. Whenever a group of people gather together you have politics. It is part of the rich tapestry of life. You are being naïve to expect otherwise.'

She didn't need him to remind her of that. 'Well, I've never been that into tapestries. And I found the palace stifling.'

Not to mention bitchy, but she didn't see the point of raising that.

There was a curious expression in his eyes. 'Why are women so contrary? You love to dress up and my palace will afford you ample opportunity and yet you are looking at me as though I just promised to imprison you in a dark dungeon with no food or water.'

She wondered whether it was worth sharing with him that a dark dungeon would be preferable to an hour in the company of his aunts and cousins and decided not.

'Well, maybe you just don't know me as well as you think. You never took the trouble to ask what I cared about, did you, Tariq? You didn't know what I liked and what I didn't like. Let's be honest about this, shall we? All you were ever interested in was sex.'

He studied her carefully, his expression maddeningly impassive. 'You're an extremely beautiful woman,' he drawled softly, 'and the physical attraction between us is powerful, no matter how much you would like to deny its existence. It is clear to me now that you were just too young to handle such an explosive passion. You misunderstood your feelings. It happens.'

He was so cynical about women that he'd failed to spot the real thing, she thought numbly as she looked away, trying to ignore the empty, hollow feeling deep inside her. It wasn't even worth trying to explain that all her life men had been showing interest in her money and, later, her looks. Never, until Tariq, had she met a man who'd seemed interested in her as a person.

But it hadn't been real, of course. He hadn't really been interested in her. The art of conversation and appearing interested were all part of his superior seduction technique. After all, she mused, was there anything more seductive than someone who appeared to find you fascinating? Who appeared to share your interests? Probably not, and she'd fallen for it. The brief memory of how stupid she'd been was enough to harden her resolve.

She'd been stupid once. It didn't mean she had to give a repeat performance.

'It doesn't matter what I think of your palace, because I'm not going there.' She said the words aloud as much for herself as for him and there was steel and determination in her voice as she turned to look at him. 'I want you to order them to turn this car round and I want you to take me back to the airport right now.'

His gaze was tolerant, as if he found her mildly entertaining. 'Naturally, you are surprised by my proposal. You need time to become accustomed to the idea and I intend to give you that time. There will be no wedding until you are sure.'

His belief in himself was monumental. Briefly, she

wondered what it would be like to have such unshakeable self-confidence.

'There will be no wedding at all! And taking me to Nazaar isn't going to make any difference to the way I feel about that.' She gritted her teeth and her eyes flashed. 'We could spend a century together, Tariq, and still I wouldn't want to marry you.'

'And yet once,' he reminded her in a soft, lethal tone, 'you dreamed of nothing else.'

The fact that he was aware of her most intimate secrets was deeply humiliating.

'That was before I knew what a total bastard you are.'

The sudden touches of colour that appeared high on his aristocratic cheek bones offered the only indication of his disapproval. 'As I have already said to you, Farrah, be careful. My patience is not limitless and you've clearly failed to learn the art of diplomacy over the years. Your desire to shock and flirt with danger does you no credit.'

'Which just goes to prove that I would be deeply unsuitable as a wife,' she said helpfully, 'so you might as well just turn this car round now. Either that or just instruct your bodyguards to shoot me and have done with it.'

'On the contrary, I have decided that you have all the qualities that I require in a wife.'

Her heart was thumping. 'You want a shocking wife?'

'A certain independence of spirit is to be admired.' His slow smile was unmistakably masculine. 'And fire and passion is always a bonus in the bedroom—'

'Which is the only place a woman has a role, in your opinion.' She felt her face flame and dragged her eyes away from his. 'Be careful you don't take on more than you can handle, Tariq.'

'I have never in my life had trouble handling a woman.'

'And you've certainly had enough practice,' she muttered, unable to hide the hurt and the pain.

He'd dated some of the most beautiful women in the world. Why she'd once thought she meant something to him was beyond her. She must have been really, *really* foolish at the age of eighteen.

Thank goodness she'd grown up and seen the light.

'You have no reason to feel jealous. You are the one I'm marrying.'

'I'm not jealous, Tariq. To be jealous you have to care and I don't care about you. You have no effect on me whatsoever.'

His movement was swift and smooth and came without warning. In a show of ruthless determination and masculine strength, he powered her back against the seat and trapped her mouth under his with such ferocious passion that her whimper of shock was swiftly transformed into a soft sigh of acquiescence.

Her skin tingled, heat exploded deep within her and every inch of her trembling, quivering body cried out for him. *Ached for him.*

It had been five years since they'd touched and yet it was as if her senses had retained a memory of him.

She'd dreamed so often of the two of them together. Had tried to imagine what it would be like to be with him properly. And they'd come close. *So close—*

Until he'd stopped it.

But he wasn't stopping it now and his hard body came down on hers, one muscular thigh sliding between her legs as he held her captive with his weight and the heat of his mouth. The hard thrust of his arousal touched her intimately and she shifted and arched in an attempt to bring them closer together.

She felt hot. *So hot.* Her body burned and craved. Her heart bumped against her chest and the blood raced around her body. Her fevered senses demanded that she do something to relieve the pounding, pulsing tension that throbbed deep in her pelvis.

Frustration and anticipation exploded inside her and she moved against him in an instinctive invitation that was entirely feminine.

She needed him and that need was a powerful driving force that blasted everything from her head except the primal urge for sexual fulfilment.

Dragging her mouth from his, she breathed his name and then slid her arms round his neck, traced the roughness of his jaw with the tip of her tongue and then found his mouth again.

Accepting her fevered overtures, his tongue delved between her parted lips and he muttered something that she didn't understand, sliding his hand beneath her hips to haul her closer still to his powerful frame.

With a gasp of encouragement she wrapped her legs around him and then sobbed with frustration as she realized that the thin silk of her trousers still separated them.

She reached out to touch him, her hands fumbling in her haste, but he lifted his mouth from hers and eased himself away from her seeking fingers. His eyes glittered dark and dangerous as he gazed down at her, a frown on his impossibly handsome face.

'This is *not* the right time—'

'Tariq—'

'When the time is right, you will give yourself to me and it will be good. But this is not that time.' His voice slightly husky, he sat up in a smooth movement and relaxed against the seat. Nothing about his body language suggested that only moments before they'd been on the verge of indulging in hot, mindless sex on the back seat of his car.

Torn between aching frustration and utter humiliation that he still had the control to pull away, she smoothed the jacket of her suit and waited for the hot colour in her cheeks to subside before turning to look at him.

The exotic, angular planes of his handsome face revealed nothing. As usual, his expression gave no clues as to what he was thinking. If their torrid encounter had affected him at all then there was no evidence of that fact.

By contrast, her lips felt swollen and hot and her whole body was still suffering the shocking after-effects of their erotic interlude.

'Why did you do that?' Her voice was hoarse and she just hated herself for revealing so much despite her best intentions. *'Why?'*

He turned to her, his gaze faintly mocking. 'Because you insist on pretending that there is nothing between us when we both know that we share a powerful bond. You are a complex woman. On the one hand you are almost painfully honest and yet when it comes to our relationship you are happy to deceive yourself. I wanted to prove something and I did.'

'That's rubbish.' Ignoring the insistent throb that tortured the very centre of her body, she slid into the corner of her seat, placing herself as far away from him as possible. 'All you've proved is that you're a good kisser. And you jolly well should be. You've certainly had enough practice.'

'I've just proved that, when I decide the time is right, you will come to my bed willingly.'

'The only way you'll get me anywhere near your bed is if you drag me,' she threw back at him and he smiled.

'I think we both know that isn't going to be necessary.' He was so blisteringly confident of his own attractions that she was suddenly filled with an almost overwhelming desire to slap him again.

Normally she considered herself to be a very easygoing person, but around Tariq she turned into a boiling cauldron of exaggerated emotion.

'Has anyone ever told you that you have a whopping ego?'

'I have a healthy appreciation for my own abilities and

achievements. That's a good thing, *laeela*. Unlike the English, I do not consider success to be distasteful.'

And he'd had enormous success, she knew that.

Educated at Eton, Cambridge and Harvard, he'd taken over the running of the country after his father, the Sultan, had suffered a stroke. And all were in agreement that, thanks to his exceptional business talents, the oil rich state of Tazkash had moved into a new age of peace and prosperity.

She licked her lips. 'So why do you suddenly feel the need to get married?'

He turned to look at her, his dark eyes slumbrous. 'Because it is time. I am ready to take a wife.'

Take a wife. She ignored the sudden warmth that oozed through her traitorous body. 'Your views on marriage are positively Neolithic. You don't get married just because the alarm clock is buzzing,' she said, her tone thick with contempt, 'you get married for love. But that's something you don't know anything about, do you, Tariq? So tell me, why me? I'm not so stupid as to believe that you care about me, so why have you picked me for the dubious honour of matrimony?'

'It's not true to say that I don't care about you. The connection between us is very strong. We will be good together. I can feel it and so can you.'

Her flesh still yearned for his touch and she shifted in her seat, denying the insistent throb deep in her pelvis. 'No, we wouldn't be good. We'd be a total nightmare.'

He gave a faint smile. 'Are you still so naïve that you don't recognize powerful chemistry between a man and a woman?'

Something dark and dangerous shimmered inside her. Temptation. Shocking, delicious temptation. *Oh, yes, she recognized the chemistry*. And that was the reason that she knew she had to get away from him. 'I could never be happy with you, Tariq.'

'I think I just proved you wrong.'

'You're talking about sex again but marriage is supposed to be about so much more than sex. It isn't going to happen. For the first time in your life you're going to have to come to terms with hearing the word *no*.' And that was going to take some practice, she thought dryly. He was the Sultan. No one dared to say no to him. Everyone around him bowed and scraped and rushed to do his bidding.

He saw, he coveted, he took.

She lay back against the seat, still dazed and disorientated from his kiss and feeling exhausted after such lengthy exposure to his autocratic, forceful personality. Being with Tariq could never be described as restful, she thought desperately, as she tried to subdue the feelings that were still tumbling through her sensitized body.

Nothing had changed. He still only had to touch her for her to lose all sense of reason.

Being around him was dangerous. She didn't trust herself, *didn't trust her body*, not to respond.

But this time she knew that it was just physical, she reminded herself, staring out of the window to hide her confusion. And once she'd got away from him, the squirming, nagging ache deep in her belly would fade to nothing but a distant memory. She'd be able to forget him.

And she had every intention of getting away.

If he wouldn't take her back to the airport, then she'd have to find another way to get herself home.

And the airport wouldn't be an option. Even if she did make her own way there, she'd be stopped the moment she showed her face.

No. She had to find her way into the neighbouring state of Kazban. Nazaar was less than a four hour drive from the border. If she could cross safely into Kazban then she stood a chance of getting home. She was an intelligent, independent woman. How hard could it be?

Preoccupied with planning, she was silent for a while, but not once was she able to forget his presence beside her.

She watched the dunes roll out into the distance, a strangely beautiful alien land that had captured her heart and her imagination from the first moment. She watched as the sun rose higher in the sky and played with the colour of the sand. Burnt orange, browns and yellows all merged together as the wind breathed life into the dunes, creating strange ridges and patterns.

The desert had always fascinated her and it fascinated her still.

'There is a storm coming.' He spoke the words quietly. 'It is predicted to hit in the next twenty-four hours.'

A storm?

She'd never witnessed a sandstorm but she knew that they could be lethal, obscuring roads and reducing visibility to zero. *And turning the desert into a deathtrap.*

It would affect her plans. She couldn't travel in a storm, she thought, and then her mind moved one step further. On the other hand, who would follow her or even notice her absence if the weather conditions were severe?

With the right sort of four-wheel drive vehicle and satellite navigation, it could be done.

'Have you ever been in the desert in a storm?' She turned to him and his eyes narrowed.

'Of course. I have lived in this country for most of my life and I know the desert as well as I know the city. Far from being romantic, I can assure you that it is an experience to be avoided. Fortunately we have sophisticated weather equipment that allows us to predict such an event with a fair degree of accuracy and behave accordingly. No one would choose to be out in the desert in a storm.'

No one, Farrah thought silently, except a woman who was desperate.

And she was truly desperate.

She sat back in her seat, decision made.

She was going to take a four-wheel drive, cross the border and return home.

And His Royal Highness, Sultan Tariq bin Omar al-Sharma was going to have to look elsewhere for a bride.

Women.

Why did they always have to play such elaborate games?

Why did they have to be so difficult, their actions so utterly incomprehensible?

Having spent the entire journey to Nazaar engaged in verbal warfare, Tariq paced the tent in barely contained exasperation, his dark hair still damp from the shower, the fine silk of his shirt clinging to the muscles of his broad shoulders.

It was so obvious that she was as hot for him as he was for her and yet she persisted in her ridiculous pretence that she had no desire to marry him.

Of *course* she wanted to marry him.

Why wouldn't she?

Marriage was what she'd *always* wanted. What every woman ultimately wanted.

The past still lay between them, he decided with a frown. Once, five years previously, he'd refused to offer her marriage and obviously he'd dented her pride. She was playing games.

But, unfortunately for her, he knew everything there was to know about women's games. He'd had firsthand experience of them since he'd been old enough to speak. And Farrah was no different from all the other women he'd ever known.

Of course, in an ideal world he wouldn't have chosen to *marry* her but, given what he stood to gain from such a union, he was more than prepared to make the sacrifice, particularly now he'd been reacquainted with her charms.

Remembering her uninhibited reaction in the back of the car, he gave a smile. He knew *exactly* which buttons to press and now he had her here at Nazaar, he had all the opportunity he needed to press them as often as necessary.

CHAPTER FIVE

ANGRY with Tariq and exhausted from the drive, Farrah followed six female servants into the tent that had been allocated for her use.

As she was led through folds of creamy canvas, across richly carpeted floor, her anger fell away.

The room was enchanting. Dreamy. And richly exotic. Much more so than the one she'd occupied during her stay five years previously.

The huge bed was draped in silks and velvets and piled high with sumptuous cushions that just invited a person to collapse into their welcoming comfort, a canopy of filmy fabric providing just a suggestion of privacy for the occupant.

No roughing it for Tariq, she thought dryly as she looked at the carefully selected books on the low table next to the bed, the handcrafted furniture and the mixture of traditional ornaments.

Outside the wind was rising and she could hear the faint scrape of sand against the canvas of the tent.

A storm was coming.

And that storm would hide her escape.

Eager to rest while she could, she dismissed the hovering staff, lay down on the bed and slept.

When she woke she was feeling much refreshed.

'His Royal Highness sends his apologies.' A pretty girl entered the tent and gave her a shy smile. 'He has pressing business matters to attend to and is unable to join you for lunch. But he wants you to know that he will take dinner with you later.'

Oh, no, he wouldn't, Farrah thought to herself, because she wasn't going to be here for dinner. By dinner time she'd be at the airport in neighbouring Kazban, negotiating to be allowed on the first flight back to London.

She wasn't hungry, but she knew it was important that she eat something. She was going to need energy and she needed to take some food with her. It came as a relief to discover that Tariq wouldn't be joining her.

'It doesn't matter. I'm quite happy to have lunch here. I'm thirsty, could I possibly have more water, please?' Water, she knew, would be a key part of her escape. No one in their right mind would risk a journey across the desert without water.

She dined alone and managed to stash away the food and water that she needed. Then it was just a question of waiting until the maids left her alone in the tent.

Although the wind had risen, there was no sign of the promised storm as she made her way through the bright sunshine to where the vehicles were parked.

In terror of being caught at any moment, her heart banging painfully against her ribs, she sidled up to the nearest one and saw the keys in the ignition. With a sigh of relief, she opened the door gingerly and slid inside.

There was no sign of anyone. No guards. No one, but still she winced as the engine burst into life with a throaty roar.

Expecting to be stopped at any moment, she put her foot hard on the accelerator and aimed for the road.

A labyrinth of sand dunes stretched ahead of her but she

kept her eyes fixed on the dusty track that she knew led towards the border and the neighbouring state of Kazban. And safety.

Just drive, Farrah, she told herself grimly. Drive and don't look back.

'Miss Tyndall has gone, Your Highness.'

'Gone?'

Hasim clasped his hands in front of him, his expression that of a man who would have preferred to be elsewhere. 'It appears she has taken one of the four-wheel drive vehicles and has driven into the desert. Alone. It seems entirely possible that she wasn't as excited at the prospect of marriage as you originally predicted.'

Lost for words for possibly the first time in his adult life, Tariq found himself in the grip of an entirely new emotion. Shock. And surprise. Never before had a woman chosen to walk away from him. He had always been the one to do the walking away. He had been the one to end each relationship when he decided that the time was right.

It hadn't occurred to him that she would go to such lengths to avoid him and he frowned in incredulous disbelief, forced to concede that he had clearly misjudged the situation badly.

But why would she reject him when her response to him was so powerful?

With single-minded focus, he traced back through their conversations and his mind came to an emergency stop at one word. Love. Somewhere in their conversation hadn't she flung in the fact that he didn't love her? Was that what was holding her back from saying yes?

With startling clarity, everything suddenly became clear and he cursed himself for his own stupidity and lack of vision.

At the age of eighteen Farrah Tyndall had been a dreamy-eyed romantic and clearly nothing had changed.

She'd loved the legend of Nadia and her Sultan. She'd

sighed and smiled over the wonder of their relationship and had been appalled at the Sultan for refusing to marry his love.

For her it had been all about love and romance and not about practicalities.

Cursing himself for crass stupidity, Tariq winced as he recalled just how lacking in emotional embellishment his proposal of marriage had been. He knew only too well that some women had a deep-seated need to engulf every relationship in a bubble of emotion and he also knew that Farrah was one of those women. He should have remembered that at the age of eighteen all she had done was talk about love.

How could he have made such a mistake? This was a business deal, after all, and he excelled at negotiating business deals. He was a master at evaluating his opponent and pressing all the right buttons. Only in this case he'd totally missed the mark.

It was immediately clear to him that he hadn't made his proposal of marriage anywhere near romantic enough to appeal to the dreamy nature of a girl like Farrah.

But the situation was retrievable, he assured himself, providing he found her before she drove the four-wheel drive into a sand hole or turned it over.

The thought sent a chill down his spine.

Suddenly the need to reach her before something happened to her seemed increasingly urgent.

His expression grim, he turned to his adviser. 'What is the weather forecast?'

'Not good, Your Highness. The wind is rising.'

'All the same, even in good conditions she knows *nothing* about driving in sand.'

'I shall arrange a search party,' Hasim murmured but Tariq shook his head.

'No. I will go myself.'

And hopefully she would see it as a romantic gesture on his part, he thought dryly.

Hasim didn't hide his shock. 'That would not be a good idea—'

'My plans for Farrah Tyndall did not include her dying in the desert,' Tariq reminded him, his mouth set in a hard line. 'I will take the helicopter.'

Hasim licked dry lips. 'I understand that you have a love of extreme sports, Your Excellency, but it is unsafe to fly and—'

'Life cannot always be safe. She has a head start. There is no other way of reaching her. Was the tracking device on her vehicle switched on?'

Hasim nodded, visibly disturbed by the prospect of Tariq taking the helicopter. 'Yes, Your Excellency. But if you insist on flying, at least allow your staff to accompany you—'

'I will not risk any other lives. With luck I will reach her before she does herself permanent damage. If not—' If not then he'd have ample time in which to regret underestimating the Tyndall heiress.

It took less than an hour for Farrah to admit that driving into the desert alone had been a stupid idea. The 'road' soon vanished under the drifting sand and she was forced to rely on the unfamiliar equipment within the vehicle she'd taken.

She'd let the air out of the tyres as she'd seen others do, but the sand was soft and she gripped the wheel hard as she tried to hold her course up a steep dune. Maybe if she made it to the top, she'd be able to get her bearings. Perhaps the road would be visible.

She hit the accelerator and aimed straight for the top of the dune but, as she felt the vehicle slow and the wheels bed down into the soft sand, she automatically flung the wheel to the right, trying to turn. The world tilted and the wheels bedded in deeper.

She was stuck.

Helpless and frustrated, she sat back in her seat. Stay calm, she told herself firmly. Stay calm. But it was hard to stay calm when the wind was rising, night was falling and there was no prospect of digging herself out.

Intending to see whether she could put something under the wheels, she slid gingerly out of the vehicle, still concerned about tipping it over.

And then she saw the helicopter. Like a threatening black insect, it raced above the dunes towards her and then set down on a dusty flat patch of desert, the whip of the deadly blades clouding the air with particles of sand. The pilot leaped down and his broad shoulders and muscular physique left her in no doubt as to his identity.

Tariq.

She swallowed hard and felt her heart bang against her chest. Which was worse? she wondered helplessly. Getting lost in the desert, never to be seen again, or being taken back to Nazaar by the man from whom she'd been trying to escape?

She braced herself as he reached her and lifted her chin. 'I'm not coming back with you.'

His robes billowed out behind him in the strong wind and his handsome face was hard and devoid of humour. 'I accept that I have made many mistakes in my dealings with you but this is not the time for such a discussion. Had you forgotten that a storm was forecast?'

'No.' The wind whipped her blond hair across her face and she reached up and anchored it with her hand, her eyes narrowed against the wind and the sand. 'I hadn't forgotten. But I thought you wouldn't follow me in a storm.'

He looked momentarily stunned at her confession. 'My proposal of marriage is that abhorrent to you?'

'Where I come from, marriage should be about love, Tariq, and we don't love each other. I don't want you in my life. I tried that once before and it didn't work out.' Even as she spoke, the wind rose and swept harsh, biting sand into their faces. She choked and tried to cover her face with her arms and he muttered something that she didn't understand.

The next thing she knew he was wrapping a soft strip of silk around her mouth and nose with firm but gentle hands.

'This will help. We need to get out of here while we still can. There will be time for talk later.'

'I'm *not* going with you, Tariq.'

He braced himself against the wind and stared at her with naked incredulity, clearly at a loss. 'You would rather stay here and risk death?'

'Than be bullied by you? Yes.'

He stared at her with ill-concealed exasperation. 'I give you my word that, once we have spoken, if you wish to return to London then I will fly you there myself. Is that good enough?'

'What if you're lying?'

Those dark eyes flashed a warning. 'You question my word?'

The wind howled in her ears and, despite the scarf, the sand stung her eyes and seemed to find its way through her clothing to her sensitive skin. Suddenly she realized just how bleak and dangerous their surroundings were. 'All right. Let's get out of here. Back to the helicopter.'

'No helicopter. The conditions are now too dangerous. Visibility is reducing by the minute and I cannot lift off in this.'

'Then what do you propose?'

'We use your four-wheel drive.'

She glanced at it guiltily. 'Ah, well, there's just a bit of a problem with that. I was just getting out to see if I could do something about it.'

He looked at her feet for the first time and his mouth tightened into a grim line. 'In sandals? Don't you know the risks of walking in the desert like that? This isn't London, *laeela*,' he said with sardonic bite. 'Here you walk amongst snakes and scorpions.'

Snakes and scorpions? She squashed down a ridiculously girly instinct to leap up on him and cling round his neck so that her feet were well out of harm's way. The truth was she hadn't been thinking about the desert dangers when she'd planned her escape. She'd been thinking only of him. And getting away.

'The car is stuck,' she muttered and he breathed out sharply.

'The car,' he informed her helpfully, 'is not designed to go sideways down a dune.'

'Well, I know that! I didn't go sideways on purpose! I was aiming for the top but the wheels were just digging deeper and deeper—'

'If you failed to go forwards then you should have gone backwards. Driving in shifting sand, particularly sand that has been softened by the heat of the sun, presents particular challenges. I will move the vehicle and we will return to the camp in that.'

Searching for the rest of his entourage, she glanced over his shoulder and saw no one. 'Where are your bodyguards?'

'There is a storm coming and this is the last place anyone should be because there is no shelter.'

'But you flew—'

'You are my responsibility. I cannot allow others to risk their lives to save yours. The visibility was good when I left Nazaar. But we won't be able to take off again. We will need to return in the four-wheel drive.'

It was her turn to be surprised. He'd come for her alone? 'Your fancy car is totally stuck.'

'Then we will need to unstick it.'

From the gleam in his dark eyes she had a feeling that he was relishing the challenge. Instead of appearing disturbed by the rising wind and the sharp sting of sand against their faces, he merely wrapped something over his own mouth and set to work. Then he slid into the driver's seat and proceeded to manoeuvred the vehicle out of the sand.

He let still more air out of the tyres and then did something clever with the brake, the accelerator and the steering wheel and the vehicle finally sprang to life. Watching the smooth, confident movement of his strong hands, she realized that he made it look easy. And he'd made it look easy five years earlier. Which was why she'd thought that she'd be able to do it herself.

'I was silly to try and drive on my own,' she conceded, clutching the seat as he roared to the top of the dune. 'But you made it look easy.'

'I was born here.' His hands were hard on the wheel and she gave a soft gasp of alarm as they crested the dune. The sand fell away steeply and she clutched at her seat, her eyes wide.

'Tariq—you can't go down there; it's a cliff!'

'Are you afraid?' He turned to her with a gleam of challenge in his eyes. 'I've never asked you if you like roller coasters, *laeela,*' he purred. 'But I'm about to find out. Hold on to your seat.'

Grateful that the swirl of sand obscured at least part of the vertiginous drop, Farrah gripped the seat tightly. 'I hope you're at least half as skilled as you are confident,' she muttered. 'Otherwise we're going to be ending our days at the bottom of this dune.'

Concentrating on the driving, he didn't look towards her but there was a smile on his mouth as he manipulated the wheel with a sure and skilful touch and she realized with a flash of shock that he was enjoying himself. 'There are many things you don't know about me, Farrah, but we are going to remedy that.'

Somehow they were safely down and only then, as the nose of the vehicle rose and she felt the tyres bite into a more solid surface, did she realize that she'd been holding her breath.

'I'm almost relieved I didn't make it to the top,' she muttered. 'If I had, I wouldn't have known what to do about coming down.'

'You should never turn. Turning too sharply has the same effect as slamming on the brakes. If you drive even at a slight angle, the weight transfer is to the downhill wheels which dig in and make the angle even worse. You will roll over. I know.' He dealt her a wicked smile. 'I did it several times when I was younger.'

The smile made her heart and stomach flip in unison and she issued herself a sharp reminder about the dangers of falling for the charms of the Desert Prince.

He'd always enjoyed risking life and limb—she remembered that now. Remembered reading that he'd been forced to curb his more dangerous activities once he'd become the ruler of Tazkash.

'I've driven a four-wheel drive before and I thought it would be similar.'

'Driving on a sliding, shifting surface takes much skill.' He glanced across at her. 'Drive too fast and you'll rush into quicksand or a sinkhole, drive too slowly and you won't have the momentum to get up the slope.'

Hearing him spell out the difficulties, she realized how foolish she'd been even to think about driving into the desert. Gloomily, she stared out of the window, frowning as she saw the sky darken and the visibility reduce. 'The storm is getting worse.'

'And we are less than twenty minutes from Nazaar and safety. You can relax, *laeela*.'

'Twenty minutes? That's not possible.' She glanced at him, shocked. 'I'd been driving for over two hours.'

'In circles. You were lost.' His eyes were fixed on the road and she studied his strong, handsome profile, wondering if he'd ever had a crisis of confidence in his life.

'How can you possibly know that when you weren't there?'

'Because the vehicle is equipped with a tracking device. That was how I was able to find you so easily.'

Realising that she'd never stood a chance, she flopped back against her seat. 'Why me, Tariq?' Impulsively she turned to him. 'I can't understand why you would suddenly want to marry me. You, who always hated the idea of marrying anyone. Why me and why now?'

'Because it is right.' He brought the vehicle to a halt in a cloud of dusty sand and immediately a horde of people descended on them. Briefly his eyes met hers. 'This is not a conversation for now. You will dine with me tonight and we will talk.'

Mildly embarrassed at everyone's relief at their safe return, Farrah accepted the offer of a scented bath and a massage and then slipped back to the sanctuary of her luxurious canopied room. Her scalp still tingled from the application of shampoos and scented oils and her hair fell damp and glossy over her shoulders.

A girl, who introduced herself as Yasmina, had been sent to help her dress and for once Farrah didn't resist. She felt completely exhausted, but whether from the strain of her ride through the desert or the stress of being back with Tariq again, she wasn't sure.

All she knew was that she didn't have the energy to resist when the girl started to dry and brush her hair.

'You have beautiful hair. It is easy to understand why His

Highness requested that it be left loose this evening,' the girl murmured as her hands stroked and soothed.

In receipt of that totally inflammatory piece of information, Farrah tried to summon up the energy to instruct the girl to fasten her hair up on her head, but she decided that she'd had enough confrontation for one day.

Instead, she reminded herself that Tariq had promised to fly her back to London if that was what she wanted. And that *was* what she wanted, she told herself firmly. So she'd dine with him and make sure that he got that message, get some rest and then travel home in the morning.

Satisfied with the plan, she realized that Yasmina was showing her a dress. 'It is an extremely generous gift from His Highness,' the girl breathed. '*How* he honours you.'

How he fails to understand me, Farrah thought wearily as she allowed the girl to slip the dress over her head. Made of the finest silk, different shades of green and blue merged and blended together like the colours of a peacock feather. The fabric was of such superior quality that it was like wearing nothing next to her skin and Farrah reached down to touch it.

Should she refuse to wear it? Probably, but she had to wear *something* and obviously she hadn't been given the opportunity to pack anything of her own.

Yasmina stared at her in admiration. 'You look beautiful enough to ensnare a sultan.'

Farrah frowned as she slipped her feet into strappy sandals. She didn't want to ensnare anyone. She just wanted to go home. Back to her life. *Back to the riding stables*.

And if Tariq thought that one pretty dress was going to change her mind, then he was as far off the mark as he ever had been.

Tariq paced the length of the tent, ignoring the staff who were carefully arranging various delicacies on the low table.

Everything was in place, he thought.

She wanted romance and now, thanks to a sudden flash of inspiration on his part, he had an entire team of staff working flat out to deliver nothing but romantic gestures. Massage, candles, dresses, jewellery—as far as he could see, he was ticking all the boxes. How could he possibly fail?

There were certain courtship rituals that a woman expected and he'd neglected those rituals because he'd thought the connection between them was enough. Clearly it wasn't and he wouldn't be making that mistake again.

When a whisper of silk announced her entrance into his tent he turned to her with a confident smile. The smile froze on his lips as he saw her. Something dangerous and unfamiliar shifted inside him and for a brief moment he forgot that the relationship he was trying to forge with this woman was all about business.

She looked like a woman designed specifically to tempt a man from the straight and narrow. A woman who would wrap herself around a man's mind until all coherent thought had been squeezed out.

The sleek fall of her hair shone pale gold, gleaming under the flickering light of the candles that had been arranged around the tent by his staff in accordance with his instruction.

Exquisite, he thought to himself, indulging in a brief erotic fantasy that involved all that glorious hair trailing over his heated, naked flesh.

Lust stabbed through him and, with a flash of masculine frustration, he momentarily reflected on the fact that a woman's requirement for romance invariably acted as the brakes on the roller coaster ride towards sexual satisfaction. Before he could take her to bed and give them both what they needed, he was expected to jump through all the right hoops.

But he was well on his way, he assured himself as he

dragged his gaze away from her lush, glossy mouth and forced himself to concentrate.

He'd arranged for her to be pampered, he'd presented her with a dress. Now on to the next thing on his list. Compliments and jewellery. Both were easy.

'You look very beautiful.' His voice was soft and he reached for a velvet box in midnight blue that had been delivered only moments earlier. 'I have something for you which I think you'll like.'

She opened the box and he silently congratulated his staff on their excellent taste. The diamond necklace was a truly exquisite piece. Rare and tasteful. Preparing himself to be on the receiving end of an appropriate amount of female gratitude, he dismissed the staff with a wave of his hand and was taken aback when she snapped the box shut and slipped it into her bag.

'Thank you.'

This was not the reaction he'd expected. 'You're not going to wear it?'

'Possibly. I suppose it depends on the occasion. It seems a bit over the top for dinner in the desert in a tent. To be honest, it's not really my style.'

Never before having witnessed such a lack of enthusiasm for jewellery, Tariq looked at her with frank incomprehension. 'Diamonds are every woman's style.'

'But I'm not every woman.' She gave him a sympathetic smile and walked gracefully over to the cushions. 'Sorry to be difficult. I'm sure most of your conquests would be well and truly sewn up by now. Pretty dress, candles, diamonds—you should be on to a sure thing.'

Her tone told him that he was missing something crucial and he racked his brains for inspiration. 'They are the things that matter to women.'

'No.' Her smile faded and she looked him straight in the

eye. 'They're the things that matter to the women you usually mix with, Tariq. That's not the same thing. I'm not like them and yet you persist in thinking that I am. That's always been your mistake.'

'I don't make mistakes.'

'You're making so many mistakes you're falling over them,' she said sweetly. 'Your mistakes are the reason I drove your car into the desert. We are operating on entirely different wavelengths. It's clear to me now that you will *never* understand me.'

On the receiving end of this less than encouraging announcement, Tariq was filled with a previously unknown urge to defend his actions.

'You are a woman who lives to dress up—'

'So you think.' She sank on to the pile of cushions in a graceful movement and he inhaled deeply, hanging on to his patience with difficulty. Being with a woman was supposed to be relaxing, he mused. But life with Farrah was one long game of cat and mouse. She was infuriatingly unpredictable. Surely he'd done everything that was required of a man? What more did she expect?

'I suppose you have a rich father to buy you all the diamonds you need.'

'Yes.' Reaching forward, she helped herself to a glossy black date. 'But you see, Tariq, I don't need diamonds.' She slid the date into her mouth and he felt tension throb through his body as she licked her fingers. 'Has it ever occurred to you that you and I are actually very similar?'

Disturbed from the pleasurable act of contemplating their differences, Tariq looked at her blankly. 'How?' At that precise moment he wasn't interested in exploring similarities.

'We were both born with sufficient wealth and influence to ensure that we could never be entirely confident of another person's motives.'

Her mouth was perfect, he reflected, struggling to ignore his increasing arousal. 'I don't know what you mean—'

'No. You probably don't.' She reached for another date and popped it into her mouth. 'And that's always been your problem. You don't really care what women think about you because you only connect with them on one level. But I'm not interested in that one level. You have absolutely no idea who I am or what I want and you've never bothered to take the trouble to find out. All you're really interested in is sex.'

And who could blame him?

His eyes still on her mouth, he watched as she sampled the food with slow, sensuous relish. Never before had he watched a woman eat with such obvious enjoyment. All the females he'd ever known had appeared to regard food as a threat and eating as nothing more than a distasteful social obligation to be undertaken under sufferance and preferably without the consumption of a single calorie. Watching Farrah lick her fingers, it was clear that she held an entirely different attitude to food. Showing none of the inhibitions characteristic of her sex, she studied each plate with enthusiasm and helped herself to a selection of local delicacies.

In the grip of a severe attack of lust, Tariq struggled to deliver the conversation that was so clearly required of him. 'Why would you always be suspicious of people's motives?'

'Because I've learned to be that way. And I'm suspicious of yours, Tariq.' She leaned forward and selected an olive from the bowl in front of her. 'Why would you want to marry me? It doesn't make sense.'

It made perfect sense to him. In fact, as he watched her nibbling and licking her lips, it was making increasing sense. His body was wound so tight that he thought he might explode and it felt as though his entire brain was sliding south. Suddenly there was only one purpose in his life.

He wanted Farrah Tyndall and he wanted her to himself.

And what better way was there of guaranteeing exclusivity than marriage?

Marriage would mean that she could take up permanent residence in his bed. Captive. No other man would have a chance with her. No other man would see her as he was seeing her now, her fair hair trailing on to the cushions, the delicate silk of her dress skimming her amazing body. For the first time in his life he realized that the institution of marriage came with significant benefits.

She would be his. He would own her, body and soul.

At that precise moment he had forgotten that the purpose of his own marriage was supposed to be all about business because all thoughts of business had been blown from his mind. With her lying in front of him he could focus on nothing except pleasure.

'We would be perfect together. You saw that five years ago.' His voice was husky as he lowered himself on to the cushions next to her. 'Am I to be punished because I was a little slower than you to recognize what it was that we had?'

'So you're saying that you've spent the past five years pining for me?' There was a hint of sarcasm in her tone but the tiny pulse beating in her throat told him that she wasn't as cool and indifferent as she pretended to be.

'You weren't the obvious choice of a wife,' he confessed, remembering that women were purported to like honesty, 'but never has any woman affected me the way you do.' The discovery that the second part of his statement was nothing more than the truth came as something of a shock.

Up until now, the women in his life had been more or less interchangeable. Society clones with the right pedigree. Women paraded in front of him by his family in the hope that he'd select one, marry her and produce the necessary heir.

'Well, if I wasn't the obvious choice five years ago, why would that have changed?'

'Perhaps it is I who have changed,' Tariq muttered, still reeling from the implications of his discovery. It was just because their relationship had never reached the obvious conclusion, he assured himself, a frown touching his black eyebrows. Had the relationship developed in the way he'd anticipated, he would have had no problem moving on in the same way that he'd always moved on. 'I am no longer prepared to marry for political reasons.'

In fact, he wouldn't have been prepared to marry at all were it not for the fact that he was able to seek a divorce after forty days and forty nights.

'You want to take me to bed.'

'If that was all I wanted, then why would I marry you?'

Her gaze was fixed on his. 'I'm still asking myself that question.'

'Then allow me to answer it for you. I have seen enough marriages fail to know that there must be something more than political gain in order to make the relationship work.'

'And yet you never thought that Nadia should have been more than the Sultan's mistress.'

Her voice was pleasant but he tensed, sensing a trap. 'You still think of that legend?' He leaned forward to fill her glass. 'We are not talking about history now. Things change and progress. We are not living the lives of our ancestors.'

'And what would your family think of this marriage you're proposing?' For a brief moment he saw the flash of hurt in her eyes and his eyes narrowed as he remembered the reaction of his family to Farrah Tyndall.

'My family must accept my decision.' And they would, he mused, because the senior members of his family had been informed that the marriage was designed to benefit Tazkash. 'You are my choice. That is all there is to be said.'

'Oh, I'm sure they'll just welcome me with open arms.' She pulled her hand away from his and drew her knees up, her position as defensive as a child. 'Your cousins, uncles, aunts—none of them wanted me near you, Tariq. I was seen as a threat. They made sure that my time in your palace was as unhappy as possible.'

He decided that the pursuit of his goal dictated that he overlook the criticism of his family. 'Because you were the first woman who had ever truly interested me. You threatened them with your outspoken ways and your dazzling looks.'

And by her pedigree.

The reputation of Sylvia Tyndall and her subsequent death had attracted sufficient negative press attention to ensure that her daughter was viewed with the same suspicion.

Farrah lifted her chin. 'Five years ago I would have believed that, but you taught me not to be naïve. You taught me that actions always have a reason. I want to know your reason.'

Why, he asked himself with mounting exasperation, did she pick this particular moment to suddenly discover the meaning of cynicism? 'Once, we were the best of friends. Give me the chance to prove to you that we can be so again. Give me the chance to prove that we'd be good together. Two weeks, that's all I ask. Stay with me for two weeks. If at the end of that time you still wish to return home, then I will arrange it. You have my word.'

'Why would I agree to stay for two weeks?'

He lifted a plate of delicacies that she'd almost finished. 'Because what we have is worth exploring further. No man has made you feel the way I make you feel.'

'You're arrogant.' But he heard the husky edge to her voice and smiled, knowing that he was winning the argument.

'I'm honest, *laeela.* And if I am wrong, how can you lose? In two weeks you can walk away.'

And she'd definitely be walking away in six, leaving him with control of her father's company.

She licked her lips. 'And what are we going to do for two weeks?'

'All the things you enjoyed on your last visit.' Relieved to see her wavering, he kept his tone was warm and persuasive. 'If it helps, think of it as a holiday.'

She hesitated, her eyes on his face. 'I don't think so. A holiday is the last thing I need—'

'Maybe it's exactly what you need. I know that I hurt you. You have never been involved with another man since me,' he said quietly. 'Isn't that true?'

Her eyes widened with shock. 'How do you know that? Are you having me followed?'

He made a mental note to destroy the file he had on her that was currently locked inside his desk back in the palace at Fallouk.

'No, but you still wear my ring.'

Her chin lifted defensively. 'I've already told you why.'

'I don't think so, *laeela*,' Tariq murmured 'You wear the ring because our time together was special. The least you can do is give us a chance to see what might have been.'

She eyed him warily. 'That would make me stupid.'

'That would make you sensible,' he contradicted swiftly, bestowing a smile on her anxious face. She was deliciously transparent and always had been. *She still wanted him but, like a typical woman, she needed to justify the need that burned inside her*. 'If a love is so great that it keeps you from forming a relationship with another man, is it not at least worth another look?'

Their eyes held and he felt the tension rise between them, saw indecision as her mind fought the battle between common sense and the powerful connection between them. The rational and the irrational.

'I can't just take time out of my life without warning,' she muttered finally. I'd have to make some phone calls. I wasn't expecting to take a holiday.'

Wondering how one could take a holiday from a life that contained nothing but social engagements, Tariq gave a nod. 'Of course. You shall make whatever calls are necessary to give you peace of mind.'

Having won the battle, he was willing to make whatever minor concessions were necessary in order to allow her to feel comfortable with her decision.

She must be mad.

Why hadn't she just insisted that he put her on a plane and fly her home? She'd gone into his tent intending to demand exactly that. But somehow he'd talked her into staying.

Appalled at herself, Farrah called the riding school where she worked and explained that she wouldn't be able to come in for two weeks. Then she called a couple of close friends and told them she was going to be travelling for a while.

It wasn't an entirely ridiculous decision, she told herself as she paced the length of her tent, too wound up to even contemplate sleep. Tariq *had* haunted her dreams for five years. He was right when he claimed to be the reason she'd never become involved with another man.

Maybe spending some time with him was just what she needed to help her put him out of her mind, once and for all.

Once she saw that they had nothing in common, it would be easier to walk away.

Having justified what appeared to be an utterly ridiculous decision on her part, she slipped out of her dress and climbed into bed, her mind still spinning. She'd spend the next two weeks doing all the things she enjoyed doing, she decided. And two weeks of non-stop exposure to Tariq should be more than enough to remind her what a cold-hearted, arrogant individual he was.

And then she'd fly home. And she'd move on.

No more sultans for her.

CHAPTER SIX

THEY spent every day exploring the desert.

Tariq took her dune driving and wadi bashing, speeding along the empty river beds until Farrah gasped at the sheer exhilaration of the experience. And then he let her take a turn behind the wheel and taught her to do it. And he proved to be a gifted and patient teacher as he showed her how to drive in sand, how to alter the tyre pressure and how to use the sophisticated global positioning system.

'If I'd known how to do this a few days ago I'd be back in England now,' she said dryly and he dealt her a smile that was disturbingly attractive.

'Then I'm thankful that I have postponed the lesson until this point. Are you interested in the local wildlife?'

'Snakes and scorpions?'

His smile widened. 'On this occasion, no. I had something more fluffy and appealing in mind.'

'Fluffy and appealing?' Despite her resolutions not to be affected by him, she couldn't stop the laughter. 'Is that another one of your stereotypical views of women? We like the fluffy and appealing?'

'You would, perhaps, prefer the scaly and poisonous?'

She shuddered, still laughing. 'No, thanks. On this occasion I'm happy to fall into the box you've designed.'

'Box?'

'Yes. You put all women in the same little box because you believe that we all have the same characteristics.'

'For you, Farrah,' he said dryly, 'I have designed your own, private box. And now look—' He gestured for her to turn off the engine and leaned across, sliding an arm across her shoulders as he pointed across the sand dunes. 'There. What do you see?'

He was so close she could hardly breathe. Her nose picked up his elusive masculine scent and her eyes were drawn to the dark hair that clustered on his forearms. He had strong arms, she thought absently, trying to concentrate on what he was saying. Following the line of his gaze, she gave a soft gasp of delighted surprise. 'Oh—Tariq.' The animal stood still, eyes huge, as if sensing danger. Even though they were inside the vehicle, Farrah dropped her voice to a whisper. 'It's gorgeous. What is it?'

'A type of gazelle. They were hunted almost to the point of extinction,' he told her, 'but this is now a protected area and the numbers are recovering. That particular project was a success in conservation terms.'

Farrah stared at the creature, fascinated. 'A protected area? It looks like desert—'

'And, of course, it is—' his tone was amused '—but this particular part of the desert is protected. We restrict the amount of off-road driving because it damages the vegetation and threatens the animals. There are several such sites in Tazkash.'

She turned to look at him and caught her breath. His head was close to hers as he leaned forward to get a better look at the animal. The dark stubble on his jaw seemed merely to intensify his masculinity and she swallowed.

'I never knew you were interested in conservation.'

His eyes slid to hers, his gaze faintly mocking. 'As you are always pointing out, there is much that we have yet to discover about each other.' His eyes dropped to her mouth and lingered, leaving her in no doubt that he was referring to more than his dedication to local wildlife. 'It is my responsibility to act as custodian for this country. Part of my job is to protect our heritage for future generations and that includes the wildlife.'

'Your job?'

'Of course.' He gave a casual shrug and withdrew his arm, leaning back against his seat. 'Mine is a job like any other.'

'*Not* like any other,' she said dryly and he smiled.

'Perhaps not. Although, in truth, my role bears similarity to that of any other chief executive of a large organization. It certainly comes with the same number of major headaches.'

And she knew that he'd made an enormous success of the business. 'Most CEOs don't have the autonomy that you have. You just give an order and everyone stumbles over each other to carry it out.'

He threw his head back and laughed in genuine amusement. 'How I wish it were that simple, *laeela.* I spend my life playing politics. Persuading people. Preparing arguments. It's like an ongoing game of chess. I must anticipate every move that my opponent is likely to make and act accordingly. Introducing just small elements of change often requires months, if not years, of careful manoeuvring on my part.'

She looked at him, interested. 'What do you want to change?'

'It is important that Tazkash remains competitive and a real force if our people are to thrive and be safe.' His handsome face was grimly serious. 'But progress must not come at the expense of our heritage. The preservation of our culture is important. My job is to find a way of weaving the past into the future so that the people benefit. Oil will not support us for ever and we need to find alternative ways of generating revenue.'

'You really care about the people who live here.' It was a statement rather than a question and he nodded.

'Of course. It's important to understand the way of life of our people. Where we came from and where we are going. We are used to exploiting a harsh environment and it's important to understand the problems our people face. Lately we have been exploring water courses and irrigation systems—'

She listened in fascination as he outlined the various projects that were currently ongoing to make life easier for the people. And she asked endless questions and added her own thoughts.

Their conversations continued over the days that followed, becoming more complex and stimulating, often lasting well into the night as they ate by the light and warmth of a bonfire.

He taught her to read the stars as his ancestors had once done and showed her how to watch for signs of changes in the weather.

'You love it here, don't you?' She stared at his face, bronzed and handsome in the flickering firelight. Saw him nod.

'In the desert, life is simple.' Idly, he tossed a stick into the fire and watched it flame and crackle. 'I suppose in a different life, this is where I would belong. Where I would choose to be.'

She hid her surprise. She'd assumed that he enjoyed the luxury and pomp that was part of palace life at Fallouk. It hadn't occurred to her that maybe he was playing a part, just as she did.

'I can understand that.' Her voice was soft as she laid back on the cushions and rugs that had been placed by the fire for their comfort. 'It's blissful. I love everything about it.'

'And yet, by now you must be bored. You don't have to pretend with me.' He shot her an amused glance. 'You are young and very beautiful. I'm sure you must be missing your usual round of parties. Here in the desert, we lack that many excuses to dress up.'

Part of her wanted to tell him the truth—confess that she hated the constant round of parties and meaningless mingling. But he was a man who expected a woman to fulfil that role—expected a woman to be like her mother. Having been so utterly consumed by Tariq in the past, *having trusted him enough to bare her very soul to him*, could she risk giving him a glimpse of what lay behind the glittering shell that she'd so carefully created? Did she dare confide her innermost secrets? No. Such a confession would make her too vulnerable. Fortunately she'd grown so used to concealing her true self from all but a few close friends that deception came easily. 'The desert has many charms,' she said finally, 'and life isn't all about parties, although I do miss my friends, of course. I have a few good friends that I've had from childhood and I'd trust them with my life. I've learned to be wary of strangers. Haven't you? Is there anyone that you truly trust, Tariq?' She turned her head towards him. Saw the tension in his broad shoulders.

When he finally answered, his voice was quiet. 'No,' he replied. 'There isn't. But that is the price you pay for being in my position.'

She couldn't imagine being without her friends. 'It's a high price.'

'Not to me. I've never felt the need to confide in people.'

'Everyone needs someone,' Farrah said softly, wriggling into a more comfortable position on the rug. 'Being loved for who you truly are is the best thing in the world. The only thing that really matters. The rest of it—the money, the lifestyle, that isn't real.' She knew that better than anyone. *Had seen her mother seduced and destroyed by the empty glamour.*

'I thought you loved all the glitter and bright lights.'

She quickly realized how much she'd betrayed. 'I do,' she said hastily, 'but there are other things that matter too…' Her voice trailed off and he lifted an eyebrow in question.

'So—' his voice was low and persuasive, his eyes gleaming dark in the firelight '—what else matters to you, Farrah Tyndall?'

For a moment she thought about the children she worked with. About her job at the riding school and the fact that no one knew who she really was. How her identity, her money, didn't matter. But her other life was her last defense. She had to keep that part of herself locked away from him. 'Oh—er—'she struggled to think of something plausible '—charity work, that sort of thing.' She sounded intentionally vague and he studied her for a moment, his dark eyes searching.

'You can do charity work in Tazkash if that is what you wish. As my wife, it would be expected of you.'

Her heart flipped. Every angle of his strong, handsome face was designed to make an artist drool. He was every inch the arrogant prince and she couldn't look at him without catching her breath. Being so close to him for the past two weeks had been a delicious kind of torture. But he hadn't touched her. Not once. This was the first time he'd mentioned marriage since the night of her attempted escape and her reaction worried her. She should have leaped to her feet and run for cover; instead, she felt drawn to him. 'Your wife?' Just saying the words sent a thrill running through her body and she closed her eyes to hide what she was feeling.

She'd done it again.

Despite her best intentions, despite everything that had gone before, she'd let herself fall in love with him again. She'd opened her heart and let him in.

Not the Sultan, she realized as she opened her eyes and looked at him. She'd never been interested in his status. Like Nadia, she'd fallen in love with the man, not the title or the promise of riches. It was the man who interested her. The man that she saw whenever they were here at Nazaar. There was a part of him that he only seemed to reveal in the desert.

He was watching her. 'We agreed not to talk about it for two weeks. That time is up tomorrow. Until then the subject is banned.'

She stared at him, suddenly uncertain. Did he still want her? Was he intending to renew his proposal? Or had two weeks in the desert with her been enough to convince him once more that she was unsuitable wife material? Suddenly she needed to change the subject. 'Did your parents bring you here when you were young?'

He tensed and a muscle flickered in his strong jaw. 'No. My mother loved life in the Palace. She would rather have died than spend time in the desert. She needed civilization at all times.'

It was the first time he'd ever mentioned his mother. The first time he'd ever told her anything remotely personal about himself. Maybe it was the darkness or maybe it was the intimacy of the conversation, but suddenly she felt truly close to him for the first time. It was just the two of them and the crackling fire. 'And your father?'

'My father was busy with affairs of state.'

'But you were his only child. He must have spent some time with you.'

His face was expressionless. 'Raising a child wasn't his role.'

'What about playing with you? Reading to you?' She thought of her own father and the hours of fun they'd had together. 'Surely you must have spent some time together?'

'He allocated time each week to teach me what he thought I'd need to know about ruling Tazkash.'

Ruling? She wanted to ask about play. Wanted to know whether he'd ever had any fun with his parents, but the answer was in his face. 'That sounds pretty lonely.' She felt a twist of sympathy for what he'd missed.

'On the contrary—' he gave a bitter laugh '—to be lonely would have been a blessing. I was surrounded by staff from the moment I was born. I had three nannies, several tutors and a whole team of bodyguards briefed to watch my every move. To be lonely was never more than an elusive dream.'

'You can be surrounded by people and still be lonely,' she said quietly. 'If the people around you don't love and understand you, then you can be extremely lonely.'

'Are you speaking from experience?'

Her eyes flew to his. 'No, I—' She broke off and licked her lips as she tried to make good her mistake. 'My father worked very hard, of course, but my mother was always around.'

'You are close to your father?'

'He's my hero,' she said simply, reaching her hands towards the warmth of the fire. 'Despite her faults he adored my mother, and he never found another woman who meant the same to him. He brought me up to believe in one special love and never to settle for anything less.'

She couldn't read his expression. 'That's a very romantic view.'

'It's how it was for my parents,' Farrah said quietly. 'Tell me how you came to spend time in the desert. If your parents didn't bring you here, then who did?'

His eyes lifted to hers and he stared at her for a long moment. 'When I was seven, one of my tutors decided that I needed to broaden my education, to understand my roots and the ways of our people. He brought me to Nazaar.'

'And you loved it.'

'Oh, yes.' He leaned over and topped up her glass. 'I shall steal one of your over-the-top romantic expressions and say that it was love at first sight.'

She lifted an eyebrow in mockery. 'Getting soppy on me, Tariq?'

'Perhaps.' He flashed her a smile that was so charismatic she felt her stomach perform a series of acrobatic moves. 'Blame the stars.'

She stared up at the tiny dots that sparkled and patterned the sky. 'Did your parents love each other? Were they happy together?'

He hesitated. 'To answer that, I will have to shatter your romantic illusions. They were *extremely* unhappy. And the result of that was that they spent virtually no time together. It was very much a marriage of political convenience.'

'Then it's no wonder you don't believe in love.'

His eyes narrowed. 'How do you know I don't believe in love?'

'Nadia and the Sultan.' She sat up and rested her chin on her knees, her expression dreamy. 'When we talked about it you always disagreed with me. You could never understand the degree of passion that might make death seem a better option than losing the love of your life. You were always practical. Now I understand why.'

'Perhaps I just don't believe that marriage is the only way of expressing true passion.'

'Ah—so finally we're back to sex again.' Her eyes gleamed and his mouth curved into a sardonic smile.

'You have the two so neatly separated in your head. Do you not know that sex can be an expression of love?'

Oh, yes, she knew that. Suddenly breathlessly aware of his body close to hers, she felt her heart stop. In the two weeks they'd spent together he hadn't once touched her. But it had been there between them all the time. Simmering passion. He was biding his time and she knew it. And she had to admit that the slow build of anticipation had only added to her own excitement.

Never could she have imagined that it was possible to want a man as much as she wanted him.

He lounged by the fire next to her and her gaze was drawn to his lean, muscular legs and upwards to his broad shoulders. He had a powerfully athletic physique and suddenly she knew that if he chose to touch her now she wouldn't be able to resist him. He was the one. The only man she would ever love. The only man she would ever want. Like Nadia, she knew she would never be able to be with another.

And something had changed between them over the past two weeks.

He was gradually opening up to her. Revealing parts of himself that he'd kept carefully hidden. Confiding in her, even though she could tell that it was difficult for him. Would he do that if he felt nothing? Would he do that if all he cared about were sex?

Aware that he was watching her with those disturbing dark eyes, she scraped her hair away from her eyes and gave him a self-conscious smile.

'Where are we going tomorrow?'

His gaze didn't shift from hers and he didn't hesitate. 'To the Caves of Zatua. Time to indulge your passion for our legend, *laeela.*'

'I haven't been there for five years.'

'Then we must hope the trip lives up to your romantic expectations.'

There was something in his lazy drawl that made her look at him searchingly but there were no clues to be found in his slightly amused gaze.

Was it coincidence that he'd chosen to take her there at the end of the promised two weeks? She wanted to ask whether they'd be on their own, but she wasn't sure whether she wanted that to be the case. In fact, she didn't know what she wanted anymore. Her resolve to stay away from him had been weakened by their growing intimacy and the slow throb of unfulfilled passion that grew stronger each day.

She didn't know what she wanted anymore, but it was time to decide because she knew that a man like Tariq wouldn't be prepared to wait much longer.

Tariq lay by the fire long after she'd retired to bed.

What, he wondered to himself, *had come over him*? Never before had he felt even the smallest desire to discuss his past with a woman, let alone a woman that he intended to divorce a mere forty days after the wedding.

He wasn't the confiding type—had never felt the need to spill his guts to anyone, man or woman. It wasn't his style and never had been. From childhood he'd been taught to control and contain his emotions, and that was what he'd always done.

So why had he just spent a long evening telling Farrah Tyndall things about himself that even his closest advisers didn't know?

He'd even talked about his mother and that was something that he'd *never* been driven to do before.

With a soft curse he ran a hand over the back of his neck and put his uncharacteristic behaviour down to physical frustration. He saw her on a daily basis but he'd made a strategic decision not to touch her. To give her the space she so obviously thought she needed. He was not accustomed to exercising such self-denial but, on this occasion, he was willing to do whatever it took to bring this deal to a successful conclusion.

And the strangest thing of all was that he'd actually found himself enjoying her company on their lengthy trips together. She'd shown herself to be surprisingly intelligent and well informed.

But, he reminded himself quickly, that was only because he'd removed all opportunity for her to indulge her party habit.

Given the right set of circumstances, he had no doubt that Farrah Tyndall would revert to type and become the shallow socialite again. It was fortunate that he had plans for curbing her addiction to the empty lifestyle that she enjoyed so much. He'd decided to make the most of their limited time together.

For the short duration of their marriage she would remain confined to his bed.

After two frustratingly long weeks of unnatural celibacy, letting her walk away untouched had tested his control to its limits but he told himself that it was only for one more night.

Everything was in place. Everything was arranged.

He'd given her two weeks to make up her mind and the two weeks was up tomorrow.

Tomorrow she would be his.

Their marriage would take place. The shares would be his.

And after forty days and forty nights he would divorce her.

They left at lunchtime, driving across the dusty sun-baked dunes towards the Caves of Zatua.

Farrah sat in silence, painfully aware of the feverish tension that was building between them. He was so close and she was aware of every move he made. Ignoring him had become impossible. What was it about this man that made it so difficult to breathe? Why was it that she couldn't look at him and not think about sex? She wasn't like that and never had been. She had plenty of male friends and she never *once* thought about sex in their company. With Tariq it seemed she could think about nothing else.

The attraction she felt was becoming almost intolerable. It was hard to be in such a confined space and not reach for him. She wanted to slide her hands through that luxuriant black hair, run her fingers along his roughened jaw and sink her teeth into his bronzed muscular shoulder. She wanted to strip his clothes off and see him naked! And yet not once during the fortnight they'd just spent together had he made a move in her direction.

After that first steamy kiss in the car on the way to the camp—a kiss that had been merely a manoeuvre on his part—he hadn't made a single sexual overture.

They'd talked, he'd taken her on endless trips and they'd eaten meals together. Occasionally his hand lingered on hers a moment longer than was strictly necessary and sometimes she caught him looking at her with that deadly gleam in his eyes. But he hadn't kissed her again.

And yet neither of them could fail to be aware that the fortnight that he'd promised was now complete. Today was the last day.

When was he going to ask her for her decision?

And what was her decision going to be?

As she walked towards the entrance of the caves she thought of Nadia. Was this how she had felt before she'd plunged into her passionate affair with the Sultan? Had she had doubts or had love and passion swept away common sense?

In his usual decisive fashion, Tariq grasped her hand, his long strong fingers closing over hers.

'Come.' It was a command and she followed his lead, walking next to him into the huge cavern that guarded the entrance to the labyrinth of caves.

The first cavern was alight with flickering candles and intricately woven rugs had been placed on the ground. Tariq glanced around him with satisfaction.

Everything had been carried out exactly as he'd instructed.

He heard her shocked, delighted gasp and knew that the effort on his part had produced the desired response.

She turned to him, her gaze a mixture of delight and confusion. 'It's so beautiful,' she breathed. 'Who did this?'

'I did. I'm trying to demonstrate that I'm capable of romance.' His smile held a hint of wry self-mockery. 'You've always loved these caves. They mean a great deal to you, which is why I have chosen to bring you here to ask you the question that has been on both our minds for the past two weeks. Marry me, Farrah.' He watched with satisfaction as the breath left her body in a soft rush.

'That sounded more like a command than a question.' She lifted a hand and placed it on the centre of his chest, her touch light and teasing.

'I want you as my wife. I've been patient for two weeks. Now I need to hear your answer. If the answer is yes, then you will marry me here.'

She stilled, a flare of shock lighting her green eyes. 'You want to marry me here? Now? In the caves?'

'What better place than where Nadia and her Sultan first discovered their love and where we too first discovered our feelings for each other?'

The thoughtful silence that greeted his words was not what he had expected. He felt his tension levels soar, although why that should be the case escaped him. He was a man who positively thrived on complex business negotiations. The safe and the predictable bored him. He preferred the impossible to the possible. Having reminded himself of the facts, he waited for the usual adrenaline buzz that accompanied the climax of each major deal. Instead he felt something more akin to—panic?

He dismissed the thought instantly, reminding himself of the far-reaching implications of failing to close this particular deal. It was natural that her answer should take on greater than average importance, he assured himself.

Determined to sway her decision, Tariq slid an arm round her waist and clamped her against him. 'Say yes. And say it quickly,' he commanded. 'My patience is running out.'

'What patience is that? It seems to me that whenever you want something, you just dish out orders and it happens.'

'So I know what I want and I go after it. What's wrong with that?' He gave an arrogant lift of his head, deciding that he'd had enough of tiptoeing round the edges. 'I want you in my bed and in my life. And I have shown a great deal of patience up until this point. No other woman has *ever* made me wait the way you have made me wait.'

And he'd had enough of waiting. Staring down into her soft green eyes, he felt lust spear his body. She was exquisite and really he was to be congratulated for having waited this long.

She raised an eyebrow. 'Learning to wait for something has probably been good for your emotional development.'

'My emotions are in excellent health, thank you,' he groaned, lowering his head and kissing her neck. *She smelt of paradise*. 'I'd be grateful for an answer any time you feel ready to give it. Just make sure it's in the next three seconds.'

'I feel as though I'm standing on the top of one of your highest sand dunes,' she confessed in a soft voice. 'I don't know whether to step back and opt for safety or whether to plunge forward and risk the danger of falling.'

His eyes gleamed. 'Life with no danger becomes nothing more than an existence. Danger is what makes the miracle of life so precious, *laeela.* Only when you take risks can you know what it is like to truly live.'

'Spoken like a devotee of extreme sports,' she said dryly. 'Before I give you my answer, I need to ask you one question, Tariq.' She stared up at him, a strange light in her eyes. 'And I need you to answer honestly.'

Immediately on the defensive, Tariq racked his brains in an attempt to work out if he'd overlooked something. If he had, then it was going to be difficult to provide it at this late stage. 'Ask your question.'

She hesitated, almost as if she were afraid to voice what was in her head. 'Why do you want to marry me?'

He relaxed. 'That's easy—' He gave a confident smile. 'You're beautiful, you're good company, I enjoy talking to you and you amuse me. I even like the way you speak without any attempt at censorship—' He broke off, astonished at the length of the list and by the fact that the question had been so easy to answer.

'What you've described is friendship, Tariq.'

He frowned, wondering why she wasn't as impressed by the length of the list as he was. 'And shouldn't a good marriage be about friendship?'

It was more than his own parents had ever had, he thought bitterly.

'Of course, but there has to be more than friendship.'

Deciding that physical contact was called for, Tariq gave a smile and pulled her firmly into his arms. 'Of course there is more to marriage than friendship. There is also an amazing attraction between us.' He slid his hands over the rounded curve of her bottom, mentally applauding himself for having displayed such uncharacteristic self-control up until this point. In view of his restraint, it was surely impossible for her to misinterpret his intentions. 'That goes without saying.'

She pushed at his chest, trying to hold him at a distance. 'That's sex, Tariq. So far you've mentioned friendship and sex. Neither of those are reasons to get married. The most important ingredient is missing.'

Alarm bells rang in his head.

It was obvious what she believed the missing ingredient to be.

Like a cornered lion, Tariq felt rising apprehension and discomfort. That feeling of panic took him by the throat. It was clear to him that she wanted him to say, *I love you*. Every muscle in his body tensed and a sheen of sweat broke out on his brow as he steeled himself to say the three words he'd spent his entire life avoiding.

Still trying to circumvent the issue, his mind quickly ran through a few possible alternatives. *You're very beautiful. I want you in my bed. You're good company.*

He'd already tried all those and *still* she wasn't satisfied. One glance at the expectation in her shining eyes was sufficient to convince him that substitute words were not going to suffice.

He took a deep breath and licked his lips. How hard could it be?

'You're an amazing woman—'

'Thank you.' Her eyes gleamed with ironic humour. 'I'm glad you think so, but it isn't a reason to marry.'

Was she doing this intentionally to torture him? 'I—' He ran a hand over the back of his neck and she gave a soft laugh and wrapped her arms round his neck, her eyes dancing, her smile warm and trusting.

'Just three little words, Tariq. How hard can it be?'

Very hard, as he was fast discovering. He stiffened and steeled himself to make the effort that was so obviously required of him but she hugged him tightly and stood on tiptoe to kiss his cheek.

'You've never said those words to anyone before, have you, Tariq?'

He shook his head, his eyes wary. She was smiling. *Why was she smiling?*

'I know you love me.' She said the words quietly. 'But I'm going to need to hear you say it. Often. So you're going to have to practice. And yes, I'll marry you.'

She knew he loved her? How?

He was so busy wondering exactly *which* part of his behaviour had suggested to her that he was in love that it took him a few moments to realize that she'd given him the answer he'd been waiting for.

'You will marry me?' The degree of pleasure he experienced at her words surprised and unsettled him. But then he reminded himself that this marriage was the final part of an important business deal on his part. A deal that had proved far more complex than he'd anticipated. Of course he had every right to be pleased. He would take over her father's company. The pipeline could be built. The future of Tazkash was secure. 'You're saying yes?'

'I'm saying yes because you've finally proved that you understand me,' she said softly, her expression dreamy as she looked up at him. 'You didn't arrange for some enormous formal wedding with loads of boring guests. You arranged this—' She waved a hand around the illuminated cave. 'And this is the most romantic thing you could have done. It's just you and me. It's about the two of us and no one else. And that's how I know you love me.'

Slightly stunned at her interpretation of what he'd considered to be no more than an elaborate business plan, Tariq smiled. 'Obviously we need someone to marry us and witnesses—'

'And, knowing you, there are several of your staff waiting at this moment to receive your call.'

'How do you know that?'

'Because you're a very controlling personality,' she teased, 'and I know you wouldn't have set this up without having thought of everything.'

He found the fact that someone knew him that well vaguely disconcerting. Never before had he gained the impression that women had even the remotest understanding of the workings of the male sex. Farrah was proving to be disturbingly astute.

'So—' she glanced down at herself with a rueful smile, '—did you think of clothing, or am I getting married in my jeans?'

'Yasmina has brought you a dress.'

'Good.' She reached up and kissed him. 'So let's get on with it, shall we?'

CHAPTER SEVEN

FARRAH stood in her wedding dress, trying to remember a moment in her life when she'd felt happier.

She'd just married the man that she loved in a place that had always been special to her. And it had been *incredibly* romantic.

Vows had been exchanged in front of witnesses. She was wearing his ring.

It was hard to see how life could be better.

Overwhelmed with happiness, she turned to Tariq and hugged him tightly. 'I love you so much.' His powerful frame went rigid in response to her unguarded declaration and she felt his immediate withdrawal. Pulling away slightly, she tipped her head back so that she could see his face. Thick dark lashes shielded the expression in his eyes but his mouth was hard and unsmiling. She felt a sudden flash of uncertainty. And insecurity. 'It makes you uncomfortable, doesn't it, when I hug you?'

His hesitation was barely perceptible. 'It's not a problem. You may hug me if you wish. I understand that women have a greater need for affection than men.'

As answers went, it wasn't entirely reassuring. 'I don't think that's true. It's just that men aren't always comfortable with their emotions.'

But she was going to make him comfortable, she decided. She was going to make him open up and confide in her.

He studied her, a curious expression in his eyes. 'I've never met anyone quite like you before,' he confessed, his voice slightly unsteady. 'You're very affectionate. You don't hold anything back. You don't hide anything.'

She felt a sharp pang of guilt, aware that there was a *huge* part of herself that she was hiding. Concealing her true self had become second nature to her, so much so that even now, when everything had changed between them, she couldn't quite bring herself reveal the person she really was.

Anyway, what was the hurry? Tariq needed a wife who was prepared to socialize. He didn't want or need to hear that it wasn't her favourite pastime. Hadn't he approached her a second time because she'd shown that she was capable of holding her own on the social scene that he frequented?

She smiled, thinking that part of the fun of their marriage would be making discoveries about each other. 'I certainly think it's important to tell someone that you love them.'

And if she was a little disappointed that he still hadn't said those words to her, she pushed the emotion away. After everything he'd told her about his childhood, was it really surprising that he had trouble showing his emotions? They were difficult words to say if you'd never been encouraged to say them, and clearly Tariq had never been allowed to express his emotions in any way. She'd be wrong to expect too much of him too quickly.

She understood only too well the impact that one's upbringing could have on behaviour.

Food was served against the backdrop of the setting sun, but Farrah found it hard to eat anything at all. Her nerves were jumping and her stomach was churning and she was breathlessly aware of Tariq, lounging on the rug right next to her.

He was as much at home here in the desert as he was in

his palace, she thought, watching as he selected various delicacies and placed them on her plate.

'You're not eating, *laeela.*' His voice was low and seductive and his eyes swept her face in question. 'You have lost your appetite?'

The way he looked at her sent a jolt of awareness through her body and she managed a shaky smile. 'I'm not that hungry.' They were surrounded by a discreet army of staff and yet it was as if they were alone.

Casting a final lingering glance in her direction, Tariq rose to his feet in a smooth athletic movement and dismissed the staff with an imperious wave of his bronzed hand.

'Why are you sending them away?' Farrah watched in surprise as the staff melted away to the Jeeps. 'We still have to drive back to the camp.'

'Not tonight.' He drew her to her feet, very much in command of the situation. 'Tonight we stay in the caves.'

'Here?' She looked up at his arrogant, proud features and her heart thudded against her chest. 'We're *sleeping* in the cave?'

His answering smile was both seductive and dangerous. 'I don't anticipate much sleeping, *laeela,* but yes, we are spending the night in the cave. Like Nadia and her Sultan.'

As she watched the last of the convoy pull away from the caves Farrah licked her lips and her eyes slid back to his. 'On our own?'

His eyes held a hint of mockery. 'For what I have in mind, I don't require an audience.'

Her pulse rate surged at an alarming rate. 'I can't believe you've arranged this—'

'Despite what you say about me, I am trying to understand you. You grew up dreaming of Nadia and her Sultan, together in this cave. Their relationship was the centre of all your childish fantasies.' His voice was husky and he lifted a hand

and withdrew the pins from her hair, allowing it to fall unrestrained around her shoulders. 'And I am more than prepared to indulge your fantasies.'

'Tariq—'

His hand tightened over hers and he led her along the narrow passageway that led through the rocks to the second cave. Again it was lit with candles and the rugs were strewn with cushions and velvet throws. The atmosphere was seductive and intimate.

'Oh—' She stared in amazement. 'You planned all this?'

'Of course. I remembered that you didn't like the dark when we first came here five years ago. And now that is definitely enough talking. For two whole weeks we have done nothing but talk.' He groaned and hauled her against him in a decisive movement. 'Have you *any* idea how long I've been waiting to undress you?'

Her stomach flipped over with nerves. 'You married me just so that you can undress me?'

'I was getting to the point where I would have done almost anything in order to win the right to undress you,' he confessed unsteadily, his arm anchored firmly around her hips.

Held against his hard, muscular strength she felt her limbs weaken. 'Are we going to blow out the candles?'

'No. Definitely not. I want to see all of you.' His voice was husky as he trailed burning kisses down her neck. 'I want to see your face when I finally make love to you.'

His words sent a wicked thrill through her body. 'Tariq—'

'I have *never* wanted a woman as much as I want you—'

Breathless and trembling with anticipation, she told herself that it didn't matter that he couldn't actually bring himself to say the words she wanted to hear so badly. He'd married her and the ceremony had been full of romantic gestures. He'd *shown* her that he loved her. That was enough. Finally she'd met a man who loved *her*, rather than her money or her father's influence. In time she'd teach him how to be comfortable with his emotions.

'You haven't touched me for the past fortnight—'

'Because I didn't want you accusing me of only wanting you for sex,' he muttered as his mouth hovered over hers. 'I've taken so many cold showers that my staff are beginning to question my sanity. And I've been trying so hard to understand you that my brain is aching.'

He slid a hand into her hair and tilted her head back to allow him better access. His mouth was close, so *close*, and the heat and anticipation built inside her.

She'd waited so long for this moment. She'd imagined, she'd dreamed—

'So—' He raked his fingers through her long hair, his gaze hungry as he scanned her face. 'What did the Sultan do next, do you think, *laeela*?'

Her heart pounded against her ribs. 'I expect he undressed her slowly.'

'Slowly?' One ebony brow lifted and there was a sardonic gleam in his eyes. 'In that case I think we could have hit our first problem.' His gaze holding hers, he released her and stepped back. Then he reached inside his robes, withdrew a dagger and with a swift, precise movement of the deadly blade he cut her dress from neck to waist.

The priceless white silk slithered into a pool at her feet and she gave a gasp of shock. 'Tariq—'

He tossed the dagger casually to one side and gave an apologetic shrug of his broad shoulders. 'It is entirely possible that I'm not as patient as your Sultan,' he confessed in a regretful tone that held more humour than sincerity. 'Where you're concerned, I don't do "slow". I've waited five years for this moment and that is long enough.' His eyes glowed dark with purpose and her breath caught in her throat.

What woman could fail to be flattered by the burning need

she saw in his gaze? What woman could fail to feel powerful and feminine when on the receiving end of such a blatantly sexual appraisal?

He wanted her. *He wanted her so much that he couldn't even be bothered with a few buttons.*

Tariq muttered something unintelligible under his breath and then shed his robes in a few smooth movements. Totally unselfconscious and with his usual arrogance, he swept her high in his arms and lowered her gently on to the piled cushions, his eyes fixed on hers.

'At last, you are mine—' The words were a clear statement of possession and she gave a shiver of longing.

'Kiss me,' she breathed against his mouth, the excitement inside her building to breaking point, '*please kiss me*—'

And he did.

'I'm going to discover you piece by piece.' His mouth was hot and demanding, the skilled and subtle probe of his tongue an erotic and intimate prelude to what was to follow. The chemistry between them exploded with frightening force. She felt breathless and dizzy, as though she were poised on the edge of something dangerous, *something that would change her for ever*, and instinctively her arms slid round his neck, seeking his protection.

The flickering candles provided just enough light for her to see the harsh planes of his handsome face, for her to make out the burning intent glowing in his eyes.

He shifted slightly, covering her with his lean, powerful frame as his mouth took hers. His kiss was possessive and urgent and she was breathlessly aware of the hard heat of his body. She arched in an involuntary movement, hearing his groan of approval as he lifted his mouth from hers and transferred his attention to her breasts.

The skilled flick of his tongue over her nipple sent sharp stabs of sensation shooting low in her pelvis and she pressed against him in an instinctive attempt to soothe the throbbing ache that was building within her body.

It was only as she felt the cool air of the cave whisper over her bare skin that she realized that he'd somehow removed the last of her clothing. She was naked under him and she felt the leisurely, seductive stroke of his hand over her thigh.

'I'm going to torture you with pleasure,' he promised in husky tones and proceeded to do just that. He kissed and caressed every part of her body except that one most intimate place that ached to be touched. He licked the top of her thigh, dragged slow kisses over her stomach, always withholding what she wanted most. She shifted and moved and the ache inside her intensified until it was almost pain and desperation rose to screaming pitch.

Did he know? she wondered. Did he have any idea what he was doing to her?

And then he lifted his head and she saw the wicked self-satisfied gleam in his eyes.

He knew.

'Tariq, please—' Losing all her inhibitions, she reached for him, her fingers touching him intimately for the first time. She gave a violent shiver of excitement as she felt the power of his aroused manhood, registered his size with a flicker of trepidation. But, before she could think, he reached down and finally touched her where she was longing to be touched.

Sensation merged and mingled until she could no longer distinguish exactly what he was doing to her. His fingers moved with skill and awareness as he touched and teased until her entire focus was on the incessant, blinding ache deep inside her.

Everything went from her head except the desperate need for him. She wrapped her legs around his waist, urging him on with her body and he slipped an arm under her hips and raised her.

'Look at me—' His command was hoarse and urgent and her eyes flew wide with shock and breathless abandon as he entered her with a purposeful thrust that joined them in the most intimate way possible.

Shocked by the size of him, her body instinctively tightened and she felt him pause, his eyes darkening as he stared down at her. 'Farrah?'

'Don't stop! Oh, please, don't stop now,' she groaned and he drew in an unsteady breath and moved again, but this time more gently.

Sensation flashed and exploded and she gave a gasp of pleasure that he misinterpreted.

'I don't want to hurt you—' He looked strangely uncertain and she shook her head.

'You're not—please, Tariq. I need—I want—' She broke off and closed her eyes, unable to verbalize exactly what it was that she wanted but hoping that he could make the necessary translation.

He did.

He moved again and the feelings in her body escalated until every thought in her head was eclipsed by a sensation so wild and all consuming that she could do no more than cry out his name and move in the way that he urged her to move as he guided them both towards sexual oblivion.

When the explosion came it took them both together in a shower of sensation so intense that she clutched at him as if he was the only one that could save her from the madness.

And perhaps he felt it too because he drove into her hard and then held her against him, murmuring something against her neck while his body throbbed into hers.

Tariq lay in the dark with Farrah wrapped around him. Her head was on his chest, strands of blond hair were spread over his arm and the cushions beneath them and her limbs were tangled with his. Listening to her peaceful steady breathing, he knew that she slept.

In the aftermath of the most incredible sex of his life he was being forced to re-evaluate almost all his preconceived ideas about marriage. He was shocked to discover that he actually enjoyed the idea that she belonged to him and no one else. And the biggest shock of all was the discovery that she'd been a virgin.

It was true that the file on her that currently lay in his desk contained no evidence of her involvement with a man, but never, not once, had it crossed his mind that she might be innocent.

The knowledge that he'd been the first and only man to experience the seductive passion of Farrah Tyndall brought a soft smile of masculine satisfaction to his face. But the smile faded the instant he remembered that in forty days and forty nights he would release her from the bonds of matrimony, which would leave her free to link up with any man of her choosing.

And, given the degree of male adulation she'd received when she'd strolled on to the catwalk, she wasn't going to find any shortage of willing candidates.

At the mere thought of Farrah with another man he was suddenly filled with a possessiveness so intense that he contemplated creating a landslide that would trap them in the cave for ever.

He had no intention of *ever* sharing her with *anyone.*

Which left him facing a situation he hadn't anticipated.

He'd entertained the idea of marriage only because he knew that it would be short-lived. The fact that he might not want to divorce her at the end of forty days and forty nights hadn't crossed his mind.

Why would it? Farrah Tyndall was no one's idea of good wife material. She was flighty and shallow and her priorities were all wrong. It would be impossible for him to persuade his people to take a woman like her to their hearts. The marriage had been no more than a business deal designed to give him ownership of her shares.

He'd married her only because he knew that divorce would follow.

And yet why would he even contemplate ending something which had brought him the greatest pleasure he'd ever experienced?

The solution was simple, he decided, tightening his grip on her soft, curvaceous body. He wouldn't divorce her. They would remain married.

Instead of taking over the company, he would work in partnership with her father to build the pipeline. He had no doubt that, now that he'd actually married Farrah, Harrison Tyndall would be prepared to reopen negotiations. She need never know that the company was his original reason for marrying her.

And, as for her unfortunate partying habit—he frowned slightly as he searched for a solution. She was surprisingly intelligent and she'd coped well with life in the desert. He just needed to make sure that she was kept well away from charity balls and fashion shows. If he kept her on a tight leash and watched her every move in public, could it not work?

Of course it could. All he had to do was to arrange for her to have an extensive staff to watch her every move when he wasn't around to do so himself.

With that in place, she could stay as his wife and his plan to divorce her would stay well and truly buried.

Why risk upsetting her unnecessarily when that situation was now in the past?

Having found a satisfactory solution designed to keep her by his side for ever, he slid a hand down the smooth skin of her back and decided that she'd *definitely* slept for quite long enough…

* * *

Farrah woke feeling deliciously warm. Her body ached in unusual places and she was instantly aware of Tariq's arms holding her securely against him.

The memories of the intimacies they'd shared during the night brought a touch of colour to her cheeks and she lifted her head with a shy smile.

'Have I told you that I love you and that I think you're incredible?'

His dark eyes locked with hers and flashed with fierce determination. 'You are mine and you're staying that way,' he said decisively and she frowned slightly, wondering why he felt the need to say that after they'd been through a marriage ceremony. *Of course she was his.*

She pressed a lingering kiss on his bronzed shoulder. 'You're possessive, do you know that? Domineering, controlling and overprotective.'

His arms tightened around her. 'Never before,' he said huskily, 'but with you, yes. I have discovered the meaning of all those words. You are mine, always, for ever.'

Basking in a warm haze of masculine appreciation, Farrah lay back and watched as tiny fingers of light found their way into the cave. 'I don't ever want to leave here,' she whispered softly. 'It's perfect here.'

Tariq tensed. 'It *is* perfect, but sadly we cannot spend the rest of our lives in this cave.'

'How about the rest of the day?'

'Not even that, I'm afraid.'

'What's happened to your controlling, demanding personality? You're the Sultan. Everyone has to obey you.' She rolled on top of him, blond hair tangling with dark. 'You can tell everyone that this is where you're going to live from now on. They can drop off food parcels.'

He reached up and pushed her hair away from her face,

his expression fierce. 'It is what we share that matters, *laeela,* not where we choose to share it.'

'Oh—' Her heart skipped and danced and she lowered her head and kissed him. 'That's the most romantic thing anyone has ever said to me. And, just for that, I'll forgive you for saying we have to leave. Are we going back to Nazaar?'

'Not to Nazaar.'

Something about the way he was looking at her made her suddenly anxious and she drew back slightly. 'Where, then? Where are we going?'

'We have to return to Fallouk.'

Fallouk.

The word made an ugly dent in the smooth, warm atmosphere. Farrah sat upright, blond hair sliding over her shoulders, horror on her face. 'No.'

'It was inevitable that we would have to return there.' His tone was level. Unemotional. 'It is my home. And my home is now your home.'

'We can't go there, not yet.' Her own tone was frantic and clogged with emotion. 'That was where everything went wrong last time.'

'Things will not go wrong this time,' he assured her immediately, reaching out and pulling her back into his arms. 'You are my wife and no one can change that.'

It was true, she assured herself as she relaxed against him and tried to make the most of their last moments together in the cave. She *was* his wife. But even that knowledge couldn't dispel the sick feeling of unease that rose inside her.

Farrah sat silent in the back of the chauffeur-driven car, her feeling of foreboding growing stronger with every mile they drew closer to the capital city and the Palace.

As if to match her dark mood, thunder and lightning flashed through the sky and she stared into the deepening gloom wondering if the worsening weather was an omen. A portent of things to come?

Telling herself that she was being ridiculous she tried to forget, but instead she found herself remembering every minute detail of her last visit to Fallouk, the ancient capital city of Tazkash…

After a month living in the desert camp at Nazaar, Tariq's father's ill health dictated that they all return to the capital city. Tariq insisted that she return with him.

Madly in love, convinced that it was only a matter of time before he proposed, Farrah readily agreed but found herself more than a little daunted by the opulence and formality of palace life.

The truth was, to the constant chagrin of her sociable mother, she wasn't comfortable at glitzy parties and functions.

'I don't know what to do or what to say,' she'd confessed to Tariq a few days later but he'd brushed her fears aside, suddenly remote and distracted and nothing like the man whose company she'd enjoyed so much during their time in the desert.

'Any of my family will help you,' he'd assured her with a faint frown. 'If you have questions, you only have to ask.'

She wondered if she ought to point out that, after the initial introductions to endless cousins, uncles and aunts, none of his family had come near her. She'd spent the last few days on her own in her room, reading.

'I hardly see you—'

'My father is unwell. I have urgent matters of state to attend to—'

She smiled, feeling horribly guilty for being the one to put extra pressure on him. 'Of course, I'm sorry—don't worry, I'll be fine.'

'There is a formal dinner tonight—' Distracted and unusually tense, his eyes flickered to one of his advisers who hovered anxiously at a discreet distance, obviously eager to escort him to yet another meeting. 'I will arrange for someone to help you prepare.'

And from then on it had been downhill all the way.

Racked by insecurities and longing for just five minutes alone with him so she could ask him some questions about how she should be dressing and behaving, Farrah spent ages selecting something suitable to wear for her first formal dinner.

Finally satisfied with her choice, she was just adding some discreet jewellery when a young woman strolled into her room.

'I'm Asma, Tariq's cousin. He asked me to come and help you dress.' Her faintly superior air and slightly mocking smile suggested that it was the last job in the world she would have chosen. 'Oh—' She ran her eyes over Farrah's slim frame and pulled a face.

Already lacking in confidence, Farrah bit her lip. 'Something's wrong with the way I'm dressed?'

His cousin opened her mouth and then closed it again with a faint smile. 'Not at all. You look delightful.'

Farrah glanced down at herself. She'd chosen the dress so carefully. 'I thought it was discreet.' Determined to get it right, she'd chosen to wear long sleeves and a high neck. 'I want to make the right impression.' She didn't dare admit that she didn't even enjoy formal functions that much.

'Of course you do. But Tariq is a man used to being with *extremely* beautiful women. You're never going to hold him if you dress like a nun,' Asma murmured, her huge dark eyes roving over Farrah with something approaching pity. 'My cousin appreciates beautiful women.'

Farrah bit her lip. The cruel reminder of Tariq's reputation with her sex made her stomach sink and all her youthful insecurities rush to the surface.

Why would he possibly be interested in her? He mixed with sophisticated mature women who knew exactly what games to play to keep him ensnared and interested. Whereas she—

She caught a glimpse of herself in the mirror and let out a sigh of frustration.

She was just a girl and it showed. She laughed at the wrong times, talked at the wrong times and dressed in the wrong clothes. Her own mother had despaired of her. What could a man like Tariq possibly see in her?

In the desert she'd felt that they'd connected, but here—here amongst the splendour and the formality she felt totally out of her depth.

But then she remembered the kiss they'd shared at the caves of Zatua. He loved her, she knew he did. And she would learn everything there was to know about palace life, she told herself with a determined lift of her chin. She could *learn* to be the sort of wife he needed and wanted.

'All right—' Turning away from the mirror, she started to unzip her dress. 'Tell me what I should be wearing, Asma. I need your help.' Instinctively trusting, she turned to the other girl for advice.

'Something short and low-cut,' Asma said immediately, reaching for something from the rail. 'This looks good.'

It looked like something her mother would have chosen. Farrah looked at it doubtfully. 'I wouldn't normally wear anything that revealing.'

'But do you normally date guys like Tariq?' Asma's smile did little to conceal her disbelief at her cousin's current choice. 'He dates the most sophisticated women in the world—princesses, actresses, models—'

'All right, thanks, I'll try it.' Farrah interrupted her hastily, not wanting to hear any more about the type of woman Tariq usually chose. Her confidence was at an all-time low and she didn't need the fact that she was an unusual choice for him battered home by a member of his family.

He was single, wasn't he? So obviously he'd never been in love before now. And that, she told herself firmly as she wriggled into a dress that made her blush, was the difference between her and the competition.

She stared at herself doubtfully in the mirror and tugged the neckline upwards. 'You're sure this is suitable?'

'Absolutely,' Asma replied smoothly. 'I think we can safely say that if you wear this tonight Tariq won't be able to take his eyes off you.'

Her prediction proved to be correct, but not for the reasons that Farrah had assumed. Far from being dazzled by her beauty and glamour, Tariq had looked at her with a frowning disapproval that he hadn't attempted to conceal.

'That dress is *not* suitable. You should have asked my family for advice on how to dress,' he said coldly and she gritted her teeth, ignoring the sting of tears behind her eyes, trying not to feel hurt at his complete lack of understanding.

And, as for Asma—she realized, too late, that the girl clearly had her own agenda, but she was nowhere to be seen and Farrah was forced to endure a hideous evening, aware that she'd committed an enormous social *faux pas* and had embarrassed Tariq as well as herself.

Why Asma had chosen to put her in this position was a mystery to her.

Furious with herself for being so naïve and trusting and feeling miserably self-conscious amongst the formally dressed women, Farrah picked at her food and kept her mouth shut, afraid to risk expressing an opinion. She'd already put her foot in it. She didn't want to risk making another mistake. She didn't want to draw attention to herself. And she was just mortified at having been so gullible and not having followed her own instincts when it came to matters of dress.

As a result of her own desperate embarrassment, she met all Tariq's attempts to converse with monosyllabic answers and tried not to mind when he finally gave up and started to talk to the beautiful redhead seated to his right.

As far as she was concerned, the evening couldn't end soon enough and she escaped back to her room at the earliest opportunity.

He sought her out the following morning. 'You should have asked for advice on what to wear. I will arrange for one of my aunts to talk to you.'

'If she's related to Asma then please don't bother,' Farrah muttered, trying not to sound sulky. 'I think I've just about had all the help I can stand from your family.'

His gaze was chilly. 'What is that supposed to mean?'

'Well, they're not exactly welcoming, are they? It is perfectly obvious that they don't want me here. They resent me.' Asma had blatantly set out to embarrass and humiliate her in front of Tariq.

'That's nonsense.' His brows came together in a frown. 'Why would they resent you?'

'I have no idea,' she said flatly. 'Unlike you, I don't have a PhD in palace politics.' She looked at his rigid profile and suddenly the fight drained out of her. 'Don't let's argue. I love you, Tariq.'

His gaze softened slightly. 'Things have not been easy since we arrived here, I understand that. There is something I have to ask you and perhaps this is a good time.'

Her heart suddenly skipped and danced. The humiliation of the previous evening was forgotten as excitement took its place. This was the moment she'd been waiting for. This was the moment that Tariq was going to ask her to marry him.

Poised to say yes, she held her breath and waited expectantly.

He took her hand in his and lifted it to his mouth in a

strangely old fashioned gesture. 'I suppose things are more difficult because people are unsure of why you are here. Your role hasn't yet been defined.'

She couldn't hold back the smile. *It was now*. He was going to ask her now. 'I'm sure you're right—' She'd never known such happiness. She wanted the delicious sense of anticipation to last for ever.

'So you will move into my apartment today. I'll announce it straight away. It was foolish of me to delay.' He slid an arm round her waist and dropped a lingering kiss on her mouth. 'After all, you are perfect mistress material.'

Her happiness died a dramatic and rapid death. 'Perfect mistress material?'

'Of course.' He smiled, supremely confident. 'To wait any longer would be madness given the powerful chemistry between us.'

'Perfect mistress material?' It was such a shock that she had trouble getting her tongue round the words and she stared at him blankly. 'That's what you're planning to announce?'

'You are extremely beautiful and I find you amusing company,' he assured her. 'You can move in with me. You won't even have to appear in public much. You can just keep to my suite of rooms.'

In other words, he was ashamed of her and didn't want to display her in public, she thought miserably.

And, just like that, her dreams fell to the ground and broke into pieces.

A tight band squeezed her heart. 'Let me get this straight.' Her voice shook slightly. 'You've decided that I'm good enough to have sex with you?'

He frowned. 'I'm offering you a great deal more than that.'

Her temper started to simmer. 'What, exactly?'

'A place by my side. Access to certain aspects of palace life.'

Certain aspects. 'Until you decide that you've had enough of me.' She hid her pain behind anger. 'I'm worth more than that, Tariq.'

He released her and stepped back, his bronzed hands spread in a gesture of masculine exasperation. 'I am honouring you—'

'No, you're insulting me,' she said flatly, turning away so that she didn't have to look at him. *Wasn't tempted to just throw herself in his arms and accept him on any terms*. 'You're every bit as bad as the sultan in the legend. He was ashamed of Nadia, just as you're ashamed of me.'

'You are as dreamy and impractical as Nadia. But now we reach the truth.' His voice was silky smooth and she tensed as he strolled up behind her. 'You were expecting marriage.'

The fact that he was aware of her hopes simply added to her humiliation and she turned angrily, blinking back tears.

'I realize now that Nadia was an utter fool! Instead of killing herself, she should have killed the Sultan for being such a short-sighted, selfish *bastard*,' The word came out on a sob and he inhaled sharply.

'Our legend has twisted your thinking, but—'

'My thinking is perfectly straight, thank you,' she yelled, ignoring the fact that her voice could probably be heard halfway round the palace. She didn't care! She just couldn't believe what he was saying. She loved him. 'It's you that's twisted! You're not capable of loving anyone except yourself. All you think about is yourself.'

Proud and unyielding, he threw back his head, his dark eyes ablaze. 'You are angry because you wanted the position of my wife,' he said coldly, 'but—'

'You make it sound like a job application!' She flung the words at him like stones. 'You just don't get it, do you? Why do you think I wanted to marry you, Tariq?'

His shoulders were tense and he was very much a man on

the defensive. 'For the same reason that the peasant girl wanted to marry the Sultan. For power and position.'

She turned away, not wanting to reveal the depth of her feelings. Not only did he not love her, but he didn't believe in her love for him.

The past few weeks had obviously meant nothing to him. He thought she was interested in glitz and glamour. He thought she wanted access to his lifestyle.

How could he have misunderstood her so greatly?

And how could she have been such a gullible fool?

But the answer to that was obvious. She'd been a gullible fool because she'd fallen in love with him, she told herself miserably. And love was always generous and optimistic. She'd trusted him. She'd believed in him.

And he'd proved he was a total rat.

She needed to get away fast, before she gave in to her misery and did something totally uncool like begging him…

Dragged back to the present, Farrah gave a tiny laugh. She'd been an innocent, trusting fool, she reflected. So trusting that she hadn't seen the malice in Asma. Hadn't expected even for a moment that she had been doing her best to sabotage a relationship.

But she would never have been able to have sabotaged it without Tariq's help, she reminded herself. He'd been so willing to see the worst in her.

Suddenly everything about her had been unsuitable.

Every step she'd taken in the Palace, her foot had slid right in it up to the thigh. And in the end she'd stopped taking advice from his family because it had been so clear to her that they'd wanted her out of his life.

It would be different this time, Farrah assured herself as the convoy of vehicles gradually approached the ancient walled city of Fallouk.

This time she was arriving as his wife.

They'd spent time together. They enjoyed each other's company.

In his own way, he loved her. *She knew he loved her*.

It was just important to make sure that nothing went wrong. In a sudden panic, she put a hand on his arm. 'You need to tell me how to dress for everything. What's expected of me—'

'Calm yourself, *laeela*,' he said with an amused smile. 'I will take care of everything. There won't be a problem.'

As long as his family didn't interfere, she thought gloomily, wishing that she had his confidence.

'Aren't you worried that your family won't accept me?' she asked, just hating herself for appearing so insecure but, at the same time, needing something in the way of reassurance.

He hesitated and then turned his head away from her. 'My family will welcome this marriage.'

There was something in his tone that made her feel slightly uneasy but she decided that she must have imagined it. She was just apprehensive, which was entirely natural after what had happened on the last occasion she'd had a taste of palace life.

Her apprehension increased as she was escorted to an enormous suite of rooms that led on to a balcony. Stone arches overlooked a courtyard garden below. Feeling confined after the freedom of the desert, Farrah immediately stepped on to the balcony. A gushing fountain formed an impressive centrepiece to the pretty courtyard and exotic plants tumbled in an array of rich colours down the walls of the palace.

She turned to Tariq, who had followed her outside. 'What am I expected to do with my day?'

'You are my wife. Do as you please. During the day, when

I am involved in matters of state, you can enjoy the Palace.' He cupped her face with his lean, strong hands and lowered his head to kiss her. 'You are my Queen. Go anywhere you please. Command as you please.' He surveyed her with benign amusement.

'And at night?' Her heart thumped as she stared up at him. 'What happens at night, Tariq?'

Watching the hot flare of desire in his dark eyes, she felt her limbs weaken alarmingly.

'At night you are mine and mine alone. I share you with no one,' he delivered in his usual arrogant style and she felt her heart miss a beat.

It was going to be all right, she told herself firmly as he released her with obvious reluctance and strode out of the room.

She was his wife and nothing his family did or said could change that.

What could possibly go wrong?

CHAPTER EIGHT

IN HER anxiety not to be late, Farrah dressed for dinner far too early and had time on her hands.

Deciding to spend the spare half an hour exploring the Palace, she wandered down corridors, her heels tapping on the marble floor as she admired paintings, furniture and the ornate ceilings.

She was on the point of returning to Tariq's private apartment when she heard hysterical sobs coming from a room close by.

Instinctively wanting to comfort anyone in so much obvious distress, she gave a sharp frown of concern and hurried towards the sound, pausing by the open doorway as she heard voices. Clearly someone else had had the same idea as herself.

'I hate her,' sobbed an anguished female voice. 'I hate her *so* much. I hate her perfect blond hair and her long legs. I hate her smile. But most of all I hate the fact he actually *married* her.'

'Calm down, Asma,' urged another voice. 'He may have married her but you know he doesn't love her.'

Farrah froze. It was Asma and her mother, Tariq's aunt. And they were talking about *her*. She wanted to leave, to run back down the corridor as quickly as she could, but her feet were glued to the spot. What, she wondered, had she ever done to Asma to deserve being on the receiving end of so much vitriol?

'He's married her,' Asma hiccoughed, her voice rising to a hysterical pitch. 'Despite everything we did five years ago to make sure that she wasn't suitable, he's *married* her!'

'Be silent!' Her mother's voice was sharp. 'The marriage is nothing more than a business deal.'

Asma was sobbing quietly. 'That's rubbish. Of course it isn't a business deal. I saw her face when she arrived in his car! She's crazy about him and she always was.'

'Possibly. But she doesn't know that after forty days and forty nights,' the older woman said crisply, 'he will divorce her.'

There was a long silence, punctuated by a few sniffs as Asma tried to assimilate this latest piece of information. 'Why would he do that?'

Yes, why? Farrah wondered numbly from her position outside the doorway. *Why would he?*

Asma's mother helpfully supplied the answer. 'Because he doesn't love her. Tariq married her only for her shares in her father's company.'

'He's married her for her shares?'

'And they became his on marriage. In forty days he can and will divorce her,' came the firm reply. 'Leaving him free to marry whom he chooses.'

'Which would be me—' Asma's voice shook. 'It would be me, wouldn't it, Mother?'

Unable to hear the answer to that question because of the loud buzzing in her ears, Farrah wondered in a vague, detached way whether she might be about to pass out. There were disturbing clouds around the edge of her vision and suddenly she felt removed from reality. Tariq's aunt must have made some mistake, she thought numbly.

Tariq hadn't married her to gain possession of her shares.

He'd married her because he loved her. She knew he loved her.

But had he actually ever used those words?

Shocked and dazed, she backed away from the open door like someone in a dream and almost fell over a statue behind her.

Why would Tariq need her shares?

She needed to speak to Tariq. She needed to phone her father. *She needed to be sick.*

'Your Highness—'

Dizzy with horror, she turned and recognized the smooth, expressionless features of Hasim Akbar. She remembered him from the desert camp at Nazaar. Wasn't he one of Tariq's most senior advisers? 'I need to see Tariq,' she whispered, so badly in shock that she could barely form the words, 'and I need to see him right now.'

'His Excellency is currently involved in extremely delicate negotiations with the Kazbanian foreign minister and can't be disturbed, but I could—'

'I said, *right now*.' Something in her tone must have hinted at the gravity of the situation because Hasim gave her an anxious look, drew breath and bowed.

'If you would follow me, Your Highness.'

The walk down the marbled corridor was sufficiently long for her to examine the facts. Sufficiently long to ensure that by the time they finally reached the large double doors that led to the private audience chambers, she'd reached boiling point. The guards on either side of the door stood to attention and she eyed the swords that they wore as part of their ceremonial uniform, contemplating violence for the first time in her life. Shock had given way to anger. She felt outraged and affronted and so blisteringly angry that she wanted to kill someone.

Something of her undiluted fury must have shown in her face because Hasim shot her an uneasy look.

'I will announce you, Your Highness,' he began, but she swept past him and the guards without bothering to answer him.

She didn't need a sword, she thought grimly. The way she was feeling at the moment, she was more than capable of killing Tariq with her bare hands.

Utterly shattered by the realization that their marriage was a sham, she stalked through an outer chamber, ignoring the startled looks of those who were waiting to be given an audience with the Sultan, ignoring the confusion on the faces of the guards who were standing by the final doorway. In other circumstances she might have felt sorry for them. Clearly they had no idea whether they were supposed to stop her or not.

But at that moment the only person she felt sorry for was Tariq. He had no idea what was coming to him, she thought grimly as she pushed open the door and walked into the room, head held high. If he'd known then he would have run for the hills.

His dark glossy head was bowed over a set of papers but he looked up with a frown of irritation at her surprise entrance. Astonishment was replaced by caution. 'Something is wrong?'

'You're quick,' she said sweetly, 'very quick. I need to speak to you and I need to speak to you now.'

He threw down the pen he was holding and sat back in his chair, his expression falling a long way short of encouraging. 'Farrah, I am in the middle of negotiating a—'

'What I have to say could be said in public,' she said, working hard to keep her tone well modulated, 'and it probably should be. But in the interests of diplomacy I will allow you precisely sixty seconds to get rid of your guest and save yourself public humiliation.'

With a sharply indrawn breath, Tariq rose to his feet, his eyes never leaving hers. 'Faisel, if you will excuse me for a short time,' he said, 'we will resume this meeting very shortly.

My staff would be honoured to offer you refreshment if you care to go next door.'

Clearly riveted by the scene playing out in front of him, the Kazbanian foreign minister rose to his feet, abandoned the pile of papers in front of him and slid silently out of the room.

'For your information, I hate scenes. And in particular I hate public scenes.' Tariq sat back in his chair, dark eyes glittering with anger, his long fingers drumming a steady rhythm on the polished table. 'I don't appreciate being disturbed in the middle of a meeting.'

'And I don't appreciate discovering that you married me for my father's shares. Allow me to say that I find your romantic streak less than overwhelming, Tariq.'

The atmosphere in the room changed in an instant.

'You're not making sense.' He uttered the words in a bored tone but his fingers stilled, his eyes narrowed and she could see his sharp brain shifting through the gears. It was the final confirmation that she needed.

Rat.

'Oh, I'm making perfect sense. And if you hate scenes then you married the wrong woman because I'm not prepared to stand by with my head bowed while you walk all over me.' Torn in two by the agony of his betrayal and the effort of holding on to her steadily collapsing emotions, she walked across the room and stared out of the window. Then she turned, her voice little more than a whisper. 'You bastard.'

Something flickered across his face. He had the look of a man who knew he was under attack but so far hadn't managed to identify the enemy. 'Farrah—'

'I thought you cared. This time I *really* thought you loved me. And what sort of a fool does that make me?'

He rose to his feet in a fluid movement, his hands on the table. 'We need to—'

'All those things we did together—' she lifted a hand to her forehead and rubbed '—all those things you said to me. And you didn't mean *any* of them.'

'You're being hysterical—'

'Too right I'm hysterical! Forty days and forty nights—' Her voice cracked as she gave voice to the words. 'You married me knowing that you were going to divorce me after forty days and forty nights. What sort of man does a thing like that? *What sort of scumbag gets married with the intention of divorcing his wife after six weeks?*'

He inhaled sharply but she didn't give him a chance to speak.

'Are you sure you can stand me for that long, Tariq? I can't *believe* what a fool I've been. It all makes sense to me now. I thought that getting married in a cave was a romantic gesture on your part but the truth is that you were afraid of marrying me in public in case someone gave the game away. Was that what all the candles were for? To make sure I couldn't see what I was doing? I thought that the time we spent at Nazaar was special, but you were simply doing what was necessary to get your own way, as usual. You are a ruthless, conscienceless rat and I can't believe that I actually slept with you!'

Muttering something in his own language, he moved so swiftly that she didn't see it coming until his fingers gripped the tops of her arms, until she had her back against the wall. 'That's enough! You have had your say, now it is your turn to listen.'

'I don't want to listen.'

'You *will* listen to me—'

'Why? So that you can tell me more lies?' His powerful body pressed hard against hers and she felt the familiar curl of excitement low in her stomach. The instinctive response sickened her. Even now, knowing what she knew, her body failed to recognize the man that he was. 'Face it, Tariq, there's no way you can dig yourself out of this hole. You're in so deep that even a rope and a ladder wouldn't save you now.' She tried to push him away but he planted an arm either side of her head, blocking her escape.

'I insist that you calm down and listen to me. Already I have allowed you more leeway than any other woman.'

'And that's supposed to flatter me? No other woman had the shares you needed, did they, Tariq? It's amazing what you can get away with when the stakes are high enough.' She could feel the tension pulsing through him and wondered with a flicker of alarm whether she'd gone too far.

'Listen to me,' he growled, 'or so help me I will make you and you may not like my methods.'

Eyes clashed, breath mingled and the atmosphere snapped tight around them. She had a feeling that his methods would include his mouth on hers and she wanted to avoid that at all costs.

Even after what had happened, she knew herself well enough to understand that if he kissed her she was lost.

'Speak, then. Make your excuses. Tell me it's all a lie.'

'It isn't a lie.'

The flat, simple statement sent a sharp pain through the centre of her chest, killing off the final flicker of hope that it had all been a terrible misunderstanding on her part.

'Then I truly, truly hate you and there's no excuse for what you've done,' she whispered. Her knees sagged and she would have slid into a heap on the floor if he hadn't caught her.

'I do not intend to make excuses. The pipeline project is essential for the future of Tazkash and it is my responsibility to protect that future. Since our talks with your father collapsed five years ago we have explored a number of other options but none of them are viable. If I have ownership of the company I can make it work. I *have* to make it work for the sake of my people. I bought up all the available shares, but—'

'Hold on a minute—' Her voice was little more than a whisper as she lifted a hand to stop him in mid flow. 'So, as well as using me, you're preparing to smash my father's life too? Preparing to take over a business he's spent his life building? Have you no conscience?'

He tensed. 'You are making it look bad, but—'

'I fail to see how even someone as ruthless and machiavellian as you could put gloss on this situation,' she said, trying to stop her teeth chattering. 'You were prepared to lower yourself to marry me for a few barrels of oil. No matter how many times you rephrase that, it isn't going to look good.'

'You too have gained from this marriage,' he said in a raw tone. 'You have always had money so I understood I couldn't give you that, but now you have royal connections. There is no party list that will not contain your name. Your position as my wife will gain you access to any event that takes your fancy.'

'Don't you mean my position as your ex-wife? You don't have a *clue* about women, Tariq. And you have even less of a clue about *me*!' Thank goodness she'd never told him the truth about herself! Her shell was her protection. His firm hold on her was the only thing preventing her ignominious descent on to the smooth marble floor and perhaps he realized that because she felt his grip tighten.

'You are overwrought and your pride has been damaged, but—'

'Pride? I've just discovered that I'm married to a lump of *slime*, and you talk about pride?' She flung the words at him, mortified as she felt her voice crack with emotion. The fact that, even having spent time together, he knew so little about her depressed her utterly. 'You seem to think I want to spend my entire life at parties—'

'There is nothing wrong with that,' he assured her quickly

in a smooth tone. 'Women are interested in different things than men; it's a fact of life and one that I have long since accepted. You like dressing up, you are addicted to shoes, you find fascination with make-up—' His helpful summary of what he clearly saw to be the main characteristics of her sex left her virtually speechless.

Surely by now he must have at least a vague inkling that she was more than a frivolous socialite?

'So why,' she annunciated when she'd finally recovered sufficiently for speech, 'if this is the sort of person that I am, have I just spent two happy weeks in the desert wearing hiking boots?'

'Because stilettos aren't good on sand?' There was a glimmer of humour in his dark eyes but she was too angry and upset to respond with anything other than a fierce glare.

'You think I lead this empty, useless life and you've never taken the trouble to get to know the real me.'

His expression was instantly guarded. He was a man on the spot and he knew it. 'I don't think you are useless and I've been very touched by how well you adapted to living in the desert,' he returned, his dark eyes scanning her face for a reaction to his words of praise.

'Let me ask you a question,' she said, her tone dangerously quiet. 'If I had to spend the rest of my life in the palace or in the desert, which would I choose?'

He didn't hesitate. 'Of course, the palace. Any woman would.'

'Wrong answer, Tariq.'

His brows met in an impatient frown. 'But you love parties—you spend your life at parties. It's what you do with your life—'

'You deal in stereotypes, Tariq. You've put all women into the same box and you can't even see—' She closed her eyes and shook her head.

What was the point in trying to correct him? The truth was she was so shattered by what she was hearing that she couldn't think of a single thing to say. She just wanted to curl up in a tiny ball and protect herself from any more hurt.

He didn't know her and he never would. *She wasn't going to give him that privilege.*

'You agreed to marry me so *clearly* you believed that this marriage would be advantageous to you also,' he said stiffly and she winced.

Advantageous?

They were just so different. How could she possibly have thought that this relationship would ever work?

'What's clear to me is that the inner workings of my mind are a total mystery to you. And actually they're a mystery to me too, because why I would choose to make a fool of myself over the same man twice in one lifetime I really don't understand,' she muttered and he looked at her with ill-concealed exasperation.

'Then *tell* me how you feel—'

'Sick?'

Sick that she'd been so stupid and trusting. That she'd let herself love him again. But clearly the words had meant nothing to him. And she wasn't about to remind him how open she'd been in her affections. For him marriages were all about mutual benefit. Another type of business deal.

'We are good together. Last night in the cave—' his voice became husky and he stroked her hair away from her face with a gentle hand '—it was incredible, *laeela*. And I decided then that forty days and forty nights with you would not be enough. You can relax because I will *not* be divorcing you.'

His complete lack of sensitivity triggered the burst of emotion that she'd been struggling to hold back and he stared at her with disbelief and no small degree of frustration as the tears spilled down her cheeks.

'You are making no sense whatsoever!' He jabbed his fingers into his hair. 'You are upset because you believed that I planned to divorce you and yet when I tell you that this is not the case, you start crying. Why?'

'Because I've never been more miserable in my life,' she said flatly, scrubbing her palm across her face and sniffing hard. 'You marry me to gain possession of the shares in my father's company but then you decide not to divorce me as originally planned because the sex was actually better than you expected. Forgive me for *not* being flattered, Tariq.'

Two spots of colour appeared on his perfect bone structure. 'You misinterpret everything I say—'

'I don't think so.' Needing to escape before she lost the last of her dignity, she wriggled out of his arms and walked over to the door. Only when the handle was safely under her fingers did she risk turning to look at him.

His handsome face might have been carved from stone, his powerful body tense and unmoving as he watched her. He looked like a man who had his back up against an electric fence. It was clear that he was trying to anticipate her next move and if the situation hadn't been so tragic she would have laughed. It was the first time ever that she could remember seeing Tariq unsure of himself. He didn't know what her next move was going to be.

And neither did she, she realized miserably. Even while her dignity and common sense told her to leave the room—leave him—a tiny, stupid part of her wanted to hurl herself into his arms and lie there safe and warm while he used his diplomatic skills to talk his way out of this vile situation and made it possible for her to forgive him.

'I want to go home, Tariq,' she said, hanging on to the last of her dignity.

'You are my wife and you are not going anywhere.'

One glance at the rigid set of his hard, handsome features

told her that argument was useless. For some reason he wanted her here. And you didn't have to be a genius to know what that reason was.

The sparks in his eyes, the sexual awareness that even now pulsed between them, all gave her the answer to that question.

She sucked in a breath, suddenly knowing what had to be done. *What would hurt him most.* 'You want me to stay? Fine, I'll stay. You thought you were going to have to endure forty days and forty nights with me, Tariq,' she breathed, 'and that's what you're going to do. You've proved that the only things that interest you in life are power, money and sex. Finally I understand the person you really are. You're right when you say the chemistry between us is powerful. You're right when you say that our wedding night was amazing. It was. But that was it. That was all you're ever going to get from me. From now on you can look, but you're not going to touch. Prepare yourself for forty days and forty nights of hell, Your Excellency.'

CHAPTER NINE

'WHAT do you mean, you can't find her?' Tariq paused in the act of prowling the length of his apartment, his dark eyes fierce, evidence of his usual self-control distinctly lacking. When she'd promised him hell, he hadn't anticipated that her first move would be to disappear.

Cold, hard logic told him that her unfortunate discovery of the truth had no bearing on the outcome of the deal. They were married. The shares were already his.

Mission accomplished.

So why did he suddenly feel as though his entire life was unravelling?

He was in the grip of emotions hitherto unknown to him. He was a man who had never in his life felt the need to explain his actions to anyone and yet suddenly he was filled with a burning need to explain every tiny detail. But the only person he wanted to explain himself to couldn't be found and the knowledge that she'd been *extremely* distressed immediately before she'd disappeared only served to increase his state of unease. Frustration and concern mingled with a severe attack of conscience.

Hasim Akbar clasped his hands together. 'She appears to have vanished, Your Excellency.'

Blasted out of his usual cool by that less than helpful statement, Tariq rounded on him. 'It is impossible for anyone to make a move in this palace without at least ten people witnessing the event. She must be somewhere. *Find her.*'

On the receiving end of that icy tone, Hasim tensed. 'No one has seen her since she left the audience chambers.'

The less than subtle reminder that he was the cause of the current situation left Tariq on the point of explosion.

'Find her,' he repeated in a soft, lethal voice that had Hasim backing towards the door. 'I want every corner of the palace searched, I want guards out on the streets. If necessary get helicopters up in the air. No one rests until her whereabouts are discovered.'

She'd been *very* upset when she'd left him. She could have wandered out of the Palace and into the seedier parts of Fallouk. *She could be in extreme danger.*

As the list of potential disasters lengthened in his mind, Tariq started to pace again, pausing only briefly to question precisely *why* his anxiety levels were running so high.

It was obvious, he told himself. Despite what she thought about him, he wasn't such a louse that he enjoyed seeing a distressed woman leave his Palace with absolutely no knowledge of the surrounding area.

Someone needed to find her.

Faced with the prospect of idleness or, worse still, introspection, he decided to join in the search himself.

Farrah sat curled up in the corner of one of the stables, indifferent to the future appearance of the long silk dress she was wearing. Her high heeled shoes had been discarded and lay half buried in the straw and she'd removed the pins from her blond hair, allowing it to fall loose down her back.

It was dark, it was late and she'd cried so hard that she didn't dare imagine what her face looked like. Given that she was only sharing the stable with a horse, she didn't see that it mattered.

The reminder that she was no longer dressing for a prince brought fresh tears to the surface and she brushed them away with an impatient hand. Enough crying, she told herself firmly. *Enough.*

Eventually she'd get over him. It wasn't possible to hurt like this for ever. And in the meantime she was going to give him forty days and forty nights of total celibacy. For a man as red-blooded and virile as Tariq, knowing how much he wanted her in his bed again, being deprived of sex would be a just punishment.

But, before she could face returning to the Palace, she needed to allow herself the self-indulgence of a good cry.

She deserved that, at least.

'I suppose you think I'm mad,' she muttered to the pretty Arab mare who was munching through a pile of hay. 'Making a fool of myself again, over the same man. I'm obviously not great at learning lessons. And it's not just me—' tears welled again '—I've lost my dad his company because I was too blind and stupid to check exactly what marriage to Tariq would mean.' Would her dad be able to sort things out? If she hadn't been so miserable, she would have laughed because the one person in the world who was probably a match for Tariq was her father.

The horse turned her head and blew gently through her nostrils.

'I just feel like a total idiot,' Farrah confessed softly, curling her long legs underneath her. 'I thought Tariq loved me. I know he's arrogant and controlling but he really can't help that and I felt sorry for him because he's obviously had a pretty grim childhood. I thought I could teach him to be more demonstrative.'

The mare stamped her foot and dragged some more hay into her mouth.

'It turned out that the reason he wasn't demonstrative was

because he didn't love me and, frankly, I don't believe he's capable of loving anyone,' Farrah said flatly, leaning her head back against the wall and closing her eyes. All the anger had drained out of her, leaving her limp and exhausted and unable to make a decision about anything. 'I just can't believe that I was such a gullible, stupid fool that I let the same man hurt me twice.'

The horse gave a whicker of sympathy and nuzzled Farrah's hand.

She opened her eyes and stroked the mare's velvety nose. 'I don't honestly know what I'm supposed to do now,' she mumbled. 'I don't have a single friend in this place. No one I can talk to. His family all loathe me. My dad's working on some project in the back of beyond so I can't get hold of him either and warn him what's happening. My life's a total mess.'

'Your life is *not* a mess, my family certainly doesn't loathe you and you can talk to me. In fact, I wish you would.' The deep, masculine tones were drawn tight with stress and she shrank back against the wall as Tariq walked into the stable and bolted the door behind him in a decisive movement that ensured that she wouldn't be escaping in a hurry.

Farrah flinched as she heard the finality of the clunk. She would sooner be trapped with scorpions and snakes. 'What are you doing here? I don't want to talk to you because you're a truly *horrible* person. Go away.'

Picking up the tension, the mare threw up her head and stamped her foot and Tariq reached out and stroked a soothing hand down her neck, his touch skilled and gentle.

Manipulative rat, Farrah thought dully as she watched him calm the horse with a few soft words and the gentle caress of his long fingers. Wasn't that exactly what he'd done to her? He'd soothed and charmed until he'd had her exactly where he wanted her.

'Have you any idea what an uproar you've caused?' Tariq

demanded in a tense, driven tone. 'We have been searching for you for hours. The entire palace guard is out looking for you.'

It occurred to her that she'd never seen him look anything less than suave and well groomed. But tonight he looked anything but. He was dressed in the same suit he'd worn for his meeting with the Kazbanian foreign minister, but the jacket and tie had long since been discarded and what had started life as a crisp white shirt was now crumpled and dirtied. She wondered what he'd been doing. 'Why are the palace guard looking for me?'

'Because you vanished from the face of the earth. We needed to know where you were. I thought you might have had an accident. I was worried about you.' He frowned slightly, as if that confession was as much of a surprise to him as it was to her.

'Worried about your investment, you mean. But it wouldn't have mattered if I had had an accident, would it, Tariq? You've got what you want. You married me and the shares are yours.'

He sucked in a breath. 'Whatever you may think, this is *not* about the shares.'

'Of course it is.'

He dragged a hand through his glossy dark hair and glanced around him in disbelief. 'I can't believe we're having this conversation in my stables in the middle of the night. Come with me now and we'll talk.'

She didn't move. 'I don't want to talk. And I'll come when I'm ready and not before.'

'You mean you don't want to talk to *me*.' A muscle worked in his jaw and there was a wry gleam in his dark eyes. 'You've been talking to my horse quite happily for the past hour.'

She wondered just how much he'd overheard and then decided that it didn't matter. She'd already made an utter fool of herself over him. It really couldn't get any worse. 'I happen to like your horse.'

He gave her a curious look, momentarily distracted by her comment. 'I never knew you liked horses.'

'What difference would it have made?' she snapped. 'You weren't remotely interested in me as a person, were you, Tariq? You just wanted to manoeuvre me into marrying you and once I did that the rest was all irrelevant.'

'If that is the case, then why am I standing here now?'

'Damage limitation?' She leaned her head back against the wall and studied him in the dim light of the stable. 'You're a man who hates emotions. You've probably seen more today than in your entire lifetime. I'm sure you just want it all to go away. As you just pointed out, your normally ordered palace is in an uproar and you wanted to find me before I could disturb any more of your meetings.'

'Certainly the foreign minister of Kazban has rarely been so thoroughly entertained at my expense,' Tariq admitted with a rare display of humour. 'And what I really want is not for you to disappear but to come back to our apartment so that we can talk properly. It's freezing in here, you're wearing next to nothing and you cannot spend the night in my stables.'

'Why not? They're nice stables. And your palace is full of rats.' She gave him a pointed look and saw his eyes flash dark.

'We can work this out.'

'I don't think so.' She tilted her head to one side, her slightly sarcastic tone hiding layers of pain. 'This time you've really excelled yourself. But it doesn't matter, does it? Because you were never thinking about me, only yourself. It's what you're really, really good at.' Her voice rose and the mare threw up her head in alarm and stamped her foot.

Tariq put a reassuring hand on the horse's neck and turned back to Farrah.

'Are you going to be reasonable?'

'Probably not. I don't feel reasonable. If you really want to know, I feel stupid and gullible,' she threw at him. 'Discovering that you've been thoroughly manipulated isn't really the best incentive to be reasonable.'

But she was starting to shiver and felt his gaze fix on the tiny bumps that appeared on her skin.

'That's enough discussion. Being angry with me is no reason to risk pneumonia. You can sulk and ignore me in our apartments as easily as you can ignore me here,' he pointed out, stooping and sweeping her into his arms without further attempt at negotiation.

'I never sulk. And I want you to put me down,' she muttered, pushing at his chest, feeling the hard muscle under her fingers. 'You're always dragging me off. You need to learn the art of conversation instead of kidnap. And I don't want to be married to you anymore. I don't like you.'

'You're married to me and that's the way it's staying,' Tariq said grimly, tightening his grip on her as he strode from the stable. 'And I think this is one of those occasions when you should probably stop talking.'

'Why?'

'Because you might say something you'll regret later.'

'Offhand, I can't think of a single thing that I'd regret saying to you. The only thing I regret is the part where I said "I do",' she muttered but he simply tightened his grip and strode across a courtyard and through another door.

She was dimly aware of people staring and bowing but Tariq ignored them all, taking the stairs two at a time with her still in his arms.

At any other time she might have admired his impressive athletic ability, but now she simply glared at the hard ridge of his darkened jaw, which was within her line of vision.

'Don't you want to throw a bag over my head in case anyone spots that we've been having a row?'

A muscle worked in that same jaw. 'I'm not interested in anyone else's opinion. I am, however, interested in getting you out of that non-existent dress before you catch your death. The nights here are very cold and you're wearing very little.'

'It's not like you to complain about that, Tariq,' she said sarcastically just as he reached the door of his apartment.

Guards snapped to attention but Tariq ignored them, striding through the door with her still in his arms and kicking it shut behind him. He carried on walking, through the three luxurious and ornate living rooms, down a marble corridor and into the huge master bedroom, dominated by a massive bed.

A bed that she hadn't even had the chance to share with him yet.

And never would, she told herself firmly, ignoring the sudden rush of awareness that engulfed her as he deposited her firmly in the middle of the large bed. There was no misinterpreting the purposeful gleam in his eyes as he lifted a hand and unbuttoned his rumpled shirt.

'Don't even think about it, Tariq,' she warned, scooting up the bed out of reach of those dangerous, skilful hands.

He dropped the shirt on to the floor, his eyes still locked on hers. 'Why deny yourself what you know you want? The chemistry between us is all that matters here.'

The sight of his bronzed muscular chest was almost enough to make her believe him. Almost, but not quite.

'Yes, well, it would make it very convenient for you if I believed that. You think that everything can be solved by sex, but it can't,' she muttered, ignoring the banging of her heart and the buzz in her ears.

Rat, she reminded herself as she dragged her gaze away from the fascinating sight of dark, masculine body hair that followed a trail down his body and disappeared temptingly beneath the waistband of his trousers. *Neverland*, she thought to herself. She never should have gone there. *Major* rat.

As he reached for the button on his trousers she felt her blood heat and knew that urgent action was necessary to prevent her from doing something that she was going to sincerely regret later. Sliding off the bed, she made a run for the bathroom without giving him a chance to stop her. Pushing the lock home, she leaned against the door and slid slowly on to the cold marble floor.

Forty days and forty nights, she reminded herself.

She was going to make him suffer for forty days and forty nights.

And then she'd go home and spend the rest of her life trying to get over him.

Apart from fulfilling her role in certain social engagements, she devoted her time to avoiding Tariq.

She spent her nights dozing fitfully behind a locked door in the large dressing room that was part of the master suite. The door was locked for her sake as much as his. She didn't trust herself to be around him and not give into temptation. He was so unbelievably sexy that it would have been all too easy to just forget what he'd done and sink into his arms. But she wasn't going to do it. And every time she felt remotely tempted to unlock that door, she reminded herself what he'd done to her and to her father.

She'd tried over and over again to contact her father to warn him what was happening but so far it had proved impossible to track him down and she was growing more and more anxious.

What was he going to say when he discovered what she'd done?

Trying to distract herself, during the day she explored Tariq's palace. She discovered secluded courtyards with hanging gardens and bubbling fountains, she found a library, stocked floor to ceiling with books, but her most important discovery was the one she'd made on that first night. His stables.

Over the days that followed, she got to know each and every one of his horses by name and personality. Deciding that as her marriage was a sham then so was her role as Queen, she found herself a pair of jodhpurs and a loose, comfortable T-shirt and spent her time riding and caring for his horses. And if his staff thought her behaviour in any way odd, they concealed it.

It was a week after they'd arrived in Fallouk that she heard a sound that was entirely familiar to her. The uncontrolled yells of a child in the middle of a major temper tantrum. Acting on instinct, she put down the body brush she'd been using to groom the Prince's favourite stallion, left the stable and went to investigate.

Tariq's aunt was standing looking frustrated and out of her depth while a boy of about seven years old lay on the pristine lawn in front of the stables and drummed his heels into the ground. His jaw was clenched, his arms and legs rigid as they flew up and down, threatening damage to anyone daring to approach.

'If you cannot control yourself then I will leave you here until you can!' Tariq's aunt turned away from the boy, saw Farrah and quickly controlled her expression. But not before Farrah had seen the sadness and the desperation in her eyes. She recognized the look because she'd seen it in the eyes of other parents.

She knew immediately that there was more to the boy's behaviour than just an ordinary temper tantrum. Unsure of what to say, Farrah stood for a moment but Tariq's aunt merely straightened her shoulders defensively.

'Rahman suffers from behavioural problems,' she said stiffly. 'He is very difficult to handle. He must be left to come out of his temper by himself. Whatever you do, don't touch him. He hates being touched. It makes him worse.' And with that she walked off, leaving the child on the grass, screaming.

Farrah let out a sigh of disbelief, shook her head and dropped onto her knees next to the boy. She wouldn't touch him, but at least she could keep him company. 'If it's any consolation, this place makes me feel like screaming too,' she muttered but Rahman took no notice because he was making too much noise to hear her.

Farrah sat quietly, her mind absorbed, remembering a child with similar problems who had been sent by the family doctor to the riding stable where she worked.

The animals had helped him—really helped.

Looking at the boy now, she wondered whether anyone had ever taken him near the stables. Certainly there were several ponies in Tariq's stable with the right temperament to carry a child. Wasn't it worth a try?

She pondered the problem through an incredibly boring formal dinner that evening and when, the next morning, she found Rahman screaming on the grass again she made up her mind. What was there to lose?

And so Rahman became her project.

She took him with her to the stables every day. At first he just sat, silent and uncommunicative, on a pile of straw, watching while she tended the horses. Farrah took to grooming the quietest, most docile pony in the stables on a daily basis and eventually held out the brush to Rahman in silent invitation. He stared at her for a long moment and then he reached out and took the brush.

'Circular movements,' she said calmly, 'like this—' She demonstrated what she meant and then stood back, careful not to crowd him.

Tentatively he started to groom the pony himself, his movements growing more and more confident.

Several days later, she persuaded one of the grooms to help her take him for his first ride and Rahman smiled—really smiled.

And eventually the temper tantrums lessened, just as she'd hoped they would. She watched in satisfaction one morning as he hugged and stroked the pony.

'He really likes that,' she said quietly. 'Hugs are very important.'

'I'm glad you think so,' came a deep, drawl from behind her and she turned to find Tariq standing there, a sardonic expression in his dark eyes. 'You seem to have taken up permanent residence in my stables—' His voice tailed off as he noticed Rahman and he gave a sharp intake of breath. For a moment he watched while the boy fussed over the pony and then his jaw tightened. 'Farrah. I need to talk to you. Immediately.'

Worried that his icy tone would upset Rahman, Farrah slid out of the stable without arguing, moving just far away enough that they couldn't be overheard but not so far that she couldn't see the boy.

'What's the matter now?' Her tone was flippant. 'Share price dropped? Oil wells gone up in flames?'

'Get the child out of the stable now. He shouldn't be in there.'

Affronted by what she saw as a totally unreasonable command, Farrah opened her mouth to argue but then saw the look of concern in his eyes. He was worried. Which was something in his favour at least, she thought to herself.

'Rahman's fine. He's great with the horses.'

'How well do you know him? If he loses his temper he will frighten them and they might hurt him,' Tariq said quietly and she nodded.

'Yes, I'm sure you're right. But he doesn't lose his temper around the animals. I've seen it before. Children often relate to the horses in a way that they just can't seem to relate to adults. It's amazing really.'

His eyes narrowed. 'What do you mean, you've seen it before? When have you ever come across a child like Rahman?'

She hesitated. She was so used to hiding that part of herself. But why not tell him the truth? The time for games was long over. 'All the time, actually. I work in a riding stable and children with different disabilities are sent to us from all around. The horses can't always help, of course—' she gave a tiny shrug '—but mostly they do. It's amazing to watch. We have children who have never been able to move under their own steam before and then we put them on a pony and you see their little faces as they walk across the yard for the first time—' She broke off and blinked, aware that Tariq was looking at her with a strange expression in his eyes.

'You work with children?'

'Well, I work with the horses, really,' she confessed, pushing her hair out of her eyes. 'My talent is knowing which horse will be good with each rider. I don't pretend to be an expert on anyone's medical condition. There are other people who do that. I just do the pony bit. Horses have personalities, you know that, just like humans. Some of them are kind and they seem to sense whether they have to be gentle or not. They're so clever. That pony of yours over there—' she gestured with her hand to where Rahman was still grooming '—he's wonderful. Just the right type.'

'I bought him for one of my little cousins but she was never interested,' Tariq said and Farrah shrugged.

'Oh, well, her loss, Rahman's gain, I suppose. Is he your nephew?'

Tariq nodded. 'Yes. He has seen an endless round of doctors and psychologists and none of them have been able to cure his terrible rages. It seems you've managed to do in a matter of weeks what specialists have failed to do in years.'

Feeling suddenly awkward, Farrah rubbed the toe of her boot along the ground. 'Not me, the horses.'

Tariq breathed out heavily. 'How often do you work in the stables?'

'At home?' She looked up at him. 'Every day. I get there at five-thirty and I leave after the last child has gone. It's a pretty long day, but I love it.'

'You work in a stable every day?' He said the words slowly, as if he was having trouble comprehending and she nodded.

'Apart from Sundays. And I even go in on Sundays if they're really desperate.'

'And you didn't think this was something worth mentioning to me?'

'No. It's a part of my life I don't share with anyone. It embarrassed my mother because she could never understand why I'd rather be up to my knees in mud than dressed in designer heels. I'm sure you're equally embarrassed, but actually I don't care.' She lifted her chin defensively. 'I do it because I enjoy it and because I'm useful.'

He ran a hand over the back of his neck, a strange light in his eyes. 'We told each other many things in the desert and yet you didn't think to mention it.'

'Well, you didn't think to mention that we were only getting married for forty days and forty nights, so you can't really accuse me of keeping secrets,' she pointed out, moving back towards the stable.

He grabbed her hand in an iron grip. 'You are the most contradictory, infuriating woman I've ever met.'

'And I bet you've met a few, so that's probably a compliment. I need to check on Rahman—' She yanked her hand away from him and walked back into the stable, murmuring quiet words of praise to the boy and the horse, aware that Tariq was watching, simmering quietly from the other side of the stable door.

She could feel his gaze burning into her back as she took the brush from the boy.

'Time for your ride, I think. Let's saddle him up, shall we?'

She waited for Tariq to become bored and leave but instead he followed her out to the paddock she'd been using to give Rahman lessons.

'Don't you have anywhere to be?' Holding the pony's reins, she shot him an exasperated look. 'War could break out while you're hanging around here with me.'

'War is undoubtedly going to break out if I don't have five minutes alone with you soon,' Tariq promised in an undertone and she felt her heart jump in her chest.

'Forget it.'

'You are such a little hypocrite,' he breathed in a menacing tone. 'You want *exactly* what I want but you pretend otherwise.'

'I don't want anything, Tariq, except to go home.' And with that she walked the horse forward, ending the conversation.

She concentrated on Rahman and the pony and when she turned round again Tariq had gone. She should have been relieved that he'd finally left her alone, but instead she felt—disappointed?

Which just went to show that she was as stupid about the man as ever, she thought, turning her attention back to the boy and the pony.

She went through her day feeling more miserable than ever and after Rahman had left for the day she stayed on in the stables because she couldn't face going back to the Palace.

She completely lost track of the time and when she glanced up and saw Tariq standing in the doorway she blinked in astonishment. He was dressed in a dark grey suit that seemed only to emphasize the athletic perfection of his powerful frame. His hair shone dark and glossy under the harsh stable lights and his arrogant features showed evidence of strain.

'Tonight was the formal dinner to welcome the Crown Prince of Kazban,' he informed her helpfully and she felt a stab of guilt which she pushed away.

'If I was supposed to be there, then I'm sorry. I lost track of time.'

'Obviously.'

'Was I supposed to be there?'

'You're my wife. I married you.'

'Well, not really—' She pulled a face and turned back to the pony she was grooming. Anything to stop her looking at him. He was spectacular, she thought weakly. Stunning. Gorgeous. Virile. Masculine. Ignoring the slow curl of heat low in her pelvis, she closed her eyes briefly and talked sense into herself. Rat. Bastard. 'You married my shares. And I sort of came along too, which must have been pretty inconvenient for you.'

With a harsh expletive that she didn't understand, he crossed the stable and yanked her away from the pony. 'Enough.' His voice was a low, throaty growl as he powered her against the wall and trapped her there with the strength and heat of his body. 'I have heard enough. You are determined to simplify the complicated and soon we are going to talk about that, but for now I've had enough of talking and I've had enough of being patient. I have given you space to calm down and be reasonable and it hasn't happened.'

'Let me go, Tariq—' Overwhelmed by his masculine scent, the fire in his eyes, *the sheer closeness of him*, she pushed at his hard chest, struggling against a temptation so large and potentially dangerous that her movements became frantic. 'Let me go—'

'No way—'

'Oh, God, don't do this to us—to me—' She wriggled against him in an attempt to free herself and then gave a soft moan as she felt the hard ridge of his arousal and the warmth of his breath as his mouth closed in on hers.

'You are the most *infuriating* woman.' His arms planted either side of her, blocking her escape, Tariq's voice was husky and seductive. 'I don't know whether to strangle you or kiss you.'

'Strangle me, definitely—it will be better for both of us,' Farrah gasped, her heart pounding hard against her ribs, her head swimming. 'I don't want you to kiss me. I really, *really* don't want you to kiss me—'

If he kissed her she'd be lost. If he kissed her, she'd—

His mouth came down on hers with punishing force, his kiss ravenous and desperate, trapping her sob of need. His hands slid down her arms and lifted them to his neck. He wanted her to cling and she clung, her arms wrapped round his powerful shoulders, her own shoulders pressed hard against the wall by the power of his body and the force of his passion.

She forgot that she didn't want him to kiss her. She forgot that this man had hurt her. She forgot that she'd resolved to keep her distance. She forgot *everything* except the fact that she'd kept her distance for two long weeks and now she needed him. She needed him badly.

His kiss was savage, a primitive assault on her senses that destroyed all thought and will power. Excitement whipped through her body like a loose electric wire as he stole and plundered, his body hard against hers until all she could feel was the pumped up, insistent throb of pulsing masculinity.

She felt his hand slide up to cup her breast and she arched in a desperate plea for more. Responding to her silent demand, he used both hands to jerk her shirt open in a rough, impatient gesture that sent buttons flying and made the pony throw up her head in alarm. But neither of them were aware of their surroundings. They were aware only of each other. Of the pounding hammering of hearts and the frantic lock of seeking mouths.

'I need you naked,' Tariq groaned, his hands swift and determined as he stripped her of the rest of her clothes and she was so completely desperate for him that she did nothing but urge him on. Her entire focus became the insistent, throbbing ache deep within her body that grew to monumental proportions and threatened to drive her mad with frustration.

Need made her uncoordinated and she clawed at his suit, groaning in frustration when her fingers met fabric instead of flesh.

When she felt his mouth on her bare breast she closed her eyes and gasped at the sheer perfection of the feeling and when she felt his strong fingers slide between her legs she gave a moan of frustration because his touch brought her so close to ecstasy and yet not close enough.

The hard, cold wall of the stable pressed against her bare back but she was oblivious to everything but her body and his. *Her need and his.*

Frantic for him, she reached down and fumbled with his zip and he covered her hand with his and helped her with the task. He was painfully aroused and so hot and hard that her entire body throbbed with an urgency so monumental that nothing could have stopped the inevitable.

Her desperation bordered on the indecent but she didn't even care.

'Now, Tariq—' her voice was strangled '—now, please—'

His eyes glinted dark, his breathing was harsh and he lifted her without hesitation, wrapped her legs around him and entered her with a hard, possessive thrust that brought a sob of pleasure and relief to her lips.

She felt the force of him deep inside her as he took her with barely contained violence and she moved her hips and clung to him as excitement surged through her body, caring for nothing except the need which grew and grew from deep within.

He thrust deep and he did it again and again until her vision blurred and her entire body exploded in a shower of sensation so exquisitely perfect that for a moment she ceased to breathe. She felt him shudder as he reached his own desperate climax and then there was only the slow descent back to normality. The unsteady breathing. The sudden intrusion of the outside world into their private place. The cold wall. The rhythmic munching of the pony in the corner of the stable…

Dazed and disorientated, it was only as he lowered her gently to the ground that Farrah realized that, although she was totally naked, he was fully clothed. Even his stylish silk tie was still in place.

For some reason, this stark reminder that she'd thought about nothing but her own need for him increased her mortification and she stopped quickly and retrieved the remains of her torn shirt. Head bowed, fingers shaking, she slipped it on and reached for her trousers.

Tariq caught her arm, his eyes dark and stormy, his breathing less than steady. 'We *really* need to talk—'

And that was the one thing she didn't want to do.

He was going to tell her that they might as well stay together until such time as he grew bored with her. Wasn't that more or less what he'd offered her five years before? A place in his bed until he decided that it was time to fill it with someone different?

Perfect mistress material—

Well, that wasn't what she wanted. What they shared was too powerful, but it was just sex, and sex wasn't enough for her. She couldn't live with him, knowing that he'd divorce her when the time was right. *When it suited him.*

Eventually he'd get bored with the sex and then where would she be? In love with a man who didn't return her feelings and she couldn't live with that.

He *had* to let her go. That had been his plan all along and he probably wanted it even more now that he realized that she wasn't the person he'd thought she was.

So she'd leave and make it easy for him.

CHAPTER TEN

THE following morning, Farrah went in search of Asma.

She was drinking coffee and looking at dress designs and seemed more than a little disconcerted to see Farrah standing in the doorway.

'I'll come straight to the point.' Farrah closed the door so that their conversation couldn't be overheard. 'I want to leave this place, but I can't do it on my own so you're going to have to help me.'

Asma closed the book and gave her a cold look. 'Why would I help you?'

'Because you don't want me here and you never did,' Farrah pointed out and Asma gave a tiny shrug.

'I don't think—'

'Good, because you don't need to think,' Farrah said pleasantly. 'I just need you to find a reliable way of transporting me to the border with Kazban without Tariq knowing anything about it.'

The book fell from her hands. 'You're going to cross the border?'

'Once I'm in Kazban, I'll persuade the authorities to let me fly home,' Farrah explained impatiently. 'I can hardly just take a commercial flight out of Tazkash, can I?'

'I suppose not. You're seriously leaving?'

'That's right. And I want to do it quickly. You're his cousin. You must be able to arrange something. I just need transport, that's all, and a driver who knows the way.'

She had no intention of repeating the fiasco of the desert.

Asma's breathing quickened, as though she couldn't quite believe her luck. 'I—yes, I could, of course, but—'

'Good, that's settled, then. Tariq is tied up in meetings with the Prince of Kazban all day. I want to be gone long before he comes looking for me.'

Asma rose to her feet. 'I'll order a car for you. It will be outside the stable gates one hour from now.'

'Good.'

Which left only one further thing to do before she left.

Farrah returned to Tariq's apartment and found her bag. Inside was an envelope she'd had sent out from England only two days earlier.

She opened it up and stared at the contents, her eyes filling with tears. Then she blinked them away, picked up a pen and got to work.

The journey was smooth and without incident.

Farrah told herself that she was hugely relieved that Tariq hadn't chosen to leave his meeting early and hadn't suspected anything. She wouldn't have wanted him to follow her. She really, really wouldn't.

So why was it that no sooner did she brush away one tear, another one took its place?

She stared out across the dark gold dunes, which stretched into the distance, wondering if she'd ever see the desert again. Probably not. She wouldn't be coming back to Tazkash for a third time, that was for sure.

The knowledge that she might never see the place again left her unutterably depressed and she was so lost in thought that it took her a few moments to realize that they were slowing down.

When she finally noticed the buildings along the road and the men in uniform, she leaned forward in her seat with a frown. 'What's going on?'

'We've reached the border between Tazkash and Kazban,' came the reply and for some reason his words simply increased her misery.

So this was it, then.

Once they drove past those guards, Tariq would be in a different country, far away from her. Oh, why was she kidding herself? She brushed the tears away angrily. Tariq had always been far away from her. He was from a different country, a different culture—he was in a different league. They'd never stood a chance. All they shared was passion and that just wasn't enough.

She was about to look back at the majestic dunes for a final time when her door was jerked open and a uniformed guard stared down at her.

'Passport.' His face was hard and unsmiling and she felt a flicker of disquiet as she rummaged in her bag and handed over the document.

He took it from her and gestured for her to get out of the car. 'Come with me.'

Farrah did as he ordered, wondering whether this was a routine happening at the border.

He led her into the stone building and then stood to one side to let her pass. 'In there.'

Wondering what was going on, she walked into the room as he'd instructed and then stopped in shock. The door closed behind her but she wasn't even aware of that fact.

Tariq stood by a desk in the middle of the room, dressed in another sleek designer suit, his handsome face taut with strain. 'Must I keep you locked up? Every time I turn my back on you, you run away. *Why*?'

She found her voice. 'What are you doing here?'

'Abandoning my royal duties, as usual,' he said in a raw, impatient tone. 'If I wasn't the one in charge I would have been fired by now for taking so much time off. If you were to take your rightful place by my side as my wife, I might get a great deal more done in my working day.'

She curled her hands into her palms. 'My rightful place is not by your side. It was never meant to be like that, was it?'

'Why did you leave me these?' He threw the envelope on to the desk and she bit her lip.

'They're share certificates, Tariq. You married me for those. I hope you live happily ever after.'

She felt her voice crack and she turned towards the door, intending to leave before she made a complete fool of herself, but he moved so swiftly that she didn't even manage to take more than a step towards freedom.

'You're not going anywhere,' he said grimly, propelling her against the wall and trapping her there with his arms.

It reminded her of that incredible night in the stable and she felt tears threaten again.

'You married me for my shares, Tariq. Those are the shares and I just can't do this anymore. I'm leaving.'

'You're not leaving.'

'The shares are yours. You can divorce me. You don't even have to wait forty days and forty nights.'

'I won't be divorcing you. Ever.'

'You're being ridiculous—'

His mouth moved closer to hers. 'You think what we share is ridiculous?'

'What we share is just sex, Tariq. And I'm not prepared to stay with you until you get bored with me.'

'Bored?' He laughed in genuine amusement. 'Bored? I would give much for the opportunity to become bored by your company, *laeela*. You tell me exactly how you feel; I doubt you will ever learn to filter what happens between your brain and your mouth and you are reliably unpredictable. Every time I turn my back you are escaping and now I discover that you have a completely secret life of which I know nothing. There are many words to describe our relationship, but boring is certainly not one of them.'

'I'm not good at palace life.'

'You haven't made any effort to become involved in palace life,' Tariq said quietly. 'And I can hardly blame you for that. On your first visit here, my relatives were horribly unkind to you and gave you advice that made you feel even more awkward and out of place and that caused me to misjudge you.'

She lifted her head and looked at him. 'You knew they did that?'

'At the time, no.' His tone was weary. 'I'm afraid that five years ago I had a great deal to occupy my mind. My father was seriously ill, the economic future of the country was under threat from different directions. The demands on my time were such that I didn't give any thought to your feelings whatsoever and for that I apologise. All I saw was that when you arrived at my palace you changed into a different person.'

'I was trying to please you. I was trying to be the person I thought you wanted me to be.'

His eyes gleamed with a certain wry humour. 'I'm aware of that now. And I'm also aware that you were led down the wrong path by my family.'

'How did you find out?'

He released her then and turned and paced back across the room. 'I was determined to discover who told you about the plan to divorce you after forty days and forty nights. It did not take a genius to trace it back to my own family. Asma has always been horribly indulged by my aunt.'

'Well, I'm sure when she's your wife she'll learn to behave herself,' Farrah muttered, sidling towards the door.

'The guards are instructed not to allow you to pass,' Tariq

informed her pleasantly, 'so there's no point in attempting another of your escape bids until this conversation is finished. And Asma will never be my wife.'

'Does she know that?'

'She does now. I made a point of speaking to both her and my aunt and pointing out that the role is no longer vacant because I am married to you and that is the way it is staying. There will be no more misunderstandings from that quarter. And anyway, my aunt has revised her opinion of you since you have worked such a miracle with Rahman. You will find her eager to secure more of your help in that direction.'

Farrah closed her eyes. The heat in the room was intolerable and her head was throbbing after her sleepless night. 'Why would you want to stay married to me? Because the sex is good?'

'No, because you are the woman I want to spend the rest of my life with.'

'I embarrass you.'

'That's *not* true. Five years ago I was completely charmed by you and then we returned to the Palace and I saw a different side of you.' He hesitated and his mouth tightened. 'This does not reflect well on me, but I confess that I was concerned that you were like your mother, a concern that my relatives used to their advantage when they gave you such unfortunate advice on how to dress and behave.'

It was painful hearing it and yet at the same time his words created a flicker of hope inside her. He hadn't *wanted* her to be like her mother. 'So when you discovered that you would have to marry me you must have *hated* the idea—'

He ran a hand over the back of his neck, visibly discomfited. 'Marriage to *anyone* was never at the top of my wish list,' he said honestly, 'and I think I only agreed to it because I knew that a divorce was possible. I wasn't really thinking about you. I only thought about me. I realize that confession does me no credit,' he added hastily, 'but you have to understand that I had a completely false impression of you at that point. It didn't occur to me that a divorce would bother you at all.'

'So you came after me purely for business gain.'

His gaze was wary. 'You are making it sound very bad but that is all in the past and it is the future that matters. The future that I am determined that we will have together.'

Her heart stalled and she swallowed hard. It was time to be honest. 'You don't know me, Tariq. You have no idea who I am.'

'And whose fault is that?' He turned on her, his dark eyes flashing, his mouth grim. 'You accuse me of not knowing you, you are quick to blame me for all the faults in our relationship, but are you not at least partly to blame too? You were careful to keep so much of yourself hidden away. Think about it, Farrah.'

'You think I'm a lightweight party animal. You think that of all women. You think all we care about is hair and shoes.'

'Because up until now that has been true of the women I have had the misfortune to mix with. But you gave me no reason to question my own prejudices. In fact you chose to perpetrate that image, did you not?' One ebony brow lifted in challenge. 'Is it not true that you turn up at high society events looking like a million dollars and socialize?'

'Yes, but—'

'And you appear to be enjoying yourself. Do you advertise the fact that you were working with disadvantaged children in a grubby stable only minutes before you slip on your high heels?'

'No, but—'

'It is true that I'm perfect in many ways,' Tariq drawled in a slightly mocking tone, 'but even I have yet to perfect the art of mind-reading and it's time that you offered the odd explanation for your own behaviour in all of this. You placed certain facts in front of me. You built an image for yourself over the years. Why did you do that?'

Farrah swallowed. 'Because I was always a disappointment to my mother. She wanted a girly girl and instead she got me. As I child I was overweight, clumsy and I loved being outdoors. I was useless at ballet but good at riding horses. I spent my teenage years treading a fine line between pleasing myself and pleasing her.' She took a deep breath. 'And I also changed my image because of you. When you told me that I wasn't good enough to be your wife, that was the final spur I needed to reinvent myself. You hurt me so badly that I thought I could put a protective shell between myself and the world and so, from then on, I lived two very different lives. And the glamorous socialite bit wasn't as empty and useless as it sounds. I raised lots of money for the charities I cared about.'

'And during the day you worked with horses and children.' He raised a brow in question. 'So, having heard that story, can you honestly blame me if I chose to believe the image you portrayed? I interpreted the facts as you presented them to me and was that not exactly what you wanted and expected people to do?'

Farrah stared at him. He was right, of course. She *did* present a certain image to the world. An image very different from her real self. In fact, she relished the fact that, even in such public times, she'd managed to keep a large part of herself so private.

'Wealth makes you suspicious of people and their motives.' She bit her lip as she made a feeble attempt to explain. 'My mother found the real me highly embarrassing so I've learned to hide who I am. I suppose I'm not used to trusting anyone with my secrets.'

'And neither am I. In that way, at least, we are similar.'

She'd never thought of it like that, but it was true. How could she blame him for forming the wrong opinion of her, when she herself had been at least partially responsible for giving him that opinion? 'Five years ago you invited me to be your mistress—'

'I was under a great deal of pressure at the time. My father was desperately sick but not so sick that he couldn't interfere with everything I was doing.' Tariq strode around the room, his expression fierce. 'My time in the desert with you was an oasis of calm in my life. I wanted you to stay with me but suddenly we returned to the Palace and everyone in the Kingdom found reasons why I should not be with you, reasons that you supported with your manner of dress and your behaviour.'

'It should have been about us, Tariq, not anyone else—'

'You have no idea how often I wished that to be the case. How often I wanted to heave the responsibility on to someone else and ride off with you, as we did for so many months on the beach. A man and a woman. You dreamed of Nadia and her Sultan and yet I was weighed down by the responsibility of running the country in my father's place. You saw everything as simple and yet, for me, the simple did not exist.'

She felt a stab of guilt and realized suddenly that, until that moment, she'd never really understood the monumental pressure that he'd been under. 'I only ever thought about our relationship,' she admitted, aware that she'd been hideously self-absorbed and selfish. 'I thought you were ignoring me.'

'I was up to my ears in palace politics, as you so accurately call it,' Tariq said dryly and Farrah blushed.

'And I was naïve. I admit it. I should have realized what Asma was doing, but I didn't have any confidence in myself. Have you any idea of what it is like to be just eighteen and in love with the sexiest man in the world?' She swallowed. 'My mother destroyed my confidence in myself and your palace was full of gorgeous women, far more sophisticated and worldly than me. There was no way I could compete.'

'But I did not want a woman who was sophisticated and worldly. I wanted you. Which is why, when the opportunity to come after you presented itself, I snatched it.' He walked over to her and took her hands in his and she stilled.

'What are you saying?'

He lifted her hands to his lips. 'I'm saying that even the need to gain control of your father's company wouldn't have been enough to tempt me into marriage unless that was what I wanted.'

Her heart pounded. 'But you needed my father's company.'

'That deal could have been achieved in other ways,' Tariq said quietly, still holding her hands tightly. 'The truth is when I was offered an excuse I grabbed it, not because of the shares but because I wanted to marry you. I only realized that myself recently.'

'You're just saying that because you're in a tight spot.' He was a master negotiator—she knew that and she'd made a fool of herself over this man twice. She wasn't going to do it again.

'I told myself that I was marrying you for your father's shares because I was not ready to admit, even to myself, that my reasons could be more complex than that.'

'Tariq—'

'Don't interrupt me. I'm trying to say something I've avoided saying for my whole life and it isn't easy.' He released her hands and paced over to the other side of the room before turning back to face her. 'I love you. I married you because I loved you, although I don't think even I recognized it at the time, and I want to stay married to you because I love you. There, I've said it three times and it's getting easier already.' He gave a self-deprecating smile and for a moment she couldn't speak. Couldn't respond.

'You love me?'

'Unbelievable, isn't it?' He spread his hands in a fatalistic gesture. 'Finally I fall in love with a woman who loves me in return, but it is all in jeopardy because of my stupidity in linking our marriage with a business deal. How am I ever to convince you?'

She wasn't ready to give in that easily. 'How do you know that I love you in return?'

'You have always loved me,' Tariq said softly, 'but it has taken me a long time to recognize that too. You see, I'm not used to seeing love. My parents didn't love each other and none of the women I have been with have loved me any more than I loved them.'

'You married me intending to divorce me—'

'That may be true. But I made up my mind on our wedding night that I would *not* be divorcing you.'

'But Asma—'

'Our marriage is no one's business but our own.' He folded his arms across his chest and lifted an eyebrow. 'And now it seems to me that I've been doing a great deal of grovelling and apologizing for a Sultan and I'm hearing very little from you in return.'

That statement sounded so much like his usual arrogant self that she gave a slow smile, hope building inside her. 'What do you want to hear?'

'A declaration that you intend to stop running away? Something about you being crazy about me, loving me madly—' there was a glimmer of humour in his eyes '—that kind of thing.'

'We're different, Tariq—'

'A fact for which I am grateful on a daily basis,' he drawled, strolling towards her and dragging her into his arms. 'Enough argument. We *are* different, it's true. But we are supposed to be different. Different is good.'

'You're arrogant and stubborn—'

He gave a dismissive shrug. 'And you speak without thinking. It's part of the person you are and I love you for it.'

'You always command and order—'

He slid his hands either side of her face and dropped a gentle kiss on her mouth. 'And you are ridiculously, extravagantly, impractically romantic, but I love you for that too.'

She stared up at him. 'You don't know me—'

'I know everything you have allowed me to learn,' he said softly. 'I look forward to discovering the rest if you'll allow me to do so.'

'But—'

'I know that you love horses and children, that you are kind and giving. I know you like the simple life but are also comfortable at formal occasions. I know that politics and intrigue make you uncomfortable but I'll teach you how to cope with it. I know that you love our desert, enjoy our food and that you are not safe to drive on a sand dune.'

She gave a gasp of outrage. 'I drive well on sand!'

'You will, after more lessons,' he said confidently and she laughed.

'You're assuming I'm staying.'

'Why would you leave, when you know that you love it here? Despite what you think, you will not have to live your life in a goldfish bowl. There are many charities who would be glad of your help and there is a riding school within Fallouk where you could help if that would make you happy.'

'It wouldn't embarrass you?'

'On the contrary—' his voice was soft and there was a strange light in his eyes '—I never thought it possible to be so proud of my wife.'

She felt colour touch her cheeks. 'And your pipeline?'

Tariq released her and took a step backwards, his expression serious. 'The pipeline is a crucial project. I spoke to your father a few days ago and explained everything to him. He was surprisingly reasonable, given the circumstances. I will no longer be taking over the company but we have agreed on a partnership that will benefit both parties.'

Relieved that her father's business was no longer in jeopardy, Farrah smiled. 'He's a man who understands love.'

Tariq nodded. 'Obviously. Now that you are my wife, he is coming here tomorrow to reopen discussions on how to proceed with the project. So all that remains is for you to decide what you are going to do when he arrives. Should you still wish to leave, I'm sure he would be happy to take you home. Alternatively, he can join us for some belated wedding celebrations.'

For the first time she saw uncertainty in his eyes and it was that uncertainty that made up her mind.

'I am home, Tariq.' She walked towards him and reached up to hug him. 'You know I love you—'

'Yes, I do know that.' Tariq's voice was unsteady. 'But I didn't know if you would be able to forgive me for the less than conventional route we took to reach this point.'

'The thing about love is that it's generous and forgiving,' she breathed, 'love is kind and everything good. And love can perform miracles.'

'That I know to be true.' Tariq leaned down, his mouth hovering temptingly close to hers, 'because I found you. And that truly is a miracle.'

'If I stay married to you, do I have to dress like a queen?'

'Only part of the time,' he promised in a husky, sexy drawl. 'The rest of the time you will be *undressed*—'

And with that he kissed her, leaving her in absolutely no doubt that as well as being generous, forgiving, kind and good, love was also perfect.